Here's what Amazon Readers are saying about Sarah Vail's Books:

All I have to say is WOW. Sarah Vail's books are riveting. I loved every second of them. Very well-written characters and plots. Every detail flows so perfectly—as if you watched it unfold with your own eyes and a part of the action. So much suspense I couldn't turn the pages fast enough!

I recommend Sarah Vail's books to those who enjoy murder mysteries riddled with suspense, compelling characters, and plenty of action. Vail's writing hooked me within the first three pages and never let me go. She is skilled at dropping clever clues for the reader to follow that generate suspicions and theories; sometimes misleading, but always relevant. I happily give her books five stars, and if the scale went higher, I'd give it more.

. . . .The characters are always complex and very believable. The mystery and story lines are so juicy I just have to know what happens next. I can't wait for more Sarah Vail novels!

The writing and the way the events unfold so smoothly show us the talent of Sarah Vail's writing, her attention to detail is outstanding. You get hooked into the story pretty quickly, from the first few pages I couldn't stop. I highly recommend it to crime and suspense lovers.

. . . . kept me on edge all the time, kept me speculating and the ending could not be more satisfying, also the romance part was so hot. In Summary very well written crime thriller in which the hero saves the day with the help of his team.

LIGHTNING RIDGE ROAD

Sarah Vail

ACKNOWLEDGEMENTS

I would like to express my heartfelt appreciation to my editor, Suzanne Holland, for her expert help with editing this book. Her insights are impeccable.

I would also like to thank my writers' critique groups for their help and suggestions that kept me on track and moving forward.

AUTHOR'S NOTE

This is a work of fiction. Names, characters, places and incidents, organizations and dialogue either are the product of the author's imagination or are used fictitiously. Any resemblance to actual persons, living or dead, events, or locales, is entirely coincidental.

In this book, many locations are fiction. No Tenville River, Tenville Ridge or Reservoir, no Crystal Falls Campground, Little Crooked Creek, Crystal Falls City, or Sugar Maple Lodge exist, though they may somewhere. These were entirely made up for the story's benefit. Make-believe is part of the fun and freedom writing fiction provides to readers and authors alike.

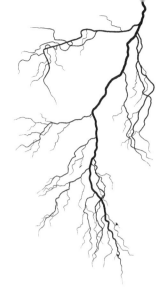

PROLOGUE

D AVID BERKSTAD TOOK the elevator to the forty-fourth floor. The old man had the ten-thousand-square-foot penthouse overlooking the Potomac River. He was always surprised by the opulence. The space was decorated with priceless antiques, hand-loomed oriental rugs, paintings by the old masters worth millions, and some, Berkstad speculated, were stolen.

Rumor had it the old man was a remnant of the Stalin communist regime, though he'd only been seventeen at the end of the Second World War. No one knew where he'd amassed his vast fortune; they just knew it was there. Forbes magazine listed his net worth at a hundred billion, but there were whispers—it was closer to three hundred billion, as much as the annual budget of a small country.

The butler took Berkstad's coat, hung it in the closet by the door, and guided him to the study. He could see the old man's silhouette against the city lights beyond the floor-to-ceiling glass window. He stood straight and tall for a man of 93.

This room always smelled of expensive cigars, leather-bound books, and fine whiskey.

"You wanted to see me?" Berkstad asked. The old man turned. His appearance always startled him. His face was a landscape of wrinkles and deep folds as if draped with old cheesecloth. The skin around his eyes was puffy and red, but the eyes were unexpected—bright blue, as if a young man was trapped in an ancient mummified body.

"Patterson has been indicted and arrested?" His voice was surprisingly strong for a man of that age.

"Yes," Berkstad answered.

"I told him long ago to temper his appetites. Patience, I suggested. But he let power go to his head." The smile on his craggy face seemed to hold on to a memory of pleasure for the moment. Pleasure, in which he could no longer participate. Berkstad felt his stomach clench in disgust. But he'd heard the rumors.

"Yes, sir."

"The new world is coming and can't be stopped. Patterson will talk, and we can't have that. Take care of him, will you?"

"Yes, sir." Berkstad knew what the old man asked. He could arrange a prison yard altercation. Patterson had lied, made campaign promises he couldn't, and never had any intention of, keeping. Everyone hated him. It would be easy. He wouldn't be missed.

"Tell me about Elias Cain's new boy, McAndrews. Can he be bought?"

"He's married to money, lots of it. Daniela St. Clair."

"Lucky man. She's lovely. But her wealth is nothing compared to mine."

"Sir, I don't think the usual enticements will work. Roxie says he's a real hurray-for-America kind of guy."

"Ah, Roxanne, speaking of incorruptible, how is my little vixen?" Berkstad knew the old man had always found Roxie irresistible. He actually enjoyed their adversarial combat. He'd even let her win the battle when it suited him.

"She's fine."

"Fine? If I were a younger man . . . ." Again, the faraway look, the remembering of a past time. "Never mind. McAndrews—can he be turned?"

"He's just a profiler. He isn't important to our cause," Berkstad argued.

"Rich, intelligent, young, innovative. Sounds to me Mr. Baseball-and-Apple-Pie is important. He was the driving force that brought down

Patterson. Even though it's not a loss, it is an inconvenience. And you know how I hate to be inconvenienced." The old man smiled, deepening the trenches radiating out from the corners of his eyes.

Berkstad should just walk and pull the lever on the old man. But now that he was in the middle of a divorce, he needed the money the man generously sent his way. To land Roxie, he'd need to prove he could pay child support, alimony, college educations, and provide for her, too. He'd never meant to fall in love with her. But now, living without her wasn't a possibility.

"My time is short. You have two options, David. You turn McAndrews to our side, or you eliminate him."

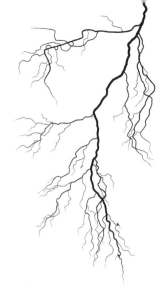

CHAPTER ONE

"**Y**OU SPEND MONEY like we won the lottery!" Dad screamed. Jamie covered his ears and cringed in his hiding place.

"You're just cheap!" Mom shrieked, close to Dad's volume, only at a higher pitch. "But you don't have a problem with spending on yourself!"

Jamie Randall hated it when his parents fought. When they moved their battle to the motor home's bedroom, he crawled out from under the dining table.

That's all they seemed to do anymore. They fought about everything. They especially fought about money. At least that's what they were bickering over when he'd had enough and left the camper. He let the screen door slam behind him like an exclamation point at the end of a sentence.

He and Dad were supposed to go fishing, but that was off. When his parents yelled at each other, all promises were broken.

Jamie climbed up the sturdy limbs of the gnarly oak he spied beside the hiking trail. To his left, from his perch, he could see the sparkling green water of the Tenville River rushing over boulders. Off to his right, from the heart of the forest, the little Crooked Creek babbled and splashed down the cliffside rock face to the river below.

Yep. His parents fought and fought, and it ruined the camping trip. He wished he'd stayed home with his neighbor and best friend, Chubbs

Martin. He wished Chubbs could've come up here with them. Oh, he'd asked, but then his parents went off on that idea!

Jamie wasn't ever gonna get married if all you do is fight, even if the girl looked like the babes in the posters hanging in Chubbs's dad's garage.

Shoot! He leaned against the tree's trunk and scratched his back like an old bear rubbing to and fro. He sure wished he had somebody to play with. If Chubbs were here, they'd build a fort in this tree. It had two big branches almost at the same level. With the lumber left over in the back of Dad's truck, they could frame a platform right across. He imagined curling up in his sleeping bag and looking up through the canopy of leaves, watching the stars. Betcha they could see all the constellations in the night sky up here in the mountains. Yeah! If Chubbs were here, they could sleep in this old tree.

For a moment, he stared up at the white cotton puff clouds that hung in the pale-blue morning sky. He gazed down at the stream lapping and crashing over rocks and fallen trees on its way to the river. The creek seemed to be laughing, maybe laughing at him. Anyway, it invited him to play.

Jamie knew there were crawfish in that creek. Last summer, he caught a whole basket full. One of those big suckers grabbed Chubbs's finger. Must'a hurt like heck, too, 'cuz Chubbs bawled like a baby. Jamie laughed out loud.

Jamie slithered down the fat tree trunk and jumped the last couple of feet to the hiking trail. He crammed the rest of his candy bar in his mouth and shoved the wrapper in a crevice at the junction of two branches.

He decided to get some of those crawdads. Mom could stick 'em in the big black kettle on the open fire. Dad loved crawfish with hot pepper sauce. Cajun style. That's what he called it. Maybe that would keep Mom and Dad from fighting tonight.

All the thoughts about cooking crawfish made him fiercely hungry. His belly rumbled. He peeled off his nylon jacket, tied it around his waist and headed down the slope and into the creek. He could tell it would be a scorcher today. The icy water seeped into the canvas of his high-top tennis shoes, and it felt great.

The blackberry brambles, growing in tangles alongside the creek, smelled just like sugar. Jamie stopped, picked some ripe, juicy berries, and stuffed them in his mouth.

He wandered up the creek bed, jumping from stone to stone. This looked like as good a spot as any. He turned over a rock, and sure enough, a greenish-brown crawfish scurried away from him, seeking shelter under the next rock. There were going to be lots and lots of crawfish. He removed his jacket and tied the sleeves together, creating a bundle. Carefully, keeping his fingers away from the snapping claws, he grabbed his prey and dropped the first of his catch into the jacket.

After a while, he had a good number and decided to return to camp with his prize. His parents would be so pleased. And maybe, just maybe, they'd stop fighting.

Jamie noticed a big flat rock; the dry top reflected the sunlight above the creek's water line. He opened the sleeves of his jacket for a peek inside the bundle. A mass of green bodies wriggled around against each other. He must have a hundred of those suckers in there. He re-tied the make-shift pack together again and started down the creek bed.

Up ahead, at the top of the slope that ran down from the dirt road to the creek, he saw two men, one taller and bigger than the other, struggling with a heavy bundle. The smaller man wore camouflage clothing and a blue baseball cap, and the taller one dressed in a gray and black jacket with a hood and khaki shorts. Their faces were in shadow, so he really couldn't make out their features very well. He could hear them puffing and grunting as they wrestled with a brown plastic tarp.

Boy! Howdy! Jamie's dad would be spittin' mad. He hated people who came to the woods to dump their trash, ruining the countryside just to save the few bucks it took to go to the landfill. When he grew up, he planned to have lots of money. That's all there was to that! Money so he wouldn't have to fight with his wife; money so he could afford to go to the stupid dump.

They finally got the bundle over the lip of the embankment, and it began to roll down the rocky slope, causing a mini landslide. Rocks from above were pulled loose by the trash and splashed into the creek in front of him.

Transfixed, Jamie watched the filled plastic roll over and over, followed by a cloud of dust. As it tumbled, the plastic fell away from the contents inside. It only took a few seconds for Jamie to realize what he saw.

"A dead body? That's a dead body!" Jamie couldn't stop the scream from leaving his throat.

The men straightened and glared down the creek bed. For one breathless moment, the bigger man's stare locked with Jamie's. He saw Jamie clear as day.

Jamie dropped the crawfish and ran.

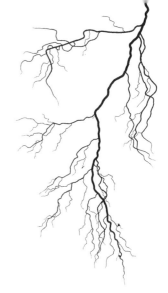

CHAPTER TWO

TIM MCANDREWS HELPED Lettie dismount her horse, taking her into his arms as she slipped off the saddle. Before letting her go, he whirled around with her, making her laugh and giggle and beg for more.

"Now me!" Chloe cried out.

"It's your sister's turn," Tim teased, waiting until Lettie's feet were on solid ground before turning loose. "Love you," he said.

"Love you, too, Dad." He paused for a moment, unable to stop the smile swelling like the emotion inside. He hadn't expected Lettie to call him Dad yet, which made him happier than she knew. Lettie acknowledged him with a sheepish grin.

Tim took the reins from Chloe and handed them to Brenda, their horse trainer. An accomplished and winning rider, Brenda filled the position of the girls' full-time instructor perfectly. Brenda had needed a place to go. Tim knew his soft-hearted wife, Dani, offered the apartment next to the barn to help Brenda escape her abusive boyfriend. Dani never shied away from helping people in need. He loved that about her.

Tim stood by the horse's left side as Chloe dove from her saddle into his arms, the momentum nearly knocking him off balance. He twirled her around like he had Lettie. Before releasing her, he felt her wet, slobbery kiss against his cheek.

"Love you, Dad." Chloe mimicked her sister.

"Love you, too," he replied. When Chloe's feet touched the ground, she grabbed Lettie's hand, and they sprinted toward the house.

"Whoa, ladies!" He called after them. "We need to help Brenda cool down these horses. Mom would never let you get away with this." The girls looked at each other and shrugged. They started back.

Tim picked up his mare's reins and waited for the girls to return and take charge of their horses.

"Mr. McAndrews, it's okay. I can handle it." Brenda offered. Tim admired her practical, loving, and common-sense approach to horses. He knew she could, but this dad business was new to him. He could only reference what he thought his dad would do.

"I know you can. But cooling out the horses and grooming them is part of horse ownership, and they need to learn it," he smiled. "Dani explained the chores to them, and they agreed to do them."

After the girls took charge of their horses, Brenda walked ahead. The tack-up area consisted of three separate matted grooming stalls with crossties to secure the horses while removing the saddles, bridles, and blankets. Tim helped the girls take off the bridles, exchange them for halters, and connect the crossties to each side of the mares' halters.

Tim hadn't been for the horse thing at first. The girls were so young. Lettie was a timid and shy five; in contrast, Chloe was a bold and fearless four. But the horses turned out exactly as Dani had predicted. The sweet-spirited Arabian mares were gentle and protected the girls when they rode. The mares seemed to know they carried precious cargo.

Tim learned a lot about horses in the last few weeks. He hadn't expected to like them; he'd always been wary of them—until now. He wouldn't admit it, not out loud anyway, but he had even developed a fondness for the mare Dani had chosen for him.

Brenda helped the girls remove their saddles, and Tim caught the clean scent of damp leather mixed with salty horse sweat as she passed by to put the tack away. The girls were still too small for that chore, but Tim would make sure they learned and took on the responsibility as they grew older. He didn't want them to become spoiled brats depending on the help.

Brenda passed out wipe-down towels and brushes to each of them.

"Well, girls, how'd I do?" Tim asked about his performance during the riding lesson, knowing the answer. He was no equestrian, but he'd try his best to become one to get extra time with the girls. Both girls were quite accomplished for the short time they'd been riding. So, if they could do it, he could, too.

"You need more lessons," Chloe said boldly. Outspoken Chloe always gave her assessment with complete honesty, and he laughed to himself.

"What do you think, Lettie?"

"She thinks you need more lessons, too," Chloe tipped her chin, her blue eyes full of confidence. Her blonde curls fell in Shirley-Temple-ringlets around her face as she answered for her more reserved older sister.

Chloe easily settled into life with her new adoptive parents while Lettie struggled. Tim wanted Lettie to know she belonged—because she did, and that they loved her—because they did.

"Is that what you think?" Tim had to persuade Lettie to speak for herself. When she finally joined in, Lettie always enjoyed it, especially if it included teasing him. So, he encouraged her.

"I think you need more lessons, too," Lettie answered, slowly raising her gaze, her dark brown eyes meeting his as if begging for his approval. When he nodded, a smile erupted on her face, and she toyed with one of her chocolate-colored braids.

"Yeah, I think you're both right." He grinned at her and watched her whole body relax. "Maybe tomorrow we can take another lesson together."

Sometimes, Tim saw Lettie as the terrified little girl he'd found, cowering in the closet, hiding from the traffickers who had kidnapped her. When he did, emotion would overwhelm him for a second. If he'd been able to, he would've taken all fifty children they'd rescued that day home with him.

Lettie's therapist said she would take a while to heal. Tim and Dani would see to it—she'd have as much time and love as she needed. They hoped to change her terror into trust—her fear into love.

"Can we go on a trail ride?" Chloe asked.

"We'll see what Mom says," Tim answered. The big sliding barn doors across from the tack-up area were open, and a breeze spun dust and chaff up from the barn floor. It tickled against his cheek, making him turn and look outside.

A former racehorse breeder's place, their luxurious new home had everything any horse lover could want. The huge pristine barn contained a 200-foot long by 160-foot-wide covered riding arena and sixteen 12 x 24-foot stalls with turnouts. Gently rolling hills were covered with brilliant green irrigated pastures and dotted with Maple trees along the fence lines.

The two-hundred-fifty acres were encircled by a specially prepared 16-foot-wide trail the former owners used for breezing their Thoroughbreds. Like a racetrack, both sides of the road were bordered by white three-rail fences, making it a safe place for the kids to ride. Large Maple trees full of translucent emerald leaves arched across the path, offering shade from the summer sun. White cumulus clouds formed on warm updraft thermals in the sky, looking like towers built from cotton balls. It was a beautiful Saturday morning, and he looked forward to spending it with his family.

"Maybe Mom can go on a trail ride with us," Tim said, watching Dani walk up the trail from the house. Disappointment curved her full lips into a frown, and she held his iPhone out to him.

Or maybe not. He thought to himself, blowing out breath. The look on his wife's face said it all. Though he'd been promised a three-day weekend, criminals didn't take time off. He traded the brush he held for his phone and kissed Dani on the cheek.

"It's Elias," Dani said. A tight smile crept across her lips, but she wasn't a complainer, at least not in words. Supervisory Special Agent Elias Cain wouldn't call Tim in unless it was an emergency.

"Sorry." He mouthed to her, waiting for her look of forgiveness. When she smiled, he answered the call by pushing the speaker button.

"McAndrews."

"Tim, it's Elias. We have a new case. Meet me at headquarters in an hour." The Behavior Analysis Unit of the FBI occupied the basement of the building at the Marine training grounds at Quantico and had become one of crimefighting's most important assets.

"Yes, sir," he answered, wistfully looking down the barn aisle at his family, joking, laughing, brushing horses, and making plans. He wished he could stay with them, yet the thrill of hunting down bad guys competed with that emotion. Tim found satisfaction in taking dangerous criminals off the street.

"A helicopter will be waiting. I'll give you the details when you get here."

"On my way." Tim disengaged and stuffed his phone in his shirt pocket. He turned to face his family and shrugged. "Looks like I have to go to work."

After his last case, his entire team volunteered for the FBI's Child Abduction Rapid Deployment (CARD) Unit. They quickly responded when notified of a lost or missing child or a suspected child abduction. They'd profile the kidnapper, help local law enforcement's rescue efforts, and arrest the perpetrator. Tim believed wholeheartedly in their mission.

Dani slipped her arm around his waist. "Be careful, okay?"

"Always," he answered, resting his arm over her shoulder, and pulling her tight to his side. The girls glanced at each other, giggled, dropped their brushes, and ran to him, making the horses fidget in their crossties. Each girl grabbed one of his legs as if that would keep him here. Tim couldn't help but laugh. He loved being loved by his family.

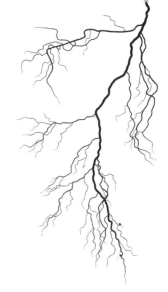

CHAPTER THREE

L IKE A RABBIT pursued by a predator, heart thundering in his chest, Jamie froze. He concentrated on the hiking trail from the shelter of the dappled shadows and tangle of branches and leaves in his hiding place. He watched one of the men stop at the intersection of the trails. Only a few feet away, Jamie could see the bottom of the killer's khaki shorts, dark skin, hairy legs, and Nike Athletic shoes as he turned in a slow circle, scanning all around. The man leaned forward, bending down in his direction, and squinting into the brambles. Jamie covered his mouth, choking off the scream rising in his throat. The man finally stood, turned away, and sprinted toward the river.

Jamie panted, almost hyperventilating. He couldn't stay here. He waited to see if the other man stood nearby. If the first man returned, he'd surely find him. His thoughts were scrambled, not settling in any direction until he remembered another hiding place. At the top of Tenville Ridge, nestled in a small clearing, a Forest Service Cabin would provide shelter. There was a phone inside connected to the main Ranger Station at the entrance to the campground. He could call, tell the Forest Rangers about the dead body and the killers, and hide until help arrived.

Carefully, he wriggled from his current hiding place on hands and knees, stood, turned a full three-sixty, making certain he was alone, and ran, as fast as he could, up the hiking trail as soundlessly as possible. From time to time, he dashed off the trail, sank to a crouch, and listened for footfalls on the gravel. When he heard no sounds but the forest, he continued.

The small cabin was little more than a warming hut. He and Chubbs found it as they hiked and played along the trail last summer. They hadn't told his parents about it. They would've been in big trouble for straying so far from the campground. His parents wouldn't even know to look for him there. His spirit sank, and he suddenly felt alone—but he remembered the phone on the wall next to the kitchen sink. The sign to the side read: FOR EMERGENCY USE ONLY. *Well, this was an emergency if there ever was one!*

Jamie realized the killers had taken the back way into the campground and probably thought they were miles away from people when they dumped the body at the creek. *Would the killers know about the cabin?* He had to chance it.

After crawling from his current hiding place, Jamie sprinted up the trail again. This part of his path was an easy climb. The steep rise from the river valley started at about the two-mile marker. Then, the gravel trail switch-backed up the hillside until it stopped at an outcropping of jagged rocks just before the top of the ridge.

Once there, he had to be careful. His way would be impeded by the occasional rough steps chiseled out by the rangers for the summer hikers. The stairs were full of loose pebbles and shifting round stones held in place with old railroad ties. Chubbs fell last year and scraped up both knees and both palms. They found a first aid kit at the cabin, but the box held iodine instead of a painless antiseptic. Boy, did Chubbs throw a fit. After applying it, he cried and danced around the cabin for about ten minutes. Jamie couldn't help but laugh out loud. Then, he and Chubbs opened a can of baked beans and cooked them on the stove inside, though they knew they shouldn't.

Jamie's thoughts circled back to the killers, so he slipped behind some bushes off the road and waited for a minute or two. Like a squirrel running on the top board of a backyard fence, a shiver of fear ran along his shoulders. Wishing Chubbs were here now, he finally returned to the trail and resumed this part of his climb at a brisker, more urgent pace.

An hour later, he reached the jagged rock ledge—the last part of the climb. He turned and studied the trail below. Almost all of it was visible from this height, and the men weren't anywhere. A small surge of relief washed over him, but he knew better. He'd seen them dump a dead body. They would come looking for him. Jamie's tongue felt thick and dry.

He needed a drink of water and plopped down on a patch of grass hidden between two big boulders to rest. The sun was merciless, but he thought he heard the distant rumble of thunder and looked up. He picked a piece of tall grass, peeled away the thick outer leaf, and chewed on the slightly sour, soft center shaft inside. It wouldn't satisfy his hunger, but it would cause him to salivate and help with his dry mouth. His father had taught him that trick.

If his parents hadn't been fighting, he'd be fishing with Dad right now. He remembered the peaceful feeling of drifting in the boat down the deep, slow water and finding holes near the rocky banks where the trout would hide.

He reclined into the sweet-smelling grass, catching his wind, and watching big cotton puff clouds shapeshifting in the sky overhead. After resting for a few minutes, he stood. From his position high on the mountainside, through the pine branches and maple leaves, he studied the campground below. The section of the Tenville River in front of their camp snaked its way slowly to Crystal Falls, where it plunged dramatically thirty feet to a rocky pool below. A twinge tightened the pit of his stomach. He missed Mom and Dad and wondered if they'd stopped fighting—looked for him. Should he abandon his climb and sneak back? No. The cabin was closer, and he hoped, safer.

Jamie resumed his climb. Scrambling up the rocks on the artificial steps, he lost his footing and fell, scraping one knee. He needed to be careful. When he finally reached the ridge top, he saw the cabin with its rough-hewn log porch under the blue peaked metal roof. He remembered the wicker rocking chairs with the flower print cushions he and Chubbs sat on to rest their last time here.

The bright red *Coca-Cola* Machine containing his much-needed drink still sat beside a stack of seasoned firewood. The vending machine full of chips and candy bars practically called out his name. Mouthwatering at the thought, he felt his pockets for change. None. At least, inside the cabin, there were supplies. If he remembered correctly, the kitchen's small pantry was stocked with bottled water, canned chili, and various other goods. There was a box on the counter beside the door for contributions so the rangers could restock. He could borrow a few quarters to buy a coke, candy, and chips. His parents could pay it back when they found him. Most of all, though, he wanted to get to the black phone on the wall. He had to get help, and he had to report the dead body.

Off to the west, the sky darkened as a rain cloud passed in front of the sun. Jamie finished his trek to the cabin. As he stood on the porch steps, he turned. A lightning bolt zig-zagged from the cloud, striking the ground on the path, close enough to tingle his skin and cause the hair on his arms to stand. A deafening clap of thunder rattled the whole porch, and big raindrops made little dust explosions when they hit the path behind him. He smelled the mixture of dust and ozone in the air. As the rain intensified, a burst of hail clattered noisily on the metal roof. Jamie dashed inside the cabin and picked up the phone.

"Hello?" He said, his voice trembling. No reply. "Hello? Is anybody there?" He waited. "Hello?" A strange electrical crackling sound was the only reply.

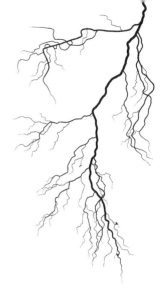

CHAPTER FOUR

WHEN TIM WAS a child, he remembered days like this. He and his friends relaxed in the cool, sweet-smelling clover in his backyard. As they watched the hot breeze flutter through the broad leaves of the sugar maples, they would try to see creatures and faces in the clouds billowing up in the afternoon sky.

Like the memory, today, in the sweltering heat, clouds formed and towered majestically against the emerald slopes of the Western Appalachian Mountains.

After their hour-long helicopter ride, Tim and his partner, Miguel Gonzales, picked up an SUV from the Virginia FBI branch office in Crystal Falls City. Miguel was a good partner, far more experienced than Tim, and had a fun-loving edge to his personality. He loved to joke and kept even the darkest moments light. Like Tim, he was tall and military fit, matching Tim's six foot two. In contrast, Miguel's hair was black, Tim's sandy blond and Miguel's eyes were espresso brown while Tim's were ice blue.

They followed the SUV's onboard GPS to a parking lot on the back edge of the Crystal Falls Campground and parked. The deputies they were to meet from the sheriff's department hadn't arrived yet.

Tim closed the door to the passenger side of the SUV, went to the back of the vehicle, and opened the hatch. After slipping into his FBI vest, he replaced his shoulder holster and hung a pair of binoculars around his neck. Miguel did the same.

As the deputies pulled into a parking space beside them, Tim started to shut the hatch but paused. Quickly, he stuffed two extra magazines for his FBI-issued Glock 17 pistol in the pockets of his vest. He joined Miguel at the trailhead to the Crystal Falls Campground, where they waited for the deputies to catch up.

Tim chuckled out loud.

"What's so funny?" Miguel asked as he looked up at the clouds.

"I was thinking about my childhood and watching the weather on days like this," Tim smiled. "Did you do that when you were a kid? We used to count seconds between a lightning flash and the sound of thunder to guess how far away the strike was from us."

"Yeah, all kids do that," Miguel answered, nodding. "What brought that on?"

"That big thunderhead," Tim pointed to the west and the storm building against the mountain ridges. He wiped away a big raindrop that splashed on his forehead from a small passing cloud.

"When I was a kid, there were thunderstorms nearly every afternoon in the summer in Venezuela." Miguel smiled, and a far-away look filled his eyes.

"Do you miss it? Venezuela, I mean." Tim asked.

"Oh, hell no!" Miguel answered, shaking his head. "I don't know how anyone survives there." Miguel's family had escaped from Venezuela when Chavez's rule turned bad. They were the lucky ones. In the years since he'd done an eight-year stint in the Navy. From his position on a SEAL team, he was recruited by the FBI.

"Where I grew up, in the Pacific Northwest, this time of year, thunderstorms meant forest fires. Still does," Tim answered.

"Sure is pretty out here today." Miguel stared up through the trees at the sky.

"Your idea of pretty is out of whack," Tim removed his hat and wiped his shirt sleeve across his brow. The humidity made him feel like he needed another shower and wearing the FBI-issued vest worsened that feeling. "Hot. Humid. Real pretty," Tim laughed. He watched as Miguel slapped a mosquito dining on the back of his neck. "Not to mention bug-infested," Tim added.

While waiting on the sheriff's deputies to collect their gear, Tim looked down the tree-filled draw. Miles away, the clouds seemed to bunch up together, and the telltale anvil shape of a thunderstorm spread aloft in the wind.

"How can a storm look so beautiful and soft but be so angry," he wondered aloud.

"Just like a woman," Miguel replied.

"Careful," Tim chuckled. "Remember, one of our deputies is a woman." Tim tipped his chin in the direction of the deputies as they approached. And just like that, Miguel dialed up the charm, directing a big guilty grin at the female deputy.

"I'm SA Tim McAndrews, and this is SA Miguel Gonzales." Tim reached out his hand to complete the greeting.

"Deputy Shannon Cleary, and this is my partner, Deputy Lane Tegner," The young woman said, giving them both a studied once over.

Deputy Cleary was a handsome woman, but her eyes, a brilliant shade of green, flashed with intelligence spiced with anger, like hot sauce on chicken wings. Her flame-colored hair showed from under her Smokey-Bear hat in curls tied back into a low ponytail.

"So, what have we got, Deputy Cleary?" Miguel asked.

Deputy Cleary's tight smile and the annoyed tick to her left eyelid immediately extinguished the flirty grin on his lips. *The Latin lover put into his place by a fiery redhead?* Tim smiled to himself.

"Missing boy, age nine. The sheriff's afraid it might be a kidnapping. That's why you're here," Cleary said, giving Tim the same cold stare. Almost as a *so-there*, she adjusted the weight of her police belt on her hips. Tim was happy he wasn't obligated to wear one, especially in today's heat.

"Have there been others? What's the connection?" Tim asked, turning his mind to the task at hand.

"There have been two, but they don't seem connected to me. They resulted from custody fights. I don't know why Sheriff Montgomery called you," she answered, lifting her shoulders in a shrug. "The sheriff and forest rangers are with the parents now."

Tim smiled at her and nodded. Cleary had an attitude Tim decided to ignore. He'd been here before; not every sheriff's department relished interference from the FBI, even after they'd initiated the call for help.

Elias Cain wasn't arrogant and insisted his team be respectful. They were here, with all the FBI's resources, to help find lost and abducted children and that's exactly what Tim intended to do.

As the group trudged along the gravel trail, Tegner looked up at the sky. "We'd better find the kid. It looks like that storm is moving our way and going to break wide open."

"Oh. That storm is miles away. We won't even get a drop." Shannon laughed, rejecting Tegner's assessment outright. Tim knew that wasn't true. He'd been splatted by a big raindrop only minutes ago. Though it was from a small cloud, the humidity in the air had an afternoon thunderstorm written all over it.

"If you say so," Tegner retorted, a glare as sharp as a knife in his eyes.

Deputy Cleary's whole demeanor was defensive as if she battled Tegner daily. She increased her pace, almost like she didn't want to walk with them. Tim hoped it wouldn't interfere with the search.

"I don't think she likes me," Miguel whispered aside to Tim, laughing.

"Or me. And don't make it worse by teasing her," Tim chided his partner as a big grin slid over his face.

They walked briskly along the hiking trail toward the campground. Tim stared down at the boiling waters of the Tenville River. The fragrance of mint growing along the side of the trail brought back memories. It had been years since he'd been drift fishing in a river. The sight of the swift flow reminded him of tagging along with his older brothers when he was a kid. He remembered rafting the river, the summer sun warming his skin, and the sugary smell of ripening blackberries on the riverbank. He wondered if his daughters would like fishing. When they were a little older, he'd take them.

A frantic woman rushed up the trail toward them when they reached the campground. She had to be the missing boy's mother.

"Thank God you're here. Jamie's been missing for six hours. I'm scared to death. This isn't like him. He never misses a meal, and when he didn't come back for lunch…." The woman finally paused to take a breath. Worry and tears had left her cheeks covered with red blotches, the same color that ringed her swollen eyes. Tim immediately felt empathy. He'd be a mess if either of his daughters went missing.

"Okay, Ma'am. We're here to help you find him." He reached out and put a comforting hand on the woman's shoulder, but it didn't help. She burst into a flood of tears and sobs.

"I'm a terrible mother. I should have watched him more carefully."

Mr. Randall joined the crowd, gathering around Tim and the deputies. Tim immediately didn't like him. His mousey hair was pulled back in a scraggly ponytail, and his face was rough and unshaven. He knew he should give him some slack; the guy was camping, after all. But Randall reminded Tim of a crackhead, and his cruel eyes didn't reflect the worry he expected from a loving father. Suspicion made him carefully study his body language. Mrs. Randall, on the other hand, gushed with enough tears for both.

"All right, folks, step back and give us some room," Tegner spread his arms out wide and encouraged the other campers to back away from the Randall's camp.

"We just want to help." A fat, balding man volunteered.

"Great," Tim said, taking a notepad from the breast pocket of his vest. "If you could list names, addresses, phone numbers, and license plate numbers for the people who'd like to join the search, that would help." He handed the man the pad and pen. Smiling, the man hustled off to complete his task.

"Where's Sheriff Montgomery?" Tim asked Deputy Cleary.

"With Ranger Marcum. They're finishing up the interviews with each of the campers here."

The campground swarmed with police, and volunteers arrived from the city of Crystal Falls fire department's search and rescue. Miguel joined in organizing the search parties. Tim decided to interview the parents.

The Randalls were working middle-class. Jamie's parents' camping equipment was tattered, well-used, and dated. That fact left a hole in the pit of his stomach—children from that background were seldom taken for ransom, and the other reasons for kidnapping were horrible and hard to contemplate. He breathed deeply and let it out, trying to expel anxiety.

He turned his attention to Mrs. Randall. "First, how old is Jamie, and can you give me a description?" He guided her to sit at a picnic table near their spot and sat on the bench across from her.

"Would you happen to have a picture of Jamie?" Tim asked additional questions about what clothes he might be wearing.

Mrs. Randall sorted through the photos stored on her iPhone and handed it to Tim.

While he slowly scrolled through the images. Mrs. Randall continued, "Jamie is nine, but he's really smart. He has skipped one grade already. He's especially fond of science and math."

Jamie was a good-looking kid. Shaggy brown hair fell to about mid-ear, and his big brown eyes were clear and curious. His looks confirmed Mrs. Randall's description.

"Are you or is your husband in a custody dispute over Jamie with an ex-husband or ex-wife?" Tim remembered Deputy Cleary's explanation of the other abductions as custody battles.

"No. Jamie's dad and I have been married only to each other. We've been married since High School," she answered.

Tim tried not to react. Stranger abductions statistically had terrible outcomes. Tim's spirit sank. From what he'd learned, Tim guessed Jamie was a very smart guy. But was he smart enough or lucky enough to escape or survive a kidnapping?

"Can you email this picture to me?" Tim chose a full-face picture of Jamie. When he received it, he updated the Amber Alert and sent it on to Elias to inform police departments all over the country.

"I don't want to scare you, and Jamie may just be temporarily lost. Maybe he wandered off...."

"My husband and I walked every inch of this campground. We've talked to every camper here. Jamie was told to stay close. He was supposed to go fishing with his dad. He loves fishing. He would've never missed that." Mrs. Randall sniffed.

"Did you find something, see something that makes you believe he's been kidnapped? Is there a ransom note?" Tim asked. He studied her response, rubbing his thumb and index finger on opposite sides of his face.

She shook her head, "No. I just feel it."

Tim understood that this phenomenon was very real. Lots of guys dismissed it. But he'd learned when he was a prosecutor that victims' mothers often described knowing or dreaming their child was in trouble and could *feel* it when they were injured or dead.

"We've camped here for the last three summers," Mrs. Randall volunteered. "He's never been gone this long before."

"That's encouraging. Jamie might know his way around and be playing somewhere perfectly safe. Maybe he just lost track of time," Tim said to ease her worry. He needed to talk to the sheriff to find out why the man believed Jamie was kidnapped. There had to be evidence, but it was also okay with Tim if it was to pull in the FBI's CARD resources. A lost child was enough of a reason in Tim's book.

Miguel signaled to Tim that they were ready to go.

"I know you want to go on the search, Mrs. Randall, but you need to stay here in case Jamie returns." Tim waited until she acknowledged his words and joined the crowd of about twenty deputies, search and rescue members, and campers who'd offered to help. They gathered in front of a picnic area under a log gazebo.

Tim and Miguel stood in the back of the crowd and studied each volunteer discreetly but carefully. They knew perpetrators often joined in a search just to throw off suspicion, cover their tracks, figure out what evidence the police had, or sicker yet, to relive their crime.

Tim knew he couldn't tell by looking at someone if he was good or bad. He wished they had *evil scumbag* stamped on their foreheads. Normal-looking, soft-spoken, nice guys sometimes turned out to be monsters.

"Alright, folks." The sheriff clapped his hands to get everyone's attention. He was a big man—imposing, yet his brown eyes were filled with kindness. He cleared his throat, and his bass voice boomed out information efficiently. "Jamie is wearing blue jeans, a yellow t-shirt with Mason

County Bolts Little League printed on the front, a blue nylon jacket, and black high-top tennis shoes. He has brown hair and eyes, is about four and a half feet tall, and is around 75 pounds. Your group leader will have a picture. I want you all to take a look. Group A will head south. Deputy Tegner will instruct you on how to proceed. Group B, head north, and Deputy Cleary will be your team leader. It will be dark in about seven hours, so let's find this kid."

Miguel turned to Tim. "Anyone stand out to you? Bother you? Make your hair stand on end?"

"The guy in the gray and black jacket...." Tim tipped his head in the man's direction. "He wasn't paying attention to the boy's description or the sheriff's instructions. Kept looking around." Cautiously, Tim glanced in the man's direction, ensuring he didn't observe the scrutiny. "Why is the sheriff assuming it's a kidnapping?"

"At this point, it's a lost kid, but the sheriff says he's had two kidnappings from this campground. One last year, one the year before. He doesn't want to rule it out."

"Didn't Cleary say they were custody disputes? Were we called?" Tim frowned.

"She did. And yes. FBI was called, but not Elias's team. I ordered the files from the DC Field Office. Once they get here, we need to look for connections," Miguel answered, pulling his communication gear from his pocket, and pressing a wireless earbud in his left ear. "Keep in touch with me."

Tim nodded his agreement.

Miguel was the senior agent, and in charge of their part in the investigation by default. Tim trusted his judgment completely.

In the distance, he heard another rumble of thunder from the towering clouds. Tim pushed his communication bud deeper into his left ear. They needed to find Jamie before that storm hit.

Tim waited until the man in the gray and black jacket chose a team. Then he followed suit.

"I'll join Group B. You go with A," Tim said.

"If you find the kid or any evidence—let me know," Miguel said, tapping his left ear.

"You'll be first." Tim smiled. As Team B headed north, Tim lagged behind to watch all the members.

The forest shade was at least ten degrees cooler than the parts of the trail in direct sun. Light filtered through the translucent leaves, painting the trees in varying shades of green. Between the periodic calls of Jamie's name from the searchers, the river bubbled and babbled its music. The spicey scent of the deciduous trees and wet river rocks left Tim wishing he were here for a different purpose. He set his thoughts of his family aside. He had to find Jamie. Alive.

He searched for any sign of the boy in the brush bordering the river. Though this part of the river looked smooth and quiet on the surface, dangerous currents and eddies could be swirling beneath the calm. Tim hoped Jamie hadn't fallen in and drowned, but it was possible. The sheriff thought so, too. If the boy wasn't found, he had scheduled dive teams for later this afternoon.

Tim paused when he reached a large oak with branches reaching across the trail and out over the river below. *No boy could resist climbing this tree,* he thought, walking around it. Stuffed in a crevice between branches, he found a wrinkled candy wrapper. Trash cans were placed regularly along the hiking trail, but it would be just like a kid to stuff a wrapper here, or it could be nothing at all. He pulled an evidence bag from his pocket, marked it, took a picture, and notified Miguel.

"What have you found?" Deputy Cleary walked up to him.

"Candy wrapper," Tim said as she leaned forward and closely inspected the find.

She stepped back and curled her lip, and her green eyes flashed disapproval. Surprised by her reaction, Tim wondered if he was the problem or if resentment of the FBI played a role. Unfortunately, that animosity still prevailed. It shouldn't. They needed each other.

"Hey, Sheriff Montgomery called us," he said, grinning defensively. "And you never know. If it's Jamie's trash, we're going in the right direction." *Err on the side of caution.* He thought. In return, she narrowed her eyes at him.

"All right. Let's fan out. No more than four feet apart," Cleary ordered. The group obeyed the instructions, some on the gentle slope that bordered the river, some on the other side of the trail.

A wooden bridge crossed Little Crooked Creek about thirty feet before it spilled in a waterfall into the river. Tim took out his iPhone and looked at the forest service map he'd earlier downloaded. The creek meandered along the contours of a box canyon and up the hill to the west—a one-lane dirt road wound alongside the creek's path. A small engraved wooden sign with an arrow pointing west read *Lightning Ridge Road*. He found it on his phone's map. When he glanced up to get his bearings, he saw the man in the gray and black jacket slip away from the group, and fade into the trees and brush along the creek bed.

Tim ducked behind a tree to watch. Twice now, the man turned back, almost as if checking to see if anyone shadowed him. Whether for innocent reasons or not, he snuck off and didn't want anyone to see it. His actions dialed up Tim's suspicions. He ran his tongue across his upper teeth, arched an eyebrow, and decided. Like it or not, tracking this guy was *exactly* what he would do. He would do it inconspicuously. If his misgivings had gotten the better of him, he could quietly rejoin the search group.

"Miguel, I'm headed up Little Crooked Creek. Monitoring the guy in the gray and black jacket."

"Roger that. Coming your way," Miguel's voice responded in his earbud.

Tim let the man get several seconds ahead and then trailed behind him. Though the forest thickened here, he heard the man stumble in the rocks.

Tim emerged from the edge of the thicket and noticed a brown tarp, a part of which fluttered in the increasing breeze. The man in the gray and black jacket stood over the tarp for a second. When he turned toward Tim, a cruel, devious smile crept over his face, and his eyes went dark, and his stare void.

He reached into his waistband.

In an instant, Tim knew he'd drawn a gun. *What the hell!* He thought as a round whistled past his shoulder. He twirled, slamming his back against a tree for cover.

"Shots fired," he reported to Miguel over his throat mike. As a reflex, he drew his Glock, pulled back the slide, and armed the firing chamber with a nine-millimeter hollow point from the magazine.

The man sent a barrage in his direction. Splinters of wood exploded from the tree, hitting his arm, cheek, and shoulders. Tim lost count of bullets in the echo bouncing off the canyon walls. The smell of gunpowder and hot lead wafted in the air.

The shots ceased, and Tim spun into the open meadow. He prepared to fire, taking a shooter's stance with his finger ready on the trigger. While Tim was pinned down behind the tree, the man had increased the distance between them. Realizing Tim could return fire, he ran, and rocks clattered together as he scrambled up the creek bank to the road. Tim gave chase. He climbed up the hill, he lowered his profile in case the man had replaced his magazine with a new one. Tim was wary of an ambush. Instead, he heard a car engine crank over. He dashed for the sound. When he crested the rise, the passenger side door of a dark green Jeep closed. The vehicle raced away in a cloud of brown dust. Tim caught sight of the Virginia license plate and memorized the number.

"License plate number seven, four, eight, bravo, tango, alpha. Dark Green Jeep," he called it in, reporting the direction of travel. The man and his driver had no choice but to pass by the campground entrance, and deputies would collar them there.

Tim cleared his weapon, engaged the safety, and replaced the Glock in his shoulder holster. He headed for the brown tarp. *What was in there that made a man shoot and run from the police?* He balanced himself like a skier starting down a run as the rocks rolled underfoot. Deputy Cleary and several of the search and rescue team emerged from the woods and approached from the direction of the river at a dead run.

"Are you hit? What happened?" Cleary stopped and looked at him up and down. Her eyes had softened, and her attitude changed.

"I'm not hit. But a guy in a gray and black jacket tried to use me for target practice."

"What did you do?" she asked with a smirk. Obviously, she believed Tim caused the exchange of lead.

"I guess he didn't want me tracking him," Tim answered. He brushed bark and leaves from the sleeves of his white shirt. The debris had broken off from the tree he'd used for cover when bullets started to fly. "Or finding whatever that is." Pointing to the brown tarp close to the creek's edge, he walked in its direction.

He approached closer. Tim flinched away from the sickening-sweet smell of death and swallowed back his revulsion and gag reflex. He knew he had to look. It was his job and duty to do so. Still, he hesitated. Slowly, he lifted an edge.

"Oh, for crying out loud, McAndrews!" Deputy Cleary said, stopping beside him, thoroughly disgusted. She stepped forward and yanked the tarp from his hand, and away from the contents inside.

"Oh, God," a mutual groan erupted all around him, and Cleary stumbled back two steps in horror.

It was a body, and the woman was definitely dead. At least it wasn't Jamie. However, there was no relief in that.

Tim studied the woman for a moment. A hint of recognition tickled his mind. But from where? She was a middle-aged black woman, fully clothed in expensive tan slacks and a white silk blouse stained with blood. She lay on her back, her fixed, glassy eyes staring at the sky.

A slim gold braided watch encircled the wrist of her left hand lying across her chest. Two of her red-painted fingernails were broken to the quick—evidence of a struggle. A gold cross necklace fell to the side of her throat. One brown leather loafer was at her side, the other still on her right foot. Tim looked for ligature marks around her neck, and none were visible.

On closer inspection, he noticed the tell-tale powder burn of a close contact shot in the center of the bloodstain on her blouse. By its location, he guessed she died from a shot to her heart. One shot. She'd been murdered elsewhere and dumped here like trash. He stood straight, choking back emotion. He turned away.

"Why?" he whispered, shaking his head, and trying to detach himself from sadness and grief. He called for backup.

In his peripheral vision, he noticed Miguel and Deputy Tegner approaching at a jog. Instead of waiting to update them, he faced the creek, watching the clear water sparkling over the darkened rocks in the sunshine, trying to calm his mind. The man in the gray and black jacket murdered this woman. *I know what you look like.* Tim thought. Unfortunately, he hadn't seen the driver. *But where was Jamie? Was he still alive?*

Tim glanced at the creek again and spotted something blue rippling under the water's surface. *Jamie?* Quickly, he waded into the shallows to get a better look. Blue fabric caught by a submerged tree stump undulated with the current.

Nearly underfoot, the creek bed swarmed with crawfish. Tim had never seen so many together in one place. Most scurried away from his steps, but some stood their ground, raising their claws and threatening him. He picked up the material, realizing it was a nylon jacket—*Jamie's blue jacket.*

He scanned the opposite bank of the creek. A small tree branch, broken in the middle, hung halfway across a deer trail. Tim sloshed across the stream and inspected it. The break was brand new. The sap still beaded and dripped like syrup onto the leaves below. He stood erect. Suddenly, a vision of the boy running, stumbling in the creek, and scrambling up this trail filled his mind.

Tim blew out a breath and licked his lips. He was pretty sure he understood what had happened here.

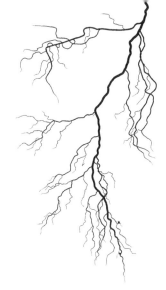

CHAPTER FIVE

W HEN HURRICANE CARLOTTA first hit the Gulf Coast, fifty-year-old Walt Harper had feared this turn of events. He rolled his chair away from his desk and computer, still watching as the predictive radar played out on the screen. He looked up at the big monitors above his head displaying the North American Continent and the various active weather systems moving in real-time across its surface.

Only once in his career as a meteorologist had he seen this phenomenon as part of the aftermath of a hurricane. As the remnants spread northeastward from the Gulf of Mexico, it was predicted to join a moisture-laden low-pressure system from the west rather than being sheared off by the jet stream. The previous time, vast thunderstorms formed in the afternoon and unloaded over ten, sometimes twenty inches of rain in hours on the higher elevations of the Appalachian Mountains. Then water did what water does, and the runoff from the downpour oversaturated the soil and swamped the streams and drainage creeks. Rivers swelled quickly to the flash flood stage.

Doppler radar and his computer models indicated just such a weather event was taking shape, high in the mountains, at the headwaters of the Tenville River. The difference between this storm and the other was the strength of the dissipating hurricane. This time it would still be tropical storm force when it collided with a squall line forming ahead of the cold front along the jet stream. While one storm cell dumped its rain, another would blossom, intensify, and move into place, like freight train cars at the unloading dock. The unstable conditions could last for hours.

Currently, the mountains' eastern slopes enjoyed bright and sunny weather. The deluge caused by this weather phenomenon could send torrents down on unsuspecting people recreating in the sunshine and warmth in the campgrounds below. Or worse yet, hit them while they slept, feeling safe and secure in their campers and tents at night.

"Bill, come take a look at this." He coaxed his colleague to get up from his computer station and join him. Bill Cox stood behind him as he played the computer forecast on the screen.

"What really worries me is that we know the flood control dams were weakened from this year's heavy spring rains," Harper commented, taking in a deep breath. Anxiety rolled in his stomach like a bowling ball.

"What's your prediction?" Bill asked.

"The air is so saturated—worst case, this could cause the Tenville River to crest well over flood stage, and if just one of the flood control dams fails...catastrophe!" Harper wrung his hands and turned to stare into Bill's eyes. Equally disturbed, Bill pulled up a map of the cities and towns along the river on his computer screen.

"We need to issue Flood and Flash Flood Warnings all along the Tenville River," Bill said.

"I agree," Walt answered, quickly typing up the alert and sending it to his National Weather Service superiors with a copy to the Corps of Engineers.

"Should we recommend evacuations?" Bill asked. Harper rubbed his hand across his chin. He didn't want to be one of those meteorologists who cried wolf every time it rained. Just last winter, he'd predicted nighttime tornadoes over six states in the Midwest and South twelve hours before it occurred. Still, with all the warnings, hundreds died.

"I think we should," Harper answered, trying his best to keep calm in his voice. He rolled his chair back to his desk.

"Betty, can you get me the Trask County Sheriff on the phone?" Bill stepped aside so Harper could make eye contact with his secretary. Immediately, Betty started to work. They were a great team.

"Sheriff Montgomery is on line five," Betty called out after a few seconds.

"Sheriff? Walt Harper from The National Weather Service, here." Harper could hear the rush of the river in the background. "I've got some bad news." He had to hold the receiver away from his ear. Apparently, the sheriff had enough bad news for the day. He cussed a stream for a good five seconds. When he finally took a breath, Harper calmly said, "There is a massive storm headed your way. Big enough to flood the Tenville River. We ask that the Crystal Falls Campground and the City of Crystal Falls be evacuated immediately."

Harper pulled up a map on his computer, still listening to the Sheriff's exasperation. From his location in Silver Springs, Maryland, he could be in Crystal Falls in an hour and a half by helicopter. He figured the storm would hit in about three to eight hours, and the flooding would follow about three hours after the rain started. They had plenty of time.

Betty joined them from the reception counter. "Isn't Tenville Canyon where that little nine-year-old boy is lost? I thought I heard something about it on the news." Harper watched her grab up her iPhone. "It is. There's an Amber Alert." She turned the face of her phone toward him so he could see.

He turned slightly away from her. "I understand, Sheriff. What resources can we send to help—all right, sir. You've got it." Harper disengaged and sat in shock before his adrenaline kicked in. In addition to the coming flood, the sheriff was dealing with a lost boy, and a dead body—likely a homicide. *Whew!* Harper was glad he wasn't a cop.

"Bill, you call the governor. We'll need an evacuation order. I'll call the Mayor of Crystal Falls. Betty, see if you can round up a crew to help notify people in the city to evacuate. Call all their radio and news stations and ask them to get the word out. We may need to go door to door. I'll call the Coast Guard. They have swift water rescue teams I can put on standby." Harper barked out his orders.

An eerie silence settled over the office when all the notification tasks were complete. *Had he thought of everything?* Harper wasn't sure he had. The only thing left to do was to go.

"Chopper's here," Bill announced.

Harper stood and grabbed his worn brown leather coat from the back of his chair and slipped his arms through the sleeves. He positioned his Indiana-Jones-Fedora on his head, covering his thick salt and pepper hair.

"Shall we?" He motioned for Bill to go first.

Harper stopped for a moment at Betty's desk. When she looked up at him, she ran her fingers through her tight sable curls and then repositioned her reading glasses on the bridge of her perfect upturned nose. Betty was an incredible beauty for fifty, looking at least ten years younger than her chronological age. Harper considered asking her out about a hundred thousand times over the last few years. She lost her husband to cancer about the same time his wife left him. But each time he mustered the courage to ask, something stopped him, and he didn't. He leaned forward on her desk, pressing his weight into his hands. An invitation formed in his thoughts; he could feel the words rising in his throat.

"Betty…." He stared into her dark brown eyes and watched a shy smile curve her lips. *Tongue-tied!* Again, he was tongue-tied!

"Your steed awaits, Sir Knight," she grinned, setting his field computer for notes on the counter between them.

He gave in to timidity. "I guess I'm outta here." He picked up the notebook and saluted a stiff goodbye. She wouldn't ever consider going out with him anyway. He was just a nerdy scientist, spending his time reading his weather maps and plotting models of the changes on the computer.

Harper left the office, turning back to wave as the glass doors closed behind him. Betty was beaming. *Okay, then!* He'd take that image with him while he dashed off to study this storm. He ducked under the spinning helicopter blades.

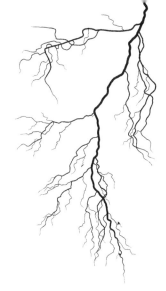

CHAPTER SIX

TIM STOOD AT a "Y" junction in the hiking trail. One section turned right and headed toward the river; the other bordered a small meadow and meandered upward to Tenville Ridge. The meadow grass and wildflowers were not disturbed or crushed—no sign of a struggle, no blood on the leaves and grasses.

Powdery dust covered the trail to the river's edge, and though footprints were distinguishable in the loam, there were too many to characterize a single set or a clear direction of travel. On the other hand, the path to Tenville Ridge, overlaid with loose gravel, held no footprints on the rocks.

He closed his eyes for a moment. He could hear the gurgles and splashes of the river as it dashed over boulders and stones on its way. Even though Tim could still feel the sun's heat on his skin, distant thunder threatened on the mountain tops. Birds warbled out their songs, and flying insects hummed as they gathered nectar from wildflowers poking their purple heads toward the sun in the grassy meadow.

With Nature's music all around him, Tim imagined what had happened. Jamie saw the unsubs dump the body, ran, and the killer or killers chased him. Simple. The question they had to answer—did they catch Jamie? Did Jamie successfully elude them? Did he fail? Was he now another body, hidden somewhere in the forest?

Clearly, the man who'd shot at him was involved. Tim needed to prove it. But first, he needed to find Jamie, dead or alive. He felt a swirl of anger in the pit of his stomach. Instead of Jamie running from killers, what if it were one of his girls? The thought made his heart beat faster. He drew in a gulp of air.

Tim opened his eyes and studied the landscape around him. Deep inside, he believed Jamie was still alive—because he had to. No evidence gathered so far supported his death. Maybe it was only hope, but Tim maintained that Jamie hid somewhere in the dense forest. Otherwise, the perps would've driven away and disappeared. Jamie was the only witness to the body dump.

Instead, he'd gone to the campground. There were motives for that. One, he'd murdered Jamie and wanted to find out what the cops knew. Two, he pretended to be a searcher, planning to find the body *accidentally* to shift suspicion away from himself. Or three, he lost Jamie, assumed the kid circled back to the river and campground, running to mommy and daddy for protection. A reasonable premise.

But Jamie spent the last three summers here. Tim imagined himself at nine. To his parents' dismay, he would've known every inch of this place. He'd know the trails. He would've found caves, hollow logs, bramble dens, and climbing trees. By the third year, he and his friends would've probably built a fort.

Without hesitation, Tim looked left to the hiking path that climbed up toward Tenville Ridge. Because the search and rescue teams would scour the trail along the river, he felt justified following the gravel path up to the ridge.

Tim assured himself that the deputies would have the shooter in custody by now, so that concern disappeared from the table. Still, he could double his chances of finding Jamie if Miguel were with him. He took out his iPhone and searched for landmarks and places of interest along the trail as he walked back toward Little Crooked Creek. He needed to find places Jamie might hide.

As he approached the creek's bank, he noticed a crowd standing on the other side, surrounding the body. He slid down the bank and sloshed his way across the shallow water. He found Miguel in the assembly and slipped up beside him.

"I think I know where Jamie is," he said, just above a whisper.

"What? Where?" Miguel asked, reflecting the same hushed tone. He adjusted his sunglasses so he could peek over the rims.

"There's a fork in the hiking trail. If Jamie's still alive, I think he took the left fork and climbed up Tenville Ridge." Tim pointed to the location on his iPhone screen. "According to this map, there's a forest service cabin just beyond the top of the ridge. If I were a kid, that's what I'd head for. Shall we go, see?"

"Aren't you interested in the murder? Deputy Cleary thinks it's Judge Evelyn Waterford."

Incredulous, Tim slowly raked his teeth over his bottom lip. "Judge Waterford? Wasn't she the President's nominee for the Fourth Circuit Court of Appeals? Oh, boy...."

Miguel tipped his head slightly and raised both eyebrows. "What a coincidence, right?"

"Does Elias know?"

"Yep. The Medical Examiner still needs to confirm with finger-prints at the autopsy. Judge Waterford's husband reported her missing twenty-four hours ago. He panicked when she didn't show up for a prearranged dinner engagement. He found her empty car in the restau-rant's parking lot."

Judge Waterford was recently in the news for adding prison time to the sentence for the convicted killer, Deshawn Murdock. She reasoned that his crimes were so heinous that he should never walk the streets again, and if capital punishment hadn't been abolished in the state, she would've condemned him to death. She'd caused an uproar.

"So, little Jamie's out gathering crawfish...wrong place at the wrong time. The deputies caught the unsubs, right?"

"No, they drove the jeep off-road into the forest, and got stuck and could go no further, they disappeared on foot. We ran the license plate. The Jeep is registered to Samuel Greer and reported stolen." Miguel informed him. "Sheriff's ordered in a couple of Canine Units."

"They escaped? That's not good. The Canine units are, though." Tim clenched his jaw. Worry descended like hundred-pound weights on his shoulders. He heard a breaking twig and turned to see his boss, Supervisory Special Agent Elias Cain, Special Agent Roxie Stauffer, and of all people—Counterintelligence Section Chief David Berkstad, approaching them from the river trail.

"What the hell is Berkstad doing here?" Miguel asked under his breath. "Covering up for another politician?"

A frown pinched Tim's brow. In their last case, Berkstad tried to warn them off a suspect before the DNA results were back from the lab. As it turned out, their person of interest, Congressman Aaron Patterson, contributed that DNA. Now, he lived at the Federal Prison in Leavenworth, serving life plus forty with no possibility of parole.

They'd found no hard evidence Berkstad knew about the Congressman's misdeeds, but suspicion still lingered. Tim didn't trust Berkstad. At the very least, he was a bungling fool. Worst case, he was complicit in trying to cover up a murder-for-hire plot. But either way, he put politics before justice, making Tim bristle. Even at twenty-eight, Tim knew powerful men wielded their influence to intimidate and stay in some imagined ether above the law. *But no one was above the law.*

"Would it surprise you?" Tim asked.

"Ah, nope. You heard about the pedos they found in the CIA just after we closed the Patterson case?"

"I did. I hope we had a hand in busting that wide open," Tim said.

"I think we did. Did you hear back from Kandar on the files we hacked from Berkstad's computer?"

"No. Did you?"

Miguel dipped his head once. "They're downloaded to my phone, but I haven't had a chance to look. He sent them to you, too."

When he and Miguel brought their suspicions to Elias, he acquired seventh-floor approval, and a surreptitious operation was set in motion. No one could buy that Berkstad, the chief of Counterintelligence, had Congressman Patterson surveilled and didn't know about his disgusting secret life.

"I can't wait to dig into that light reading." Tim laughed.

Miguel guiltily raked his hand through his black hair, signaling they should terminate their conversation.

Elias, Roxie, and Berkstad joined them.

"Tim, Miguel, what have we got?" Elias asked without greeting. Tim noticed a difference. After nodding a hello to the other agents, he studied Elias's face.

"You shaved off your mustache. I like it," Tim finally said. He never thought Elias would lose his signature handlebar. He'd worn one for as long as Tim could remember.

"I did. Clare loves it. She says I look like Denzel Washington, a taller and fatter version, though." Elias laughed. "So, what have we got?"

"While searching for the lost boy, I stumbled upon the body." Tim tipped his head in the sheriff's direction and the group of deputies encircling the brown plastic tarp.

"Judge Waterford—I heard," Elias said, his voice quiet and laced with dread. "And the boy?" Elias studied Tim; his eyebrows peaked with hope.

"I'm guessing he witnessed the body dump and ran," Tim said.

"Do you think he's still alive, then?" Elias asked.

"I do," Tim answered. "He's been camping here with his family the last three summers. That's what his mother told me. I think he knows the area. My guess—he's scared and hiding."

"Good. Let's go with that premise unless we find . . .otherwise," Elias answered. "You and Miguel, continue the search. We'll see how we can help the sheriff with Judge Waterford."

"We're on it." Tim nodded, turned, and jogged with Miguel back to the SUV to gather supplies.

Berkstad followed and stood in his usual observational role, arms folded across his chest, expressionless face, almost in a defensive posture. He always left Tim with the impression he was up to something and not a good something.

"I'm going with you," Berkstad said, out of the blue, making Tim take a step back and gawk. Miguel pinched off a snicker by covering his mouth with his hand. Berkstad hadn't dressed for a hike in the woods.

"Sir...?"

"Do you think I'm not fit enough? Let me assure you, young man...." Hostility flashed from his eyes, and the muscles along his jaw ticked with anger.

"No. I'm sure you're fit. We have to be," Tim answered, studying Berkstad's expensive suit and polished Italian leather shoes. He and Miguel had dressed in long-sleeved shirts, jeans, and hiking boots when they'd learned they'd be joining search and rescue in the woods. "You'll need to get changed, sir."

"I'm fine," Berkstad insisted, narrowing his eyes—daring Tim to dispute him.

"If you say so. Let's go. Time's a-wasting," Miguel said, tossing a backpack to Berkstad. The older man caught it by a strap just before it touched the ground.

"What's this for?"

"If we find the boy, he may be injured, dehydrated, and hungry," Tim answered. Berkstad spent the last few years of his career riding a desk. Though he'd come up through the ranks, rumors were that he acquired his office by playing politics rather than first earning it as a field agent. Any outdoor skills he learned were likely rusty, if not forgotten. He left the physical work to the junior agents in his charge. Tim wondered why he didn't do that now. "Have you ever participated in a search and rescue?" Tim asked.

"This is my first," Berkstad grinned, proud of himself.

Tim nodded. He studied the SUV's trunk contents for a moment and decided. He added three thirty-round 5.56 magazines to his gear. After placing his carbine into the backpack's scabbard, he slipped his arms through the straps, adjusted it to balance the weight, and closed the clasps around his chest and waist.

Berkstad moved left, then right, trying to decide what to do with his suit coat. Tim took it from him, folded it lengthwise, and laid it across the back seat. Babysitting the section chief would slow them down, and it irked him.

"Are you...expecting trouble?" Berkstad asked, choking on his words.

"With the killers armed and on the loose and Jamie the only witness to the body dump—yeah, the odds of trouble are pretty high," Tim said. He smiled at Miguel as Berkstad grabbed several extra magazines for his pistol and quickly stuffed them in his trouser pockets.

"Ready?" Miguel swept a hand through his black hair and put on a camouflage baseball cap with FBI embroidered across the brow.

"Ready," Tim answered, closing the SUV, and pressing the lock button on the key fob. He put on a cap and handed Berkstad one. The section chief curled the left half of his lips, tipping his head slightly to the side with an unspoken question.

"Ticks," Tim answered calmly, and Berkstad quickly slapped the cap on his head.

They stopped at the bank when they reached the creek, waiting for Berkstad to catch up. Tim and Miguel watched in amazement as Berkstad sat down on a boulder, removed his shoes and socks, and rolled up his trouser legs. Gingerly, Berkstad waded into the creek.

Miguel rolled his eyes at Tim, shook his head, chuckled, and said, "It's going to be a long day."

"Maybe one of Jamie's crawfish will get him." Tim grinned.

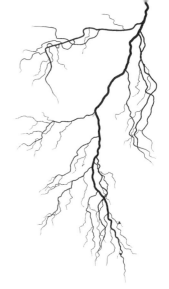

CHAPTER SEVEN

"**GO WITH THEM!**" Deputy Shannon Cleary elbowed her partner Lane Tegner in the ribs and pointed to the FBI agents crossing the creek downstream.

He slapped her arm away and glared at her. "I take my orders from Sheriff Montgomery, not you."

"You're still mad at me? Get over it, Tegner. We're going to have fights," Shannon said disdainfully. His envy annoyed her. They'd fought about the FBI agents since they'd first seen them in the parking lot. Yes, they were young and handsome. She couldn't help but notice, especially SA Tim McAndrews. The tall, blue-eyed blond was very polite but discouraged any friendly conversation with his *just-the-facts-ma'am* attitude. Besides, he wore a diamond-encrusted wedding band that screamed married at her from every sparkling jewel. Why was it good-looking guys were such assholes? He could be married and still be nice. But that would've infuriated Tegner even more.

Shannon and Lane "Teg" Tegner had been sweethearts since high school. After college, they'd gone to the police academy *together*, joined the Sheriff's Department *together*, and just a year ago, they'd moved in *together*. Hell's bells, they did everything *together*. What possessed him to drop the ultimatum on her head this morning? They were very happy just as they were.

"Marry me, or else I'm moving on," he'd said, perfectly calm, but his voice had an icy edge, making her shiver through her shoulders. He'd never sounded this serious before. *Was he?*

She'd tried to brush it off, but that didn't work. It made him madder.

"All right, if we're still a couple in a year, I'll marry you." She thought it was a compromise. They'd had fights, but never a fight to this degree. They were both fast approaching thirty. She knew it was time to settle down, buy a house with a white picket fence, start a family, and all. But why did her stomach lurch like the last moment before a rollercoaster's first downhill at the thought? It wasn't like she didn't know everything there was to know about Teg.

Though she tried not to let it, the battle spilled over to work this morning. And handsome FBI agents just fueled Teg's jealousy. It was her fault he wasn't one of law enforcement's "glamor boys" and was stuck in this backwater county. He'd been recruited by the FBI right out of college—she wasn't. So, he chose to stay with her. Was he sorry? He'd never said so until this morning while driving to the campground.

"Hey, Teg," Sheriff Montgomery called out from where he stood next to the body. "Why don't you go with the FBI agents and help them find the boy? We need a deputy on the scene in case they find him."

"Yessir," Teg said, tossing Shannon a smart-ass grin as he jogged to catch up.

~

Jamie stuffed a handful of corn chips in his mouth and washed them down with a coke. He'd bought the food and drink with the change he found in the contribution box by the phone. Watching the meadow through the big picture window from inside the cabin, he wondered, were his parents looking for him? Or were they still fighting about money? Never in his life had he felt so alone and scared.

He hadn't decided what to do now that the phone was dead. Should he stay here or go? Outside, the sky darkened. He heard the ping-ping-pang of small hail pounding on the metal roof. Jumping to his feet, he ran out to the covered porch as the small stones pummeled the ground, slapped the tree leaves, knocked down weak branches, and covered the meadow grass with white ice. Dad always called hail nature's pruning shears. The weather answered his question for him. *Stay.*

When he first arrived, he'd inventoried the supplies and figured worst case; he'd be okay for a night. Again, he thought of Mom and Dad. Were they looking for him? Were the killers? He felt fear trickle down his spine like sweat, and tears pooled in his eyes and streamed down his cheeks. He quickly wiped them away. Tears were no help. He had to think.

He wondered, *Can I rig up some booby traps like Kevin McCallister in "Home Alone?"* He sprinted back inside and looked in the kitchen drawers, the pantry, and the side tables in the living area. No defense measures, no ingeniously engineered spring-loaded traps came to mind. His best option was hunkering down in the dark with the cabin door locked.

He imagined the killers coming up the porch steps, testing the door, finding it locked, and going away. The next vision wasn't so cheery. Instead of leaving, they persisted and kicked open the door. Jamie realized this was the more likely outcome.

Frantically, he cleared all evidence of his presence in the cabin, putting his empty soda cans in the recycling tub and his trash in the bin under the sink.

He carefully scanned the room, searching for a hiding place. A big storage box with a padded seat sat under the main picture window facing toward the meadow. He lifted the lid. Inside were folded blankets, pillows and bedding that could be used to make the sofa into a sleeper. He could climb inside and pull the bedding over top of his body. Would this be the perfect place to disappear? He opted against it.

Next, he opened the pantry. There was room for him to squeeze inside. But this was the first place the killers would look. Jamie turned to leave, but then he thought about all the can goods. He could hurl the cans at them if they looked in here. It wasn't a good option either. He carried a couple of cans with him. If he hit the bad guys with one, it would hurt and maybe buy him time. He was smaller than they were, but he might be faster. Also, he knew this part of the forest because he and Chubbs had explored it over the last three years.

He stood in the doorway, heart pounding in his chest. He wanted to go back to the motor home—start this whole day over. He wanted Mom and Dad. Jamie dropped his head into his hands and began to sob.

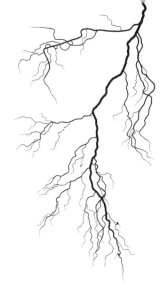

CHAPTER EIGHT

A LIGHTNING BOLT DREW Harper's attention to the distant clouds billowing skyward in convection currents. The helicopter pilot glided above the treetops, searching for a clearing near the campground to land.

He remembered his father's stories of how the King of Thunder built magic castles with cottony towers in the air on warm summer afternoons. As a six-year-old boy, he believed those fairy tales, but the grown man knew the truth. Warm air rose from the Earth's surface, and water vapor carried in the updraft condensed into clouds in the cool atmosphere. Nonetheless, he still thought of thunderstorms as magic castles and was filled with wonder and awe each time he went to study them.

Harper directed his pilot to fly closer to the developing storm. He loved watching the separate cells connect—creating the maze of turrets and towers, hallways, tunnels, and caverns in the cloud structure. Mesmerized by the bright white, reflecting sunlight and darker shades of gray and blue in the shadows, he stared out the helicopter window. Alive with upward movement, always morphing into new shapes, against a backdrop of brilliant blue, the storm changed before his eyes into the super-cell mesocyclone his computer models predicted. Beauty and terror married in front of him.

"Let's find a place to land near the campground," Harper said into the microphone part of his headset.

They found a clearing in the trees, a meadow beside a small stream his map named Little Crooked Creek. As the helicopter started to hover, he saw the crowd around a brown tarp. A man in uniform, he assumed was Sheriff Montgomery, waved him down.

~

Tim looked up when he heard helicopter blades slicing through the air. The side of the bird had a government seal and NWS printed in bold letters on the side.

Automatically, he stared toward the top of the ridge. Their destination was shrouded in white that descended in a ragged curtain from the clouds to the ground.

"Now what? The National Weather Service is here," Deputy Tegner said, repositioning his hat on his head.

Tim pressed his earbud deeper into his ear. "Elias?" He paused, waiting for a reply. "Let us know why National Weather Service is here," Tim said, catching a curious glance from Miguel. Tim slowed his pace and lifted a palm to quiet the group. Berkstad slipped and fell to one knee. Tim bit his bottom lip holding back his annoyance. The forest trail was definitely not the place for slick, leather-soled shoes.

In the distance, a steady hissing sound, like boiling water, seemed to emanate from the forest above them. He'd heard the noise before; an ancient memory from boyhood tickled his mind—an "oh-shit!" memory.

"Hail!" Tim cried out just as a few small pellets started to bounce on the trail in front of them. The men dashed for cover under a tree—probably the worst place to be in a lightning storm. Tim wriggled out of his backpack and retrieved the plastic ponchos from inside, tossing his extra to Tegner.

Tim ripped open the package, shook out the plastic, and slipped it over his head. Berkstad struggled, so Tim helped him out of his backpack just as the wall of hail arrived. The stones were small, but because of their velocity, they still stung when they hit bare skin. The noise grew louder. Leaves and small branches began to fall and litter the ground.

Berkstad struggled to open his gear, and Tim quickly lent a hand. His thoughts raced to Jamie. If the boy had made it to the cabin, he'd be safe; if not, would he be all right? In this part of the country, hailstones could be huge. Tim dropped to a crouch, making himself into a tight ball, and lifted his backpack over his head, copying Miguel. Within a couple of minutes, the hail turned to rain.

"Tim? Can you hear me?" Elias' voice squawked in his ear.

"I copy," Tim answered, pulling out his phone and putting it on speaker so everyone could hear.

"We're calling off the search, Tim. Do you hear me? The search is terminated. National Weather Service has issued a Flash Flood Warning. We are evacuating the campground."

Tim gasped, and his heartbeat quickened. He shook his head as he said, "We can't leave Jamie, not out in this!"

A long pause charged the air. Tim realized he'd just bucked orders for the second time in his short FBI career. Once again, he thought of Dani and all he'd asked of her when he chose to join Elias's team. The cross-country move, the new house, the new wine shop, uprooting his daughters, and moving horses weren't easy feats. Dani had taken charge without complaint. What would he tell her? *Hi, Honey, I'm home. I just got fired.* He sucked a breath through his teeth and stifled a groan. But at least Dani would know what a jerk she'd married. But that didn't matter right now. He couldn't leave a nine-year-old alone and scared in this storm. Even if they evacuated the campground, he decided he would continue the search on his own.

"All right. You and Miguel keep looking for Jamie but be careful," Elias said. "I can't afford to lose either of you. Sheriff Montgomery wants his deputy to return to the campground."

"Get up to higher ground!" He heard an unfamiliar voice call out in the background.

"Weather Service guy says you need to get to higher ground."

We'll be at the top of the ridge in about an hour, and there's a forest service cabin there. I'm guessing that's where Jamie went. His mom says he's very resourceful."

"I hope you're right. The sheriff has called off the canines. If we get the rain Harper says we will; things will get dicey," Elias warned.

"We'll be all right," Tim replied. Yeah, he said it; he wasn't sure he believed it.

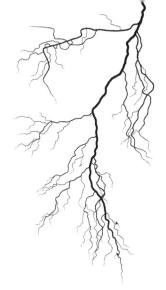

CHAPTER NINE

"**J**AMIE! JAY-MEE!"
Jamie stirred awake at the barely audible sound of his name. A steady rain thrummed on the roof, raced through the gutters, and slapped the splash blocks that channeled water away from the cabin. The voice was unfamiliar, but still, he strained to hear his name again. *A dream?* He wondered, slipping off the sofa to his feet and starting to the cabin's front door. Had someone finally come to rescue him?

"Jay-mee! Are you in there?"

Jamie stopped short. The menace and mockery in the voice made the hair on the back of his neck stand, and a shiver, like a warning siren, hummed in his brain. He spun against the wall next to the door and forced his weight against the logs as if he could disappear into the wall.

"I know you're in there. Come out, come out, wherever you are. Little pig, little pig, Let me come in." The sing-song from outside continued, like the big bad wolf in "The Three Pigs" fable. Goosebumps stood on Jamie's arms.

The cops would never play this kind of game. Wouldn't they just say, *Police. Open the door?*

Panting with fear, Jamie silently slid down the cabin wall to a crouch on the floor. Why had he let himself fall asleep? Should he open the door? No! He was too scared. Where should he go? Where should he hide? Pressing his lips tight, he stifled the whimper rising in his throat.

The door handle rattled as the man on the porch tested it. Jamie heard heavy boots clomping against the wooden deck as if he had now walked close to the window. Jamie imagined him pressing his face against the glass and peering in.

"Go away. Go away. Go away," Jamie whispered, his eyes squeezed shut, his heart pounding furiously in his ears.

Lightning flashed. The loud crack of thunder instantly followed the double strike.

"Shit!" the man said out loud. Then, in what sounded like two forceful strides, he was off the porch. Jamie heard twigs breaking under his weight as if he dashed into the forest. The crunching noise faded the further he was from the cabin.

Trembling, Jamie curled into a fetal ball. He waited frozen for a few minutes. *Got to get out! Got to get out of here!*

Jamie stood, panic and terror driving him toward Mom, Dad, and the campground. He opened the cabin door, stepped outside, and closed it behind him. As he turned to run through the meadow to the ridge path, he saw flashlight beams dancing on the curtain of raindrops. He scrambled back to the cabin door. He grabbed the knob, but it wouldn't turn. *Locked!* He'd forgotten to twist the center button and had locked himself out. Frantic, he searched the porch for a hiding place.

Lightning streaked across the sky, and for that second, Jamie saw a ghost, its dark robe eerily fluttering in the wind. It stood in silhouette at the far end of the meadow. Thunder rumbled, and rain pelted the roof at a heavier beat. A beam of light skimmed across the meadow grass. The killer was searching for him, coming for him. Jamie knew he was smaller, but maybe—just maybe—he was faster.

Scrambling, Jamie slipped into the small space between the coke machine and the stack of firewood by the cabin's front door. He could barely think. But he had to think. By staying perfectly still, he had fooled the killer once before. Could he do it again? When the killer kicked in the door and went inside, he'd run as fast as he could. He prepared and crouched like a sprinter in the starting block. And then he remembered the cans, one in each pocket. He'd use them if he had to. There was no other choice. He had to get home.

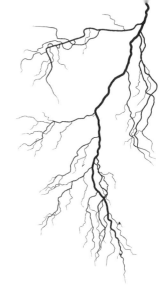

CHAPTER TEN

D URING A FLASH of lightning, Tim thought he saw a child's small frame slip behind the stack of firewood on the cabin's porch. He stopped and lifted his night vision scope to his eyes. Even through the raindrops, the semi-darkness turned to an alien landscape of shades of green, and the image of a small body darted in and out of view as if he peeked from behind the woodpile, then retreated. Tim switched to infrared. The scope now read a heat signature and pierced through the woodpile and the rain. The child lit up in a rainbow spectrum—bright white and yellow, where the skin was exposed and various shades of red, magenta, purple, and blue, where his clothes retained body heat.

"I think we found Jamie," he said to Miguel, as he crested the last few feet of the ridge trail. Tim exhaled a sigh of relief.

"Where?"

"On the porch, behind the firewood." Tim passed the scope to Miguel.

"I see him," Miguel answered. The two men grinned at each other and without any further conversation, approached the cabin at a jog, rather than wait for the team's straggler.

"Jamie? Jamie Randall, is that you?" Tim called out as thunder rolled overhead. He mounted the porch's stairs two at a time. From behind the woodpile, a can of corn flew in his direction and crashed in the gravel behind him. A second came his way, and he dodged it by ducking to his left.

Suddenly, from between the coke machine and stacked wood, a loud guttural scream broke through the rain and thunder. A yellow blur raced from the shadows. The small figure plummeted toward him, head down like a charging bull. Tim reached out and hooked him around the waist, tangling the boy in his rain poncho. Jamie tried to spin away, but Tim held on. With his free arm, he deflected the flurry of blows from the child's tightly clenched fists. Jamie wriggled, screamed, and kicked to get free, giving Tim one good blow in the shin.

"Ouch! Jamie! Stop! Calm down, son. FBI here to rescue you," Tim shouted. Finally, he wrapped his arms around the boy, locking Jamie's hands at his sides, corralling him against his chest. "Jamie. Do you hear me? FBI. We're here to take you home."

Carefully, he set Jamie down, holding the boy's shoulders. Tim knelt so they could meet eye to eye.

"You're safe now. Do you understand?" Tim said softly.

Jamie studied him; his muscles were tight like a coiled spring. Clearly, the boy was ready to bolt. But something made him change his mind. Tim thought maybe he read the FBI acronym printed on his hat and decided to trust him. Every muscle in the boy's body went limp in complete surrender. Jamie collapsed against his shoulder. Tim could feel him begin to shudder with sobs. Tim felt every ounce of fear, every second of distrust and confusion releasing from the boy as he trembled in his arms.

"I've got you. You're safe." Tim surprised himself. He had never expected to grow up and be so—so fatherly. Now, he was drawn to rescuing kids as if pulled by a magnet. It had become a calling or maybe an obsession. He wasn't sure which.

Jamie stood back and wiped away his tears as if trying his best to man up. At nine, he had no obligation to do so. Tim thought of himself at nine. He would've faked a tough bravado, too. But, he had never faced what Jamie had. He'd never seen killers dump a body and realized by instinct he'd be hunted down. Jamie was an incredibly brave boy. Tim removed his hat and put it on Jamie's head, receiving a big toothy grin back from the boy. It was the best reward.

"Are you ready to go inside?" Tim asked. He stood and reached for Jamie's hand. The boy hesitated for a moment, then placed his fingers on Tim's palm. He looked up into Tim's face, utterly vulnerable. "Trust me, Jamie. I won't let you down."

Jamie nodded but asked, "Why did you scare me?"

"Did we scare you? We never meant to scare you. We are here to get you home," Tim smiled.

"But why did you talk to me in that wolf's voice?" Jamie asked as Tim unlocked the cabin door, and they walked through.

"Wolf's voice? Do you think I have a wolf's voice?" Tim stopped cold.

"No. But a few minutes before you came up the steps the second time, you looked in the window and called me little pig. I was so scared."

"That...wasn't...me," Tim muttered mostly to himself. Suddenly, like the flash of lightning behind him, Tim realized the killer had reached Jamie before they did. Lucky for Jamie, they'd arrived when they did. Tim turned and scanned the treeline on the north side of the cabin.

"Miguel, can you take Jamie inside?" Tim asked. His protective mode automatically engaged, like push-button four-wheel-drive in snow.

"Hey, Jamie, do you want something to eat?" Miguel directed the boy into the cabin.

"I'll call it in," Tim said. Miguel agreed with a tip of his chin. Tim turned and stepped back onto the deck, closing the door behind him. For several seconds, he watched a flashlight beam pointed skyward at the meadow's far end; Berkstad finally crested the ridge trail. Tim speculated the perps had seen their flashlight beams, knew they were the cops, searching for Jamie, and hightailed it for the woods.

With his night-vision scope, Tim slowly scanned the forest around the cabin. The scope was military grade and could see up to four hundred yards depending on obstacles. The infrared mode could see further and would pick up a heat signature through fog, rain, dense brush and even walls. He recognized two deer standing at the west edge of the forest, waiting for the rain to slow and the cabin's visitors to disappear inside before returning to graze in the meadow. He heard Berkstad noisily clomping up the deck steps behind him. Berkstad shook the water from his raincape with a loud plastic snap. Tim couldn't help the annoyance flooding through his bloodstream. Berkstad was a menace and had no practical field experience. They needed to be quiet, even though Tim was sure the perpetrators already knew they were there.

"What are you looking for?" Berkstad asked, full volume.

Tim didn't respond but continued his reconnaissance, flipping the scope to infrared. Other than the two deer, the forest was hushed. Even the nocturnal woodland creatures decided to skip hunting dinner in this steady, hard rain.

"Did you find the boy?" Berkstad asked, placing a hand on Tim's shoulder.

"He's inside with Miguel," Tim answered. "You should go in and dry out. I'll call it in."

Tim walked to the other end of the porch, tossing Berkstad a tight smile as he passed by. He retrieved his iPhone and dialed.

"Elias?" He asked when he heard him pick up. "We found the boy. Tell Jamie's parents he's safe, frightened, a little dirty, but okay."

"Where are you?"

"Top of the ridge, in the forest service cabin. It's raining like Noah's Flood up here," Tim said.

"The campground is evacuated. I need you to stay put. We'll get a helicopter up to you as soon as we can. I've emailed you and Miguel information on Judge Waterford. Take a look. I received a call from the director. They want a profile ASAP. The president is involved now. He wants to know who killed his favorite nominee and why."

"We have a problem," Tim let out a deep breath. "Her killers may be up here, in the forest. They came for Jamie just before we arrived. They must believe the boy can identify them."

"Do you think they're armed?"

"I know one of them is. He's already shot at me. Send in the cavalry. We need to search the forest and get these guys."

60

"You need to stay put. The river is over its banks, and some roads and bridges are already washed out. All flights are grounded for now. I couldn't get the cavalry to you if I wanted to."

Tim raked his teeth across his bottom lip. "Okay. We'll set up a defensive perimeter and wait." It was his job to protect the witness, and he would do it without hesitation. Let the killers come to them and try to take Jamie. Yeah, let them try.

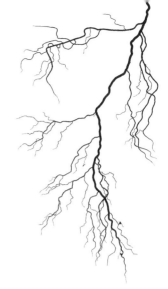

CHAPTER ELEVEN

ONCE THROUGH THE cabin door, Tim wriggled out of his backpack and set it on one of the chairs at the dining table. Miguel walked over from the small two-burner stovetop and spooned soup from a saucepan into the bowl in front of Jamie.

"Want some chicken noodle soup?" he asked.

"No thanks. Not yet," Tim answered. He was hungry, but the cabin's menu wasn't appealing. "They're sending a helicopter for us as soon as the storm allows," Tim continued. "We need to stay sharp. I can take the first shift." He didn't want to discuss strategies in front of the boy; he'd been frightened enough for one day. But Tim had no choice. They needed to prepare for an armed assault. The people who murdered Judge Waterford wouldn't give up that easily. They stayed to find Jamie when wiser folks would've fled.

Tim removed his rifle from the backpack's scabbard, extended the carbine's buttstock and adjusted the scope. When he looked at Jamie, he noticed the boy had stopped eating mid-spoonful and studied him with extreme interest.

"Have you ever fired a rifle, Jamie?" Miguel asked, refilling the boy's bowl with another ladle of soup.

"No, sir," Jamie answered, shaking his head, but his eyes were wide with little boy curiosity.

"Does your dad hunt?" Tim asked.

"No. But I want to learn how." He seemed to stare at the rifle with a healthy mix of inquisitiveness and fear. Tim remembered the feeling. He had learned how to handle firearms early on. Gun safety and proficiency were one of his father's priorities.

Every fall evening during hunting season, he'd heard his father's and two older brothers' stories about the sport. Dad said he could go with them when he reached his eighth birthday. When he turned eight, he was invited to go. He was thrilled to get the chance to belong to the hunt club composed of his father, two older brothers, and their friends. It was a rite of passage in their family. The taunts of "Momma's Boy" would be at an end—he'd be a man—one of them.

Tim remembered seeing his first stag, standing alert and elegant, at the edge of a Cascade Mountain forest. The trophy buck stood in the rifle scope's crosshairs, his head crowned by a perfectly balanced six-point rack. Tim couldn't pull the trigger and wanted to let the magnificent creature live and go free. His father silently came to help him sight in.

"Go ahead, son. Take your shot," Dad whispered. Tim closed his eyes and squeezed the trigger, missing the animal. The buck bounded into the woods and away from danger. His brothers had audibly groaned and complained that they wouldn't have missed.

Dad patted Tim's shoulder. "Good try. You'll get the next one." And he did. Later that day, he shot a spike, and with his father's help, field-dressed it and carried it home. Ironically, he didn't feel the elation he'd imagined he would. He felt horrible, sad, and grieved for the life he'd taken. These emotions he kept to himself. He never said a word to anyone about letting that first buck go, though he suspected his older brothers knew and maybe understood.

A rifle meant something very different these days. Now, Tim hunted men—miscreants and murderers, robbers and rapists, pornographers, and pedophiles. It was his job to keep others safe and bring those who broke the law to justice. He didn't feel the same empathy for them as he did for innocent animals. Though he preferred to take criminals into custody without a fight, he would do what he had to do. He inserted the magazine into his rifle. Right now, keeping Jamie safe was his main concern.

64

"Jamie, did you see the people who disposed of the body?" Tim asked, wiping the rifle down with a microfiber cloth.

Jamie hesitated and then slurped the spoonful of soup. "Yes."

"Can you describe them for me?" Tim looked across the table, making eye contact. "Take your time. Try to remember anything you can. What were they wearing?"

"The bigger guy was wearing tan shorts, a camo t-shirt, and a black and gray jacket. I saw him the most, once while I was hiding in the black berries alone on the trail. I was really scared."

Tim stared. He had to get this kid in protective custody. "You saw him on the trail?"

"Down by the creek. He turned toward the river, and I ran up here."

"Can you remember anything else?"

"I think so. The big guy had on a dark blue baseball cap and red, black, and white Air Jordans. I could see the black checkmark. The smaller guy seemed weaker and wore all camo. Not like real military camo, but what my dad calls *fashion camo*." Jamie made a limp-wristed gesture, apparently mimicking his dad's prejudices. "He had on a blue hat, too. I don't remember his shoes."

"Were they white men? African American? Latino? Could you tell?"

"Oh, yeah. They were both black men," Jamie said confidently. "But I really didn't see their faces very well."

"Do you remember enough to have a sketch artist do a drawing?" Tim asked.

Jamie's face brightened, almost as if he was in a TV police drama. "Yeah."

Berkstad broke Tim's chain of thought, emerging from the cabin's bathroom in a cloud of soap-fragranced steam. Because he'd had no choice, Berkstad had to dress in his same dirty clothes. Tim could tell he wasn't happy by the scowl on his face. Berkstad's wet socks and nearly ruined leather shoes were almost dry on the brick hearth surrounding the woodstove.

"What's up?" Berkstad asked, toweling his hair dry. Tim was tempted to ask him to stand the first lookout shift.

"The storm has washed out the roads and bridges in the area. We will need to hole up here. We'll need to post a lookout overnight—take shifts," Tim said, putting on his bulletproof vest and slinging the rifle over his shoulder.

"Wait? What? You can't be serious. You want me to be a lookout?" Berkstad whined.

Miguel stirred soup at the stove, and Tim could hear him snicker even with his back turned.

"Did you volunteer to search for Jamie? I thought I heard you volunteer for this job." Tim glared at him and walked out onto the porch, frustration making his cheeks flush hot. He resigned himself to his fate. He had a job to do, and indulging the section chief was now part of it.

Walking the perimeter of the cabin's wrap-around porch, Tim studied the forest at the meadow's edge through his night-vision scope. All seemed quiet; even the deer he'd seen earlier were bedded down.

The thunderstorm had lowered the temperature by at least thirty degrees. Tim could feel the cool air on the sweat-dampened parts of his shirt. The steady beat on the roof, splashes through the gutters and downspouts, and rustle through the tree leaves let him know the storm's pace was still on full tilt. He barely heard the cabin door and footsteps following behind him. He turned.

"It's cool out here," Berkstad held out Tim's lightweight nylon jacket. It was a conciliatory gesture. At least he was smart enough to recognize Tim was pissed off at him.

"Thanks," Tim took it, and for now, draped the jacket over the back of one of the chairs on the porch.

"Listen, Tim. I joined the search hoping to have a moment to talk to you alone."

"I'm at work. I was called to duty by the CARD team. You could've used the phone or email." Tim looked him up and down, focusing on his ruined shoes.

Tim lifted the scope to his eyes, hoping to cover his frown. For a moment, he wondered if Berkstad knew he'd hacked his files on Congressman Patterson. If the man was under surveillance when Berkstad said he was, he had to know Patterson drugged and raped children. And he would've continued right under Berkstad's nose if Elias's team hadn't caught him.

"All right. Talk," Tim said, his tone far less than welcoming. He slowly started circumnavigating the cabin's porch again, scanning the forest in infrared mode this time.

Berkstad cleared his throat, making Tim suspicious. He thought. *Just spit it ou*t.

"Tim, have you ever thought about working in counterintelligence?"

Tim laughed. "Me? No. When a job's done, I think about getting home to my wife and kids."

"Lots of men in counterintelligence work are married with families. I was."

Tim nodded. Yeah, Berkstad was married; until he started his affair with Roxie Stauffer, one of Tim's team members. *What a schmuck.*

"I'm flattered you asked," he lied. He wasn't soft-soaped in the slightest. "I'm a criminal lawyer—a prosecutor. I think I serve the country best here with Elias's team."

"Will you give it some thought?" Berkstad squirmed as if he'd suddenly become uncomfortable in his skin. "You've been more than just considered. The director is interested in recruiting you. Let's just say he found your work on the Patterson case—inspiring."

That wasn't true, and Tim knew it. "David, you know my backstory. Elias rescued me just before the King County Commissioners could throw me onto the trash heap."

"We know it was a self-defense shooting. Besides, you'd be perfect for CI, Independent, married to wealth, and able to travel in international circles without restrictions. Your 'backstory' is made for this."

"Have you talked to Elias?" Tim asked, continuing to scan the horizon.

"It was better to ask you first."

Tim dropped the scope, letting the nylon strap around his neck catch it. He looked Berkstad square in the eyes. "I'll think about it," he said, mostly to get him to lay-off. Tim wouldn't leave his wife and family if he didn't have to.

Berkstad kicked at loose dried leaves on the deck. He had more to say. "And?" Tim asked.

"Tim, there's evidence someone on the inside, one of our agents, is selling classified information to Russia and China. We've narrowed it down to a few suspects. Because you are new, we could use you to infiltrate one of their offices undercover as an aide," Berkstad looked up at Tim. Both eyebrows peaked as if he hoped Tim would be intrigued.

Tim ran his tongue on the bottom edge of his upper teeth. "As I said, I know criminal law. I don't have the training for spy work."

"I'll authorize your training and see that you won't have to leave the country. We—well, I believe my electronic files have been hacked. There is barely a trace of evidence, a footprint, they call it, but it's there. My best IT guy tried to follow the trail but couldn't. It leads back to my office's servers."

"So, it's a guy in your office? Is your computer compromised? Will assigning me as an aide help? I don't know that much about computers," Tim frowned. Once again, he looked through the night vision scope to cover emotion. Counter intel guys were masters at micro-expressions, and Tim didn't want to give his duplicity away.

Tim and Miguel had gone to Elias with their theory that Berkstad covered the crimes of DC power players and more. Probably for money. If anyone sold secrets, Tim believed Berkstad could easily be the one. With the director's authorization, they'd had their IT guy, Kandar Singh, hack in, copy files, and cover his tracks. That he'd looped it all back to Berkstad's servers was news. But, Kandar did have a unique sense of humor.

Tim and Miguel hadn't even had a chance to search through the stolen information. Maybe Berkstad was wary of *him* and offered the position to lead Tim away from the truth. It was like playing a game of three-dimensional chess.

"Think about it, will you, Tim. I really would like you on my team."

"Sure." Tim let a small smile tick across his lips. "But just so you know, the James Bond thing isn't my kind of martini, whether or not it's shaken or stirred."

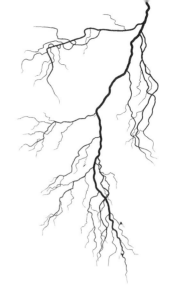

CHAPTER TWELVE

T IM'S LOOK-OUT SHIFT was up, and Miguel joined him on the porch. The incidence of lightning and thunder had diminished, replaced by steady, heavy rain. Light from inside the cabin glimmered on the puddles of standing water that formed in the meadow in front of the cabin.

"Is that a waterfall, I hear?" Miguel said, announcing he'd come to replace Tim.

"Yeah, sounds like the ridge trail is flooded." Tim could hear the cascade as it crested over the lip of the canyon and roiled down the artificial steps.

"That's not good," Miguel commented. He moved so he stood close enough that only Tim could hear him. "Do you mind if I ask, what did Berkstad want?"

Tim looked around and lowered his voice before answering. "He wanted to recruit me to do covert spy crap because I'm new to the FBI, and no one knows me. He believes someone on the inside is selling secrets to Russia and China." He and Miguel slowly walked the full circle of the cabin's covered wrap-around porch.

"That's Berkstad's MO. He made a run at me to join CI a couple of years ago. Elias was furious. So, what do you think? Is there a spy on the inside?"

"What do I know? I'm new," Tim grinned. "Why do I imagine *he'd* be the one selling secrets—if anyone is? He knows someone hacked his files."

Miguel leaned in and quietly asked, "Do you think he knows who did it?"

"He may suspect. But I think he was fishing," Tim scanned the horizon through his infrared scope again. Nothing stirred in the forest except the flutter of maple leaves as the raindrops hit them, rolled off, and splashed on the forest floor. The rain on the roof had become a constant thrum.

"Are you going to do it? Join Counter intel, I mean?"

"No. That's not for me. It's a single man's gig," Tim answered. "I want to spend my nights with Dani and the girls."

"I understand when Berkstad was young, he was quite the dashing CI agent."

"How does that happen? From a fearless spy to pain in the ass?" Tim asked. "He wasn't prepared for this mission."

"I noticed he ruined his Bruno Magali's," Miguel chuckled and got Tim to laugh with him. "Roxie thinks he's trying to stay in the game and grab that last spark of youth before the bureaucracy swallows him whole."

Tim stared at Miguel. "I guess I understand."

"The way Roxie tells it, he was sweet-talked into a promotion, given assistant supervisory special agent, which turned out to be a desk job, and in time, he lost his daring-do. He was promoted to section chief ten years ago."

"Then he needs to act like a section chief. He knew this was a search and rescue mission in the forest." Tim sat on one of the porch chairs.

"I don't think he planned to go with us. I think it was a spur-of-the-moment decision," Miguel repositioned his ball cap and sat in the chair next to Tim. "I think he wanted to impress Roxie."

"Good thing she's not here to see him in action. He can make up a big story just for her," Tim laughed and then became serious. "I'm wondering why he showed up in the first place. You don't think he's...."

"Involved in the Judge's murder?" Miguel finished Tim's sentence for him. Tim inclined forward, resting his rifle in his lap. He turned his head to catch Miguel's glance. Miguel tipped his head slightly and gave him a half-smile. "Could be. You know I think he covered for Patterson. Rumor has it he's in big with Nicolai Solenov."

"Solenov? The billionaire? Isn't he anti-law enforcement?"

"Some say Solenov is a Russian spy."

"We need time to get through his files." Tim had heard the name before, but thought he was just a rich philanthropist meddling in politics.

"It would be nice to know if Berkstad's with or against us," Miguel mused.

"Judge Waterford was a law-and-order judge. She was no-nonsense, very logical, and fair. She always considered the victims. As a prosecutor, I would've loved having someone like her as the judge on my cases," Tim said. He furrowed his brow. "Did you have a chance to read the crime scene notes?"

"No. I didn't."

"Elias said he needs our input for a profile. But I think we can get these guys here. One of them threatened Jamie just before we arrived. I think they are lurking out in the forest somewhere. Not having very much fun, I'll bet." Tim chuckled at the thought of the killers huddled somewhere, drenched to the bone and cold.

"The bad news is—they're only a few shots away from being inside the cabin and dry," Miguel mused.

"Yeah. They're out there. If the rain lets up, they'll make their move." Tim stood and picked up his rifle. "I'm going to check on Jamie, get something to eat, and do some reading. Stay sharp and call me if you need me."

Tim watched as Miguel took up his rifle and searched the forest with his night vision scope.

His shift over, Tim entered the cabin deep in thought. He reviewed what he knew: the Jeep the killers used when the deputies chased them into the forest was reported stolen; deputies found three loaded ten-round magazines for a nine-millimeter semi-auto in the vehicle's front console— but not the pistol. Tim surmised both perps were armed.

Since they'd disposed of the body in broad daylight, Tim guessed the unsubs planned to drive out into the forest, dump the body, and drive away, completely unseen. It was a reasonable premise, but they failed to calculate the unpredictable, unknowable, random things that happen in life—like a little boy gathering crawfish for dinner.

Because of Jamie, Tim put the rifle on safety, removed the magazine, emptied the firing chamber, and slung his rifle over the back of one of the kitchen chairs. He slipped the magazine into his pants front pocket. He could quickly re-arm, if necessary.

Jamie sat cross-legged on the overstuffed sofa and dropped the book he read onto the maple coffee table. Joining Tim at the small dining table, eyeing the rifle with more than curiosity, Tim knew the boy wanted to learn how to use it.

"Can you teach me how to shoot?" Jamie asked. Tim knew that was coming—solely from the hungry look in the boy's eyes. He remembered the feeling.

"Jamie, I'll need your parents' permission. But if they say it's okay...."

"You don't have to ask them. They won't care. I won't get in trouble." It was an explosion of excitement and likely not the whole truth. It was exactly what Tim would've said at Jamie's age if in the same position. Every trick a kid tried wasn't new. Tim scrubbed a hand through Jamie's hair.

"You won't get in trouble, but I just might," Tim said, laughing. "Tell you what, tomorrow when we get you back home, I'll ask your parents if I can teach you to shoot." Tim gave Jamie a reassuring smile. "I'm hungry. What do we have to eat around here?" he asked, hoping to change the boy's focus. Jamie had already eaten all the chicken soup, but that was hours ago.

"There's all kinds of stuff in the pantry," Jamie raced over and opened the door for him. The boy was on his best behavior now that the promise of learning to fire a rifle was in his future. Tim hoped his parents wouldn't dash that dream.

Tim glanced over at Berkstad. Earlier, he'd assumed the section chief was asleep. But now he noticed the man watched him, with one eye open, like a coiled python deciding whether to strike. Tim wasn't sure how to handle his suspicion and distrust and let a few moments pass, locked in a stare.

"Are you hungry?" Tim finally asked. "Jamie and I are fixing something."

With Jamie's help, Tim fixed a concoction of "Kraft Mac n' Cheese" with processed ham that looked nothing like the label when the tin was opened—*false advertising*. Tim thought.

Jamie stood next to Tim as he stirred the mess in the pan.

"I found a bunch of crawfish in the creek when I crossed. Were they yours?" Tim asked.

"Yeah. Too bad we don't have them right now," Jamie answered pushing his lips out in a pout. "They were gonna be lunch."

"I guess macaroni with fake cheese and fake ham will have to do," Tim laughed. "Dinner, if you want to call it that, is served."

Berkstad stood from his chair and strolled to the table. He looked at the slop in his bowl and back up at Tim in disgust—colored with a touch of fear.

"Hey, I never said I could cook." Tim lifted both palms in surrender, a big open grin on his face.

Jamie dug in with gusto as if he'd had this *delicacy* before. Berkstad dipped his fork into the sauce, taking a small, tentative taste before trying a real bite.

Tim waited until Berkstad nodded, and after, Tim took a bowl out to Miguel. Finally, back inside the cabin, he slid into his dining table chair, and took a bite. The 'casserole' tasted somewhat like real mac n' cheese. It wasn't like his mom used to make, and definitely not the greatest, but he was hungry, so it would have to do.

After eating, Jamie volunteered to do the dishes. Tim let him help but didn't want him to get the impression the carbine lessons were assured.

"Your parents might not approve of you learning to fire a rifle. I don't want you to get your hopes up too high," Tim said, pressing his lips together in a tight line.

"I promise they won't care. Most of the time, they let me do what ever I want," he answered. Tim didn't believe that of Jamie's mom. When he'd called to let her know Jamie was safe, her voice on the phone overflowed with pure joy.

"Okay, we'll see." Anxious to get a look at the crime scene notes, Tim glanced at his watch. It was past nine, and he needed to get Jamie off to bed. "It's time for you to get some sleep. We probably have a big day ahead of us tomorrow."

Jamie raced over to the window box and retrieved blankets and pillows. Tim fixed the boy a spot on the sofa and pulled one of the overstuffed chairs close at Jamie's request. Before climbing under the covers, the kid brought a blanket and pillow to Berkstad. The gesture confirmed he was just a kind-hearted, helpful boy. It stirred up Tim's protective father emotions even more.

It was going to be a long night. Like Miguel so eloquently said, "The killers were one shot away from being warm and dry, and one shot away from getting to Jamie and erasing the one known witness. Tim was not going to let it happen.

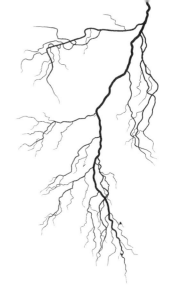

CHAPTER THIRTEEN

INALLY, JAMIE DRIFTED off to sleep. Tim took that moment to move to the kitchen table, put on his vest, and re-arm his rifle. He slipped his communication gear in place. Expecting Berkstad to be in dreamland, too, Tim looked over at him to confirm. Instead, Berkstad rose from his chair, grabbed one of the wooden spindle backs from under the table, and followed Tim to the overstuffed lounger at the far end of the couch. He positioned it next to him, and Tim speculated he wanted to continue their earlier chat.

Tim stared at him, annoyed. He leaned the carbine against the armrest, within easy reach, and sat down. As far as he was concerned, the discussions about spy craft were over. He hated being disadvantaged—Berkstad was one of his bosses. Forced to indulge him, he narrowed his eyes. Rather than conversing, Tim retrieved his phone from his vest pocket and scrolled through the email to find Elias's notes.

"You're good with kids, Tim. I didn't know that about you," Berkstad said, leaning forward and resting his elbows on his knees. Tim lifted his gaze to meet Berkstad's eyes.

"Surprised me, too," Tim said, shaking his head softly. "I didn't expect to want kids, but Dani changed all that, and the girls we adopted won me over. They're lots of fun."

"Kids are fun. Most of the time," Berkstad said with a deep sigh.

Though Tim hadn't wanted to hear about it, Roxie let snippets of gossip about her relationship with the section chief slip out in conversations at the office. Berkstad was in the middle of a messy divorce and custody battle. Tim felt sorry for the guy. But, then again, maybe starting an affair with Roxie wasn't the smartest thing to do if he wanted to keep his family together. He didn't say it out loud. Humans do stupid stuff, and Tim wasn't above the foibles. At this point, he couldn't imagine cheating. But he wasn't under the usual American middle-class stresses; Dani's wealth ensured that. He was aware of how fortunate he was.

All the same, he didn't want to engage with Berkstad about his divorce or anything else. Tim recognized his own human weakness; he didn't trust the man. Something about him had always left him cold. Berkstad was a consummate butt-kisser, guided only by the shifting winds of office politics.

"I should get to work. Elias sent me crime scene notes I need to review."

"I'll leave you to it, then." Berkstad stood, replaced the chair at the kitchen table, and sank slowly into the overstuffed love seat at the opposite end of the sofa. His slumped shoulders screamed dejection. Tim felt like a jerk. The man obviously needed a friend. He just wasn't sure he could be that friend.

"Get some rest," Tim said as cordially as possible and waited for Berkstad's nod before starting through Elias's notes.

Judge Waterford was shot at close range. Earlier, when he first lifted the tarp, he'd noted the small halo of powder burns and stippling around the bullet entrance wound on her white blouse.

Elias hypothesized the gun was a nine-millimeter, semi-auto. They'd found and counted the bullet casings at the dump site, but had surmised those were from the unsub's target practice on Tim. He'd fired ten rounds. They'd found nine-millimeter bullets in the Jeep, still in the box and new magazines. The medical examiner made an educated guess by the wound size; the Judge was killed with a nine-millimeter round. They would know more after tomorrow's autopsy.

Evelyn Waterford's husband called the police after she failed to show up for their dinner appointment. He panicked when he found her empty car in the parking lot. Tim watched the body cam video of the initial interview with the husband he'd received from Elias.

When they arrived, the responding officers found Carlton Waterford pacing frantically in the parking lot next to her vehicle. The detectives confirmed her driver's side door was open and located her purse on the floor in front of the passenger's seat. Her cell phone still sat in a Weathertech CupFone stand in the console. Surprisingly, CSI discovered no blood evidence inside her car or on the pavement in the parking lot. There were no discharged shell casings found at the scene.

No one in the restaurant or the parking lot saw or heard anything.

DC police were collecting video surveillance from the restaurant and surrounding businesses, if it could be found.

Judge Waterford's cell phone had already been turned over to the FBI Forensics Lab to be mined for emails and messages that could turn into clues.

The stolen Jeep used by the killers had been reported missing the day before the murder. Luckily, it was retrieved from the forest and towed to an impound lot in D.C. before the flood warnings and the campground's evacuation order.

How did the killers know where the judge was going for dinner? Did they know her? Follow her? Stalk her? Clearly, this was a premeditated crime. One thing Tim did know; it wasn't a robbery. None of her personal belongings were taken—not her purse, not her iPhone, not her gold jewelry—just her life.

He hated to admit it, but Carlton Waterford managed to set off his alarm bells. The man was too slick. His panic and worry almost seemed rehearsed. And ironically, he referred to his wife in the *past tense*. It could be poor grammar, but it could also mean he knew his wife wasn't missing—but dead.

He rubbed his right hand over his face, relaxed deep into the chair cushions, rested his feet on the coffee table, and closed his eyes. He concentrated. The in and out of Jamie's breathing created a barely perceptible undertone to the steady beat of heavy rain battering the cabin roof. The repeating rhythm was almost hypnotic.

All the facts of the case circled as if on a carousel in Tim's mind. He could reach for each detail, put it in place, and a movie of the crime would play out in his thoughts.

Tim imagined the scene. There were at least two people in the Jeep—one to drive, one to abduct. As Judge Waterford exited her car, the Jeep pulled into the space beside hers. Maybe she didn't notice them because she'd turned to collect her belongings. The shooter climbed out of the Jeep's door before it came to a stop. He couldn't have been more than a foot or two away from her, and maybe he called out her name. Likely, she shifted to face him.

Did she know him? Or was she confused by a stranger saying her name? As he approached, he lifted the gun level with her heart and forced her into the jeep. When he pulled the trigger, it was from a distance of no more than six inches. If he'd shot her immediately, there would be high-velocity spatter on and maybe inside the Judge's car. At this point, they only had evidence of one shot. The autopsy would confirm that information. Two shots would be the signature of an execution. Was it?

The whole incident would only take a few seconds. The gun may have been equipped with a silencer, explaining why no one in the parking lot heard anything. Then, they disappeared like a wisp of steam. Perhaps they took her hostage first and shot her in another location.

Tim opened his eyes, dropped his legs from the coffee table, and sat forward. Was it a kidnapping gone wrong? Was it a hit?

The next questions were: *Who wanted you dead, little lady? And why?* They'd have to dig into Judge Waterford's life to find suspects. Family? The responding officer's notes said the husband was inconsolable, but the body cam footage set Tim on edge. He could be faking. The Judge and her husband had no children.

Was it someone she'd sentenced? She had a ten-year judicial career. Plenty of angry criminals stewing in their cells for hours a day could have hatched the plot for revenge. From his time at the prosecutor's office, he understood that was a distinct possibility. Did it have anything to do with her recent nomination to the appellate court? Was the motive political? Was the goal to keep a law-and-order judge off the bench?

Elias confided in Tim on their last case that the director of the FBI was a political animal and hadn't come up through the ranks. Was that the reason Berkstad showed up, to warn them off Judge Waterford's case as he had tried with Congressman Patterson's? If so, he'd have to know she was dead and that they would find the body here. It was unlikely. But truth was stranger than fiction.

Though the executive branch appointed all FBI directors, Tim wondered, who in their right mind at the Senate Confirmation Hearing had voted for a man without law enforcement experience? Promoting an impartial man with the know-how to run the world's premier law enforcement agency was a better plan. Politicizing any police force, especially one as technologically advanced as the FBI, was an idea that could have terrible and catastrophic consequences.

After a few seconds, Tim knew there was nothing more he could do from here. He made a mental note. Number one: Get Jamie home to his parents. Two: Get the family into protective custody. Three: Find out who murdered the judge and why.

Tim typed an email to Elias:

> We are looking for two or three perpetrators. One to drive and one or two to lure and control the victim.
>
> This was not a robbery gone wrong or a carjacking. No possessions were taken. The car, with keys on the front seat remained at the scene. Her purse, wallet, cell phone and other electronics were located inside her car. When the body was found, the Judge still wore her expensive jewelry. The perpetrator was highly organized, and the abduction pre-planned. The shooter knew Judge Waterford, or, at least, knew her name. They stalked her or followed her to the restaurant, so they had access to her schedule or plans. There were no signs of sexual assault, leading me to believe a woman may be involved. The crime is cold, methodical, calculated, and detached. Maybe a kidnapping for ransom gone wrong or a professional murder-for-hire. DC Metro Police said the

husband seemed upset, but in viewing the taped interview, I question his sincerity. The husband said his marriage was solid and problem-free, but police should look for infidelity on the husband's part. His gym would provide access to pretty, young, and physically fit women. Police should review his banking records and see if he paid out a large sum of money to anyone, or if he gains financially from Judge Waterford's death.

Because President Tomlinson appointed the Judge, I can't rule out a hit based on political motives. Judge Waterford's reputation branded her a law-and-order judge with empathy for crime victims and their families over perpetrators.

He hit send. At least it was a start. Elias would know that's all he could do until more puzzle pieces were available.

Tim relaxed back into his chair and put his feet on the coffee table. He felt heaviness and exhaustion in every muscle in his body. He closed his eyes. He was done for now and started to drift like a raft on a still water stretch on a river adventure. Even the splashes from the downspouts transformed into shoreline ripples in his world of dreams.

"Tim! Tim! I see movement. A figure is creeping up to the edge of the forest," Miguel's hoarse whisper rang in his communication earbud. Tim jerked awake, grabbed his rifle, and was out of his seat like a shot.

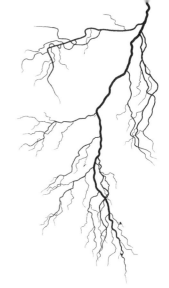

CHAPTER FOURTEEN

T IM TAPPED BERKSTAD on the knee. "We have company," he said just above a whisper. "No lights." He instructed as the section chief reached for the pull chain on the small table lamp. The man dropped his hand.

Jamie was still asleep, and Tim wanted to keep it that way. "You stay with the boy. I'll be out front with Miguel. Get your communication gear on." Tim watched for only long enough to see the Section Chief fumble with the earbuds and finally pick up his Glock 17.

"Who is it? Do you know?" Berkstad asked sleepily.

"Nope. Be ready, anyway," Tim lifted his index finger to his lips and then turned toward the door.

In quiet steps, he crossed the distance between the living room area and the door. Carefully, he turned the knob. He couldn't remember if the door was squeaky. He hesitated for a moment, crossed his fingers in his mind, and then pressed his weight against the wood.

Soundlessly, the door inched open. Tim slipped through and closed it behind him. The cool night air carried the clean, earthy scent of rain-washed forest.

Without turning to look at him, Miguel said, "The unsub is at 2:00 O'clock, just at the tree line. Behind the big maple overhanging the trail."

Tim knelt beside him at the back of the porch railing. The heavy rain beating on the metal roof masked all noise and conversation on the porch. The darkness reduced their profiles to phantoms in black on black.

He braced his rifle stock against his shoulder and lowered the barrel to the top rail. He looked through his infrared targeting scope. The invisible to the naked-eye laser painted a green dot on the intruder's chest. Tim studied the person kneeling at the base of the large tree. Though the top half of his jacket looked greenish white through the scope, Tim recognized the colors in daylight would be gray, with the lower half black, exactly like the jacket worn by the man who took potshots at him at Little Crooked Creek, and just like Jamie's description of one of the men who dumped Judge Waterford's body.

The figure crouched at the forest's edge seemed to be in the throes of indecision. Tim surmised he'd seen the flashlight beams hours ago when they'd first approached the cabin. He guessed the unsub returned to where he'd ditched the Jeep, only to find it had been towed away. Eight hours out in this rain without shelter had to be a challenging experience. Tim imagined the guy longing to be inside the cabin. It would be a double win for him. He could get his hands on Jamie, the only witness to the body dump, and be warm and dry.

"Who do you think he is? An innocent hiker caught in the storm?" Miguel asked, a grin showing beneath his goggles.

"He's the scumbag that shot at me at the creek and likely Judge Waterford's killer," Tim replied, looking straight ahead.

Miguel stood, and a smirk Tim had seen before played at the corners of his mouth. He gestured a semi-circle with his index finger. Miguel intended to sneak around behind the intruder.

"No, wait," Tim protested. "He's armed. Let's see what he has to say. Let's not start a confrontation. And where's the other guy? I haven't seen the other man Jamie described."

Miguel replied, "We have night vision—he doesn't. I've got this. Cover me."

Tim watched as quickly, and on cat's feet, Miguel made his way to the side of the cabin. With a small grunt, he launched his body over the rail and landed softly on the ground level below.

The rain slackened and changed to a gentle patter against the cabin roof. Anxiety twisted Tim's stomach into a knot. Tim strained to hear Miguel's movements but couldn't. Not a single twig snap or a rustle in the brush breached the silence. The wet leaves on the forest floor cushioned each step. Looking through his infrared scope, Tim found Miguel's heat signature and followed along as Miguel advanced into the forest behind the unsub. Miguel was a tiger, slowly, stealthily, stalking his prey.

The shooter made his move; he started across the meadow, still crouching and keeping a low profile. His whole demeanor said sneak attack with every step. Suddenly, he stopped and turned as if to listen. Tim slid his hand in position, his right index finger a hair's breadth away from the trigger. He wanted to take this guy alive. Tim needed answers. Why he killed the Judge was on the top of his list. But, if necessary, Tim would do what he had to do to keep Jamie and Miguel safe.

The perp reached around, lifting the back of his jacket. Tim recognized that movement. He'd seen this action before.

"Gun!" Tim said through his com gear. As the intruder wrestled the weapon free from his waistband, a dark blur, low to the ground, pounced from the shadows. Miguel hit hard below his center mass; the unsub's gun flew skyward as he toppled backward.

Crraacckk! The deafening sound reverberated off the mountain tops.

Tim whirled to see Berkstad standing in the open doorway. Gunsmoke rising in a wispy spiral from his pistol's barrel.

"Fuck!" Tim yelled, racing down the steps to see if Miguel was hit. Miguel untangled himself from the body when Tim reached him and slowly stood, holding the man's gun in his palm like a prize. Relieved, Tim let out a sigh.

The porch light snapped on, illuminating the meadow.

"I saw him go for his gun," Berkstad explained as he joined them.

Tim nodded and bent over the lifeless body to feel for a pulse. So, Berkstad hadn't lost his skills, after all. He'd delivered a kill shot to the face. The intruder was dead. Probably instantly.

"Well, we won't be getting any answers from this guy," Tim said. He realized Berkstad had never seen the one-man stealth-wrecking ball in action and fired, thinking he saved a fellow agent. But why didn't Berkstad know about Miguel's specialty? He had a reputation throughout the FBI for taking down active shooters. He taught the "how-to" class at Quantico. Wasn't that something a section chief would know? Hadn't Roxie mentioned it to her lover in passing? She'd seen Miguel's handiwork firsthand.

"Does he have a wallet?" Miguel asked.

Tim took a pair of nitrile gloves from his pocket and put them on. He did a quick pat down and found a wallet and a cell phone in the dead man's jacket. He handed the cell phone to Miguel for bagging as evidence and carefully opened the wallet with a pen. Inside, a North Carolina driver's license and an active-duty military ID were in clear plastic slots for easy access. Tim felt discomfort brewing deep in his core. This was all wrong, and he couldn't shake the feeling.

"There's a tarp on the porch behind the firewood. Let's cover this guy up. We need to preserve any evidence we can for the Judge's murder investigation, and I don't want Jamie to see this," Tim said, staring at the porch. He turned and strolled up the steps, looking at the open cabin door. Peeking in, he expected Jamie to be awake—wide-eyed and white with fright. Jamie hadn't stirred, and Tim watched until he observed the rise and fall of the boy's breathing.

While Miguel and Berkstad covered the body, Tim called it in to headquarters.

"[...] It was a self-defense shooting," he said uneasily. "Can you run this name for me? Jaydon Lee Jones. That's J-a-y-d-o-n Lee Jones, and yes, I'll wait," he said. Tim rubbed his hand over his eyes and down his cheeks to his jaw. It would be hours before the sheriff's deputies and an FBI Flyaway team could make it up the mountain. The Flyaway teams could be ready and deployed to anywhere in the world within four hours, but this storm may make that impossible. The teams oversaw biometric identification, and Berkstad's handiwork had made it necessary.

Glancing back to the meadow, Tim noticed Miguel standing close to Berkstad, yelling inches from his face. His voice carried across the field.

"What the hell were you thinking? You could've killed me!" Miguel shoved Berkstad backward, anger seething near the boil-over point. Tim jumped down the steps, sure he'd need to break up a brawl. Miguel turned away, shaking his head, and mumbling cuss words in Spanish.

FBI Support Agent Tiffany Rodgers came back on the line. "McAndrews?

"Yeah, I'm here."

"Jaydon Lee Jones lives at 4488 Mayfield Lane, Fort Bragg, North Carolina. He's single. He has no criminal record and is active-duty military, US Army Rangers, Delta Force," she said. "Do you need anything else?"

Stunned for a moment, Tim froze. "No. Thank you. Nothing else." He disengaged.

Delta Force? They were highly trained, hard to kill, and this was too easy. Like a car skidding on black ice, his mind careened in every crazy direction. The murder wasn't a robbery gone wrong. He knew that much. *Who wanted you dead, little lady? Delta Force? Who wanted you dead and why?* He tried but couldn't stop himself from staring at Berkstad with suspicion.

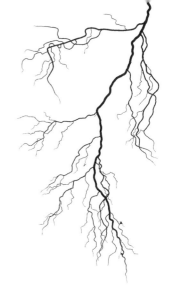

CHAPTER FIFTEEN

"**I** HAVE AGENTS IN that canyon," Elias Cain dropped his fork onto his pie plate. "And you're telling me the Tenville Canyon Dam might collapse? Are they in danger?"

Walt Harper calmly set his coffee cup down and stared across the table at the FBI section chief and Sheriff Montgomery.

They had taken charge and set up a command center here at the Sugar Maple Lodge, five miles south and west of the river and away from the pending danger of the floodwaters building in the mountains. The rustic lodge's owners kept the kitchen open for them. It usually closed at eleven, but they'd volunteered their services with the campground and Crystal Falls City's refugees needing shelter.

Harper felt Cain's stare. It almost bored through his skin like acid. He swallowed hard. None of this was his fault.

"I sent several specialists from the Corp of Engineers to inspect the dam while we evacuated the campground and Crystal Falls City. The heavy spring rains damaged the integrity of the left side spillway. It's under repair, but this storm could cause an overtopping...." Harper explained, looking out through the log-framed window to the pouring rain outside. The volume of water had overwhelmed the gutters, and water spilled off the roof in a sheet. He couldn't stop the image of a dam collapse from filling his mind. Anxiety squeezed at his chest. At least they had evacuated everyone. Well, almost everyone.

"My agents have the boy with them. Are they going to be safe?" Cain demanded. His eyes had widened and his mouth tight.

Harper pulled out his iPhone and put his map in topography mode. "The Forest Service cabin is at 3542 feet in elevation; the river channel is at 1897. They will be safe if they stay put, even if the dam—is overtopped." He showed Elias his phone's screen.

"I can send Deputies Tegner and Cleary up to the cabin another way. Lightning Ridge Road turns into a gravel road to the cell tower here," Sheriff Montgomery pointed to the location on his Google map. "From the tower, it continues along the rim of Summit Mountain to the backside of Tenville Ridge and the cabin," he stared, first meeting Elias's eyes, then swapping his gaze to Harper's.

"Do it. I want that boy safe with his parents and my agents back in one piece," Cain said.

"Wait. No. It would be much safer to wait. Once the storm moves east, we can reach them by helicopter," Harper pleaded. "There could be wash-outs on the roads—right now all roads are extremely dangerous. Mudslides are likely. We've had nine inches since 3:30 this afternoon, exceeding the normal flash flood threshold. The rain's not letting up." Harper warned about the storm's consequences, but deep inside, he was a kid at Christmas. To be here, at this moment, and able to study a once-in-a-lifetime storm thrilled him. It could be the apex of his career. He forced himself not to smile so he wouldn't rile Cain and the sheriff. After all, he was just the messenger.

The weather wasn't under human control—not yet, anyway. After seeing the results of so many *experiments*, Walt believed controlling the weather was something humans shouldn't try. He was a highly educated man and, in his younger days, participated in the HAARP ionospheric experiments. It frightened him. There were too many possible outcomes from man's meddling; some were good—others really bad—end of the world bad.

Elias's glare made Harper shift in his seat. He began tapping his fingers impatiently on the restaurant table. Elias's phone vibrated, dancing on the Formica and breaking the tension.

"Cain," he answered, keeping narrowed eyes on Harper as if it was his fault. "What? Hold on a second." Cain slapped the sheriff on the shoulder and thumbed for him to move out of the way. Elias Cain slid out of the booth and walked outside. Through the restaurant window, Harper watched him talking on his phone and pacing back and forth under the building's overhang.

~

"What do you mean it was a self-defense shooting, Tim?" Elias held his iPhone to his ear and wiped his other hand over his brow. The constant rain spattering on the concrete walkway made it difficult to hear. *If it never rained again in his lifetime, it would be too soon!* He pressed the volume up button.

"Sir, the man who shot at me at Little Crooked Creek showed up, pulled a gun, and Berkstad took him out," Tim said with a sigh. "I called it in to headquarters. But—something's all wrong. It doesn't feel right."

Elias paused, letting his mind dig into the information. "You don't trust Berkstad, I get that, but are you implying he killed this Jaydon Jones on purpose?"

"I don't know. Maybe. Miguel was taking Jones down. We could've facilitated an arrest, interviewed him, and learned something. Berkstad's impulsiveness sent us back to square one," Tim answered grimly.

"Is the boy safe?"

"Yes, Miguel's in the cabin with him. He didn't wake up when Berkstad fired. We've had so much lightning and thunder, it's likely he thought it was more of the same."

"Where are you?"

"Outside on the cabin porch."

"And Berkstad?"

"Inside where he can't hear me."

"Do you think there's more than one perp up there?" Elias knitted his brows together.

"No. I don't think so. We've been using infrared. We haven't picked up any other heat signatures besides a few deer. Still keeping watch,"

Tim answered. "But I do think more than one person was there when Judge Waterford was killed and dumped. Two. There were at least two." Tim's voice drifted as if he recreated the encounter at the original crime scene in his mind.

"Right now, we can't get to you. The storm is so dangerous that helicopters, even military ones, are grounded. The weather guy thinks the back road to the cabin is probably washed out."

"Okay. We'll make it work." There was a pause. "Do me a favor?"

"Of course. What do you need?"

"Send a couple of agents to Fort Bragg to interview Jones's roommates. We need to find the connection to Judge Waterford."

Elias liked the way Tim's mind operated. He had a grasp on detective work. Usually, age and experience were the ingredients that made a good investigator. But Tim, even at twenty-eight, seemed to ask all the right questions and assemble the puzzle. Tim liked winning and wouldn't give up until he had answers. That kind of tenacity usually led to convictions. Elias remembered it well. Tim reminded him of his younger self, and a small smile curved his lips.

"What are you thinking, Tim?"

"Berkstad shot Jones in the face. I couldn't match him to the picture on his driver's license—at the autopsy, the ME will be able to do that, but right now, I can't confirm our dead man is Jones. Support said he was an Army Ranger, a Delta. They are trained to be hard to kill, and this guy was careless. It was too easy. Can you send a Flyaway team? They could print him and grab DNA and then...."

Elias combed his fingers over his hair. "Okay. I'm on it. Stay put. I'll send help as soon as I can. And Tim, watch your back," Elias warned.

"Yes, sir."

They disengaged. Elias quickly ordered a biometric team to be on standby and scrolled through his email. Kandar copied him with the hacked Berkstad files. He had some reading to do. In this relentless storm, tonight was as good a time as any.

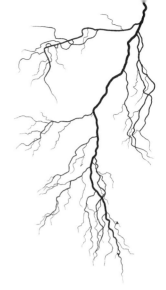

CHAPTER SIXTEEN

ROXIE STAUFFER SAT in the darkest corner of the bar at the Sugar Maple Lodge. She retrieved an unopened but slightly crumpled package of cigarettes from her purse and set them on the polished oak counter in front of her. Before opening the pack, she thought long and hard about doing so. At least ten times, she flicked the trigger on her brass lighter, watching the flame spark to life. Then she closed the lid with a snap, quenching the fire. She craved the nicotine rush of a first draw—but also remembered her addiction and struggle to quit.

Grabbing the highball glass on the bar in front of her, she downed the rest of the Maker's Mark Reserve in one swallow, relishing the burn going all the way down. She caught the attention of the bartender and signaled for another.

As a Special Agent and CARD member, she should've searched for the lost boy with her partners. She'd volunteered for the team just as they had. Her stomach lurched. Had Elias lost confidence in her? She shook her head. Her boss wasn't shy—he would've said something.

Was it Berkstad? Out of the blue, the man had appeared at Judge Waterford's crime scene without warning. He'd been *showing up* frequently, reminding her why she should end the affair. Berkstad's position and tenure gave him seniority over Elias. *Fricking office politics.* She suspected he'd put the kibosh on her original assignment. In addition, Berkstad was obsessed with and jealous of her partners, especially McAndrews. It bordered on dangerous.

Once—one time, she'd worked with Tim on a serial killer task force. She'd explained they were only co-workers a thousand times, maybe more, plus it was in Seattle four years ago, long before she met Berkstad. Even that didn't discourage Berkstad's possessiveness. Hell, she and Tim hadn't even dated; so how did Berkstad know she'd wanted more? Without hesitation, she moved to DC when Elias had asked her to join his profiling team, leaving Tim behind. When Elias hired Tim, Roxie was taken by surprise.

It wasn't Tim's fault he had good genes. She wasn't the only woman in the FBI who lost her place in conversations and felt her insides curl into a ball when the blue-eyed-blond-boy-next-door entered a room. Usually, the ladies breathed a collective sigh, to which Tim returned a rather puzzled half-smile. He didn't understand and his cheeks colored with embarrassment when they were affected by his presence.

Roxie picked up her glass again and sipped the whiskey. Whiskey! She didn't like the taste of it. But her team members did, and she'd joined in just to belong. It had taken her weeks to be able to swallow it down. But now, her body accepted it, anticipating the reward of a numbing alcohol buzz.

She shook her head, remembering the hours she spent at the shooting range, the obstacle course, and the weight gym to stay competitive with her male counterparts, only to have Berkstad complain that she didn't devote enough time to *their* relationship. Their relationship? *What a joke.* What kind of a relationship could she possibly have with a married man with three kids who'd lied to her about it? She tried to break up with him. She really had. But here she was—thirty-four, a never-been-married with a biological clock ticking so loud it was like a suburban neighborhood on the Fourth of July.

Adding seasoned wood to her bonfire of discontent, Berkstad went up the mountain with Miguel and Tim to rescue the little boy. And what did she get to do while they played the heroes? She walked house to house, knocked on doors, trying to get all the residents of Crystal Falls City to evacuate because some alarmist weather guy cried wolf. She hadn't volunteered for the CARD Team to do that.

Picking up the cigarette pack and tapping it absently against the bar, she imagined the newspaper and TV reporters swarming Berkstad and her partners when they returned. There would be grateful hugs, kudos, a ticker tape parade, and most likely pay raises. It would be a media storm. *Predict that, weather guy.*

Insides seething, Roxie took another swallow of whiskey. For revenge, she thought about dialing the tenacious and meddlesome TV reporter, Beebe Knoll. After recovering her iPhone from her jacket pocket, and punching in Beebe's private number, she stared at the call button. She had a whole row of bad choices sitting in front of her—Berkstad, cigarettes, whiskey, and her phone with SBC News's number on the screen, just waiting for her to push the green call button. It startled her when the ringtone sounded.

"Stauffer," she answered.

Without allowing her to say anything more, Elias rattled off his instructions. "Roxie, I need you to head down to Charlottesville with Deputy Cleary. There will be a flight waiting to take you to Fort Bragg. Military Police will meet you. They will pick up Tommy Pelt, our shooter's roommate, and I want you to interview him. We believe there was more than one shooter involved with Judge Waterford's murder. Let's see if he knows anything."

"Yessir," she answered brightly.

"Cleary will be by to get you."

It was late. Eleven-thirty. But she was back in the game. Excitement thrilled through her. Maybe Elias hadn't lost confidence in her after all. If he had, this chance would allow her to prove her worth.

In the mirror behind the shelves full of colorful bottles of alcohol, Roxie watched Deputy Cleary and Deputy Tegner whispering angrily at each other. When Tegner touched Cleary's arm, she shrugged free of him and stomped through the open doorway. So, Roxie wasn't the only one with relationship problems.

"There you are. I went to your room." Deputy Cleary slid into the bar stool next to her. Roxie returned her greeting with a sideways glance and a tight smile.

"Want one?" Roxie asked, fingering the condensation on her glass.

"Do I ever! But, no. Thanks. I'm driving," Shannon replied, removing her hat, and revealing a head full of thick spiral curls. To Roxie, she looked like a stereotypical Irish beauty—red hair, pale flawless skin, big, round eyes with flecks of green—a veritable Brangaene from the tale of Tristan and Isolde. It contrasted with Roxie's short brunette page-style haircut and dark chocolate eyes.

"Guy troubles?" Roxie asked. It was none of her business, but she would be spending a lot of time with Deputy Cleary, might as well make the best of it.

"Ahhh…I hoped no one noticed."

"I watched you come in," Roxie said. "He didn't look happy."

"Teg wants to get married, and I'm not sure." Shannon took a deep breath and let it out. "I mean…he's a good man. I just haven't ever dated anyone else."

"Oh, honey, there aren't that many good men out there. The prince on the white horse never really shows up. He's got a wife and three kids and no horse." Roxie laughed. "So, if Teg's single and a good man, he's a keeper."

"We better get going if we are going to make our flight on time," Shannon said.

Roxie looked at the bar and shoved her whiskey glass into the row of things in front of her. For a moment, she studied it, then grabbed her phone and canceled the call to SBC News. Tonight, was as good as any to turn her back on bad choices.

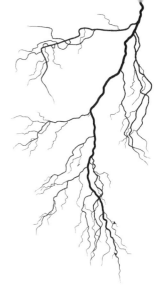

CHAPTER SEVENTEEN

WALT HARPER STARED at his mobile monitor inside a National Weather Service van in front of the lodge. The newly launched drone soared above the treetops along the Tenville River. Tributary creeks had turned the usually clear water to a muddy brown. Using its colored night vision, the UAV's camera would alert them if heavy rain overtopped the dam at the Tenville Reservoir. The thought of the flooding event worried Harper; he'd stayed up all night.

"Fly over to the left spillway." He instructed his drone operator, Major Riley Morecroft, from the Army Corp of Engineers. Morecroft adjusted the camera and zoomed in. As the drone made its way along the dam, Harper could see a small amount of water cresting and rolling over the top of the concrete and trickling down the main face, with even the slightest gust of wind. Water shot out in a powerful stream from both the right and left spillways as if from huge water cannons.

Morecroft picked up his radio. "Can you open another spillway? Over?" He needed to keep the waterline below the top of the dam.

Over the radio crackle, he heard, "There isn't another fucking spillway, Sir!"

"Go left," Harper demanded this time. "Zoom in." His heart nearly stopped. The crack he'd seen on the left spillway had widened, and he watched as it spread further to the left, making the probability of a failure of that part of the dam more likely. He noticed several chunks of concrete breakaway from the dam's edge and enter the swirling mass of escaping water.

"Oh my God," Harper gasped. The whole left concrete section crumbled on the drone's live feed, and a raging torrent of brown water engulfed the spillway and submerged the swollen river under a wall of muddy foam. "The dam is collapsing!" He shouted over the radio connected to the National Weather Service headquarters. "Issue immediate evacuation orders downriver!"

He glanced at the Corps of Engineers' map. The reservoir at Scott's Canyon would have to contain the flood, but could it? "Open all the flood gates at Scott's Canyon Dam! All of them!"

"But, sir, that will inundate the farmland for miles."

"It will be slower than a dam break and buy time so we can get all the people to safety. If this wall of water hits Scott's Canyon Dam with nowhere to go, the dam will fail. Is that what you want?" Harper yelled.

~

Tim snapped awake and jumped out of the wicker chair on the cabin porch like a sprinter off a starting block. He'd only meant to take a load off for a few minutes. His first thought was since there was another person with Jaydon Jones, he might've gotten past him and to Jamie. He glanced around. The soft light cresting the eastern horizon colored the bottom of the remaining clouds in a rose-gold hue, announcing the coming dawn. Even Venus, the morning star, was visible where night's darkness yielded to the morning light. He'd been out for at least an hour, maybe two. Too long!

Grabbing his rifle, Tim raced to the cabin door, flung it open, and flipped on the pale overhead light. Quickly, he assessed the room for trouble. As his gaze darted from right to left, he noted no sign of a struggle—everything remained as he'd left it two hours ago.

Jamie was cocooned in the handmade quilt they'd found in the window box, with only the brown hair on the top of his head showing. Berkstad slumped uncomfortably, lopsided to his right in the overstuffed chair. His feet, still in the worse-for-ware Bruno's, were propped on the small coffee table.

As the fog of too little sleep lifted, Tim reminded himself that if Judge Waterford's killers had come for Jamie, they certainly wouldn't have left him alive. His imagination had gotten the better of him.

In the other chair opposite the sofa, Miguel startled awake and snatched up his rifle.

"Trouble?" he asked quietly and glanced around the room.

Tim shook his head. "No. I fell asleep."

"I know how that goes," Miguel said, a hint of laughter in his voice. "You imagine the worst case."

"I did."

"Want some coffee?"

"Yes. Strong. Very strong. I'll take a look around outside." He walked to the doorway and hesitated. The deer from last night who had ignored him and ventured into the meadow to graze, alerted for a moment—panicked and then bounded off into the trees.

A low rumble hung in the air—like a hundred diesel engines and breaking waves—big waves, like on Oahu's north shore in winter. Tim felt something—electricity—magnetic energy—or maybe just plain old fear crawling up his spine. He tried to wrap his mind around it.

"Earthquake!" He shouted, charging back to pick up Jamie and get him out of the cabin to safety in the meadow. The dishes rattled in the cupboards, and several books fell from the shelves along the wall. Tim wrapped his right arm around the boy's waist. Jamie started to struggle, but Tim carried him, quilt and all, kicking and screaming, out into the meadow. Miguel and Berkstad followed.

"Put me down! Put me down!" Jamie pounded Tim with his fists.

"Jamie! Stop! It's me. Tim."

The boy stopped, and when Tim set him down, he looked at him, confused. "I thought you were the bad man. I'm sorry." Tears welled in the boy's eyes.

"I know. It's okay. I think we're having an earthquake," Tim explained, and the boy cowered close. Tim put his arm around his shoulders and pressed him to his side. "I'm here. I won't leave you."

The tops of the trees at the edge of the forest began to quiver and sway, and the strange sound of water crashing, hissing, and boiling against the rocks reached its crescendo, punctuated by the crack of breaking trees. Tim shielded Jamie as he turned in a circle, trying to determine from which direction danger came. But the echoes off the mountains screamed everywhere.

The ground trembled underneath them as Miguel joined the huddle. If this was a tornado, they'd done exactly the wrong thing. They were exposed. Tim groaned but suddenly recognized there wasn't even a breath of wind. The rain had stopped, and the clouds slowly moved to the east. The sky to their west was clear, dark blue, and still sprinkled with stars.

"What the hell is happening?" Berkstad shouted.

"I think it's an earthquake," Tim yelled, motioning for Berkstad to join them in the meadow's center. But it wasn't exactly an earthquake; it felt different somehow. They crouched in the meadow, sheltering Jamie with their bodies. Jamie clapped his hands over his ears and screamed. Time slowed to an unbearable crawl.

The roaring faded into the distance, leaving only the sound of river rapids. The ground stopped vibrating, and the treetops swayed back and forth, each swing smaller than the last until they finally settled and stilled. Tim stood and scanned all around him. When Tim relaxed, he realized he'd gritted his teeth so hard his jaw hurt. He massaged it with his right hand.

The cabin was in its place. Tim studied each post and beam on the porch. He'd check for damage in the interior later. The water sounds had piqued his curiosity.

"Wait here." He took up his rifle and slowly walked to the meadow's end. At the head of the hiking trail, he looked over the edge.

The Tenville River had turned to a thick, muddy brown, and swirled dangerously in eddies around the few trees left standing in its way. Free-floating logs slammed into rocks and trees as they crashed down the canyon. The campground that was supposed to be below him was unrecognizable. It was just gone—submerged under the murky flood.

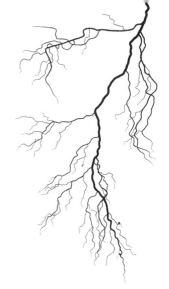

CHAPTER EIGHTEEN

ROXIE GRABBED HER small go-bag and disembarked down the C-130J Transport's gangway, with Deputy Cleary following closely on her heels. Once on the tarmac, she tried to brush some wrinkles from her dark navy pantsuit and adjusted her shoulder holster underneath her jacket.

President Tomlison had put his *RUSH* stamp on their investigation, so they received priority treatment. They were the only passengers on board the huge Super Hercules. Elias arranged for them to hitch this ride on the deadhead leg to Fort Bragg. The pilots would pick up and return some Army VIPs for a meeting in DC later this morning.

Roxie managed a few restless and uncomfortable winks of sleep on the flight and was ready to check into the hotel room Elias reserved for her. On the other hand, Deputy Cleary, wide-eyed with wonder, was like a child experiencing Disney World for the first time. But then, how many times had the backwoods, small-town deputy, taken a ride in the belly of a giant military transport plane?

"Wow," Cleary said. "I never realized how big...."

Roxie shrugged and asked, "First time?"

Cleary nodded. "You?"

"No. I've had the pleasure of doing it a couple of times. I'm looking forward to the hotel and hoping a quick shower will bring me back to life."

"I'm dreaming of food. A big three-egg cheddar omelet with bacon sounds so good right now."

"Coffee. That's what sounds good to me," Roxie sighed.

A whisper of gray light barely brightened the horizon, chasing away the stars and announcing dawn. A clear morning had arrived, greatly diminished by the sharp sting of AVGAS in the air and the constant jet take-off roar from the runways. Roxie would never be able to sleep now, even if she tried. Her body clock wouldn't let her during the day.

She trudged across the pavement toward the concrete terminal building, not paying attention to anything except how much she wanted to sleep and annoyed that she wouldn't be able to.

Surprised, she stepped back as a camouflage-painted Humvee pulled up in front of her, blocking her path. A tall, young man in military fatigues jumped from the driver's side.

"Special Agent Stauffer? Lieutenant Broady, Army CID—ah, Criminal Investigation Division. I'm here to take you to your hotel. Then on to meet with Tommy Pelt." He reached out his hand and briskly shook hers while a tight smile arched his lips. "I'm sure you'd like to get something to eat. If I drop you at the hotel and come back in a couple of hours, will that give you enough time?" He glanced down at his digital watch. "Pelt will be back from weekend exercises around ten hundred." It was barely six.

"Yes, of course. That will be perfect. Oh, by the way, this is Deputy Cleary from the Trask County Sheriff's Department," Roxie said. Cleary stumbled forward like a shy little girl and dropped a limp hand into Broady's. Obviously, the deputy had not learned the benefits of a power handshake. Roxie shook her head. Lieutenant Broady quickly picked up their go-bags, opened the passenger side and a rear door for them as he hurried by, and loaded the suitcases into the back of the Humvee, closing the circuit around the vehicle in mere seconds. Pressed and polished, clean-cut, polite, and with plenty of get-the-job-done hustle, Broady embodied the traits Roxie liked most about military men.

Deputy Cleary was out of her element, though she shouldn't be. Roxie let her take shotgun. It was penance for her unkind thought that the deputy might not be up to the job. Roxie climbed into the back seat.

Broady swiftly slid into the driver's seat, turned the key, and the diesel engine rumbled to life.

"Buckle up," he said and waited until everyone strapped in, and they left the ramp and merged into the Pope airfield traffic.

He asked the sixty-four-thousand-dollar question, "Do you want to tell me what this is all about? I was told you'd fill me in." He looked in his rearview mirror and glided seamlessly into the left lane to make a turn. "So, why does the FBI want to interview Corporal Tommy Pelt?"

"The President's favorite nominee for the Fourth Circuit, Judge Evelyn Waterford, was kidnapped Friday night, and we found the body yesterday." Roxie caught his shocked gaze in the rearview mirror for a moment.

"And you think Corporal Pelt was involved? I know him. Tommy Pelt is one hundred percent solid gold, a good soldier, and he was out on maneuvers this week. We've never had a bad encounter with him, and he has no criminal record."

Intermittently, Broady returned his attention to the road and then back to the mirror, his eyebrows pinched together, and his eyes narrowed. Roxie realized the soldier was trying to read her mind. She knew when he received his orders, he probably did a quick background search on Pelt. She would've done that, too. Fewer surprises that way.

"What do you know about Pelt's roommate, Jaydon Lee Jones?" Roxie tipped her chin to the side and lifted an eyebrow. Broady again stared at her reflection.

"Jaydon? Good guy. A decorated DELTA. You aren't suggesting…? No way. I can't imagine it," Broady shook his head, dismissing the thought.

"What is he, diamonds?" Cleary chimed in, chuckling at her own joke. "You said Pelt was solid gold."

Roxie rolled her eyes at her as Broady glared.

"He's dead. He was in a shoot-out with special agents while trying to eliminate a witness, a little boy, who'd seen him dump the Judge's body," Roxie burst Broady's bubble with the brutal facts.

"Jaydon? What? Where?" Broady said incredulously.

"He dumped the body in the forest near the Crystal Falls Campground, on the Tenville River in Virginia," Roxie reported. Broady shifted in his seat, quickly slowed, and pulled to the shoulder of the road. Gravel spinning off the big tires pinged the undercarriage until they stopped. He slammed the Humvee into park.

"That can't be true. His unit was on maneuvers all last week. They are expected back this morning." He spread his arm along the back of his seat as he turned to face her.

"Wait. Jaydon Jones is alive?" Roxie murmured under her breath, perplexed. Her thoughts shuffled the currently established facts in her mind like a Vegas dealer with a poker deck. She bit her bottom lip. "Would there be a way he could take off unnoticed? Our agents found his wallet on his body." Roxie suspected Tim and Miguel hadn't taken any MBA (Mobile Biometric Authentication) devices with them on the search for Jamie Randall. Why would they? The kid's fingerprints wouldn't be in the main databases. The boy was nine. But now, she wished they had. A fingerprint scan on the dead man would already be through the FBI, DHS, and DOD databases. They'd know if the dead Jaydon Lee Jones was the real Jaydon Lee Jones.

Roxie sank deep into her seat. Broady shifted his gaze between the road in front of him and her eyes and finally pulled back onto the road. Elias said Tim had his suspicions. Could he be right? Again?

"Listen, I'm getting ahead of myself. Let's see how this plays out. If Jones is not dead and not our suspect, maybe he knows something," Roxie said, her voice raising in a question.

"Bring them both in for an interview," Cleary chimed.

"I'll need your IDs," Broady announced as he turned right and continued down the drive to the main entry gate at the Fort Bragg Army Base. Roxie pulled her leather case out of her pocket and handed it over the seat. When they pulled to a stop, Broady presented the guard with their credentials.

While one guard scrutinized the passengers, another scanned the undercarriage of the Humvee with a camera that could detect explosive devices. This was nothing new. Roxie's offices occupied the basement at the FBI headquarters on the Marine Base at Quantico, so an explosives search was ordinary. But Broady's original demeanor had changed. Friendly and helpful had morphed into closed and dubious. They were, after all, investigating one of his comrades and a decorated DELTA.

After inspection, they were saluted and waved through. The ride to the Landmark Inn entrance became conspicuous by the silence that settled over them like an eerie fog. When they pulled to a stop, the polite and efficient Broady gathered their bags and set them on the curb, but the original sense of camaraderie had vanished.

"I'll meet you here in two hours," he said curtly.

Roxie tossed him a half smile and nodded. Standing in front of the Landmark Inn's entryway doors, she watched Broady drive away. She hoped they weren't going to be stonewalled. The pressure was on. The President wanted answers. Murder was murder, and solving the murder of a presidential nominee took precedence.

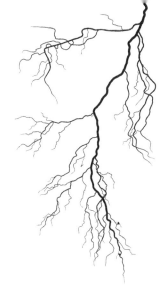

CHAPTER NINETEEN

STUMBLING SLIGHTLY, TIM stepped back from the edge of the hiking trail that dropped down more than three hundred feet to the churning water in the river canyon below. Little Crooked Creek, where Jamie fished for Crawdads, was inundated, and only muddy water raged through the remaining trees. He'd never seen a flood in person, only in images on TV. Immediately, panic overwhelmed him. *Dani.* He thought. Where was the confluence of this river with the sea? Was his family in danger? He felt suddenly disoriented.

He remembered the helicopter flight bringing him to the Trask County Sheriff's Office flew south and west, a good hour and a half from Quantico and even farther from his home. But how big was the storm? Did they get the same amount of rain? Overwhelmed by the need to know his wife and children were safe and not in the path of this stinking, filthy deluge, he called Dani.

"Hello?" Her voice was groggy with sleep, and he suddenly felt guilty for disturbing her so early in the morning.

"Baby, one of the flood control dams on the Tenville River has given way. There's a huge wall of water...."

"Are you okay? Is everything okay?" Dani's voice rose in volume and worry. "Tenville River? Is that near the cabin where you are?" Tim could hear her throw back the covers and fumble with items on the bedside table and then the noise of the television in the background.

"Yes. But we're on top of the ridge. The Sheriff evacuated Crystal Falls City and Campground yesterday."

"The news isn't reporting a flood. Are you in danger? Are we in danger?"

He scrolled through a map on his phone, switched to a weather app, and watched the radar predicting the storm would move south of his home and out to sea. "Dani, wait. It's miles southwest of you. I just wanted—I needed to hear your voice."

"Are you going to be safe? Tim, you're scaring me."

"I'm okay. You know me, I had to make sure you and the kids were out of danger." As always, he wanted to tell her everything, but he couldn't.

"We're all good." She moved around the house; he could hear the changes in the volume of her commentary and different sounds on the phone. Doors opened briefly, then latches quietly clicked shut as if she were looking in on the kids.

"Are you checking on the girls? I didn't mean for you to get up," he lied. Of course, he had. He wasn't there to protect them and wanted reassurance that his household was secure. He didn't understand the need. Whether it was learned, cultural behavior, or an innate genetic trait, the day he met Dani, providing for and protecting her became a big part of his life. Dani and his daughters were his everything.

"They're both sound asleep," Dani whispered.

Tim heard her softly padding down the stairs and the familiar swish of the sliding glass doors opening onto the covered concrete deck and the pool.

"Everything is fine here. It rained last night, but everything looks good. There's no standing water in the pastures, that I can see." Tim imagined her gazing out over the farm from the house's perch on the highest hill.

"Baby, I should let you go back to sleep."

"Can we talk a little longer? I miss you. I don't sleep well when you're away," she answered.

"I didn't sleep at all. I miss you, too."

The sun painted the underside of the clouds with a watercolor brush. Soft pinks slowly intensified to brilliant oranges and reds. He stood in awe, it was always beautiful after a big storm, like a promise. "Sunrise is beautiful this morning from here. Are you watching?"

"I'm sitting at our favorite table."

"Wish I was with you, having morning coffee." His thoughts drifted to their delicious routine. In the quiet of early morning, before the girls rose for the day and he cleaned up for work, they would watch the sunrise. His imagination dressed her in one of her negligees—the pink one that caressed her body in shimmery satin. They would talk, and when they finished their coffee, he would encourage her to join him upstairs—he could almost taste her kisses and exhaled.

"What are you wearing?" she asked, laughing a little. It was a code between them they used when he was away, a reminder that she wanted him as much as he wanted her.

"We better not go there...." he teased, tamping down the exciting thoughts. "I have to get Jamie out of here and home. And instead, I'll be distracted thinking of you." *Too late.* His thoughts were full of her, her kisses, her silky skin. He had to make it home.

"Okay. But, I want you to think of me."

"I always do," he whispered.

"I love you, Tim."

"I love you too, Baby," he replied. "See you soon." He didn't hang up until after she did.

In his peripheral vision, he noticed Miguel had moved up to the meadow's edge and looked over.

"Well, hell. That's not good." Miguel glanced over at Tim and stepped back. He punched a number on his phone. "Elias, Miguel," Tim heard him say, "I think we're surrounded by flood water."

Tim strolled back into the meadow, took up his binoculars, and followed the trail that bordered the ridgeline between the cabin and the cell tower on the next peak. Red-brown scars marred the green landscape where the heavy rain had washed the road away. The stretches of the road still intact were severely undermined to the point even foot travel might trigger a mudslide. The river side of Tenville Ridge was no longer accessible.

Surveying the meadow in front of the cabin, Tim tried to determine its size. Even a small helicopter probably couldn't land here. With his left hand, he kneaded the muscles tightening in the back of his neck. *Damn.* If a helicopter couldn't land, they might be stuck for at least another day. Maybe more. He groaned.

"You're not going to believe this. On second thought, yes, you will," Miguel said as he approached Tim in the meadow. He held out his phone.

Tim sucked in a breath through his teeth, "McAndrews," he answered.

"Listen, Tim. Roxie said Army CID believes Jaydon Jones is alive, out on maneuvers. The guy Berkstad shot might not be Jones," Elias delivered the news, his voice barely above a whisper. Tim's jaw tensed, and he turned and glared at Berkstad. Luckily, the man's back was to him. "She's interviewing Jones and his roommate at ten this morning."

Tim glanced at his watch. It was only six-thirty. "Can you get us down from here?" he asked. He'd love to be a part of Roxie's interview, but first things first. He knew how this would go down. Get Jamie back to his parents, and into protective custody, then stand with Elias for the press interview. Hopefully, he wouldn't be asked to speak. Then, he could determine the next steps in investigating the Judge's death.

"Miguel says a helicopter may not be able to land. Can you make it to the cell tower? There's a good pad there."

Tim looked across the canyon. Shaking his head, he answered, "It's probably ten, maybe fifteen miles. Easily an all-day hike. The road along the ridgeline is washed out and undermined. Dangerous with the boy. Hell, dangerous with Berkstad. The man's a menace. And then there's the body."

"The Trask County Sheriff said he could send an S-92 rescue chopper. It would require lifting you one at a time in slings. Do you think the boy can do that?" Elias asked.

The rescue craft was a tried-and-true platform, but would Jamie be too afraid to go alone? Tim imagined the scene. What could go wrong? Anything, everything. It was a risk they'd need to take.

"I think he'll enjoy it. He's a brave kid." Tim chuckled, remembering how Jamie charged them when they arrived at the cabin.

"That's what we'll do. I'll let you know when Trask County Rescue is headed your way."

"What about the body?" Tim asked. "I haven't let the boy see that."

"I've ordered the Flyaway Team you requested. I'll add a Forensic team. They will arrive right after we get you out. They'll be in and out as fast as possible and take the body to Quantico. Since our dead guy is probably not Jaydon Jones, we need to know who he is. Who he is will help us determine why and the others involved."

"Good."

"You take the boy. Miguel can escort the body."

"Okay."

"The weather guy said there's some sort of atmospheric pulse headed our way, whatever that means. I think he means another storm is brewing, and our window for this operation is tight."

"All right. We'll be ready," Tim answered, and they disengaged.

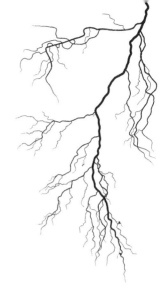

CHAPTER TWENTY

D ANI MCANDREWS STROLLED to the kitchen, cherishing the warm feeling wrapping around her as if Tim were here, holding her in his arms. She loved her husband more than anything on earth. Just hearing his voice this morning filled her with joy.

But Tim's talk of flash floods frightened her, and she quickly turned on the flat-screen television mounted in a recess on the wall opposite the kitchen island.

Dani's favorite morning news hosts talked about a schoolboy who had started a charity for the homeless in his community. She scrolled through the channels. None of the morning news shows said anything about Tim's flash flood. She turned back to her preferred channel. Was it real, or was she dreaming? Taking out all the coffee fixings, she inserted a coffee pod, slipped a big mug under the spout, and pressed the start button on the brewer for a sixteen-ounce coffee.

Suddenly, the television's volume seemed to increase a notch or two, and the emergency broadcast system alarm screeched as a robotic voice announced an evacuation alert. Dani whirled to view the screen.

"At five fifty-seven this morning, the Tenville Reservoir Dam collapsed, sending a wall of flood water down the river canyon. The following communities are under emergency evacuation orders...."

She read the names on the list as they scrolled on the screen. Each community was south of her, but still her heart pounded in her chest.

The news hosts returned to the screen.

"Our SBN News affiliate out of Charlottesville has just received drone footage of the dam's collapse from the National Weather Service." They played it.

A crack on the left side of the dam opened slowly at first, but a large block of concrete crumbled as the water began to spill out. It was only a second or two later, and the whole left wall of the dam gave way. An unmanned drone captured the event in its rear-facing camera. A huge surge of brown foamy water inundated the canyon, removing everything in its path.

Dani felt her legs grow weak and braced herself on the marble countertop. Once steady, she sank onto one of the stools at the kitchen island. The next image on the screen was a highlighted area where the flood was anticipated to go. She and the girls were out of danger, but Tim—Tim was in the middle of it.

Oh, no. Oh no. Tim told her he was safe. She forced herself to breathe. He told her he was safe, and she had to believe him, but still, she couldn't stop trembling and from anxiety tying her stomach in knots. She dialed him on her iPhone.

~

Roxie Stauffer picked up her small suitcase and walked through the Landmark Inn doors to the lobby. Behind the reception desk a big flat-screen TV was tuned to the morning news. She dropped her bag and stood frozen at the registration counter.

"Oh. My. God." She briefly turned her head to catch Deputy Cleary standing next to her. "Roxie Stauffer, I have a reservation."

The attendant typed on his computer. "Yes. I have you. That flood is just awful isn't it," he said.

Roxie nodded. Speechless.

"What flood?" Cleary asked and let her suitcase fall from her hand. She followed Roxie's gaze to the big screen TV. The drone footage of the moment of the dam's collapse replayed.

"Tim and Miguel are up that canyon with the lost boy. Oh, and David," Roxie shook her head, recognizing immediately Berkstad was an afterthought. A grimace brushed across her lips. *Time changes things.* It was past time for her to break free of their relationship.

"But they're at the top of the ridge—aren't they?" Deputy Cleary stared at her as if Roxie had all the answers when she had none. "Teg...." Cleary whispered. The young man at the registration desk handed Roxie her keycard.

"Deputy Tegner is warm and dry at the Sugar Maple Lodge, remember? I thought you were dumping him." Roxie sarcastically lifted an eyebrow and returned her attention to the screen. "That's the weather guy, that Walt Harper guy," she said as he appeared by remote. Now everyone in the lobby was watching the TV screen. Whispers buzzed in the background.

"[...] If the lower dam at Scott's Canyon holds, there is the potential for flooding here." Harper narrated as a graphic image flashed into view. The map was covered with an oval pictured in green. The darkest green represented the area with the most likelihood of serious flooding, and lighter shades depicted inundation at lesser degrees.

Adrenaline surged through Roxie's bloodstream. Powerless to help anyone from here, she tried to contain her emotion by tapping her closed fist against her thigh. *Focus. Damnit. Focus.* Squeezing her eyes shut, Roxie forced herself to think of Judge Waterford and Jaydon Lee Jones. She grabbed her keycard from the counter in front of her.

"Get cleaned up. I'll meet you in the coffee shop in half an hour." She directed her comment to Deputy Cleary, snatched up her suitcase and bolted for the elevator.

~

"The helicopter can't land in the meadow, so they will send down a basket or a harness and lift us up," Tim explained, facing Jamie in his chair on the porch. "It'll be like a carnival ride, only the real thing."

Jamie squirmed and bounced in his chair. "Will it be scary?"

"Maybe a little. But the men who do this practice all the time. They know what they are doing and will make sure you're safe. You just have to do exactly what they say," Tim smiled and reached out, setting his hand on Jamie's shoulder.

"Are you going with me?" Jamie pleaded.

"I'll be in the helicopter with you. But they'll have to take us up one at a time. You'll be fine. I'll be right behind you." Tim did his best to reassure the boy. But he'd never done this before, either.

Miguel mounted the porch steps.

"Are you going with us?" Jamie directed his question to Miguel.

"Naw. I'm on the second chopper. I have some clean-up to do." Miguel narrowed his eyes and let out a sigh. Tim knew what he meant, but discouraged any explanation to Jamie with a quick shake of his head.

"I did the dishes," Jamie volunteered.

"Not that kind of clean-up. But thanks for doing the dishes." Miguel patted Jamie on the back.

Tim glanced at the cabin and noticed Berkstad listening behind the screen door. No matter how hard Tim tried, he didn't like the guy. Elias assigned Miguel to escort the body to Quantico's autopsy lab with the Flyaway team. Tim thought Berkstad should do it. He shot the guy; he should fix his mess. Like Tim, Elias shared the same trust issues, but Berkstad was one of the seventh-floor higher-ups. Like him or not, he was one of Tim's bosses.

In the distance, Tim heard the rhythmic beat of helicopter rotors.

"Let's go," Tim said, tapping Jamie on the shoulder. He picked up his gear, took Jamie's hand, and headed for the meadow.

He looked up to the sky. Some of the Northern white pine and pitch pine trees in the forest surrounding the cabin were easily eighty to ninety feet tall. The helicopter would hover about ten to twenty feet above the crowns. When the craft came into view, the treetops began to shudder, and he could feel the wind from the down draft against his skin. A fall from this height would be fatal. Tim kept that thought to himself.

Jamie stepped closer and reached for his hand. For a moment, Tim held it reassuring the boy everything was okay.

The helicopter's side door slid open, and a deputy in a bright orange jumpsuit scooted to the edge, suspending his feet in the air. Before beginning his descent, he placed a yellow rucksack between his knees.

"Here we go," Tim said with a confident smile. The rotor wash pressed the wet grass down around them, but still, they both watched, fascinated.

"Wow. That's so cool," Jamie shouted over the noise.

Slowly, the deputy was lowered to the ground and detached from the steel cable. He made it look easy.

"I'm Deputy Matt Harlow."

"Tim McAndrews and this is Jamie Randall." Tim reached out and shook his hand. "This is David Berkstad."

"Storm's moving in, so we need to make this quick. Who's going with us?" Harlow asked.

"Jamie, me and—."

"And me. First," Berkstad wrestled his way to the front, practically shoving Jamie aside.

"The rescue boys will decide the order of ascent. They know what they are doing," Tim answered, clenching his jaw to keep his anger in check.

Harlow smiled, "We'll send all your gear up first, then Jamie, you'll go, and then you, Mr. Berkstad. Finally, McAndrews and I will follow up together."

Tim nodded in agreement.

"Here, help me get Jamie into this." He unzipped the bag and took out a harness. "It fits just like a vest." Harlow threaded a piece between Jamie's legs and hooked the corners together with a big carabiner. "Okay. I'm going to lift you, so you know how it feels, okay?"

"Okay," Jamie said with excitement.

"It's going to be fun. You'll have lots of stories to tell your friends," Harlow lifted Jamie a foot or two off the ground. "Mr. Berkstad, this is your gear. I'll have you carry your backpack between your knees."

Tim helped Berkstad and then put on his rigging.

"All ready?" Harlow waited for a nod from everyone. "Ready for pick up." He reported over his radio. When the cable lowered, Harlow connected Jamie. After attaching a stabilizing rope to the underside of Jamie's vest. Harlow made a circle gesture with his hand, and Jamie was on his way.

"It's like flying!" Tim heard Jamie say, followed by delighted laughter.

Once Jamie was safe inside. The new storm on the horizon decided to announce itself. A flash of lightning brightened the dark sky off to the west, and thunder rumbled in the distance.

"Better get a move on," Harlow said. Picking up his pace and with an economy of words, he fastened Berkstad to the cable and sent him on his way. Suddenly, a burst of wind competed with the chopper wash, sending Berkstad swinging wildly under the helicopter. The ground control line was yanked from Harlow's hands and snapped like a whip as it flew across the meadow. Uncontrolled and dangling, like a spider clinging to a whisp of silk, Berkstad whipped from side to side, almost tipping the helicopter over. The cable operator reversed the direction, and Berkstad plummeted twenty feet before jerking to a stop and bouncing in the air like a yo-yo on a string. One of his Bruno's, the left, flew off his foot and plummeted to the ground. Tim and Harlow raced to gain control of the stabilizing rope. Together they grabbed it and leaned their weight like a tug-of-war team. The swinging finally slowed and steadied. Harlow signaled, and the cable operator winched Berkstad upward and two men inside the chopper pulled him to safety.

Tim looked at Harlow and spat out a burst of nervous laughter. He raked a hand through his hair. "Whew."

"It happens. Good thing you were here."

Tim jogged across the meadow, grabbed the shoe, and stuffed it in his jacket pocket.

Harlow secured them together, Tim slightly higher than the deputy, and signaled for the cable operator to bring them up. Tim swallowed back the anxiety in his throat. He hoped their weight would keep them stable. He had no desire to go through what Berkstad had.

"Ready? Let's get going," Harlow said, completely calm. In reply, Tim let a tense smile tick across his lips. This was the way out, and he wasn't about to let a little fear keep him from getting Jamie home.

Halfway up, Tim looked down around him. To the west, he could see the reservoir's broken dam, the swollen river channel, and the new storm billowing up into the sky. A flash of lightning zig-zagged against the gray, reminding him they still had a way to go before they were safe.

Tim felt a hand on his shoulder; the rescue team helped him inside and unhooked him from the cable. They gave him a headset, and he slid next to Jamie across the floor. He uncoupled his backpack from the others, set it beside him, and slipped an arm around Jamie's shoulders.

"We're taking you to the Sugar Maple Lodge," Harlow said over the microphone. "Jamie's parents are waiting for him there."

Through the open side door, Tim noticed the FBI helicopter passing them on their left side. He breathed out with relief. Miguel would beat the storm, but unfortunately, he'd have to fly an hour and a half to Quantico with a dead body.

Tim frowned at Berkstad, reached into his jacket pocket, and tossed the missing shoe into his lap.

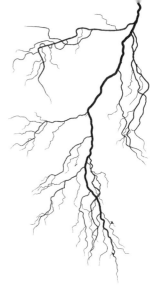

CHAPTER TWENTY-ONE

ROXIE FOUND THE Landmark Inn's DIY breakfast in the hotel's lobby dining room. The four-person tables were placed on a clean but dated gold-colored carpet. Against the room's solid wall, a neatly laid-out buffet had a great selection of breakfast items: Waffles, scrambled eggs, sausages, bacon, biscuits, and gravy. Very few patrons were out this morning; it was an off time, too late for most. Busier earlier in the morning, she guessed. When Roxie saw Deputy Cleary in the doorway, she raised her hand to help her locate their table in the breakfast area. She'd grabbed two cups of coffee and the fixings before Cleary took her seat at the table.

"Feeling better?" Cleary asked while adding sugar and cream to her cup.

"A little." Roxie glanced at her iPhone in front of her. "I called Broady and told him he could pick us up early. Then, he reminded me that Jones and Pelt wouldn't be back from maneuvers until ten."

"I checked in with Sheriff Montgomery about the flood. He said he reassigned Teg to rescue duty. They've got pontoon boats on the water, and calls for rescue are inundating the 911 center. And it's raining again." Cleary stirred her coffee with a spoon. Worry pinched her brow.

"Cain called and said Jamie, Tim, and David were rescued by helicopter and are on the way to the Sugar Maple Lodge. Miguel is taking an

FBI chopper with the body to Quantico's Forensic Lab with the Flyaway team. At least they're all safe."

"What do you think about Broady telling us Jaydon Jones is alive?"

"We will have to figure out what happened. Is Jones involved in Judge Waterford's murder in some way? Did he lose his wallet or give it to someone? Did someone steal it? The unsub used a stolen Jeep. Why not muddy the waters with a pinched ID?" Roxie asked, watching Cleary's expression change to wide-eyed innocence, like a kid discovering astronomy for the first time. "When we interview him, we'll have to tease out any leads we can."

"Can I ask you a...question?" Cleary stumbled between words.

Roxie lifted an eyebrow. Cleary hesitated for some reason. "Ask away." Roxie encouraged her before sipping her coffee.

"I wondered...what's it like to work with McAndrews?"

"Uh, oh. Has the McAndrews bug bitten you?" Roxie lifted her gaze and laughed.

Cleary's cheeks turned a brilliant shade of red. "Well, he's so...."

"Handsome, charming, intelligent?" Roxie grinned. She knew she egged her on, but the tease kept her from revealing her own crush.

"I'm sure he's all those things, but how'd he figure out where to find Jamie?"

Nice recovery, Roxie thought. Cleary lied; the pupils of her eyes contracted. She'd been bitten, all right. Roxie could read it all over her face. She knew the symptoms because she'd lived them.

"That's what we do, Shannon. As profilers, we try to read a person by their actions. Tim needed to find Jamie, so he imagined himself in Jamie's place. What would he do if he were Jamie's age and had just seen a body dump? Who better to find a nine-year-old boy than a guy who was once a nine-year-old boy?" Roxie explained.

Cleary stared for a moment, digesting the information, but Roxie felt she wanted more. After a few moments, Cleary asked, "Did the McAndrews bug ever bite you?"

At first, Roxie didn't want to answer that question. Cleary had confided in her about Tegner, but Roxie kept her cards tight to the vest. Four years ago, her FBI team and two King County Deputies from the Sheriff's department had contacted Tim, the assistant DA assigned to their case. They needed him to review a search warrant affidavit for them and present it to a judge. No one, not even her friends in the King County Sheriff's Department, had warned her about him. He breezed through the conference room door in a light grey three-piece suit and a tie with a sky-blue design that just happened to be the same color as his eyes. Tall, blonde, and tan, with a smile as warm and inviting as the summer sun outside, he turned her insides to mush. She remembered she'd even sighed like a high school girl.

"Naw, I escaped that malady," Roxie perjured herself. Fortunately, Tim spared her by not taking her up on her uncharacteristic advances. He adeptly turned her down in such a gentlemanly way; he'd made her feel good about it. She chuckled to herself and shook her head.

"Yeah, well, he's pretty stand-offish and conceited, a stick in the mud, I'd say." Cleary pouted.

"He's confident, sure, but he earned it. He's not conceited," Roxie mused. She denied her crush. Admitting it—admitting he didn't return her affection—that part she didn't want to do.

"Arrogant?" Cleary asked.

"No. That doesn't fit, either. I met him four years ago. He worked with me as an assistant DA on The Fynn Creek Serial Killer Case. You read about that one, didn't you? I busted that creep. That summer, we needed Tim for our search and arrest warrants. The last weekend, when we arrested Randy Jo Harper, you'll never guess where I found Tim."

"Yeah? Where? Some bar?" Cleary asked.

"No. His family owns a cabinet shop. McAndrews and Sons. I walked into the place, a big warehouse-type building. There was a showroom, a sample kitchen, and a sample bathroom decorated with these nice upscale cabinets. The man in the showroom took me to the back when I asked for Tim. I found him dressed in jeans, a long-sleeved Henley, and a pair of those dumb-looking safety glasses working a wood lathe. He was covered in sawdust. The slick prosecutor was just a regular, but very handsome guy, building cabinets for a foreclosure house he and his brothers were remodeling to flip."

Cleary's mouth dropped open, but no words came.

"I was speechless, too. He motioned for a guy to take over, cleaned up, wrote our arrest warrant, and found an available judge to sign off in less than two hours." Roxie said. "He knows the law. In the end, the DA appointed him as the lead prosecutor. He used our evidence and presented an irrefutable case. The defense couldn't even offer a rebuttal," Roxie paused to snicker. "They sounded amateurish and unbelievable. The jury returned a guilty verdict in twenty minutes." Roxie clicked her tongue on the roof of her mouth. "You weren't trying to flirt with him, were you?"

"I just tried to be nice." Cleary raised the pitch in her voice.

"You realize that women are always after good-looking men. A guy either loves it and becomes a cad, hates it, and becomes a hermit, or ignores it and hopes he'll be seen as just another coworker and maybe a friend. We objectify men as much as they do us."

"I didn't flirt!" Cleary said with too much force.

"No?" Roxie knew better and licked her lips while she smiled. "Well, Tim gets intense regarding situations involving children. We all do. That's why we volunteered for the CARD team. He probably wanted to get to the search. Time is our enemy in a lost or abducted child's case. After twenty-four hours, the chance of finding a kid alive isn't so good."

~

The Sugar Maple Lodge had been converted from an old log mansion built in the early 1800s and updated and expanded over the years. The owners added all the amenities normal for a high-end resort: an eighteen-hole championship golf course; an Olympic-sized swimming pool in a glass enclosure; tennis courts; and a horse barn and riding trails. Tim could see all this through the helicopter's window, confirming his online research. After talking to Elias last night, he'd mapped out a strategy for protecting Jamie.

When he interviewed the boy at the forest service cabin, Jamie stated with certainty he'd seen two men dump the body. Tim believed more perpetrators were involved with the Judge's murder. Kidnapping for ransom was one of his top theories. Maybe she fought for her life, they killed her, and then had to divvy up the clean-up duties.

Tim studied Jamie's profile. The boy stared out the chopper's window, watching the world below go by. He turned, a big smile sliding across his face. Tim suspected Jamie viewed the helicopter ride as a big adventure. Hell, he would've at that age. With the bad guy iced, like on TV, "happily ever after" seemed just minutes away.

The lodge's main buildings and cabins came into view. They were nestled in a grove of sugar maples and were topped with green metal roofs that stood out against the broadleaf trees. The smattering of yellow in the leaves hinted that summer's emerald would soon turn to the flame colors of fall.

As they descended, Tim recognized the lodge's helipad from the pictures he'd seen last night in his research. It consisted of a concrete slab surrounded by low boxwood hedges in the middle of a grassy lawn about a football field's length away from the main entry.

Jamie intertwined his fingers with Tim's and looked up into his face. Tim smiled at the boy but read the hint of fear and sadness in his eyes.

"Just a few more minutes, and you'll see your mom and dad," Tim said.

"But will I ever see you again?" Jamie asked.

In one of his training courses, he learned about the bond that often develops between victims and their rescuers. He didn't want Jamie's family to begrudge him as an interloper.

"Sure, you will," Tim had made promises and intended to keep them. Still, Tim understood he needed to tread carefully.

The helicopter descended, and Tim noticed the gaggle of reporters rushing toward the helipad. Dread began to seep into his gut. They looked like a column of Army Ants, ready to swarm and devour their prey. He felt too tired to deal with them today, but had to suck it up. He began to cage his emotions. The minute they disembarked; the questions would start—questions he had no answers for.

The helicopter skids touched the ground, and the pilot shut down the engine. They waited until the blades stopped spinning, and the deputies opened the sliding door. Before stepping out, Tim studied the crowd.

He wanted to be sure that the man they'd shot at the cabin was the only one who wanted to harm Jamie. Scrutinizing each reporter, camera operator, and technical assistant, Tim conceded he'd seen most of them before at one time or another. No one stood out to him as threatening—annoying—yes—dangerous—no.

"Ready?" Tim asked Jamie. The kid didn't know what to expect, but Tim did. Through the press of human sharks, the barrage of shouted questions, cameras, and microphones, he must navigate a path toward the hotel and Jamie's parents while ensuring the boy's safety.

Slipping into his backpack, he asked one of the sheriff's deputies, "Did you ever play football?"

The deputy returned a look of confusion, but nodded in the affirmative.

"Block for me," Tim said, jumping from inside the helicopter. He helped Jamie disembark. At first, Tim thought about carrying the boy on his shoulders but decided Jamie might become a sitting duck. He kept him right in front of him, guiding him with his left hand on Jamie's back. He kept his right hand free should he need to use his pistol.

Scared, confused, and stumbling through the foray, Jamie looked up at Tim as they plowed through the crowd. The deputies cleared the reporters with shouts of, "Step back and out of the way!"

The sea of reporters surged with them toward the lodge's entrance. Once they arrived at the doorway, Elias, Sheriff Montgomery, and several agents and deputies held back the crowd. Tim recognized Jamie's mom and steered Jamie toward her. The second Jamie saw Mom, he dashed for her, throwing himself into her open arms. Tim could imagine their emotions: a mixed bag of guilt, fear, and joy. It felt so good to see them reunited; it made Tim's job worth doing, and he smiled, satisfied.

Tim turned and searched for Elias in the crowd. He wanted to confirm all the arrangements had been made. After Jamie sat down with a sketch artist, he and his family would be moved and sheltered in a safe house with around-the-clock protection.

"Special Agent McAndrews?" Tim pivoted to answer the female voice addressing him. Jamie and his parents stood before him.

"Thank you." Mr. Randall reached out his hand, and Tim shook it. Mrs. Randall suddenly grabbed him and squeezed him in a strong embrace. When she released him, Jamie offered a high five.

The family, in unison, like a choir, said, "Thank you."

"My pleasure. We will send a sketch artist up to your room in a little bit," Tim answered. The best outcome for a lost child case—was delivering him safely to his family. Most didn't turn out that way. Tim knew the statistics but didn't say it out loud.

"All right, folks. Gather around," Elias's low-pitched voice boomed as he motioned for the group in the lobby to join him near the elevator. "The press is demanding a briefing. I'm scheduling that for 3:00 P.M. this afternoon. That gives everyone some time to get some rest and clean up. We'll meet here in the lobby at 2:30."

As the crowd disbursed toward the elevators, Elias said, "Tim, hold up a second." Tim nodded and waited while his boss gave directions to the remaining agents and deputies. As they received their instructions, Tim glanced around the lobby. Through the glass doors, he watched as news techs off-loaded gear from their vans and set up satellite feeds for the press briefing. He noticed the hotel staff staring at him like they were watching a television drama. Finally, in a corner by the elevators, with his arms folded across his chest, Tim caught Berkstad studying and evaluating him as if he were in the running for a college sports scholarship.

I'm never moving to counter-intel. Not doing it. Tim thought, a frown knitting his eyebrows together. During college, he focused on criminal law and had no desire to change direction. That's where the FBI needed him most, he reasoned. He had to consider Dani and his new family. Besides, in his opinion, spy craft was a single-man's gig. He picked up his backpack and slung it over his shoulder.

"Tim, I want you with me during the press briefing," Elias said. He handed him a small envelope containing his room keycard. "I'll meet you at 2:00. Hopefully, we'll have reports from Miguel and Roxie by then. In any case, we keep Judge Waterford's murder out of the interview."

"Yes, Sir," Tim answered.

"Go get some rest. See you at 2:00."

Tim watched Berkstad push himself off the wall and stroll his way. Involuntarily the muscles along his jaw tightened. He wanted to avoid the confrontation he saw brewing on the horizon. One of the elevators chimed, and Tim glanced at the envelope locating his room on the third floor. He walked forward into the car. When he turned to face the sliding door, he realized David Berkstad had followed him inside.

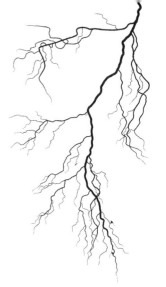

CHAPTER TWENTY-TWO

"**W**E NEED TO talk," Berkstad started before the doors closed.

"David, we need to rest," Tim sighed. "We've been up for more than forty-eight hours. I want a hot shower and to close my eyes for a while. I can barely think, let alone decide my family's future. Dani and I are taking life's journey together. I won't make a career choice without consulting her. Happy wife, happy life, as they say, whoever they are."

In the distorted reflection on the elevator's stainless-steel interior, Tim could see the dark, tired circles around his eyes.

"I didn't ever do that," Berkstad mused, a faraway look seeming to cloud his eyes.

"Everyone has unique life circumstances," Tim said, slightly tipping his head to the side. He didn't feel like listening to Berkstad's story of regrets right now. Or ever, for that matter.

The elevator stopped, and the doors slid open. "Are you on this floor?"

"Three-fourteen," Tim answered.

"Looks like I'm across the hall."

"Ummm." Tim nodded, hoping Berkstad wouldn't come knocking on his door for a 'talk' while he tried to rest.

"Do you think I did the wrong thing—shooting Jaydon Jones, or whoever he is?" Berkstad asked as they walked out into the upstairs lobby.

"No. The minute the unsub pulled a gun, he rigged the game against himself. Fire on the cops, prepare to be shot. Miguel would've been able to take him down without gunplay—I'd seen him do it before. But you hadn't."

"I didn't know," Berstad's tone was reflective. Maybe he weighed his actions. "Miguel wasn't happy about it."

"Well, he didn't know whether or not you were a good shot." Tim frowned. "It could've gone all wrong."

Next to the elevators, a small conversation area consisting of a tan leather settee and two matching chairs in front of a fireplace welcomed visitors to sit for a while. The carpet was a mixture of fall colors—brown, auburn, gold and red. Wall sconces patterned after rustic lanterns bathed the hallway in soft light, like an autumn sunset, all to charm customers into a cozy mood. Sunlight streamed through the windows, and he paused to look at the forest and the manicured lawn below. *Beautiful setting,* he thought. Bringing Dani here crossed his mind.

"I would've pulled the trigger if you hadn't," Tim said, adjusting his backpack. "It makes our job harder because we can't interview the bad guy. But, then again, who said this job was easy." He read the direction sign with room numbers and followed the arrow to the left.

"Thank you for helping me at the helicopter," Berkstad said, glancing over at Tim with a smile. "I mean it. If you hadn't stabilized the cable, I might be hanging in a treetop right now."

"You're welcome. You'd do the same for me," Tim said, but he wasn't sure that was true. The fact that Berkstad didn't agree said it all.

"Do you have any theories? Who would want to kill Judge Waterford? Do you think it was a carjacking?" Berkstad pinched his eyebrows together and shook his head once. "Doesn't make sense."

"Could've been, but they didn't take the car," Tim mused, stopping at the door with his room number.

"The husband?" Berkstad asked.

"We'll have to rule him out," Tim slipped his key card through the receptacle and heard the door unlock as the indicator light turned green. "Get some rest. I'll see you downstairs at the press conference."

Tim didn't wait for a reply. He opened his door and stepped through, clicking on the light switch as the door closed. At least Berkstad discussed the case and not whether or not Tim wanted to become a spy.

The room was typical, with a small closet across from the bathroom abutting the main hall, then opening to a bedroom with a king-sized bed. A small desk and chair were placed under the television hanging on the wall, and in a corner in front of a large window, a two-person table invited him to order room service.

He tossed his backpack into the closet, noticing the garment bag he'd brought with him and left in the SUV at the campground before they'd started their search for Jamie. It contained what he jokingly called a G-man gray suit. Elias had brought it. Tim guessed Elias wanted him dressed like a proper FBI agent for the press interview. He chuckled to himself.

Tim walked into the room's sleeping area and sat on the edge of the bed. He didn't dare lie back or close his eyes. It would be too easy to fall asleep. Feelings he'd tried to keep at bay seeped into his thoughts. He longed to see Dani, touch, kiss, and hold her. He didn't relish the thought of staying away from her for another night, and maybe he wouldn't have to. He fished his iPhone from his vest pocket and quickly searched for an airport.

He dialed her, and while waiting for her to answer, he stripped out of his shoulder holster and hooked it over the bedpost, gun and all.

"Hello, handsome," Dani answered cheerfully.

Tim laughed, "Hi, Baby. I'm at the Sugar Maple Lodge. Elias procured me a room, so I guess I'm overnight."

"I miss you." He loved her voice. It soothed him.

"I miss you, too." He hesitated to ask it and sat silently, running his fingers over the smooth satin bedspread. "Can you come?" It spilled out anyway like water breaching a dam.

"Yes. You know I will. Mitch can fly me. Is there an airport nearby?"

"About five miles west of the lodge," he said barely above a whisper.

"Is it a secret?" she asked, laughter in her voice.

"Maybe not a secret, but not exactly fair. My team member's wives can't drop everything...."

"And I can?" she teased.

He felt hope diminishing, "I shouldn't have asked. I'm sorry. I just...."

"Don't be sorry. I love that you asked. I want to see you, too," she said seductively.

"How are the girls?" He attempted to change the direction of his thoughts.

"They are fine, riding their horses. When should I be there?"

The promise sent desire shooting through his body. And he blew out a breath. "You're coming?"

"Not yet, but we'll see when I get there," she laughed.

"You tease...I'll make sure of it." He loved it when she said sexy things to him. It excited him to know she wanted him, too.

"I hope so," she murmured. "I need about four hours. Is that soon enough?"

"No. I need you now, but four hours will have to do. I have a news briefing at 3:00, so four or five will be okay. Call me when you get close to the airport. I'll pick you up."

"A secret affair, how fun," she giggled. "I'll see you around five."

"Love you," he answered.

"I love you, too."

He waited until he heard her disengage and set his phone on the bedside table. Closing his eyes and enjoying the anticipation, he slid to the edge of the bed. He wanted to ease back into the pillows, but knew he would surrender to sleep. He stood.

After a long, hot shower, Tim wrapped himself in the hotel's complimentary bathrobe, set the alarm on his phone for 2 hours, plumped up and stacked the bed pillows intending to read the crime scene notes again. He reclined into the pillows, but instead of reading, he drifted off to sleep.

~

The Criminal Investigation Division, housed in the Fort Bragg Military Police Headquarters, reminded Roxie of a medium-sized police department. A clean oak reception counter kept visitors from working patrol officers and the CID Detectives. The structure, made of reinforced concrete block, was painted stark white. Pictures of the North Carolina shore decorated some walls, but most were bare. In the background, she could hear the phones buzz in the 911 call center that occupied an alcove off to the right of the reception area.

Roxie felt her phone vibrate in her pocket and retrieved it. She studied the picture she had just received from Elias. The handsome young black man sitting on a wooden bench in the lobby matched the driver's license photo. *Oh, yeah. Mr. Jaydon Lee Jones was very much alive.* She smiled at him.

She handed her phone to Deputy Cleary to get a look.

"Well, what a waste of time," Cleary said, curling half her mouth with disgust.

"Not so fast. Somehow, someone got a hold of Jones's wallet and driver's license," Roxie said. "We should find out who, how, where, and why. The interview might get us a lead." According to a text message she received from Miguel, the dead man at the cabin was one Wilford Lenard Kincaid, a scumbag with a rap sheet a city block long. His repertoire included everything from armed robbery to identity theft and check fraud. Forgery wouldn't be out of the question.

Lieutenant Broady hustled up behind Roxie. "Corporal Jones, will you follow me?" Jones stood to his six-foot height and glared at Roxie and Cleary with suspicion as he entered the interview room. Roxie noted he looked very dashing in his camo military fatigues.

"Corporal Jones, this is Special Agent Stauffer from the FBI and Deputy Cleary with the Trask County Sheriff's Office. They'd like to ask you some questions," Broady said, looking at the women with a tight smile.

Jones's eyes widened and then immediately narrowed as he studied them. Roxie couldn't fault him. Lately, the relationship between the black community and the police had been strained by agitators. But Roxie knew the ViCAP (Violent Criminal Apprehension Program) statistics.

Roxie reached across the sturdy wooden table to shake his hand, but he didn't respond to her friendly gesture.

"Corporal Jones, I'm sure you're wondering why we're here," she started, trying to calm the hostility with a warm smile. "So, I'll get right to it."

"Thank you," he answered with cold politeness as he sank into the spindle-back chair.

"Do you know Evelyn Waterford?" Roxie looked straight into his brown eyes. *No hint of recognition there.* He tipped his head slightly as if trying to find the name in his memory bank.

"No, Ma'am. I do not," he answered, genuinely puzzled.

"No? Do you know Wilford Kincaid?"

Jones slowly shook his head and appeared more confused than before. None of the tell-tale signs of deception; narrowing pupils, rolling eyes up to the left as if fabricating a lie, sweating, or a tense jaw, changed his bewildered expression. Roxie believed he honestly didn't know either person.

"Should I know them?" His gaze flashed to Broady's face, then returned to Roxie's. "Am I in some sort of trouble?"

"Not if you don't know them, Corporal," Roxie answered. "You're not in trouble," Roxie said to reassure him. "I know you've been out on maneuvers this week, but can you tell me what you did just before you reported for duty on Friday."

"Thursday, I dropped my dog at the groomer's and shopped for his food. He's old and on a special diet. I had to get him ready for the dog sitter. Then I picked up my clean laundry and my clean dog and went home. Some friends called, and we met for dinner at the Officer's Club." He shifted in his seat. "What's this all about?"

"We'll get to that, Mr. Jones. Tell me about Friday."

"I left the house at four thirty AM and met my team at headquarters for our drill."

Roxie studied Jones's face. A good-looking guy like Jones probably didn't go home alone Thursday night. She decided it was time to get to the meat of their inquiry. "Jaydon, do you have your wallet on you?"

She almost saw the thoughts behind his eyes, working out the math and trying to connect the dots.

"Ma'am, I don't bring my wallet with me on swamp drills. I could lose it. I left it at home in my safe. There's been car break-ins, and someone jimmied open the lockers in the barracks. We all have ID badges to navigate the base."

"Did you give your wallet and ID to Wilford Kincaid?" Roxie looked over at Shannon Cleary's surprised face and then Jones's. She made sure her stare bored into his chocolate-colored eyes. Though he was unlikely to be intimidated, he'd been trained not to be cowed even under threat of torture. Roxie wished Miguel could be here. He had a deeper understanding of military training and would be able to get to the truth more quickly.

"No. I don't know Wilford Kincaid. I told you that. Why would I give anyone my wallet and ID?" Jones scooted his chair with enough force to move it from the table. "I paid for my dinner and drinks. I went home...."

"Alone? Did you go home alone?" Roxie asked. Jones's face lit up as if a lightbulb shone in the darkness.

He swallowed and bit his bottom lip, first looking at Broady as if deciding whether he should say anything. The Deltas had a strict moral code. A strange woman picked up in a bar could be a spy and compromise him or his unit in the field. "No. Not alone. I met a girl at the bar, we...." He looked down at the table, embarrassed. "No. It couldn't be. She wouldn't...."

Even though it might cost him, Jones decided on the truth, elevating Roxie's regard for him at least two levels.

"Jaydon, we found your wallet on a man accused of taking part in the murder of Judge Evelyn Waterford."

With his mouth hanging open in shock, Jones stared daggers at her. He shook his head. "Wait a minute. I...I didn't...I don't know Judge Waterberg...." His hands started to tremble, and he slid them under the tabletop.

"Ford, Judge Waterford," Roxie corrected. "Okay, Jaydon. The girl you met in the bar and took home with you, what's her name?"

"Arlina, I don't know her last name, just Arlina," he said. He stood and paced in place behind his chair.

"Take your seat," Broady demanded.

"You can't pin this on me. I didn't do anything. I would never… I was gone all week. Am I under arrest?" He placed his palms flat on the table and leaned across. Then, he sank into the chair, his breath ragged with disbelief and his carotid artery pulsing in his neck. Then he glanced up into Roxie's face. "I have surveillance cameras at my house. After the officer's club, I was home Thursday night and didn't leave. You can check."

Roxie gauged his reaction. He protested like she'd expect an innocent man to do. Good news—video didn't lie.

"Jaydon, Lieutenant Broady will go with you to your house, check your safe for your wallet, and review your surveillance footage."

"I have it on my phone. You can see it right now," he asserted after cueing up the footage.

"Better yet," she said. Jones wouldn't have a chance to alter it. She reached out her hand palm up, and Jones slapped the phone into it. Without letting her gaze leave his face, she said, "Do we have your permission to download and keep a copy of your surveillance tape?"

"Yes. Of course. Anything to get me out of here," Jones said.

Broady stood and motioned for Jones to get up. Slightly confused, he followed the Lieutenant out of the interrogation room.

"Why did you send Broady to go with Jones to look in his safe?" Cleary asked. "We already know his ID was stolen."

"Do we? It could be a forgery. Kincaid's rap sheet includes Identity theft and fraud. Under ordinary circumstances, we'd know if it was forged in a few days, but we have our answer if Jones's wallet is where he expects it to be. My question is, why did Kincaid target Jones to take the fall?"

"Maybe they look alike," Cleary answered.

"Right. Now, you're thinking like a detective." Roxie grinned at her and watched Cleary wiggle her shoulders like she was proud of herself. Roxie remembered her young and inexperienced days and was glad she had good mentors. She decided right then she would take Deputy Shannon Cleary under her wing.

"What's next?" Cleary asked.

"We'll send this surveillance video to FBI Support and my team members. Support will enhance it and see what they can find. We interview his roommate Tommy Pelt. Then we head for the Officer's Club. They'll have CC-TV inside and outside the bar. I want to find out who little Miss Arlina is."

CHAPTER TWENTY-THREE

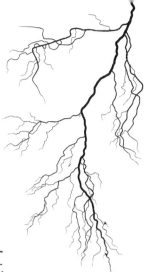

TIM SPLASHED COLD water on his face, trying to chase away the lingering shades of sleep that didn't want to let go. Studying his image in the mirror, he noted that at least the dark circles under his eyes had disappeared. He changed the water temperature to warm, drenched his skin again, and squirted a palm full of shaving foam into his hand.

Letti and Chloe called it his Santa Claus stuff and teased him about the white beard he made when he applied the cream to his upper lip, cheeks, and jaw. They'd often watch him shave at home in the morning, even mimicking his gestures to ensure he managed a close shave. Relishing the memory, he laughed and continued. He couldn't wait to see his daughters again in a couple of days, and Dani, tonight. *How did his other team members do without a family?* Tim loved his.

After he finished his shave, he ran a wet comb over his hair. As if it had a mind of its own, his hair would do what it wanted when it dried, so he kept the thick blond mass cut short.

After dressing in his clean white shirt and gray trousers, he took his laptop computer from its case and sat at the table by the window. He had an hour and a half until his scheduled meeting with Elias before the press conference. He found Roxie's email with video attached.

Tim,

I'm sending you two videos we collected. The first is from the Officer's Club Bar. The second is from Jones's home security cameras. I've edited it, so you only have the pertinent parts. Jones said he puts his wallet in his safe at night—spoiler alert—he didn't. Still, I've concluded that Jaydon Jones is not involved in the Judge's murder. I've sent both tapes and the interview recording to Support and everyone. See what you think. We'll talk when I get to the lodge.

Rox

Tim loaded the first video and watched. A gorgeous, model-like black woman slipped gracefully into the bar stool next to Jones, smiling at him irresistibly when he looked her way. Immediately intrigued, Tim concentrated. The next clip in Roxie's edited version showed Jones paying for his tab and shoving his wallet into the pocket of his jacket draped across the back of the bar stool. Tim chuckled as he watched the woman slide her hand into that very pocket while Jones turned away to speak to friends. Though he couldn't see it for sure, he speculated that was the moment the pickpocket lifted Jones's wallet. *Interesting.* Roxie hadn't mentioned the woman's name. He played the tape two more times. Roxie would bring the whole tape with her, and they'd play the full-length version. Thankful for the preview, Tim cued up the next one.

The second video told more of the story. Once Jones and the beauty were inside Jones's house, the woman led him to the bedroom. Roxie was right; he hadn't put his wallet in his safe. In the morning, while it was still dark, Jaydon appeared, dressed in his fatigues, and headed out the front door to go on his week-long drill. By the time stamp in the left-hand corner of the video on screen, Tim noted that hours later, the woman emerged from the bedroom. She cased Jones's house, rummaged through drawers, and found his safe behind a picture hanging by the bookshelf. She took the picture off the wall and set it aside, but seemed to have second thoughts and didn't open the safe. *Didn't even try.* She didn't need to; she had what she wanted. Tim paused the tape. He wished he had the wallet and could look at the contents. He remembered Miguel pulling out ID, several credit cards, and a small amount of cash, but nothing alarming.

There was way more to this story than met the eye. He pushed play, and the video started again. The beautiful woman searched for more. Was she trying to find a stash of money? State secrets? Was it merely an impulse to find valuables to steal? She returned the picture and straightened the frame. He watched that section a second time. She hadn't worn gloves; she'd left her prints. Just like Miguel said: "They always make mistakes."

Jones may have *thought* he put his wallet in his safe, but he didn't. Was he lying or distracted and duped by a femme fatale? That wouldn't go over very well with his superiors. It might even cost him his position on his DELTA team. It wouldn't be the first time a foreign government sent a pretty woman to seduce a guy in a honey trap.

He understood misdirecting the cops by using a stolen ID, but why Jones? Was he just a hapless schmuck? Wrong place, wrong time? Or was it an intentional setup? Or maybe revenge? Tim linked his fingers together and rubbed his thumbs against each other. He felt a tingle of excitement race over his skin. *Never a dull moment in this business, he thought.*

Tim dialed Roxie.

"Hello?" Roxie answered.

"Jones's lady friend pinched his wallet at the bar."

"Tim, is that you?"

"Sorry. Yes. I'm watching the video you sent me. The woman left her fingerprints on the frame around the picture covering Jones's safe."

"Yes. I know," she laughed.

"Do you know who she is?"

"Arlina—at least that's the name she gave him. No last name. Whether or not that's her real name, I guess we'll find out if we get a fingerprint hit. Army CID has a forensic team at Jones's house. He's authorized a search." Roxie stopped talking to let out a guffaw. She laughed so loud

Tim had to hold his phone away from his ear. He put it on speaker and set it on the table in front of him. "Boy! He is so pissed that she led him down that path," she continued.

"Seduction is a very successful trick," Tim said, realizing full well he soft-pedaled the failure as if he needed to defend his gender. Roxie loved to have fuel to put down men for their weaknesses.

"Come on, Tim, would you have been fooled?"

Not wanting to give Roxie more ammo against men, he answered, "No. But I'm married and love my wife. If I were a single guy, out drinking with buddies, and a beautiful woman sidled up to me? Maybe."

"He's a DELTA, for crying out loud."

"It made me wonder, who puts their wallet in a jacket pocket? Obviously, she's not a practiced pickpocket. He made it easy for her. Was it Intentional—passing information or carelessness? Anyway, she got his wallet, not state secrets," Tim chuckled.

"How do you know?"

"Okay. You're right. I don't. Good point. Are you leaning toward a political motive for the Judge's murder?" Tim asked.

"I don't know yet. It's a possibility. What do you think?"

"It crossed my mind. I guess we wait and see."

"Why are men so easy?!"

"We all want to be loved. Don't we? That's why honey traps work in the first place," Tim argued. He wanted to remind her of her own inappropriate involvement with Berkstad. She knew he and Miguel strongly disapproved. He bit his bottom lip to keep the words from dumping out. "So, here's the deal. We're the FBI. We need to find out who this Arlina woman is, why she chose Jones, and how it connects to Judge Waterford's murder."

"Did you get a copy of Wilford Kincaid's ID?" she asked.

"Yeah," Tim answered.

"Do a comparison. Look at it next to Jones's."

Tim turned his phone sideways and placed the pictures side by side. There were minor differences, Kincaid had a narrower and longer nose and smaller eyes, and his lips were not as full. Still, they could be brothers.

"Deputy Cleary thought they would be look-alikes before I did—before we received Kincaid's picture. She might make a detective after all," Roxie said. Tim could hear the delight in her voice.

"Look-alikes...distant relatives, maybe?" Tim let that information stew in the back of his mind. It would become clear with more evidence. "What did Tommy Pelt have to say?" Tim asked.

"Pelt was with Jones when little Miss Arlina made her move. He picked Jones up the next morning, early. He said around five, and they headed for their squad's meeting place. He and Tommy were together all week—along with ten other guys. They confirmed Jones's alibi."

"The Judge's murder was premeditated and preplanned," Tim mused. "Kincaid wanted to send the police on a wild goose chase...."

"Only Jamie saw him dump the body, and that kinda ruined the plan." Roxie's ideas mirrored Tim's thoughts. "So, what's next?" she asked.

Tim breathed out. "I think we get the Waterford's bank records, look for disharmony in their marriage, and check for a big fat insurance policy. The usual," Tim replied. "We find Arlina and look for connections. We scour through the Judge's friends and family."

"Are you thinking murder for hire?" Roxie asked.

"We have to rule it out," Tim stated.

"I agree. Oh, I gotta go. My plane ride is here. See you in a couple of hours."

Roxie disengaged before he could tell her to wait. He glanced at his phone. He had just enough time to slip into his jacket and tie and make his meeting with Elias. Grabbing his tie off the hanger in the closet, he walked into the bathroom and stood in front of the mirror. Absently, he wrapped the tie around his neck and placed it neatly under his shirt collar. While he tied a half-Windsor and tugged the tie into its proper place, his mind chased motives.

Whoever killed Judge Waterford knew or targeted Jones because of how much he and Kincaid looked alike. The chances they found him accidentally while drinking at a bar—improbable—a hundred, no, a million to one odds.

He crossed the room, loaded a magazine in his Glock, and slipped it into his shoulder holster. He clipped his FBI ID and badge on his belt.

Roxie dismissed Jones as a suspect too early. Maybe he was a fall guy, but on the other hand, maybe he wasn't and was involved up to his eyeballs.

Tim grabbed his suit jacket on his way out the door and donned it as he hurried to the elevator.

The lodge's lobby was awash in news reporters. Tim scanned the crowd, his guard up in case his media nemesis, Beebe Knoll, covered the story. Once he felt safe, he edged along the perimeter of the throng toward the meeting room off the front of the foyer. He slipped unnoticed through the door, closing it silently. Feeling safe, he let out a victory sigh and turned.

"There you are, Tim," Elias walked toward him. "You remember Beebe Knoll, don't you?" The intrepid reporter emerged from behind Elias's bulk and motioned for her cameraman to move in closer. *So much for avoiding her.*

"How could I forget Beebe?" He licked his lips and grinned at her. "My lucky day," he mumbled under his breath.

"Jackass! Great to see you, too," she sniped and ran her fingers through her blond bubble curls, finally reaching out to shake his hand. She made certain her best side was to the camera, pulled out a small microphone and shoved it toward him. "So, Special Agent McAndrews, what was your role in rescuing the lost boy, Jamie Randall?" she asked in her fake, news anchor voice.

Tim played along, "Well, Miss Knoll, I'm a member of the FBI's Child Abduction Rapid Deployment Team. Our job is to partner with local law enforcement to help find lost, missing, and abducted children. We were just doing our job, Ma'am."

Beebe sucked in a breath and ground her teeth together while narrowing her eyes at him. Tim realized he'd gone too far with the sarcasm, though he doubted her television audience would notice. He was surprised she didn't call him 'Jackass' on air.

"How did you know where to find the boy?" she asked, saccharine sweet.

Tim caught Elias's worried grimace. He shook his head, signaling Tim needed to be careful with his words.

"I remembered what it was like to be a nine-year-old boy and thought about where I would go with a big lightning storm coming on. I studied a Forest Service Map, chose some likely locations, and we found him in one. I'm very thankful it turned out well for the family."

"Okay, Miss Knoll, that's your two minutes," Elias said, stepping in and instantly cutting off the interview. He escorted her to the meeting room's wooden double doors as her cameraman stumbled behind her trying to keep up. "Yes, Miss Knoll, I'll answer your questions at the press conference," Elias assured her as he closed the door. "Thank God! That's over. That woman is the pushy-est woman I know."

Tim laughed and nodded his agreement. Tim felt a tug on his coat tail. He turned, and Jamie stood before him. This was perfect timing. He'd put together a photo lineup, hoping Jamie could point out the men who'd dumped the body and hoping one would be the man Berkstad killed.

"Hi, Jamie. Are you all rested?" Tim asked, watching Jamie's parents approaching.

"I came to give you back your hat." The boy didn't look up at him and scuffed the toe of his shoe along the hardwood floor.

"I gave it to you. It's your hat now." Tim tipped his head so he could meet Jamie's eyes.

Jamie brightened and a big smile broke across his face. "Gee, thanks." He faced his parents. "See, I told you he gave it to me." Jamie put on the hat and stood tall. Dressed in his charcoal suit, he looked like a miniature agent, making Tim grin.

"Can we take a seat over at the table?" Tim pointed to the round table covered with a white cloth, where his teammate, Kandar had set up a laptop computer. "Jamie, I'd like you to look at some pictures and tell me if you recognize any of these as one of the men who tossed the body over the creek bank." Tim noticed the shocked look on Mrs. Randall's face, but he needed answers, and Jamie willingly took his hand as they walked to the table. They sat down side by side. Mr. and Mrs. Randall joined them.

Tim cued up the computer and tapped on the icon for the lineup Kandar had made for him. Six face photos appeared on the screen, including Wilford Kincaid and Jaydon Jones.

"Look carefully, Jamie. And if you see the guy, touch the picture on the computer screen." Tim instructed. Without hesitation, Jamie touched Wilford Kincaid, Berkstad's shooting victim. He flipped to the next line up. Jamie shook his head No.

"You're sure, Jamie?" Tim asked, and the boy nodded vigorously. "That's all I need. Thanks." He patted Jamie on the shoulder and stood. Jamie was a solid witness. He'd pointed out one of the killers and had given the sketch artist great details for the other.

"May I speak with you?" Mr. Randall asked.

"Sure." Tim motioned to some chairs a few feet away against the wall. Mrs. Randall took charge of Jamie and walked to the center of the room as the two men took a seat.

"Thank you for finding Jamie and bringing him home," Mr. Randall said. "I'm not sure about this safehouse business, though."

"It's your choice, Mr. Randall. But we only know the identity of one of the men Jamie saw dump Judge Waterford's body. We'd like to keep your family as safe as possible. Your son is the only witness."

"But Mr. Cain said you killed the man...."

"We killed one. But the other man is still out there. Your boy's life's in danger."

"How long? You know—how long would we have to be in this safe-house?" Mr. Randall's face was tight with worry.

Tim took a deep breath and let it out. "I'm not sure. Supervisory Special Agent Cain has made arrangements with your employer for two weeks. Do that, and we can revisit this in a week." Tim searched for Elias amongst the few remaining people in the room.

"Do I need to buy a gun?"

"I would," Tim said without hesitation. He probably shouldn't have recommended that, but he thought about what could happen. If Kincaid pursued Jamie into the woods during last night's storm, the killers might not be done looking for him. "You'll have two armed agents with you at all times. But if you decide to buy a firearm, you, Mrs. Randall, and Jamie should all take a gun safety class."

Mr. Randall sat silently for a full minute, and Tim let the information process. "Thank you, Mr. McAndrews." He stood, and Tim followed suit. They shook hands. Tim watched him gather his family together and head for the door. Two agents from the DC field office closed ranks behind them. After the press conference, the family would be escorted to a safehouse at a secret location Tim didn't even know.

"Did you get Roxie's video?" Elias asked, approaching Tim from across the conference room.

Tim turned to answer, "I did."

"She thinks Jones isn't involved. What do you think?"

"Too early to tell. Are the autopsy notes available?" Tim asked.

"Tomorrow."

"I want to walk the crime scene at the restaurant," Tim said.

Elias chuckled, "The one at the campground is underwater—gone. I hope we collected what we needed. The weather guy panicked. Kept saying we were taking too long."

"He was right. The whole forest shook when the dam burst. I thought it was an earthquake. Good thing you evacuated the campground. Glad we were up high."

"All right. No mention that there's any connection between the boy and Judge Waterford's murder at the conference. Not to anyone. This is a press conference about finding the boy. That's all."

"Yes, sir. I think that's smart." Tim shifted his stance.

Elias sighed, "Damn it. Evelyn was a good judge, a fair and honest judge. A friend. When did everything get so political and go so wrong?"

It was a rhetorical question that Tim couldn't answer. He did feel empathy. "Do you think this is political?"

"I've been fighting crime my whole adult life. A high-profile judge is murdered right after being nominated to the Circuit Court of Appeals. It has political scribbled all over it. I'm bone tired," Elias said quietly, looking deeply into Tim's eyes. Tim set a hand on the older man's arm. "Well, we won the first round. Jamie's safe for now. I'm happy for that."

"Yes. Sir."

"I want you to stand with the family, Tim. Sheriff Montgomery will give the briefing. We're just props," Elias said. His brown eyes were filled with deep sadness even though he smiled. "Looks like they're ready for us, shall we?"

"I'm right behind you."

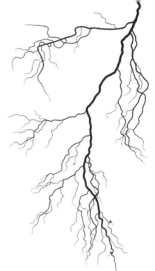

CHAPTER TWENTY-FOUR

HE PRESS CONFERENCE ended, and the TV and print newsies rushed off to be the first with the breaking story. Tim sank into one of the chairs in the front row next to the podium set up for the briefing.

Jamie and his family were off to the safehouse with two FBI special agents, and Tim felt he could check them off his worry list.

He looked at his phone for the twentieth time, hoping Dani would text to tell him she'd landed at the airport. But it was only three-thirty, and he had an hour and a half before she would arrive.

"Want to get a drink?" Elias asked, walking up to him. His face had brightened with the burden of the press conference out of the way.

"Sure," Tim answered, standing and walking with his boss to the bar. They each took a stool rather than a table in the corner, as Tim expected. With the other patrons and bartender within earshot, they wouldn't be discussing the case. Maybe that was a good thing. Sometimes information had to simmer in his mind before the connections and next steps became clear. A good detective was a well-rested detective. Tim worried he was neither.

"What'll you have?" the bartender asked.

Tim waited until his boss ordered a vodka on the rocks. He hadn't decided whether or not he wanted a drink but ordered a Maker's Mark

Reserve over ice, anyway. When the bartender set a bowl of party mix between them, Tim realized he really wanted food. Dani would be here soon, and he planned a nice dinner in his room. He'd earlier perused the menu. His mouth watered at the thought of the big juicy ribeye steak he planned to order. He took a handful of the mix, put it on a napkin, picked out his favorite pieces, and ate them.

"Claire wants me to retire," Elias said. Tim snapped his gaze to his boss's face.

"What do you want?" Tim asked.

"I'm tired. I told you that earlier. But police work is all I've ever done." He matched Tim's stare. "She's given me an ultimatum."

"Oof," Tim grimaced and bit his bottom lip. "Are you ready? I mean, money-wise?"

"Yes. That's not the problem. The girls are both going away to college next fall. Claire and I will be empty-nesters. I don't know what I'll do with myself. I'm not the stick-around-home kind of man. Besides, she'll be tired of me in about three days. Then what do I do?" Elias laughed.

"Cold case work? I understand you can do much of that from home and part-time," Tim offered. He sipped his whiskey and felt the burn all the way down.

"Part-time detective? Good grief, Tim. How would I be able to keep it part-time?"

Tim chuckled. "You wouldn't. Will the bureau let you slow down?"

"Sure, we'll just ask the criminals to work part-time," He grunted a laugh.

"You could teach. A university would be lucky to have you in its criminal psychology department. That Ph.D. of yours wouldn't be wasted."

"How do you know about that?" He scrutinized Tim with a scowl. Elias had never bragged about his accomplishments to the team. Though Tim thought he should.

"Claire told me," Tim said with a big grin.

"If I'm going to teach, I'd want to teach at Quantico. Then I'm right back to the beginning of this circle."

Tim smiled and thought about it for a moment. "What's Claire's biggest complaint?"

"She says she misses me and doesn't like being alone at night. That and the idea I might get shot isn't her favorite."

Tim suddenly felt guilty for asking Dani to fly in to see him. He hadn't thought of Elias and Claire. "What if she could join you in the evenings when you have to go away?"

"There would have to be rules. Claire would want me to go sightseeing. Imagine that in the middle of a case. And then there's the danger quotient. What if a scumbag found out she waited at the hotel for me and used it against me?" Elias shook his head. But nothing was ever lost on him for very long. "Is Dani coming to visit you?"

Lying to Elias was impossible. He could read subtle micro-expressions like reading a kindergarten picture book. Tim tipped his head slightly and smiled.

"Ah, young love," Elias shook his head as if remembering. "When we were first married and before kids, Claire and I would meet up when I'd been called away for a case."

"Dani could bring Claire with...."

"No. Not this time. We are off to headquarters first thing in the morning. But it's a thought I'll keep in mind—especially when the girls are away at college. That or I'll need to buy Claire a dog."

They both laughed.

"Don't tell the other team members about this. They're already complaining about favoritism."

"They are?" Tim sat back, surprised.

"Okay, Roxie is. But she doesn't understand the optics of TV interviews. You know how to deal with the press. You have experience there—she doesn't. Besides, you look good on TV—like a real FBI Special Agent," Elias snorted and lifted his glass, asking the bartender for another.

A commotion, including lots of giggling, filled the bar's doorway. Roxie and Deputy Cleary stood as if waiting for their eyes to adjust to the darkness of the lounge.

"There you are. Let's get a table," Roxie said, taking Elias's drink from before him. They had no choice but to do as she suggested, she'd taken Elias's vodka. Tim grabbed his drink, pivoted the chair to get out, and followed the group to the table.

Before he sat down, he glanced at his watch. Dani had said five, and he was disappointed it was only four. He slipped into the chair across from Roxie and Cleary and closest to the door for a quick escape.

Roxie bounced forward in her chair like she did when she had important information about a case that she was anxious to share. He studied her for a second, then glanced at Deputy Cleary. She looked away suddenly, and a blush colored her cheeks as if she were embarrassed. His system flooded with a well-known feeling of dread. *Oh, crap.* He thought and hoped he was wrong. He hated being in the awkward position of making a woman feel rejected. Because he was married and committed didn't mean she was less of a person or wasn't smart or pretty. It just meant he didn't cheat. He warned her off with a tight smile and looked away, hoping that would be an end to it.

The ultimate jokester, Roxie stared at him across the table with a sly, scheming look in her eyes. He shook his head NO and frowned at her.

"Are you going to tell us what you've found out or leave us in suspense all night?" Elias asked, with a grumpy edge to his voice. Roxie recoiled a little and glanced at Tim. He lifted both eyebrows, waiting for her to explain.

"Army CID sent me copies of the video they found in Jones's neighborhood. They caught a silver Equinox leaving Jones's house on a doorbell camera three houses down, and it captured the license plate. The car belongs to Arlina Kincaid," Roxie's grin spread ear to ear.

"Is she Wilford's sister or wife?" Tim asked.

"Wow. It didn't take you long to make that connection," Roxie sat back in her chair and sipped her Long Island Iced Tea. "Don't know, but Rayford Kincaid, Wilford's brother, is in prison for the hit-and-run killing of Juliette Smith, a twelve-year-old girl. She was standing on the street corner, waiting to cross with the light. Rayford was drunk and high on meth. He shot her twice with a nine-millimeter semi-auto, jumped the curb with his van, mowed her down, and split the scene as fast as possible. Of course, he claimed he was innocent and wrongfully accused. But the so-called 'accident' was caught on video, muzzle flash and all, and the van belonged to him. Judge Waterford heard his case. His attorney's talked him into waiving his right to a jury trial, and Waterford came down hard on him."

"So, Roxie and I solved the case," Cleary said gleefully.

"Revenge. One of the big three for motives for murder," Roxie continued.

Elias tapped his fingers on the side of his vodka glass as if deep in thought. Tim could tell he didn't buy it. He waited for an explanation, but Elias didn't offer one. Instead, he focused on the archway from the lobby into the bar. David Berkstad stood there, scanning the tables one at a time. His face lit up as he acknowledged them and made his way in their direction. He missed the press conference, not that they needed him, Tim thought. Berkstad appeared well rested, while everyone else looked exhausted.

Roxie tapped Cleary with her elbow, and Cleary scooted her chair next to Tim. Cleary had too much to drink, he could smell the alcohol radiating from her skin, and she'd moved far too close for comfort. He slid his chair away, making room and looked at his watch for the time.

"Excuse me," he said and quickly adjusted his chair further away when Cleary set her hand on his thigh and leaned into his shoulder.

"Oh, sorry," she blushed. But not because she'd touched him but because he reacted negatively. It was time for him to get out of this situation. Thankfully, his iPhone vibrated on the tabletop. He picked it up. Dani texted him that she would land at the small airport five miles from the lodge in a few minutes.

"Well, I've got to go study the crime scene notes. I'll see you all in the morning," Tim stood and stretched.

"But I just got here, won't you stay for one drink?" Berkstad asked.

"Let the man go," Elias interrupted. "He's been up for forty-eight hours. I'm going to order dinner in my room and watch a movie. You kids have fun. But not too much fun. It's back to work in the morning."

Elias and Tim left the bar.

"Is Dani here?"

"On her way," Tim smiled. "I need to grab a car."

"Here, take mine." Cain handed Tim the keys to the SUV. "I'll see you in the morning. Seven A.M." Tim watched Elias board the elevator. He started through the lobby toward the lodge's main doors.

"McAndrews?" He turned to the sound of his name.

"Deputy Cleary, how can I help you?" He looked down into her face. She was smaller than he remembered. He kept his voice formal, kind but reserved and allowed a hesitant smile. She'd been too flirty earlier for this to be a good conversation.

"Roxie and I wondered if you'd join us for dinner." She slurred her words; she'd had too much to drink. Roxie could hold her liquor; this girl couldn't.

"Oh, I—I have some work to do. Thanks for the invitation, but I'm calling it a day. I'll see you in the morning." He didn't wait for her to acknowledge him and started to turn away.

"Want some company?" she asked, clumsily rebalancing her weight.

Tim took a deep breath and let it out. Cleary knew he was married. "No, thank you. I'm just going to review my notes." Did Roxie put her up to this? She delighted in embarrassing him. Elias made him promise not to mention Dani was flying in. It wasn't against the rules; it just might look bad—like he flaunted Dani's wealth.

"Deputy Tegner and I broke up," Cleary added, making the implications crystal but far worse.

"Sorry to hear that," Tim said, shaking his head. He knew what she wanted; he wasn't the guy for this drama.

"No one has to know."

He lifted both eyebrows and wiped his hand across his lips. "No one has to know? Shannon, I'm married."

Cleary's cheeks turned as red as her hair. She didn't answer. He got it. He wasn't dumb, even though he was tempted to play that role. "Don't get me wrong, Shannon. I'm flattered by your invitation." He struggled. He hatred encounters like this. But Cleary was emboldened by a healthy dose of liquid courage and a boost from Roxie, who loved flustering him. "My wife, Dani and I are still very much together."

"You thought—Oh—my! You thought I was—no. Oh, no, I wasn't suggesting—I thought maybe I could help with the investigation—oh I already am...I mean research," she floundered and giggled, covering her mouth with her hand.

"Okay. Good. But, no thanks. As I said, I'll see you in the morning." He knew she lied. But he wasn't going to confront her about it. If she remembered in the morning, she'd be humiliated enough. Besides, Dani was here and probably waiting. He needed to go get her.

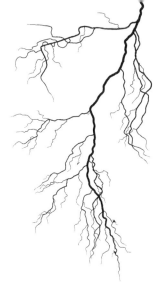

CHAPTER TWENTY-FIVE

TIM DIDN'T TOUCH Dani until they were in the elevator, alone. It had only been forty-eight hours, but it seemed like weeks. Seeing her sent him careening without brakes into a world of desire, and it amazed him. He took her in his arms, and every sense awakened when he touched the velvety softness of her lips against his. The scent of her perfume radiated in the air. He could stay lost here in this place for hours.

"Baby, I missed you so much," he whispered. She let out a small laugh.

"I missed you, too. But you love this, and you know it. Cops and robbers, the good guy wearing the badge and the white hat…." She relaxed into his embrace, and she was so comfortable there. He loved that she knew him so well.

"And riding my white horse?" He brushed her hair away from her cheek.

"My sisters say I love you because you're like James Bond."

Now, he laughed. "More like Inspector Clouseau."

"Well, Inspector, I'm glad we could meet up. I like pretending we're having a secret rendezvous," she teased him, pulling him forward and down to her lips with his tie. Her touch was so delicious, so exciting.

"We're not pretending," he chuckled. "Elias knows, but he's the only one. He thinks my team members might think he's playing favorites."

Tim admitted to himself their game was fun. It added an element of tension, an exciting, playful edge to the whole thing. They might get caught by team members, though that wouldn't be a big deal. He suspected Roxie would hook up with Berkstad tonight, and if he were lucky, Tegner would reunite with Cleary. There would be lovers everywhere and in far more clandestine and dangerous situations than he and Dani ever dreamed of being. They were the only married couple—married to each other, that is.

The elevator doors opened to his floor, and he took Dani's hand and hooked her arm through his, bringing her closer to his side. He stopped and kissed her every few steps, losing himself in pure delight. She loosened his tie and started to unbutton the collar of his shirt.

"Where's your key?" she whispered as they reached his room's door.

"My jacket pocket."

Dani leaned against the wall, tugged him to her, slipped her hand into his pocket, and retrieved the key card.

"Give me the damn thing," he wanted to get her inside the room. Teasing, she held it away from him above her head and laughed. They played like kids. Pinning her against the wall with his body, he found her lips with his and kissed her until she yielded to him. She pressed the card into his hand and wrestled his shirttails from the waistband in his slacks. She'd have him nearly undressed before he could get the door open. Tim shoved the card into the door lock slot and waited for it to turn green. He could barely think, and closed his eyes as waves of desire swamped him. The lock clicked, and he pressed the lever to open the door.

In his peripheral vision, he saw Cleary at the end of the hallway, two doors down, watching. For a moment, their eyes locked, and she chastised him with a frown.

"Crap!" he said and shoved the door open. He pulled Dani inside, leaned against the room's entryway wall, and laughed.

"Who was that?" Dani asked.

"One of the sheriff's deputies," Tim answered.

"Oops. Our secret affair isn't a secret anymore."

"No. I guess not," he chuckled.

Tim stopped cold as the door closed behind him. Something was off, and his danger alert buzzed in his ears. Dani picked up on his vibe. The mirrored closet door was open an inch or two. He remembered closing it. Dani stood on her tiptoes, trying to engage him in more kisses. He wanted that but felt a sudden chill slipping along his shoulder blades. He put an index finger to his lips and cocked his head, listening. He clutched her arms and directed her back toward the door, lifting his palm telling her to stay put. After removing his nine-millimeter from his shoulder holster, he pulled the slide, loading a hollow point round into the firing chamber. He released the safety. With a quick tug, he threw open the closet door, but only his dirty hiking clothes draped over two hangers swayed in the open space. Leading with his gun barrel, he slammed open the bathroom door, and it bounced off the rubber stop. His shaving kit yawned wide on the counter beside the sink, but he remembered zipping it shut. He yanked open the shower curtain, revealing an empty, teal-colored tub.

He caught Dani's gaze; terror had replaced their earlier fun. Once again, he touched an index finger to his lips, though he'd made enough noise to raise the dead. He crept along the wall of the short entryway and then spun into the bedroom. On the desk under the flat-screen TV, blueish light from his open laptop spilled into the room, casting eerie shadows on the wall. He'd closed it before he'd left the room. He flipped the wall switch, and the bedside table lamps flicked on. The room was empty, but the sliding glass door drapes were pushed to one side. He remembered shutting them. Cautiously, Tim crossed to the door to the covered balcony and tested it. *Unlocked.* His stomach flopped over. He hadn't left it that way. Tim didn't consider himself particularly brave, but adrenaline mixed with testosterone compelled him forward. Dani was here, and he had to protect her.

He quietly glided the slider in its track and stepped onto the deck. *No one.* But a yellow nylon climbing rope was hooked around the large wooden support beam at the far corner. He looked over the balcony's wrought iron railing. A figure eight descender belay dangled about four feet from the rope's end, reminding him of the systems used by rock climbers or SWAT team members to repel. Whoever cased his room had to exfil in a big hurry. They didn't have time to clean up or retrieve their gear.

Tim looked back inside. Dani crept forward and peeked at him from the small corridor. He cleared his weapon and went to her. He still discouraged her from speaking. Someone had likely installed listening devices and maybe cameras in his room. The thought of cameras in his room left him cold to the bone. He took hold of her hand, left the room, and led her to the sitting area in front of the fireplace by the elevators.

She was frightened, and she should be. He sat, holding her against his chest until her breathing settled into a calmer rhythm.

He stood, took out his iPhone, and called Elias.

"Someone has been in my room," Tim said after Elias answered.

"I'll be right there." They disengaged.

Tim returned to Dani and sat beside her, reassuring her she was safe. He picked up the house phone from the nearest end table.

"Desk? [...] This is Tim McAndrews, room 314. My wife has joined me and isn't happy with the room. Do you have another? King-sized bed with a sitting area? [...] Great. We'll be down in a minute." He hung up and tipped her chin so she had to look at him and hugged her. "I won't let anything happen to you. You're safe."

"I know," she whispered. But he could feel her trembling against his shoulder.

Was it Cleary? He remembered her standing in the hallway, two doors down, glaring when he and Dani entered their room. Tim held Dani's hand while waiting for Elias to arrive by elevator from his floor. No. It couldn't have been Cleary. She'd been with Roxie on the C130, returning to Charlottesville from Fort Bragg. Then they'd taken an hour and a half to drive from Charlottesville to the Lodge. That put them at the bar right when he first saw them around three-forty.

He couldn't imagine anyone involved in the Judge's murder knew about him. Even if they did, they wouldn't focus solely on him over the others on the team. He guessed he needed to make sure no one else was targeted.

Dread seeped in. Tim knew he was skirting reality. The culprit was Berkstad. Not him personally; he'd probably assigned one or two of his agents. Berkstad missed the press briefing, giving him until five o'clock to rummage through Tim's room. Berkstad wanted him to stay for another drink, buying extra time for his crew to finish planting bugs. But why? Did he suspect Tim and Miguel hacked his files? Bad news—if that was his motive, Berkstad was right.

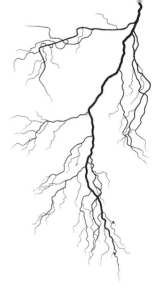

CHAPTER TWENTY-SIX

W HEN THE ELEVATOR doors opened, Roxie rushed ahead of Elias, raced to the sofa, and sat beside Dani.

"Are you all right?" she asked, genuinely concerned. She stared at Tim, her expression asking questions he had no answers for. Slipping her arm over Dani's shoulders, Roxie comforted her, practically taking over his role. Tim wasn't ready to let go, but Dani nodded it was okay.

"I'm fine. I really am. Do what you need to." She smiled at him.

Elias emerged from the elevator, followed by Berkstad, who then pulled his usual stunt of standing off by himself, observing everyone else and making judgments. He stood with his arms folded across his chest, back to the fireplace, with an infuriating smirk on his face. Tim had no doubt—Berkstad ordered the break-in. His body language screamed guilty. Tim wondered why. He wanted to confront him, bring it all out in the open. The break-in unnecessarily scared Dani.

Tim put his patience and self-control to work. His courtroom experience taught him he needed to let the facts play out. He suspected Berkstad wanted to see what was on his computer. He wanted to read his emails, snoop through his private correspondence. Did he still believe Tim would consent to be a spy? How many times would he have to say 'no?'

"Roxie, go with Mrs. McAndrews, get her keycard and settled in the new room and stay with her," Elias said; turning to Tim, he continued. "Let's go have a look at your room. I called the manager. He said they've had very few break-ins here at the lodge. I told him we'd go over the room to ensure nothing's stolen."

Tim looked at Dani. He knew she was in good hands, Roxie owed her for saving her once when trying to flee her destructive relationship. They'd become friends.

"I'll be fine. Roxie is with me." She stood and smiled, but he could tell she wasn't fine. She was scared.

He took hold of both of her hands. "I didn't mean for this to happen. I'm sorry."

"See you in a little while," she kissed his cheek, lingering there for a moment.

Now, he felt guilty for asking her to join him. She could be safe at home instead. He turned to walk with Elias. As they started down the corridor, Tim noticed Berkstad following a few steps behind.

"Do you think it was a robbery?" Elias asked.

"Maybe, but there wasn't anything to steal—dirty hiking clothes, some leftover snacks in my backpack. If they wanted that, they could have it. My rifle is in the SUV, and I have my communication gear. My laptop is still on the table. The concierge hadn't brought Dani's bags up yet."

"You interrupted them."

"Yeah. I'm sure they heard us at the door and bolted," Tim answered. "They left some climbing rope behind."

"Have any ideas—who would do this?" Elias asked.

Tim turned slightly, slowed, and studied Berkstad, lagging behind them. He ground his teeth together. Yeah, he had a pretty good idea but decided to wait before saying so. "No. No idea. I can't imagine it's anyone working the Judge's case. It isn't logical."

They arrived at the room, and Tim opened the door. He watched as Kandar Singh, his teams' electronics and IT specialist, jogged down the hall to join them. Curt Smith, one of Charlottesville's resident agents, trailed behind. After acknowledging Tim with a handshake, they entered the room. Kandar flung his backpack on the bed, grabbed a bug detector device from inside and headed first to the laptop computer on the desk.

"Why don't you get settled in your new room," Elias encouraged. "I'll call you if we find anything. Tim wanted to stay. He wanted to confirm his suspicions. "You need to take care of Dani," Elias continued.

"I'll grab my things," Tim answered, but he slow-walked his exit.

"No, leave it. I want to sweep everything," Elias said. He glared at Berkstad. "Sorry, you missed the press briefing, David. Tim was great." Elias took a position in the corner of the room, leaning against the wall, out of the way.

At first, Tim was surprised by that comment. He hadn't uttered a word at the press briefing—Elias had used him more as a prop. Then he noticed the scowl on Berkstad's face and understood completely. Elias put him in front of the TV cameras, so he'd be useless for covert and undercover work. Criminals watched television like everyone else. Tim hadn't revealed Berkstad's job offer to anyone, not even Dani. He'd never taken it seriously. But Elias seemed to know and adeptly squashed Berkstad's pirating efforts like a bug on the sidewalk. When it came to office politics, Elias was a genius. Tim admired the man more and more every day. He turned his back so that Berkstad wouldn't see his grin.

Tim's glee was cut short when Kandar found a pinhole camera attached to the bottom of the flat screen mounted on the wall. The tiny camera was disguised as the on/off indicator light at the center of the TV's bottom edge. The camera was angled to observe the laptop's keyboard, monitor keystrokes, and steal passwords. But Tim had set his computer to only open with biometric information. It unlocked when it read the print from his right index finger and recognized his face. Only a hacker as skilled as Kandar could defeat that.

"Here's another one," Kandar said. The second camera was positioned to watch the bed from the hotel clock on the left-hand side table.

Tim gasped and let out a breath. Shocked, he spun and glared at Berkstad. Did the man expect to catch him in a tryst? He sure hadn't done his research if he expected that. Tim couldn't imagine betraying Dani and his family. Suddenly, Deputy Cleary's offer to 'help' him with research in his room took on a whole new meaning. It was an old trick and usually a very successful one. *Blackmail and control.* Did Berkstad get to Cleary? Was Roxie involved?

It didn't make sense. He had no experience in counterintelligence. Why would Berkstad try to force him into a job he didn't want with a scheme like that? Tim raised an eyebrow. He knew he was missing something. Something important.

CHAPTER TWENTY-SEVEN

O N HIS ELEVATOR ride up to his floor, Tim thought about this evening's events. The candlelight dinner he'd planned was in the trash bin, and the break-in put his mood under a dark cloud of wariness and suspicion. Should he have anticipated this mess? Probably. Hacking into Berkstad's computer and phone logs was a risky move and had consequences. But in his last case, Berkstad tried to prevent his team from looking at a suspect. As it turned out, the powerful politician committed horrible crimes against children, while under Berkstad's team's surveillance. They couldn't have missed it. The FBI existed to stop crime, not turn a blind eye. Tim couldn't let it drop.

After the click of the lock when he inserted the keycard, Tim opened the new hotel room. The entry was almost identical to the one he'd just left, maybe a little bigger, but the colors were variations of the same mint green. He strolled inside.

Continuing into the room, deep in thought, he stopped short when the room opened before him. Instead of the small table by the window, a whole sitting area, sofa, love seat and one chair were arranged in front of a fireplace, adding warmth and a romantic ambiance. It almost erased his angry thoughts about Berkstad's intrusion. But they flooded back when he saw Roxie at the dining table with Dani. He wasn't being fair. It wasn't Roxie's fault her lover was a jerk.

He rubbed his left hand over his chin and jaw when he thought about what could've happened if he hadn't noticed the break-in. He shook his head.

"Evening, Ladies," he said, a fleeting smile crossing his lips. He tossed the bag of necessities he'd purchased at the men's shop on the nearest chair. Dani stood, hurried to him, and took both hands as if encouraging him into the room. At first, he resisted, but his whole attitude changed when he looked down into her eyes. She melted all his anger and distrust away. His tight muscles relaxed in a warm rush, and he embraced her. Dani was the antidote to stress. If he could bottle this feeling, he'd become a bazillionaire.

"I'm glad you asked me to come, even if things aren't perfect," Dani whispered.

"Me, too." He kissed her and lingered at her lips until she sighed. Roxie cleared her throat, reminding him she sat at the four-person dining table by the window. Begrudgingly, he stepped back.

"Are you staying for dinner, Roxie?" He lowered his eyebrows and squinted, hoping she'd read his expression and say no.

"Do you want me to?" Roxie asked.

"Isn't Berkstad waiting for you?" he countered with a question. Tim recognized his tone was accusatory. Dani looked up at him, surprised. Always gracious, Dani wouldn't want him to be rude.

"Probably," Roxie retorted. She cocked her head with a sarcastic grin. "He'll get over it."

Tim laughed. "Why do you keep him on the line if you don't like him?"

"Who said I don't like him?" She huffed out a breath.

"You like torturing him, you mean, don't you?" Tim laughed. She returned an exaggerated pout.

Suddenly, Tim felt sorry for Roxie. He remembered what it was like to be in a relationship where he wasn't fully committed. It was a halfway place, almost to love, but guilt and loneliness lingered like a hidden iceberg, ready to rip the relationship apart and sink everything that could've been good. It always ended with someone getting badly hurt. He gripped Dani tighter to his side. He never wanted to go there again.

Dani disengaged from him, but not before scowling at him. "Don't be mean," she whispered. "Stay for dinner, Roxie. We want you to," she said, biting her bottom lip, almost daring him to contradict her.

"Sure, okay," Roxie answered. She wouldn't meet Tim's glare.

Tim shrugged at Dani, turned back toward the closet in the hallway, removed his suit jacket, loosened his tie, and unbuttoned the top button of his shirt. He hung his coat in the closet, removed his shoulder holster, and suspended it over the bed's headboard. The break-in had ruined his plans anyway. Why not have Roxie stay for dinner?

He studied the bed and instantly felt tired. He hadn't slept but for an hour in the last forty-eight. Company for dinner or not, he wanted to sink into the pillows, hold Dani skin on skin and drift into the soft warmth of sleep.

Reluctantly, he sat on the edge of the bed, removed his concealed pistol and ankle holster, and set them on the table. In the background, he heard Dani and Roxie discussing items on the room service menu.

"So, do you know who broke into your room?" Roxie called out, directing her question to Tim.

"No," he stood and joined them at the table. He slid onto one of the chairs and picked up the room service menu. Looking over the top edge, he studied Roxie and reviewed the timeline in his mind. "Do you?" He dropped the menu on the table, and his jaw tightened as he focused on her body language.

"Me? How would I know?" Roxie complained, but a half-smile and her refusal to look directly into his eyes showed deception. Either she knew, or she strongly suspected someone. Someone she wasn't ready to name. He couldn't fault her for that.

"Tim!" Dani protested, set her wineglass on the table, and stared at him. "Why would you think Roxie had anything to do with that?"

He stood, strolled to the mini-bar, took out two airline-sized bottles of Jack Daniels, opened both, and dumped the contents into an ice-filled glass. He returned and sat. He asked, "Shall we order?"

"That's it? You're not going to answer my question?" Dani's mouth opened in shock. "Why would you think Roxie had anything to do with the break-in?"

"He and Miguel have this conspiracy theory about David Berkstad, that's why. If something bad happens, it's David's fault." Roxie leveled a snappish gaze in his direction. "They don't like my boyfriend. As if they have a right to decide who I date."

Tim grinned because it was somewhat true.

"We're just looking out for you," he defended.

Dani rolled her eyes. "Tim, you're not her dad! She's a grown woman."

"Brothers. Miguel and I like to think we are more like big brothers."

"That's male partners for you. Thanks, but I have a big brother," Roxie tossed her head back and laughed. She picked up her glass and drained the wine. She glanced at her watch and stood. "Is it that late? I've gotta go. I'll miss this week's episode of 'Yellowstone.'"

"No dinner, then?" Dani asked.

"Another time?" Roxie grabbed her gray jacket from the back of her chair.

"Hold on, Roxie. If someone bugged my room, they might've bugged yours, too."

Roxie guffawed. "I'm armed and dangerous. I'll be fine."

He thought it as Roxie said it, but he knew he needed to go with her.

"No. Tim will walk you to your room," Dani insisted, standing.

"Dani's right." He rose from the table, slipped into his shoulder holster, and rearmed himself. He grabbed his suit jacket off the hanger as they passed the small closet. Dani walked with him. "Don't let anyone in. Latch this door after me. I'll be back in five minutes." He kissed her cheek.

Before the door completely closed, Roxie asked, "Do you think it was David?"

"Yes." Tim shifted his shoulders to settle the holster in place. "He's checking me out. I get the camera looking for a way into my computer. What was the bedside one for?" He stared at her, perplexed.

"Don't look at me? How would I know? Maybe he's a voyeur and wanted free porn."

"Okay. That's sick," Tim laughed. "Find out for me. He's still your guy, isn't he?"

"Did he ask you to join counter intel? He's always trying to steal our profilers."

"He did."

"You aren't considering it are you?"

"No. I told him no. It's not for me," Tim answered.

"You aren't alone. He hit up Miguel before you came aboard and me before that." She hustled into the elevator, holding the door open for him. "You don't have to follow me to my room." She flashed him a grin of independence and dramatically lifted her hand so the elevator doors would close.

He quickly stepped inside. "It's only a short elevator ride. Besides, what if it wasn't David? What if it has something to do with the Judge's murder?"

"You're right," she conceded, punching him softly on his arm. He smiled.

"So, did you sic Cleary on me? She invited herself to my room."

Roxie's mouth dropped open, and her eyebrows shot up. "No, she did that one all on her own." Roxie laughed, but sobered immediately as if deep in thought. She licked her lips and pressed the elevator button for her floor. "Cleary and Tegner broke up. Maybe she thought she could make him jealous." Roxie shrugged. The elevator doors opened to a small lobby identical to the one on the floor above—rustic furniture positioned in front of a fireplace.

"Hasn't she outgrown high school by now?" He grumbled.

"You've been in law enforcement long enough to know no one ever does. Jealousy is one of the big reasons for murder," Roxie stated.

"Well, at least she didn't murder anyone." He cocked his head and scowled at her until they both laughed.

They reached Roxie's room door, and she stuck her keycard in the slot. Tim looked around. Her room was opposite and almost directly across from his old one.

"Before you go in, I want to do a sweep," Tim said. He tapped his suit coat pocket and removed the bug-finder device Kandar had given him. He showed it to her. If she was bugged, too, that would eliminate one of his *whodunit* theories.

"Go ahead," Roxie said, opening the door and genuflecting as if he were the Pope. He frowned at her.

"Tell me if anything is out of order." Tim started his search just inside.

"I threw my bag in the closet and headed to meet you guys in the bar. I really don't know what's in or out of place," Roxie's brow wrinkled with worry.

Tim scanned her bag in the closet and then the usual places, behind pictures, the television, the clock radio by the bed, headboard, chairs and table, lamps, and light fixtures. Nothing registered on the meter. He noticed her room had an adjoining door to the room next door. Berkstad's room?

"Looks like you're clear." Tim sighed. "Roxie, you can do better than Berkstad."

"Don't criticize me. I don't want to hear it."

"You're right. It's none of my business." He lifted both hands, palms up.

"You and Miguel need to stay out of mine."

He nodded in agreement and said, "Except when you need us." Smiling, he paused, reminding her of when she had asked them to help her. "I'll see you in the morning."

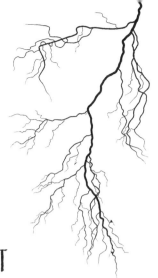

CHAPTER TWENTY-EIGHT

AFTER TIM LEFT, Roxie plopped down on the bed. She shouldn't be angry with him. In their last case, she involved Tim and Miguel in her love life when one of Berkstad's assets shot at her. If Tim hadn't insisted she wear her vest that day, she'd be dead. And speaking of not getting over high school, David had become the poster boy for jealous boyfriends. It was all well and good that he was married, but if she even glanced in another man's direction, he turned cold and would extract some sort of revenge. Usually threatening the career she'd worked so hard to obtain—so much for messing around with one of the bosses.

She remembered the night she'd met David Berkstad. She'd gone to the DC main office to help Elias profile a suspected terrorist. There were about twenty-five agents in the meeting. David stood in the back by the door, quietly observing the presentation. Tall, distinguished, with perfectly groomed silver hair, he tried to blend into the crowd, but he stood out. His eyes were an intoxicating electric blue. From a friend, she learned of his impressive reputation as a cunning and fearless agent with Counterintelligence and about his rise to Supervisory Special Agent.

She hadn't dated in three years. Though she'd denied it, especially to herself, she desperately longed for love and a family. That night, one of the senior female agents from the DC office warned her off when she noticed that she and Berkstad made flirty eye contact across the room. Roxie remembered her words. "Everyone needs love. It's part of life. But even a saltine cracker tastes like filet mignon to a starving man. Be careful, Roxie." Too bad she'd been too bullheaded to listen.

After the meeting, she joined some DC Agents she'd worked with for drinks at a local hang-out. It took about an hour for David to approach their table. The first red flag popped up when he asked if he could join them. Everyone else at the table shifted nervously and, slowly, one by one excused themselves and scampered off in every direction.

She had only an empty hotel room to rush to, and when David invited her to dinner, she willingly agreed. *Why not?* They talked for hours until the restaurant closed. Then he escorted her back to her room. She'd fallen for the dashing silver-haired spy chaser.

He'd been such a smooth and convincing liar; she didn't even do her usual homework.

Why would a fellow FBI agent lie, right? Three months later, one of her friends asked how she could, in good conscience, date a married man with three kids. At first, she didn't believe it. After doing a little research, she felt like a complete idiot. Furious, she'd tried to break it off. But not very hard. By then, she'd willingly jumped into the deep end. She loved the man—cad and liar—notwithstanding.

Then Elias hired Tim, and red flag number two waved frantically in her face. David completely lost his mind when he learned they'd worked together on the Fynn Creek Serial Killer Task Force in Seattle, Washington. Even after meeting Tim's wife, he accused Roxie of being Tim's lover.

When Tim asked about the bedside camera, she knew exactly why David had it planted there. David expected to catch her with Tim. It was projection. He accused her of *his* crime. That's why David followed her on almost every assignment these days. She'd never given him reason to distrust her. Never! She'd even agreed to this adjoining room. Anger began to do a slow burn in her belly. She had to put an end to it. Tonight.

Roxie stood, walked to the door to the adjoining room and rapped out their secret knock. David opened the door, and a big smile spread across his face.

Roxie charged him, shoving him backward with everything she could muster. "Did you do it? Did you bug Tim's room?" she screamed, barely containing her fury. She pushed him so hard that he stumbled slightly and sat heavily on the bed. He laughed at her, and that made her madder yet. "Did you do it?" she demanded.

"Why would I?" He smirked and stood, and she pummeled his chest with her fists. He grabbed her wrists, grinning at her like he enjoyed it. "He's a good guy. I like him."

"Jesus, David! Can't you stop?" Roxie knew that wasn't true. "Do you know how creepy you've let yourself become? I've told you a million times, Tim is just my work partner!"

At first, she wrestled to get free, but he pulled her close. The delicious, familiar scent of his aftershave, the warmth of his body, and the gentleness of his lips on her forehead exploded her rage into a river of tears. She sobbed as emotions mixed into a confusing cocktail. *Oh, fuck it!* She thought. Tim and Miguel were right; she deserved better. But right now, a stale saltine tasted like filet mignon, and it was better than nothing.

～

At the elevator, Tim noticed a man and a woman approaching from the left corridor. Dressed all in black, they moved like Ninjas. Both were armed—he could see the slight bulge in their jackets at the waist. He glanced down at their shoes—black leather with a waffle sole and ankle support—the very kind of shoe rock climbers and SWAT members wore. Were they the team that installed the surveillance devices in his room? Tim forced himself not to react.

He guessed they were Berkstad's agents. They both acknowledged him with a nod. He smiled but remained wary. Elias instructed the hotel desk not to give out his new room number; Tim wouldn't reveal it by letting them follow him.

When the elevator doors opened, Tim stepped inside. Acting nonchalantly, they entered. He couldn't let them get behind him and moved to the back of the elevator and studied them.

"Which floor?" the female asked, sizing him up.

"Eight," Tim immediately decided to use the trick he'd learned from Dani when she was followed by the tabloid press hounding her during her high-profile divorce from her first husband. She sent them to the wrong floor.

When the woman pressed the button to the eighth floor and no others, Tim had his answer. They shadowed him. Did they mean him harm? He didn't know. The one thing he did know—he couldn't let them get to Dani. Now, he regretted inviting her to join him.

Berkstad's buddies fidgeted, turned, and smiled nervously as the elevator ascended. The tells were obvious. Tim discreetly unbuttoned his suit coat. He rubbed his thumb back and forth along the fingers of his right hand. He would draw his pistol if needed.

"Nice evening, isn't it?" the man asked.

A new thunderstorm hit about fifteen minutes ago. "If you like rain," Tim smiled cautiously, watching their every move. The man laughed.

The elevator stopped with a small bounce. The doors rolled open.

"This is my floor. Have a good night," Tim said. They tailed him through the doors and immediately milled aimlessly in the small waiting area by this floor's fireplace.

Tim walked down the hallway to his left, and when he turned the corner, he bolted at a full run. At the end of the corridor, he hit the touch bar on the emergency exit door.

Instead of taking the stairs, he assessed the landing. When the door opened, it created a triangle barely big enough for him to hide in. If they followed, he speculated the door would shield him from view. He evaluated the handle. As he suspected, it locked automatically and, without a room keycard, wouldn't open. If nothing else, it would stall his pursuers just long enough for him to escape. He took his position.

Maybe five seconds passed, and his pursuers slammed through the door and charged down. The clatter of their steps echoed off the walls, and the smell of damp concrete and a trace of mold mixed in the air.

Once they were to the next floor's landing, Tim caught the door before it closed, rounded it, and pulled against it until he heard it latch. He'd successfully confined the hunters in the stairwell. They would need to use a keycard or rush down to the main floor and escape to the outside to get free.

Tim smiled to himself as he dashed to the elevator, pushed the button for the fifth floor and rode it down. When he reached his floor, prior to exiting, he pressed the button for the top floor of the building and stepped off. When his tail broke out of the stairwell, they'd have to wait for the elevator.

Tim hustled to the new room, hoping Dani would be ready. Softly, he knocked twice. He heard metal on metal as the bar lock released. He glanced down the hall, ensuring no one followed as Dani opened the door. He rushed through, shouldering it closed with his weight. He peered through the peephole.

"Tim? What's going on?" The blood drained from her face, and she turned pale with fear.

"It's nothing, just procedure. We're supposed to make sure we're not followed." Tim slipped his arm around her waist. "Practice makes perfect, you know." He hated lying to her but understood that Elias let him learn this lesson the hard way. There were always risks. He vowed to himself that he would never again put Dani in this kind of danger.

~

Roxie stirred when a whisper of chilled air brushed against her cheek, and the scent and patter of rain entered her dream. She felt for David, but he was no longer in bed beside her, and she sat up. A slight breeze rippled through the drapes covering most of the sliding glass door to the hotel room's deck. A sudden flash of lightning revealed a man's silhouette on the balcony.

She could hear David speaking in hushed tones but couldn't make out the words. He talked on the phone to someone. After slipping out of the covers, she donned one of the hotel's thick terrycloth robes and crept to the sliding glass doorway to listen. Her first impulse—confront him, but instead, she froze just inside while still concealed by the curtains.

"[...] I won't do it. He's not hurting our mission, and he's a good profiler. If he stays on the domestic crime side, we won't have any problems with him."

Roxie bit back a gasp. A sinking feeling crushed down on her like a lead weight. Who was on the other end of this call? She strained to hear more.

"[...] There's no proof he had anything to do with my hacked files. It could be the Chinese. [...] We couldn't get in. He's locked his computer with biometrics. [...] Sir, Cain has put him in front of Television News Cameras three times now. He could never go undercover. [...] We'll need to find someone else."

David strolled to the south edge of the deck, and Roxie stepped deeper inside the darkened corner at the opposite edge of the window. He turned, paced along the railing, and moved out of her view. She couldn't hear any more of the conversation and didn't dare stay any longer. On tiptoe, she made her way to the bathroom. If David noticed her out of bed, she could use it as an excuse. She closed and locked the door, flipped on the light, and stood in front of the mirror.

The phone call concerned Tim; she easily made that leap in logic. David had tried to recruit him. Her stomach lurched. David put her in a desperate position. She would have to choose between her partner and her lover and between her lover and her career. She hated being here.

~

Completely relaxed and comfortable, savoring the moment between lovemaking and sleep, Tim reached for Dani, encouraging her to nestle up against his side. If he were a cat, he'd be purring. He could finally get a good night's sleep—if nothing else happened. He glanced at the bedside table, ensuring he could reach his Glock.

"The girls called and said they saw you on TV," Dani said. "They're so proud of their dad for saving the little boy. So am I."

"I'm glad we found him. It doesn't always turn out that way," Tim reminded her. "I wish I hadn't missed the call."

"You can make up for it when you get home," she studied him, and he tried to deflect his worry by changing the subject.

"What are you doing tomorrow?" he asked, smoothing his hand over her hair.

"I'm going to Napa first, then Walla Walla to check on the wineries," she answered. "I need to ask you something." She hesitated as if he wouldn't like or want to hear what she had to say.

"I'm listening," Tim said, closing his eyes.

"Ummm." He felt her chest heave with a big sigh.

He chuckled. "Dani, don't worry whether or not I'll like it. Just tell me." He stroked the silky skin on her back.

"Rachel needs to come and stay with us for a while. She'll be bringing her son."

"That's it? Of course, Baby. Family is always welcome."

"I thought they could stay in the pool house. It has two bedrooms and a full kitchen so that they can have some privacy."

Tim answered with a nod. "Sure."

"They may be with us for some time…she's getting divorced."

A confusing hesitancy tinged her words. He didn't understand something he should have about this request. He tried to make his mind work, but he couldn't. It would come to him later when he was rested and had the time to think. "You don't have to ask my permission, Baby," he whispered.

"Her son is fifteen."

Tim kissed the top of her head. "Okay. Did you think I'd say she can come but her children can't? Am I that grumpy and mean?"

"You were kind of grumpy and mean to Roxie."

"That's different. She deserves it." Laughing, he adjusted the blankets around her shoulders.

"Why?"

"She's always playing tricks on us. It's part of the teams' ritual. She knows I'm joking around. Besides, I wanted to be alone with you, and she knew it. She's right about one thing. I don't like her boyfriend. Let's just say he's a bungler, causes problems, and leave it there." Tim closed his eyes and thought about the man Berkstad shot at the forest service cabin. They couldn't get any information from a dead guy. His poor decision put the investigation of Judge Waterford's murder back to square one. And those stupid shoes—great for city wear, but not for hiking in the mountains. Finally, his inept agents and their slipshod break-in and botched attempt to follow him failed miserably. What kind of spy could David possibly be?

"So, back to Rachel's son, is he in some kind of trouble I should know about?" he asked softly.

"No. No. He's a good kid, but...." she wriggled closer and kissed his shoulder.

"But...what...?" Tim asked but felt he was fading and fast.

"Never mind. I'll tell you later when you're not so tired."

That solution worked for him. Tim tried to nod, but exhaustion won. His body seemed unwilling to move. He could hear the subtle change in the rhythm of his breathing and the utter surrender of his muscles to complete relaxation. He was dropping off to sleep and didn't have the energy to fight it.

"Good night, Baby," he heard Dani whisper.

I love you formed on his lips, but he didn't know if he said it out loud.

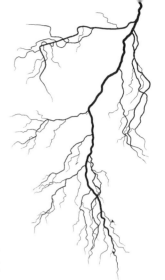

CHAPTER TWENTY-NINE

T
IM RETURNED TO the lodge after driving Dani and her pilot Mitch back to the small airport five miles away. He pocketed the keys as he walked to the entryway. He already missed her and rubbed his hand over his eyes. All night he'd been on edge and awoke to every creak and groan in his room. His distrust of Berkstad was rapidly reaching a boil-over point. To do his job, he needed a clear, refreshed mind, not one lost in the mist of insufficient sleep.

He turned and walked toward the lobby. When the doors automatically opened, it startled him. He really was in a fog. Tim shook it off and started for the conference room Elias had rented for the morning briefing.

"So, McAndrews, you have an interesting way of reviewing crime scene notes." Deputy Cleary joined him, keeping pace. She glared at him, raising only one of her eyebrows and tipping her chin up defiantly. He knew exactly what she meant.

"My favorite way," he answered, undaunted. Tim smiled at her and shrugged. She didn't reply—just seethed. After seeing Dani and him in the hallway last night, he expected curiosity would drive her to question him. He owed her no explanation. He didn't remember seeing her after discovering his room had been broken into and wondered if she knew.

He scanned the foyer for last night's Ninjas but only noticed Berkstad by the elevator in his usual stance—studying everyone as if planning to pass out grades on their behavior.

"So, who was she?" Cleary asked, bringing his attention back to her.

"My wife, Dani. I'm sorry you didn't get to meet her," Tim answered. He noticed color racing into Cleary's cheeks and let a small smile turn the corners of his mouth. He strolled toward the conference room.

"Is it okay—I mean FBI procedure for your wife to join you on investigations?"

Tim furrowed his brow. "Why wouldn't it be? I was off duty and it's my private time." He lowered his chin and stared.

"You didn't discuss the case with her, did you?"

"No. I didn't exactly invite Dani here to discuss work." He wiped his hand over his mouth to cover his grin.

"Oh?" She paused. "Oh. You're laughing at me." Another blush raced into her cheeks.

"I'm not laughing at you. I'm just perplexed. Everyone's messing around with their work partners, but apparently, it's bad for me to mess around with my wife. It just seems odd."

"Don't judge me. You don't understand...." Cleary's eyes flashed with a hint of anger.

"I'll stop if you do." He gifted her with a big smile. "Deal?"

"You're teasing me." Her face brightened.

"Yeah," Tim answered, still smiling. "Sometimes our work is a heavy lift. Teasing each other lightens it up, don't you think?"

"You're funny. At first, I thought you were too—by the book. Kind of a stick in the mud."

"Ouch." He chuckled. "I take missing kids seriously. If we don't find them quickly, they're usually dead when we do. You don't see as much of it as we do." He realized he had sucked all the fun out of their conversation.

"Well, thank goodness you found the Randall boy." Her whole face seemed to reflect a newfound respect. He hoped for that and nothing more.

"Now, let's go find out who killed Judge Waterford and why," he said, opening the small ballroom door for her. She nodded.

Elias had set up a conference table in front of a projector screen. Tim quickly realized this had turned into a task force. Elias had mentioned that the President wanted answers.

The lodge had provided coffee, juice, and breakfast pastries, and they were set out on a buffet table along the left wall. Tim chose a chair, and set up his laptop. He grabbed a mug of coffee, doctored it with cream, and returned to his seat near the far right side of the table, nearest the door. He wanted to escape quickly after the meeting.

Choosing to add some thoughts to his notes on his computer, he began to type. He realized there might be three crime scenes: the restaurant parking lot, where Judge Waterford was abducted; the unknown location of her murder; and the body dump site, now submerged under the Tenville River's flood waters.

He decided to organize his activities for the day. The autopsy was scheduled for later this morning. He wanted to meet with Miguel and attend it. Elias had ordered a helicopter to get them to Quantico on time. Though it was one of his least favorite things to do, the manner of death would support or dead-end his kidnapping-for-ransom theory.

The next stop would be the garage where they'd towed the stolen Jeep. There must be crucial evidence inside—blood, hair, fiber, fingerprints, and DNA. The man Berkstad killed at the cabin had no time to destroy everything by cleaning up. If there were other players, traces of their identities might still be found.

He was anxious to meet with Miguel and see if the DC police had interviewed the husband, again. He wanted to view that tape and harvest any leads he could.

They needed to find little Miss Arlina and her connection to all this. Deep in thought, he tapped his fingers on the table.

Roxie interrupted him. She slipped her arm over his shoulder and sat in the chair to his left.

"I've been trying to get your attention for ten minutes," she laughed.

"I'm working," Tim grumbled. Roxie scooted her chair closer and studied his computer's screen. She turned it, bunching up the white tablecloth as she did. Tim snatched it back, closed it and slipped it into its carrying case.

"How's Dani this morning?"

"Good. On her way to Napa by now."

"David says he didn't bug your room." She glanced around, studying the law enforcement personnel one by one as they started to take their seats. He followed her gaze until she stole Tim's coffee mug and sipped.

He lifted both hands. "Roxie?!"

"You weren't drinking it. It was getting ice cold." She grinned, and he shook his head, dismayed. "I don't believe him," she whispered and took another drink, looking over the rim at him.

Tim stared at her face, sat back in his chair, interlocking his fingers in front of him and rolling the thumbs one over the other.

"I think I saw his team last night. They followed me after I left your room," Tim said quietly.

She tipped her head and pursed her lips. "Soooo?"

He smiled, "I trapped them in the emergency stairwell."

"Ha! That's rich! I love it." She tossed her head back and snickered. "It looks like Elias is going to start the meeting." Roxie raked her hand through her dark brown hair and slipped out of her chair. Tim watched as she refilled his mug and a second one. She added cream and returned.

"See. I'm not as awful as you thought."

She placed the fresh coffee in front of him, turning the mug so that if he took a sip, her red lipstick mark would kiss his lips. He laughed to himself, cleared his throat, frowned at her, and conspicuously traded mugs. Berkstad should be recruiting Roxie; she was one put-together woman and a perfect Mata Hari. She had seductive moves that other women hadn't even thought of yet. Maybe she and Berkstad were the perfect couple.

When he started to say, 'thank you,' she hushed him by lifting a perfectly manicured, red-tipped finger to her lips.

As Elias finished his presentation, the conference room's overhead lights brightened and announced the end of the meeting. Elias didn't take any questions. Tim followed suit and searched for his team as the participants gathered in small groups to formulate plans. They had consented to compile the information they collected and submit it to a shared website once daily until Judge Waterford's murderers were arrested. They had all agreed that the FBI and Elias's team would lead the investigation.

It had been four days since the Judge's husband reported her missing. They stumbled on her body Saturday, and the evidence at the dump site was collected and sent to the FBI Forensic Lab before the flood waters roared down the river canyon. Tim hoped CSI hadn't missed anything important and couldn't wait to get to work.

Tim stuffed his phone with notes into his pocket and joined his group in the back of the conference room by the exit.

"Jim Quincy, the US Attorney for DC, wants to close the investigation and try Kincaid in absentia. He knows he didn't work alone but doesn't care," Roxie complained, keeping her voice low. "Quincy wants to wash his hands of the whole thing and take the easy road. Appease the President at any cost. He said the case was solved when Berkstad shot and killed the perp at the cabin. So why stir up more trouble?"

"We're not done. Others are involved," Tim replied. "Kincaid dumped the body. We don't have enough to prove he killed the Judge—yet. We need to match ballistics to his nine-millimeter, see if his DNA is anywhere on the Judge's body."

"I think a tough-on-crime show trial is a mistake and a waste of taxpayer money," Kandar spoke up. Tim's teammate surprised him with his sudden boldness. Kandar looked around the circle of team members, then stepped back, and shyness returned. Kandar scuffed the toe of his shoe along the floor, linked his fingers behind his back, and fidgeted. Each time they locked in a quick stare, Tim sensed he wanted to say something more.

"It would resurrect the President's ratings from free fall. If the President's PR team wants it, they'll get a show trial," Roxie countered.

"The Judge was murdered and thrown away like trash. She was a friend and a great legal mind. I want these guys. I want justice for the family," Elias said as he joined the group. "We are going to follow the evidence where ever it leads. No shortcuts. I don't care what Quincy wants."

Elias glared at each team member one by one for a second ensuring everyone was on board. Tim couldn't help but smile.

"All right. Tim, you're with me on the helicopter. When we get to Quantico, you'll join Miguel for the autopsies. DC detectives are interviewing Mr. Waterford at two. I want you and Miguel there to listen in.

"Kandar and Melissa, you take my SUV back down the mountain. It's loaded with everyone's luggage.

"The stolen Jeep is in the CSI garage. You see what evidence they have recovered." He reached into his pocket and tossed Melissa the keys. "Roxie, Berkstad goes with you. Drop him at headquarters in DC. Then, I want you to arrange another interview with Jones. And see if Army CID has found that Arlina woman." He paused as if waiting for complaints, but his expression was clear—he didn't want to hear any. "Let's go. We meet up at the end of the day at Quantico."

Tim walked briskly, keeping up with Elias.

"Sheriff Montgomery is pulling his deputies back. He doesn't have enough staffing as it is to handle flood rescues. When the Tenville Dam broke, we lost any evidence at that scene. He was delighted to turn the investigation over to us."

"Unless the Judge was shot in the Jeep, there's another crime scene in DC," Tim mused. Elias agreed with a nod.

The weather guy, Walt Harper, approached before they could reach the lobby doors.

"Special Agent Cain?" he asked in a hesitant voice.

"Dr. Harper...have you met SA Tim McAndrews?" Elias asked, making introductions.

"I believe I met him briefly at Little Crooked Creek," he answered.

"What can I do for you?" Elias asked. Harper furrowed his eyebrows, and his mouth turned down grimly—*bad news.* Tim thought.

"National Weather Service is reporting this area is ripe for Pulse Thunderstorms today. Localized updrafts will be strong, and wind shear very low, causing violent downbursts of hail and heavy rain. The storms could appear quickly." Harper paused to take a breath and glanced out to the waiting helicopter.

In his mind, Tim visualized the storms with dark gray rain falling in sheets to the ground. He'd seen the phenomena in pictures.

"We're heading east. Do you think we can beat the storms?" Elias asked. What would ordinarily take an hour and a half by air would take three on the ground and maybe longer if they needed to skirt flood water, Tim thought.

The way Harper eyed the chopper, Tim wondered if he wanted something more than to warn them about the weather.

"The storms will form quickly but behind you, if you're heading east, but you'd better hurry," Harper said.

"Are you looking for a ride?" Elias asked. "We can take you as far as Quantico."

"No." Harper stalled as if contemplating an exit, but said, "I'll hang out here for a few days. I want to watch the weather."

"Thank you for the heads-up. We appreciate it," Tim said. He looked at Elias and noticed his jaw muscles twitch with annoyance.

As they walked through the lobby doors, Elias mumbled, "I didn't ask for a weather report, did you?"

"No, but now we know. Thunderstorms in the afternoon." Tim snickered. They boarded the helicopter waiting on the pad near the entrance to the lodge. Tim set his computer beside him, took the headphones from the seat pocket in front of him, put them on and adjusted the sound.

As the pilot started the rotors, Tim relaxed and attached the seatbelt harness. Over the microphone, he heard Elias instruct the pilot to follow the SUVs for a minute or two before they made a beeline for headquarters at Quantico.

As they ascended and crested over Tenville Ridge, Tim could see the ravaged landscape where the flood had clawed trees, dirt, and rocks from the canyon walls. The river was still over its banks and thick with swirling mud. Behind him, new clouds billowed high into the atmosphere, promising more punishing rain. He quickly took out his phone and looked at the NOAA weather app's radar. Most precipitation would be pushed along by the jet stream south of Quantico and the farm. Dani would be safe—the skies were clear in the west. He'd be home with the kids this evening if the storms came. He hoped the King of Thunder wouldn't be pissed off again tonight.

Elias startled him by dropping two bags marked as EVIDENCE in bold red letters into his lap. He whipped his gaze to Elias.

"The bugs are FBI issue. Ours," he said with a big grin. "You're on Berkstad's shit list."

Tim lifted the bags to study the contents, stared at Elias, and raked his teeth over his bottom lip. "Yeah? Even after I saved his left shoe?" he grinned. "So, how do I get off?"

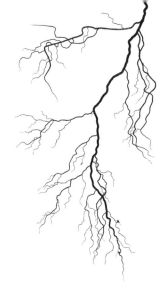

CHAPTER THIRTY

T HE STRONG SCENT of medical-grade alcohol hit Tim's nostrils, and he flinched back. Attending an autopsy was one of his least favorite things to do in life. He thought he'd be used to it by now, but he wasn't. Miguel opened the door, and an assistant medical examiner met them and passed out gowns and gloves. Tim realized they were to protect their suits, not to protect the dead.

"Dr. Samson is ready for you," the girl said. She was young and probably an intern at the University studying pathology. She helped them into the protective gowns by tying their backs and led them through the double doors to the autopsy theater.

"We just need to hear about the Judge," Miguel said. "The other guy—we know how he died." Miguel glanced at Tim and rolled his eyes.

Samson reported his findings. "Judge Waterford was shot once, in the chest. That was the cause of death. The bullet entered the body at a forty-five-degree downward angle, bisected the ascending aorta, traveled through the left lung, and lodged in the spine. She bled out quickly. If she had survived, she would've been paralyzed—probably from the waist down. There was no evidence of sexual assault." He handed Tim a deformed projectile in a small, clear plastic screw-top jar.

Tim studied it and handed it to Miguel. "Nine-millimeter," Tim said.

"Kincaid's gun was a nine," Miguel answered.

Dr. Samson lifted the woman's left hand. "As you can see, two of her fingernails are broken down to the quick, and we recovered debris under the others consistent with skin cells. I'll know for sure when I look at samples under the microscope. I think she fought like hell for her life and was shot in the struggle," Samson said. "I found deep scratch marks on one side of the dead man's neck. A DNA test will confirm if it's a match."

Sadness seemed to settle over Tim. Life was precious to him. In his imagination, he could see her wrestle for the gun with her attacker, clawing at his face and neck. Momentarily, he closed his eyes, trying to control his emotions. He needed to get justice for her and her family.

Damn! If Berkstad hadn't killed Kincaid lying on the autopsy table next to Judge Waterford, they might have had answers.

Samson went to the Formica counter along the left wall. He retrieved a plastic bag. Lifting it, he said, "We found this paper in Kincaid's jacket pocket. It's wet and in shreds, but your document department may be able to dry it and put it back together. It's typed, and the ink hasn't smeared. I don't know if it means anything." He shrugged his shoulders.

"Great. Thanks," Tim said. "I guess we'll see." He held the bag gingerly by the very top, ensuring he didn't cause any pieces to bond.

"When will you be able to send over the reports?" Miguel asked.

"By Wednesday. I've rushed the DNA samples and will try to get the reports delivered together. I received a personal call from the President."

Tim held Miguel's gaze.

"Thanks," Tim said, placing his card on the counter as they left the room.

They removed the paper gowns and deposited them in a trash bin.

"Let's get this stuff to ballistics and the document lab before we hit Mr. Waterford's interview," Miguel said. "If the President is putting pressure on the Medical Examiner, he's doing it to Elias, too."

The noontime traffic in DC was formidable. Miguel was far more familiar with the fastest traffic routes, so Tim let him drive.

At the FBI Forensic Lab, Miguel pulled into a parking place, turned off the engine, and rested both hands on the steering wheel. A frown turned down the corners of his mouth. "What's your theory on Judge Waterford?" He asked.

"When Dr. Samson said her death resulted from a struggle, I thought maybe a kidnapping for ransom went horribly wrong. Whoever did this knew how much the President wanted Judge Waterford on the appellate court. Maybe they thought he would pay money to get her back alive," Tim said.

"But when she was killed, they had a body, no chance of getting any money, and had to get rid of her," Miguel added.

"No one at the Restaurant heard a gunshot," Tim said.

"Maybe Kincaid used a suppressor. They could've still said she was alive. Either they panicked, or it was never for ransom. They drove to a remote mountain back road, thinking no one would find the body for days, if ever. They took Lightning Ridge Road and drove past the Forest Service Cabin but went too far. They didn't realize how close they were to the campground and the river." Tim rubbed his hand along his jaw.

"Do you think she was shot in the jeep?" Miguel asked, pulling the keys from the ignition.

"Could be, but the tarp…makes me think she was shot at another location we don't know about, but need to find."

"Unless the plan all along was murder," Miguel said.

"What if Kincaid wrestled her into the jeep's back seat, and it was covered with a tarp?" Tim groaned. "She'd realize he planned to kill her and would fight like hell," Tim paused, imagining the scene. Judge Waterford was a small woman, and Kincaid could've easily overpowered her.

The thought of any woman having to fight off an attacker always made emotion rise to the surface. What if's darted through his mind. At least Dani's pilot, Mitch, was always armed. Still, he'd insist Dani obtain her concealed carry permit once she got home from her trip. They'd put it off for long enough.

"Let's get this stuff to the ballistics and document labs," Miguel said as he opened his door. "I want time to read the police report and DC detective's notes before we join in the husband's interview."

"I'll drop off the document. You take the bullet to ballistics. Meet back here. Do you think it was the husband?" Tim asked as they walked to the elevator.

Miguel gave Tim a sideways glance and chuckled. "Happens all the time."

~

The 600,000-square-foot Henry J. Daly Building housed the Metropolitan District of Columbia Police Department. Sculptured reliefs were embedded in the walls, reminiscent of the Greek or Roman era, but the building was definitely "New Deal" classical modern. Tim and Miguel walked up to the main entry. On either side of the stairway, concrete columns with an embedded light fixture topped with a stylized eagle guided their way.

Inside, a beautiful multicolored tile mosaic depicting a map of the capital greeted them. They stood in a line to gain entry. Miguel elbowed Tim, prompting him to take out his leather case with his FBI identification.

They showed their IDs to the entry guard, and he waived them through the metal detector to the reception area. They approached the desk. A door at the far end was the access point to the department's busy inner workings.

"Detective Deke Cameron," Miguel announced to the young police officer managing the counter. "Tell him SA Miguel Gonzales and SA Tim McAndrews are here to see him. He's expecting us."

She pressed a button, and the door on the right side of the polished wood counter buzzed open.

Lieutenant Deke Cameron greeted them in rolled-up shirtsleeves and a loosened tie. "Good morning. Glad you fellas could come. We can use all the help we can get."

"Happy to help," Tim answered and shook hands. It was clear Cameron had been working for hours. Tim was reminded there were always more crimes than officers to solve them.

"What have we got?" Miguel asked. The lieutenant motioned for them to follow him, and they wove their way through a large open area filled with desks and busy detectives typical of a big city police department. He ushered them into his small office.

"Have a seat," Cameron said, making his way around his desk, cluttered with case files. He slid a file over to them from the top of a stack on the right side of his desk, and Tim grabbed it before it fell off the edge. Cameron lifted a thumb drive from inside the center desk drawer and inserted it into a USB port on the computer.

"This is the original 9-1-1 call. The report from the first uniformed officer at the parking lot scene is in the file. I recorded the husband's initial interview and that of a few witnesses at the restaurant." Cameron rubbed his right hand over his short-cropped brown hair. His dark eyes looked weary, and Tim wondered if he'd been up all night. "I meant to join you at the autopsy, but we had another call. I could use some coffee—you fellas want some?"

Tim nodded and opened the file he'd rescued from the edge of the desk. "Cream for me."

"Black," Miguel said as he collected one of the crime scene photos from the file.

Cameron picked up the phone and said, "Raylene, bring in three coffees. One black, two with cream. Thanks."

Tim started through the police report and looked up as the lieutenant straightened items on his desk and began to tap his fingers on the wood's edge. Cameron was bored and impatient to get on with his other cases. Tim knew the feeling. "We can go into another room. We don't need to interrupt your work," Tim said, lifting both eyebrows.

"Sorry. I didn't get much rest last night. You know how that goes. Just nod off and the phone rings." Cameron smiled. "The Cap is puttin' a lot of pressure on us. He wants this solved."

Miguel chuckled, "Our boss is getting pressure, too. President Tomlinson wants to know who killed his favorite nominee and why."

"President Tomlinson? And I thought I was getting pressure," Cameron said. "Tell you what. I'll take an empty desk out front and leave you to it. Then we'll talk." Cameron rose just as Raylene brought coffee.

The responding officer's report differed little from the information Tim had received earlier. Friday night, Judge Waterford planned to meet her husband for dinner. When she was late, he called her several times, and she didn't answer. She often worked late. Annoyed by being ignored, Mr. Waterford decided to drive to her office. But as he went to his car, he found hers—empty, the driver's side door open with the dome light on. Her keys, purse, and cell phone were still inside. He panicked, assumed she'd been abducted, and called the cops.

The crime scene photos confirmed the patrol officer's findings. Tim settled back in his chair for a second, leaned forward, stood, and signaled Cameron they were ready for him.

The detective returned to his office and took a position behind his desk. He rolled forward. "So, what do you think?"

"In his interview, the husband claimed he didn't know anything and had no suggestions for suspects. That's reasonable. The Judge put a lot of bad guys away. Plenty of suspects would be stewing in their jail cells, planning her murder, and wanting her dead," Tim speculated. "We know Wilford Kincaid dumped the body."

"Let's look at some of the scumbags she sentenced that might be on parole and see if there is a connection to Kincaid," Miguel said.

"I expected drag marks or some evidence of a struggle in the parking lot. But she was a small woman, and Kincaid could've lifted her off the ground. There was no ransom note," Tim said, staring straight into Cameron's eyes.

"No. But that doesn't mean anything. Maybe the kidnappers planned to call with their demands later," Miguel added.

"You said, kidnappers. Why do you think there was more than one?" Cameron asked.

"Two or three," Tim said. "One to drive, one to subdue. And then there's the woman on videotape who lifted Jaydon Jones's wallet. Kincaid had Jones's wallet and ID."

Cameron rubbed his brow with the back of his hand. "Makes sense."

"Here's what I don't like. In his initial interview, Waterford refers to the Judge in the past tense. Our marriage *was* great. She *was* a hard worker. She *was* a very loving and giving woman. Everyone *liked* her. If it were me, I'd be using the present tense. She was only a missing person when you first talked to him. I think he knew or expected her to be dead," Tim sucked in a deep breath.

Cameron scooted his chair back. "Man, I didn't notice that."

Tim glanced at the time stamp on the bottom left of the computer screen. "We don't have time to go to her office before the interview, do we?"

"No," Miguel answered, quickly thumbing through the file. "Are you thinking what I'm thinking?"

"The husband sounded truly worried on the tape. I don't want to get ahead of my skis, but Lieutenant Cameron, did you order a copy of credit card, bank, and cell phone records? If we eliminate the husband, we can move on," Tim answered.

"I'll do it now," Cameron said.

Miguel grinned at him and lifted an eyebrow with intrigue. "Just for fun, we should see if there's a mistress and a big, fat insurance policy." Tim knew it was meant as a joke. Cameron's expression turned to shock.

Tim laughed but sobered. "Like you said, Miguel, it happens all the time."

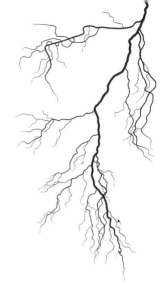

CHAPTER THIRTY-ONE

T IM HEARD HIS boss's voice outside Cameron's office and turned to see Elias with Chief Bret Reeves. They seemed to be friends.

"Good morning, Lieutenant Cameron," Elias said. "Don't get up. I'm here to talk to my agents."

Tim gave Miguel a confused but intrigued glance as he rose from his chair.

"Change of plans. Carlton Waterford has hired a lawyer, and he's postponed today's interview," Elias announced.

"He believes the husband is automatically a suspect and doesn't want to talk to us without representation," the chief added.

"The flood has held up the rest of the team. They've had to backtrack to navigate around it. Tim and Miguel, I need you to work the jeep. Get over to the garage and see what CSI recovered," Elias said. "The husband is itching to have the body cremated. I haven't released her yet, but I can't hold off forever. We've rescheduled an interview for Thursday. I'd like to have something to tell him. Maybe we can find that Arlina woman and figure out how she fits in besides snagging Jones's wallet. If there's any DNA or other trace evidence in the Jeep, we will have our reports back by then," Elias rubbed his hand over his top lip as if expecting to find the handlebar he'd recently shaved off.

"Sir, I'd like to go to Judge Waterford's chambers and look around," Tim said. What had the Judge done in the days before the murder? What did her aides and interns notice that might lead them to the others involved? Who was the last person to see her alive before her abduction?

Cameron shrugged. "Since she was abducted from the parking lot, I didn't see the need to go there."

Tim let a small smile no longer than a second cross his lips. He understood. A strained and understaffed police department overwhelmed by crime and protests took shortcuts. But he remembered the old adage—*the devil is in the details.* From his prosecutor days, he loved presenting those seemingly insignificant elements to a jury. It often took an iffy case to beyond a reasonable doubt.

"Right after you finish with the car, head over. We'll ask the court custodian to let us in. Meet us around three. To ensure there will be no problems, I'll get a warrant," the chief volunteered, glaring at Cameron as if exasperated.

"Let's get to it," Tim said to Miguel. Cameron grabbed his suit coat from the chair behind his desk and trailed behind them.

~

The FBI's forensic garage smelled like a machine shop drenched in engine oil. The five concrete bays each contained a vehicle suspected to be part of a major crime. The high-pitched whine of pneumatic wrenches and clanging tools meant the agents there were hard at work. They found the Jeep in bay number three.

"Hey, Tim, Miguel," Win Winslow, the leader of an FBI's forensic team, greeted them. He studied Cameron skeptically, then walked to the counter on the front wall of the bay. "We found three separate brands of cigarette filters in the front ashtray." He handed Tim three plastic baggies marked as evidence. In one bag, two dappled tan filters were ringed with the same shade of red lipstick prints. He passed them to Miguel and Cameron for a look.

"Well, I'll be damned. There were three perps, just like you said there'd be," Cameron commented and handed them back to Win.

"At least three," Tim replied.

"We found these," Winslow held up another evidence bag. Inside were two red acrylic fingernail fragments. A mixture of sadness and anger flashed over Tim as he thought of the Judge fighting for her life and losing that battle. He swallowed it down. He had to get justice for her.

Tim took out his iPhone and dialed the Medical Examiner. As it rang, he stepped away from the others and the noise. "Dr. Samson? [...] We found fingernail fragments in the Jeep. I'll be bringing them over for a match. [...] Yep. See you in an hour."

He returned to the bay.

"We swabbed the steering wheel, shifter, radio, the console and dashboard, door handles, everywhere for touch DNA," Winslow reported. "We found this," he walked over to the Jeep's passenger compartment. He pointed Tim to the back of the driver's bucket seat. A semi-circle of high-velocity blood spatter stained the fabric, but the bottom had a sharp, clean edge as if blocked. *The tarp?* Tim turned away, disgust and horror twisting his stomach into knots. But now they knew. Judge Waterford was murdered in the Jeep.

"I've sent samples to the lab," Win added, returning Tim's focus to him. "We also found a nine-millimeter shell casing on the floor. There's a discoloration—a heat mark on the back of the passenger's seat. The hot shell casing ejected to the right, bounced off the fabric, landed on the floor, and rolled under the driver's seat where I found it."

Tim could see it in his mind's eye. The kidnappers pulled up to the Judge in the restaurant parking lot and grabbed her, leaving her purse, phone, and keys in her car. He lifted her into the back seat, covered by the tarp. She realized she was going to die and fought for her life, breaking off two of the acrylic nails on her right hand. The perp shot her during the struggle. This wasn't a kidnapping for ransom. It was a hit. Was it personal or political?

~

The hospital's pathology department was in the basement, and the three men silently rode the elevator down. Tim looked at his comrade's faces, and the same unspeakable sadness he felt was written all over them.

The gray-green hallway seemed darker and longer than this morning at the autopsy. The same young med student waited for them in front of the double doors, offering gowns and gloves if they wanted them.

Tim smiled at her but didn't speak, and she seemed to understand.

"Dr. Samson," he said once through the door. He heard Miguel and Cameron mumble greetings. The team congregated around the sheet-covered body.

"Here you are." Tim handed the older man the evidence bag. Samson took it, and his eyes brightened with surprise.

"I can tell from here these are a match. Look how the nail polish extends past where the natural nail broke in the struggle." He took a pair of tweezers out of a drawer, uncovered the Judge's right hand, and placed one of the broken nails on her fingertip. Tim could see the jagged edge fit exactly like a puzzle piece.

"Georgianna, come take a picture of this," Samson called out to his assistant. The young blonde stepped between the doctor and Tim and snapped several shots.

"Georgianna, will you print out several pictures for the officers? Blow one up so they can see it in detail. And make a thumb drive," he instructed. "I'll take a scraping of the polish, and you can have your lab confirm it's the same polish as is on her other fingers."

Tim knew he had to watch but didn't want to. If he were the prosecutor, he'd be required to ask the forensic officer to describe how the lab determined the polish's exact color and chemical makeup to confirm a match. Also, he'd need to prove the chain of custody. For a moment, he wondered if he was cut out for this work. It was easier to detach when he was a prosecutor, and the evidence was neatly packaged up for him in reports and pictures. Real life was just a little too real.

Samson handed Tim a corked vial containing the polish and a manilla envelope containing a thumb drive and the computer-generated pictures to take. They left.

"Are you all right?" Cameron asked. "You're looking a little green around the gills there, fella."

Tim laughed. "I don't know why, it just got to me. I kept wondering what her life could've been. Supreme Court Justice, maybe? But instead,

I'm watching the ME scrape nail polish from a dead lady's fingers. Such a waste."

"It used to take me several days to get over stuff like this. With time, it gets easier," Miguel put a hand on Tim's shoulder in empathy. "I just lied. It never gets easier. We don't do this job because it's easy. We do it because someone must stand up for the victims. We have to get justice."

The elevator's doors opened, and they stepped on.

"What's next?" Cameron asked.

"The FBI lab and then the Judge's chambers," Tim answered. *Who wanted you dead, little lady?* Tim whispered in his thoughts. *And why?*

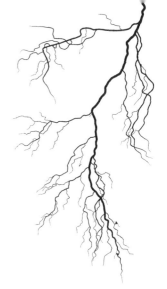

CHAPTER THIRTY-TWO

T HE JUDGE'S CHAMBERS looked like Tim expected. The walls were finished in a medium walnut, giving a sunset-like glow to the whole space. They entered an anteroom with two desks, one on each side of a closed door. Tim speculated Waterford's clerks or interns worked at these empty desks during the week. Framed pictures of families and pets were placed just behind brass name plates. He studied the pictures. Anton Williams sat at the right desk, and Tareeka Marlow was assigned to the left. Tareeka's family looked familiar—but didn't trigger a memory he could place.

He dropped a copy of the folded search warrant on Williams's desk and opened the closed door to the Judge's chambers. When he flipped the switch, the room was bathed in a soft golden light. He stood quietly and took it all in. The scent of leather mixed with freshly washed linens emanated from the back wall of bookshelves filled with bound law books. In front, the Judge's ornate cherry wood desk loomed impressively. A conference table in matching wood, surrounded by six upholstered dark brown chairs, filled the room's right corner.

Waterford had placed a tan-colored sofa beneath a signed original painting of deer emerging from a lush forest along the wall between the chamber and the anteroom. Two claw-footed credenzas occupied the left wall under a picture of Waterford with the President and several framed certificates and awards.

It was a beautiful room—tasteful, professional, and imposing. Tim speculated that if you were called to chambers during a trial, you'd know she was in charge. Her unique personality whispered from every corner.

While still at the lodge, he'd researched some of her high-profile rulings last night. She was fair, honest, and no-nonsense.

"What are you looking for?" Cameron asked, breaking Tim's concentration.

"I don't know. I guess I'll figure it out when I see it," Tim answered.

"Desk is locked. We'll need the key," Miguel said, rattling each drawer as a test.

Cameron walked over to the credenzas and tried the sliding doors on each. "These are locked, too."

Tim slowly turned in a circle taking in the ambiance. *Tell me, Evelyn. Tell me who killed you and why.* He whispered in his thoughts. *Let me get justice for you.*

His gaze settled on an ornate box on a shelf between two sections of law books. He strolled over to it and looked inside. *Too obvious.* It was just decoration and empty. He turned her swivel chair around, sat down, and rolled it next to the desk.

"If you were the Judge and needed to make sure your clerks could get into your desk, would you hide the key? Or would you give each a copy?" Tim asked out loud.

"Hide it and tell one person how to find it. That way, it has less chance of getting lost," Miguel answered, turning from reading the certificates on the wall.

After contemplating his answer, Tim remembered many times the key was taped underneath the center drawer. He bent forward and looked. Next to the rolling mechanism, he noticed a small rectangle outlined by space as if a secret compartment had been built into the bottom of the drawer. He reached under and slid his fingers over the wood. There was a difference in the texture, but no handle. He pressed upward in the center of the rectangle, and when he ceased, it clicked open. A small key fell into his palm.

"Found it," Tim said. He immediately rolled the chair back and tried it in the center drawer's keyhole. It opened. Inside, he discovered a tray. One compartment held a ring of keys, another several ballpoint pens, and a third a selection of colored paper clips. The center of the drawer contained an appointment book, yellow Post-it notes, and a blank legal pad.

"What the hell are you doing in here?" A young black man dressed in a classic navy-blue suit and tie raced into the room, holding a paper coffee cup. Tim recognized him from the photo on his desk in the anteroom. He was Anton Williams.

"Get out of here! Get out!" He screamed.

Cameron rushed him, blocking him from advancing any further.

"Who are you? I'm calling the police!" Anton fumbled with his phone.

"Hold your horses, fella. We *are* the police," Cameron said, a grin on his lips. When Williams stepped forward, Cameron slammed him against the wall, twisting his arm behind his back and spilling the coffee on the floor. "Who are you? And what are *you* doing here?"

"I work here. I'm coming back from my break," The young man defended, wrenching his neck around as if hoping the others in the room would help him.

"Enough," Tim demanded. "Let him go."

Williams turned and brushed his sleeves, straightening his clothes back into proper position. He glared first at the coffee mess, then Cameron, Miguel, and finally settled on Tim. "I'm Anton. Anton Williams. Why are you here? What are you doing?"

Tim realized the young man didn't know his boss was dead. The evacuation and subsequent flooding kept the news reporters away from the Crystal Falls Campground. Tim hadn't seen the morning news but realized Elias had squelched any reports that Judge Waterford's body had been found. Only the immediate family and the President had been informed of her death. Tim stood and walked to the doorway.

"Mr. Williams?" He waited until the confused man nodded. "Special Agent Tim McAndrews, FBI." He opened his suitcoat to show his badge and lanyard. "Have a seat." Tim directed him to the sofa.

Anton slowly sank onto the cushions, an expression of utter confusion on his face. "What's this all about? Why are you here?"

"I'm sorry to have to tell you this. Judge Waterford is dead—murdered. We found her body Saturday." There was no sense in using language to soften the blow. Williams dropped his head into his hands and sobbed.

"No, she...I just saw her Friday. She's missing, but...No. I can't...." Finally, Tim saw the change in his expression as his mind cycled through the facts. "How? Where?" He choked on the words.

"She was abducted from the parking lot of "The Lafayette" and killed Friday night or Saturday morning in a struggle with her kidnappers," Tim said. A heaviness settled on his chest. Death notifications were terrible. He usually left them to the local police, but Cameron's behavior hadn't inspired Tim's confidence. "This is a tough time to ask, but we want to catch the killers. What can you tell me about Judge Waterford?"

"She is...was beautiful," Anton started. "The most generous woman I've ever met. She's the person who helped me—gave me a chance. After my knee injury, my dream of a football career was over. I graduated from law school, but my heart wasn't in it. I sank into a state of perpetual depression. She inspired me to see my new path in law as far more valuable than I imagined." The young man looked out into the center of the room, not focusing on anything as if his memories had taken him back to a happier time.

"Do you know of anyone who would want to hurt her? Has she received any threatening phone calls or correspondence in recent weeks?" Tim asked.

"No." Williams lowered his gaze to his hands. He knew something but hesitated to tell.

"Anton, if you know something, even if it seems insignificant, tell us. It might lead us to her killers." Miguel joined them, bringing a chair from the conference table and placing it in front of him.

"It's that husband of hers!" Anton blurted out.

"Why would you say that?" Cameron asked, following Miguel by bringing another of the conference table chairs over and entering the discussion.

"She planned on divorcing him. Last Monday she met with Margaret Black, you know her, right? The famous divorce attorney. She didn't want to give up everything she'd earned to that lazy brute. He is having an affair, you know. When she found out, she was devastated. She's the one who financed his fitness business.

"He always marched in here, dressed like some big-shot gangsta, demanding money. Once, he barged in, insisting she see him in the middle of a hearing!" Anton's distaste for the Judge's husband permeated the atmosphere like a poisonous fog. It seemed a little over the top for an employee. Was there more to his relationship with the Judge than he'd told them? Tim couldn't determine that—he'd never supervised any employees.

Tim held Miguel's stare, trying to read his thoughts. Anton painted a picture of the Judge's husband that opposed the one Mr. Waterford had given in his initial interview. The happily married bromide was now in question.

"Where were *you* on Friday night?" Cameron asked, clearly skeptical.

"I was here until 5:00. I picked up my girlfriend, and we met some friends for dinner and then went dancing." He fumbled with the wallet he'd fished from his inside suitcoat pocket and produced some receipts. "Here." He handed them to Cameron. "After that, we went home and stayed there all night."

Cameron passed the receipts to Tim. The dinner one was time and date stamped. Anton paid his bill at a restaurant across town after Mr. Waterford called 9-1-1 to report his wife missing. He couldn't be in both places.

"Write down your girlfriend's and friends' addresses and phone numbers for me." Cameron offered Anton a small notepad and pen. He returned it after completing the task.

"Was Judge Waterford here when you left?" Tim asked.

"She was on the phone, at her desk. She waved goodbye and wished me a good weekend." Anton let out a low whimper. "I can't believe she's gone."

"Is Tareeka Marlow working today?" Tim asked.

"No. She only works three days a week—Wednesday through Friday."

"It would help us if you know her phone number and address. Write it down for us," Cameron said, narrowing his eyes with suspicion. Anton complied and handed the notebook back to the detective.

Tim made a mental note to call Miss Marlow and set up an interview.

"You may go. Don't leave town in case we have more questions," Cameron said.

"But..."

"It's okay. We'll make sure the office is locked when we leave," Tim said, watching for a reaction. Anton looked toward the Judge's desk and squirmed a little in his seat. Was there something in that desk he didn't want the cops to find?

"Who is going to handle her cases?" Anton asked under his breath, and it was meant to be to himself. Tim had no answer to the question. "I'm worried I don't have a job anymore," Anton's eyes sparked with panic.

"If I were you, I'd stop by the Chief Judge's Chambers. He will reassign her docket. They surely will still need you. In this business, there is always more crime than people to adjudicate it," Tim said. From his prosecutor days, he knew how the court worked.

Anton stared for a moment.

"Call me if you think of anything else." Tim pressed his card into Anton's hand. He watched him slowly turn and leave.

Tim returned to the Judge's desk and rummaged through the next drawer's contents. Stuffed behind some case files, he found a brown accordion envelope. He removed it, unwound the string from the paper buttons, and opened the lid.

Inside he found Margaret Black's business card and an asset worksheet. Anton wasn't lying about the divorce anyway. He unfolded the next document.

"I'll be damned," Tim said.

"What have you got?" Miguel strolled over to the desk.

"A two-million-dollar life insurance policy."

Cameron let out a whistle and raced to look.

Tim laughed out loud. "If Carlton Waterford killed his wife for her money, he will be pissed off when he sees this! He isn't the beneficiary," Tim said.

"Who is?" Miguel asked, reaching for the paper.

"Jaydon Lee Jones," Tim answered.

"Jones? What relationship does the policy say?" Miguel asked.

"Son," Tim answered. He continued looking through the drawer and found a file with Jaydon typed on its identifying tab. Tim took it out and opened it. Inside was Jaydon Lee Jones's birth certificate. Evelyn June Summer, only fourteen years old, was listed as the mother and Lucas Ray Johnson, sixteen, as the father. They were children themselves.

Behind the birth certificate, he located a copy of the dossier required by the adoption agency. Marcus and Elmira Jones of Fayetteville, North Carolina, adopted Jaydon through a program with the Monroe Street Southern Baptist Church. A certified copy of a new birth certificate affirmed the Joneses as the child's parents.

Digging deeper into the drawer, Tim discovered a scrapbook full of pictures of Jaydon growing up, newspaper articles of his achievements and baseball scholarship, graduation photos from high school and college, and several pictures of him in Army dress uniform. No pictures of the Judge with Jaydon existed in the book, leading Tim to believe her visits were secret. Did Jaydon or his adoptive parents even know of her presence? Was she on the outside, looking in—until she could no longer? Did she approach them and cause anger or jealousy? Did Jaydon know about the insurance policy?

The Judge gave Jaydon up for adoption, but never stopped loving him. Evelyn Waterford had no other children. Did her husband know about the love child?

Tim sat deep into the chair and rubbed his hand over his jaw. A whole new list of potential suspects and motives for murder emerged in his thoughts. He called Elias.

"It's Tim. We need a CSI team to come to the Judge's chambers and box up her paperwork, computers, and everything. This is more complicated than we thought."

"Do you have a new theory?" Elias asked. Tim could imagine his boss tipping his chin and lifting both eyebrows with curiosity.

"More than one," Tim answered.

"All right. A CSI team will be there in fifteen. I'll send Tom Redding from D.C. to oversee it. I want you and Miguel back here for our five o'clock," Elias said.

"We'll be there," Tim answered.

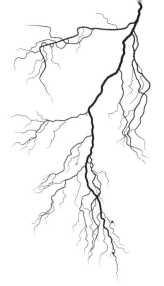

CHAPTER THIRTY-THREE

I T WAS NEARLY ten PM when Mitch turned into the driveway that wound up to the house. Dani called Winona and Mark to help her get her sister, Rachel and son, Mike, settled in the pool house. It was a nice two-bedroom, two-bath with a comfortable kitchen and a great room with a view of the pool and the pastures beyond.

They should be comfortable there for the next few months while Rachel settled her divorce. Tomorrow, they would get Mike signed up for school, buy groceries, and do anything else that might be needed.

Dani yawned. She was ready to be home. The girls would be fast asleep by this hour. Still, she planned to sneak into their rooms for a good night kiss. She warmed at the thought of Tim home—waiting for her. She imagined him in their bed, waiting for her to snuggle up to his shoulder.

The early months of Dani and Tim's marriage had been so chaotic she hadn't had time to bring him home and introduce him to her older sisters. Tim had accepted the job with the FBI and left for the twenty-two-week training while she searched for a place to live. Tim and Rachel would be meeting for the first time. Introductions could wait for tomorrow at breakfast. Dani laughed to herself. There was always some new challenge in life. How would Tim respond to her sister and son? Family was very important to him, and Dani knew he'd make an effort, but would Rachel?

She took a deep breath as dread washed over her. What about Miguel? Tim and Miguel had become close friends and work partners. Tim knew about Miguel and Rachel's long-ago love affair, but that's all he knew. Rachel's secret had become a horrible burden. When Rachel discovered she was pregnant, their father made her choose between two untenable options: an abortion or marriage to Roger Highland. Dani never understood why her father opposed Rachel marrying Miguel; he never explained it.

Dani remembered that Rachel had locked herself in her room for three days and cried until there were no more tears. She chose to marry and made Dani promise never to tell anyone about Miguel's baby. Rachel couldn't give him up. It was all she had left of her lover.

Dani wondered, should she encourage her sister to rekindle that old flame? Or leave the past in the past? She reasoned she needed to stay out of it—let things happen organically. One thing she was sure of, they would meet. Miguel often came to visit both socially and for work. She sighed. She'd think about that possibility tomorrow when her thoughts were clear, and she wasn't so tired.

With her suitcase rolling behind her, she walked up the steps to the kitchen door. Marta, her daughters' nanny, met her just inside.

"Is everyone asleep?" Dani asked, speaking quietly.

"Tim took the girls camping," Marta laughed.

"On a stormy night like this? Where?" Dani shook her head. Tim had promised a camping trip before school started in the fall. He'd made it sound like so much fun, even if it would be in the small patch of forest next to one of the horse pastures. He planned to set up tents, and ride horses to the campsite, making sure it was close to home in case the girls got scared or cold and wanted to sleep in their comfortable beds. Dani guessed he felt guilty for having to work over the weekend and let the girls talk him into some crazy adventure.

"They're *camping* in the den," Marta said.

Dani laughed. She left her suitcase, tip-toed down the stairs to the den on the lower level and opened the door. The whole milky way splashed across the ceiling and walls in magnificent color from a special projection lamp. Tim had given the girls the feeling of sleeping under the stars while safe and warm. Dani could smell the buttery scent of popcorn from the half-full bowl on the coffee table.

Tim had moved the sectional's ottomans around so the three could watch the big screen TV with their feet up. Zipped into their matching pink sleeping bags, Chloe rested her head on Tim's left shoulder and Lettie on his right. Tim was dressed in his favorite sweats and a long sleeve t-shirt, his legs partially covered by one of the throw blankets. All three were asleep.

His phone and the television remote were in his lap. His iPad rested on his chest, as if he had dropped it as he nodded off. The television played the second installment of the *Frozen* series, which the girls had watched at least a hundred times. The scene pulled at her emotions, and Dani couldn't resist taking a picture with her phone. The flash must have startled Tim awake.

"Hey, Baby. You're home," he stated the obvious but didn't move as if careful of waking his sleeping daughters.

"What are you doing down here?" Dani softly asked as she moved, sat on the ottoman, and touched his left leg.

"We're camping and watching Princess Movies. Well—the girls were watching Princess Movies. I was reading," he whispered, but Lettie stirred from his shoulder. She grinned and rubbed her eyes. He encouraged her to make room, and Dani sat beside him, hugged Lettie, and brushed a wayward curl away from the little girl's face.

Dani reached across his chest and touched Chloe's cheek. "Chloe, honey, it's time for bed." Tim sat forward, gently waking her.

"But the movie's not over, Mom," Chloe pouted.

"You were asleep. We can watch the rest in the morning," Dani answered, making sure her voice had a no-nonsense tone. She expected more protests, but the girls were ready to sleep.

After they settled the girls in their rooms, Tim and Dani made their way to their bedroom.

"Do you like Princess Movies?" Dani teased, closing the door behind her. "That's something I didn't know about you." She bit the bottom lip of her smile. Tim chuckled.

"Not necessarily. But watching with my little girls—isn't that what dads are supposed to do?" Tim grinned at her. "I don't know the rules. I've never done this before."

Dani felt a rush of love and respect flow over her. "Yes. It's what dads should do. You surprise me. I just don't expect you to be so...so...." Her voice was almost a whisper. "You take my breath away."

When she said it, Tim gazed down into her eyes like he did when he wanted to make love. She instantly became lightheaded, as if she might faint and burned for his touch. Tim's instincts were uncanny. He stepped forward and enveloped her gently in his arms, holding her against his chest. She could hear his heartbeat, and a trace of his aftershave teased the air. She'd never believed swooning to be real, just a device in a Southern romance novel, but this wasn't the first time she'd felt this way with Tim. Her skin flushed warm with desire. He tipped her chin up, and his lips barely brushed against hers, a tease that left her aching for more.

Sometimes their lovemaking was playful, full of laughter and fun. But tonight, his kisses were intense and desperate, and when he was like this, it was as if he longed to be one with her, as if connecting to another world. Dani instinctively knew he'd had a challenging day at work. She stifled herself from asking about it—he couldn't or wouldn't discuss it anyway. Instead, she offered him moments of pure pleasure and the peace that followed when they held each other. Surrendering to his touch gave them both a safe space, and she loved going there with him.

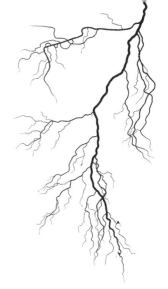

CHAPTER THIRTY-FOUR

TIM LOOKED AT the digital bedside clock. It stared glowing red numbers back at him—five thirteen AM. He could feel Dani's warmth along his back, matching the curve of his body. She'd draped her arm over his side and around his chest. He pressed it tighter to his skin with his palm, brought her hand to his lips, and kissed her fingertips.

"Do you have to get up? It's so early. It's still dark," she whispered.

"You're awake? I have some work to finish," he said, repositioning to face her. "You can go back to sleep."

Dani was disappointed; her lips curved downward into a frown. "What's on your schedule today?" she asked.

"Miguel and I are flying down to Fort Bragg to interview a person of interest."

"Will you be gone overnight?"

"I don't know. I think I should be home for dinner," Tim answered. He'd seen the skeptical look that now crossed her face before. His work often meant an overnight stay. At least he invited her whenever he could.

"I'm buying a helicopter. That way, Mitch can fly you to work, and you can sleep in with me," she stated as if it were a real solution.

"Headquarters are on a military base. They take down unknown helicopters invading their airspace. Don't waste your money," he teased but sobered quickly. "You hate this job, don't you?"

"No. I know you need to do it. I love you for it. I just want you here a little longer."

He pulled her close and gently petted her hair. He wanted to stay in this space. Dani and the girls were his escape, his fantasy world, a safe place millions of miles away from the dark side of life where men visited every sort of evil on each other. Each time he arrested a bad guy, he made his family safer, and he made the world safer. At least, that's the way he saw it.

Judge Waterford's murder intruded and swirled around in his mind, even though Dani's touch made him want to linger. He stared into her eyes, sighed, and sat up, kicking off the covers. He grabbed last night's sweats from the bedside chair and dressed.

"Go back to sleep," he leaned forward and kissed her cheek. "I'll be in my office."

~

Tim read through the crime scene notes and watched the video of Arlina stealing Jaydon Jones's wallet at least seven times, searching for any indication that Jones was more than an innocent bystander. But it wasn't there. Jones chatted and joked with his friends; unaware the woman had pinched his wallet. Yet, it was odd that he'd slipped it into the pocket of his jacket hanging over the back of his barstool. Most men kept their wallets in a pants pocket. He also didn't put his wallet in his home safe. Catching a guy in lies was as good as a confession.

Most bars and nightclubs have security cameras, and a military officer's club certainly had them. Did Jones know Arlina before this encounter, unlike the story he'd told Roxie? Had they planned this theater, hoping to throw off suspicion?

Tim decided on today's approach. He knew he had to find evidence Jones knew the Judge was his biological mother, and that she had named him the beneficiary on the insurance policy for his new theory of the crime to work. He and Miguel needed to gather as much information as possible before interviewing Jones for the second time. He'd run it by Elias and the team at this morning's briefing.

A familiar tap tap on his office door let him know Dani brought him a cup of coffee, as she often did when he worked early in the morning. He had to admit it was very welcome.

Tim shut down his computer and stood as she opened the door. He took the steaming mug from her hand, walked with her onto the small balcony out of the room's glass-paned French doors, and sat at the table. Since her sister was here, Dani had already dressed for the day, defeating his hopes that they might play in the shower. She looked beautiful in her stylish jeans and soft pink blouse.

The sun had crested the distant hilltops and chased away the morning chill. It heralded a beautiful day. Refreshed by last night's rain, the pastures were a brilliant green. With the dust washed away, the trees revealed hints of yellow amongst the darker green foliage predicting the coming autumn.

"Tough case?" she asked between sips of coffee.

"Confusing case," he answered. "Thank you for this. I needed it." He lifted the mug and then took a taste—it was perfect. Dani knew him so well, almost as if she'd studied and made notes on pleasing him. He adored her and knew he should show her that more often. He took her hand in his. They sat silently, enjoying the fresh air and stillness of the early morning before the chaos of children and work began.

Something troubled Dani. He could see a hint of worry in her eyes. Tim suspected she wanted to ask questions about the investigation. She knew he couldn't tell her anything while the case was still active. Even though he was the only person she would discuss it with, the rules were the rules. Even inadvertently, a leak that found its way to the press could contaminate a jury pool and compromise a conviction.

"I'd better get ready for work," Tim squeezed her hand and gulped down the final swig of coffee in his mug. He stood.

"Tim, remember Rachel and her son are here. I want to introduce you," she said, but she didn't meet his gaze. Whatever worried her couldn't be that important, or she'd tell him. They usually had very open communications.

"I'll be down after I shower and dress." He felt unsettled. "Is something wrong?" He asked.

She took a breath, started to speak, but paused and then instead said, "I love you."

"You don't have to be shy about that. I love you, too. And I love hearing you love me," he answered. He felt confused, but women had always mystified him a little. She smiled and pecked his cheek.

After a wake-up shower and shave, he dressed in his FBI uniform, a gray wool flannel suit, and descended the stairs to the main floor. He heard voices in the dining room and decided to put on his suit coat. Dani, his daughters, and the staff were used to seeing him in shirt sleeves and a shoulder holster, but he wasn't sure Dani's sister would approve. When meeting her for the first time, he didn't want to start off on the wrong foot.

"Tim!" Dani rushed to him and pulled him deeper into the room. "Tim, this is my sister Rachel. Rachel, my husband, Tim." Dani seemed pleased to show him off. He liked the fact that she was proud of him.

Tim smiled and shook his new sister-in-law's hand. The resemblance was immediately recognizable. Both women had the same big blue eyes, though Rachel had streaked her light brown hair with blonde, and Dani had left hers natural. They were both slender and fit, though Dani was a little taller.

"This young man is Rachel's son, Mike," Dani beamed.

The boy filling his plate at the buffet table turned, and Tim felt shocked as if struck by a lightning bolt. Automatically, his courtroom poker face fell in place like a mask. The light suddenly turned on. Now he understood why Dani had told him Rachel's history—how their father had *bought* her a husband while Miguel fought in the war and became a Navy SEAL. He hadn't really paid attention. All he'd gleaned from the stories was that Miguel and Rachel had a teenage romance. He left for the Navy, and that was that. *How did he miss this?* Dani never mentioned Rachel's pregnancy. No doubt about it, this fifteen-year-old boy was Miguel's offspring. He embodied the very image of his father. Tim studied Dani's face, then Rachel's, and their expressions said it all. *Well, hell! Miguel had no idea he was a father.*

"Nice to meet you, Mike," Tim reached over and shook his hand. The boy smiled timidly and sat down at the table. Mike gave him the once over, his gaze stopping at the badge at Tim's waist.

"Aunt Dani said you were an agent with the FBI." The boy was full of curiosity.

"Yes, I am." Tim could barely contain his dismay. If he had a son, he'd sure want to know about it. How could they keep it from Miguel, and why? From everything Dani had told him, Rachel and Miguel were desperately in love.

"That's so cool. My dad doesn't work," Mike said, rolling his eyes as if chagrined.

So, the purchased dad hadn't worked out as well as expected. Money didn't buy love—in this case, anyway. Tim mused.

"I guess some of us don't have to." Tim fumbled. He wanted to tell Mike his dad not only worked for the FBI but was a decorated SEAL. He looked over at Dani, and his jaw involuntarily twitched tight. It seemed so unfair.

Tim went to the buffet table, filled a to-go thermal mug with coffee, and screwed on the lid to tamp down his astonishment and irritation. Miguel had often expressed how much he wanted a family and how he'd be involved in his children's lives. Tim had to collect his thoughts and take time to calm his outrage. *What a fricking mess!*

He turned to Dani's guests and said, "I'm sorry to leave so soon after meeting you. I'm looking forward to getting better acquainted this evening after work." Tim glanced over at Dani and narrowed his eyes at her. "Gotta go," he said, leaving the room.

Tim could hear Dani's footsteps following him to the carport.

"Tim, wait," she called after him. "No good-bye kiss?"

When he reached the car, he turned to face her. "You could've told me. Why didn't you tell me?"

She looked at the ground and raked her shoe across the asphalt. She leveled an angry stare at him. "I did tell you. I told you my father found her a husband. I guess you're mad at me. I was twelve years old. It wasn't my fault. Stop acting like it was."

He let out a deep sigh. "No. I'm disappointed, not angry. Give me a minute to process this. I don't want to say anything I'll regret later."

""Stop being such a lawyer," she demanded. "Go ahead. Say it!"

She was spoiling for a fight, and he didn't want to give her one. It would be their first, but anger surged over him. "I didn't understand when you told me about your sister's forced marriage. You danced all around the truth but never landed on it. Why didn't you just say Rachel had Miguel's baby? Does he know? Does he even know?"

Dani slowly shook her head from side to side. He'd guessed that much. "You're the detective. I dropped so many clues, even a neophyte would've understood them," she said, glaring at him.

"Oh, boy. That was mean." He tipped his head toward her and bit back laughter. He had to admit it was a great comeback, and he deserved it. After all, he'd insinuated she was a liar. Tim groaned. "He's my partner, Dani. What am I supposed to do with this?" He took hold of her shoulders and made her face him. He tipped her chin up, so she had to look into his eyes.

"You don't have to do anything. Rachel needs to tell him, and she will—in time," Dani said, standing her ground.

Then she did the one thing he couldn't stand, could never resist. A tear sparkled down her cheek, but it was anger, not sorrow. Instantly, she wiped it away, but his heart had already melted. He pulled her close.

"Okay," he softened his voice and pressed his lips against her forehead. "But it will be on my time, not Rachel's. I'll bring Miguel home for dinner. Rachel is going to tell him tonight."

"Tim, don't. Let them work it out. Let's stay out of it." She reached up and touched his lips. "Please?"

He took her hand by the wrist and pulled it away. "Miguel still loves her, you know. He has since the day they met."

"He told you that?" Her expression was pained and sad.

"Yes," Tim answered. "Now he has to find out he's missed fifteen years of his son's life. We need to rip the band-aid off. He, at least, deserves to know about the boy."

"My father made Rachel ashamed. She didn't want anyone to know, especially Miguel. His father is still our main vintner. He'd think she was a tramp, trying to trap Miguel and hate her. She was right, you know. You already hate her."

Tim laughed and shook his head. "Oh, for heaven's sake! Both of my brothers had to get married. Why would I care? It's life. She has an excuse. Your father made her marry. We can't keep Miguel's son from him."

Dani snuggled against his chest. "Please don't be mad at me."

"Baby, I'm not mad at you. If I was—I could never be for long." He kissed her. At least that was true. "Don't you be mad at me. But I mean it. She tells him tonight, or I will."

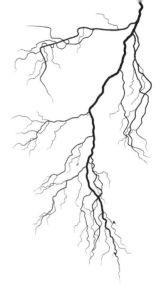

CHAPTER THIRTY-FIVE

H ALFWAY THROUGH HIS drive to Quantico, Tim argued with himself. He was sure Miguel would be devastated if he found out he had a son and hadn't been told or given a chance to be a part of his life. Tim empathized; he would be, too. Was he right or wrong to demand his sister-in-law tell Miguel the truth?

Dani had her reasons for not explaining things to him. He had to hear her out. Was it even his place to give ultimatums? Yes, the whole mess was unfair to Miguel. Yes, Rachel needed to tell the truth. Yes, it kept Mike from knowing his real father. But more than anything, Tim couldn't let Rachel's problem come between Dani and him.

He instructed his phone to call Dani and heard the ringtone through his car radio.

"Hi," her voice was timid.

"Baby, I shouldn't have talked to you the way I did this morning. I'm sorry," Tim said.

"I'm so glad you called. No. I was wrong to yell at you." He could hear relief in her voice. They were both at the same place—conceding ground to ensure their relationship wasn't damaged.

"It's Rachel's mess, but we can't leave Miguel out in the cold forever. He needs to know. Can we discuss this tonight?"

"Yes. Of course. I'll try to talk to Rachel and see what she wants to do. I promise."

"I'm at the entry gate now," he said. He couldn't let this interfere with the investigation. Life didn't let anyone have one problem at a time. It was always a dump truck full—a constant balancing act. Work couldn't interfere with family, and family couldn't burden work.

"Thank you for calling me," Dani said. "I love you, Tim. Don't forget that."

"I won't forget it. I love you, too," he said. "See you tonight."

~

After the morning briefing, Tim climbed the tail ramp into the C-130. This was his first ride in one, and he was awed. The airplane was powered by four large Rolls Royce Turboprop engines and equipped with Jet Assisted Take Off (JATO) rockets for extra power when fully loaded with cargo. It was an amazing aircraft with multiple uses, from the famous C-130 Gunships to NOAA's Hurricane Hunters. They carried troops and cargo for war, were used for fighting wildfires, and transported humanitarian aid to people in need. The sturdy airplane could land practically anywhere—including dirt and grass landing strips.

This model was originally equipped to carry sixty-four paratroopers; but now ferried military brass and, today, FBI hitchhikers back and forth from one military base to another. The forty-one-foot-long cargo compartment contained thirty-two jump seats facing inward on each side of a ten-foot-wide fuselage. That left a four-foot-wide center aisle. Tim imagined the paratroopers preparing to jump.

Inside, the metal framework reminded Tim of a whale's rib cage painted a drab gray. In between the ribs, soundproof quilting barely muffled the engine noise. There were no windows, but specially designed track lighting chased some of the darkness away. Everything was created so the interior could be reconfigured with short notice.

Tim chose one of the empty padded jump seats about midway, sat down, and buckled in. Miguel sat on the opposite side, facing him. Every time he looked at Miguel, Mike's face morphed over the top, like the images on one of the FBI's computer-generated face recognition and aging programs. Adjust the dial at the bottom of the screen, and Mike, the younger version of Miguel, appeared. Tim's Irish Catholic guilt whispered in his ear: *You're lying by omission. You're not being fair. He'll ask you when you knew and why you didn't tell him about his son.*

He felt a headache coming on and pinched the bridge of his nose. Would he be able to keep *the secret* from breaching the shore like a sneaker wave?

"You're in a mood. Want to talk about it?" Miguel asked.

That was the disadvantage of their training in micro-expressions. They couldn't hide anything from each other. Tim was in a vice. If he told Miguel, he betrayed Dani, and he betrayed Miguel by not telling him. Not really the best position to be in when he needed to rely on his partner as his lifeline.

"Dani and I had our first real fight."

"Ouch, bad?"

"Insults and all. We're good now. But fighting is exhausting," Tim said with a small smile. He let his head drop back against the seat and closed his eyes. He had to shut the compartment door on this predicament and focus on work.

The Fayetteville Police found Arlina's car and set up surveillance on an FBI request. A copy of the vehicle registration and her driver's license waited at the local police department. Tim and Miguel would confront her at her home. A search warrant for the house and car was in process and would be ready when they arrived.

"What do you think? Should we start by rounding up Arlina?" Miguel asked as a big grin spread across his face. Tim leaned forward, resting his elbows on his knees, shortening the distance between them.

"Yep. I wish the DNA reports on the cigarette butts were back from the lab. We'll take a Buccal Swab from Arlina, anyway. Then I want to interview Jones's adoptive parents," Tim said.

"Elias has initiated a subpoena for his bank, credit card, and phone records. I hope those are in my email when we arrive. If he is in financial trouble and knows about the insurance policy, he's our guy," Miguel added.

"I haven't jumped that far—yet. I watched his interview with Roxie again this morning. He doesn't seem guilty to me. But that's a feeling based on flimsy evidence. I hope Elias does the same for the Judge's husband. He referred to her in the past tense. He could be an idiot with poor grammar skills, or he knew she was dead when he talked to the DC detectives." Tim readjusted his seatbelt. "Did you catch Roxie's face when we were assigned to do the second interview of Jones? She's mad that we're bucking her analysis," Tim chuckled and leaned back in his seat.

"That's Roxie. But we have to follow the evidence, don't we?" Miguel looked down the ramp to the outdoors. "Crap. Another lucky day. Look who's joining us," Miguel grumbled. Tim whipped his head to the side, following his gaze. *Berkstad.*

"Morning," David Berkstad said, looking from Tim's face to Miguel's. "Do you mind if I join you?" He was their superior at the FBI but asked as if they had a say. Tim didn't rush to reply.

Seven officers in Army fatigues filtered in, wove their way around Berkstad and claimed seats. Once they were secure, they scrutinized the three men in suits. Tim nodded a greeting.

The ground crew signaled, and the hydraulics controlling the ramp began to whir. Slowly the daylight was shut out. Tim could hear the engines fire up one at a time.

Miguel gestured for Berkstad to sit down. He chose a seat next to Tim as a young military private passed out headphones. It surprised Tim that Berkstad would take this flight—a converted military cargo transport didn't have the luxuries and certainly not the soundproofing of commercial flights. At least Tim wouldn't have to talk to him. He put his headphones on, cutting out the noise.

When they landed at Pope Field, Lieutenant Broady from Army CID arrived to escort them to the Fayetteville Police Headquarters. CID tagged along since Jones was a DELTA and a person of interest. Broady glared at them defensively. Tim guessed Roxie had put him off with her attitude.

If he got to know her, Broady would realize she was funny, but her dark sarcasm sometimes didn't go over the way intended. He and Miguel would need to patch this up. Tim encouraged Miguel to go with the Lieutenant with a tip of his head. Miguel knew military lingo and might be able to soothe any ruffled feathers. The bad news: it left him with Berkstad for the twenty-three-minute drive to Fayetteville.

Tim climbed in the back of the second Humvee, and Berkstad joined him by sitting behind the driver's seat. They started on their journey.

Tim stared at Berkstad, grinding his top teeth along his bottom ones. He knew questioning his superior's motive was bold, maybe even reckless, but he did it anyway. "Why are you here? Thinking about changing departments?"

"Pull over, driver," Berkstad commanded. When the private complied, he said, "Wait here. We'll only be a minute."

Berkstad stepped out of the Humvee, turned to Tim, and said, "We need to talk."

Tim followed Berkstad into the woods at the edge of the road, out of the driver's earshot. Discreetly, while Berkstad's back was to him, Tim quickly slipped his phone from his pocket, pushed the RECORD button, and put it away.

A bad feeling enveloped him like toxic smoke. Tim hesitated and asked, "Have I done something wrong?"

"No," Berkstad said, looking down at his hands. "Tim, I've been offered a lot of money to influence the outcome of an investigation."

Tim scrubbed his hand through his hair. For the first time, he couldn't cover up his reaction. Tim sucked in a breath and blew it out.

"This investigation? The Judge's case?" Tim asked, searching his memory of Law School. He visualized the heading from one of his law books: **18 U.S. Code 201- Bribery of Public Officials.** "Why are you telling me?"

"Since you have a law degree, I thought I'd run it by you."

"My legal advice—don't take the money," Tim chuckled, then sobered. "The crime carries a sentence of up to fifteen years in prison or a penalty of three times the amount of the bribe or both," Tim continued. "You'll lose everything." Berkstad wouldn't be in his position without knowing this fact, even if he didn't have a law degree. Tim frowned at him.

Berkstad laughed. "I wanted your opinion on setting up a sting."

"Me? The FBI has lawyers on staff for that kind of guidance. I've been hired as a profiler and criminal investigator. My legal opinion would be worth less than zero in court," Tim explained. He rubbed his index finger over his lips and studied Berkstad. Was he supposed to be flattered?

Berkstad picked a small branch from a bush and peeled off leaves one at a time. "Let's just say someone very powerful didn't want Waterford to be seated on the court. They've offered to pay me to keep them off the suspect list. I think the person who offered me the bribe bugged your hotel room. Does that change your mind?"

"That can't be. Only you, and my team knew I was working the Waterford case two days ago," Tim said. He traced his thumb along his jaw, and studied Berkstad with suspicion.

"That's why they bugged your room. They needed to find if you were one of the agents assigned to her case."

"Did they bug your room?"

"They wouldn't dare."

"They dared to try to bribe you." Tim shrugged.

Tim didn't believe it. Berkstad's theory was implausible. Whoever offered Berkstad the bribe didn't plant cameras or listening devices in Roxie's room. Or Elias's. Would they hone in on the new kid because he lacked experience? Possibly. Maybe the briber thought a newbie wouldn't suspect someone in his own agency—he'd still be starry-eyed and naive. But, Tim knew the bugs were FBI issue. Elias had confirmed that fact.

"Do you know who it is?" Tim asked.

"No. The caller's voice was disguised. He's supposed to contact me this evening. Set up the payoff."

"Why didn't you say something earlier?"

"I was offered the money last night. I knew you were flying down here today and thought I could catch up with you." Berkstad smiled and gestured they should get going. "You'll think about it?"

For a moment, confusion ruled. Were they back to square one? Tim mentally raced through the evidence, but this wasn't the place or time. He needed quiet to connect the puzzle pieces, and Berkstad seemed to be trying to rush him and muddle his thinking with emotion.

Tim wanted to share his recording and talk to Elias before playing along. But he recalled one piece of evidence—the shredded, wet paper they'd found in Wilford Kincaid's pocket. The handwritten page was being dried and reconstructed at the forensic lab. Tim couldn't wait to see what it had to say. Would it lead to the other co-conspirators?

Tim couldn't dismiss what Berkstad told him out of hand. Theory number three just received a shot of new life. Was her murder political?

Tim smiled. "I don't know anything about setting up stings. You need to recruit someone with more experience."

"Will you think about it?" Berkstad asked.

Tim paused and then shrugged. "I'll think about it."

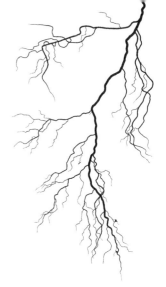

CHAPTER THIRTY-SIX

THE FAYETTEVILLE POLICE were housed in a relatively new three-story red brick building. With Berkstad trailing behind, Tim caught up with Miguel and Broady in the visitors' parking lot. Together the four men walked through the entry door.

Behind a wall of bulletproof glass, three reception officers waited for visitors to present credentials or explain what they wanted to report to the police officers and detectives working behind a painted concrete block wall.

"What happened to you guys? We've been waiting for fifteen minutes," Miguel studied Tim's face.

Berkstad shot Tim a warning glance that set him on edge.

"My fault. I forgot something in the airplane and went back for it. We started a little later," Tim said and grinned. He glanced at Miguel, hoping he recognized the lie.

Confused at first, Miguel returned his stare. "Gotcha," he said quietly to Tim, strolling past him and up to the reception desk. "Detective Johnson is expecting us. Tim McAndrews, Miguel Gonzales and David Berkstad, FBI, and Lieutenant Broady, Army CID."

The desk sergeant nodded and made a phone call. They were buzzed in, circumventing the metal detector.

Detective Hank Johnson reminded Tim of the consummate Southern gentleman. He was dressed in a color-coordinated suit and tie, and his perfectly groomed brown hair had silvered at the temples. He had kind brown eyes and a genuine smile that immediately put everyone at ease. Tim almost expected him to offer them barbecue and sweet tea. When introduced, Johnson intently listened to each name and studied each face as if committing it to memory.

"We found Miss Arlina for you," he drawled. "Her car is still in the driveway, and she only came out to water her flowers early this morning."

"Water her flowers?" That didn't sound right to Tim. He sure missed that prediction when he developed her profile. A beautiful, sexy woman could easily have a garden, but the conniving thief he saw in the Jones video—he expected her to serve drinks and lift wallets in a smokey backroom poker game instead.

"One of our patrol officers knows her. She's very active in their church."

Yeah, that wasn't in his original assessment either, Tim thought.

Johnson guided them into his office and gestured for them to sit.

"I have the driver's license picture that you requested." He handed Tim an eight-and-a-half by eleven sheet of paper with a color photo printed on it. Tim quickly gave the page over to Miguel.

"This has to be a mistake," Tim said. "This is not the "Arlina" we're looking for." He reached into his pocket, retrieved his phone, and scrolled to the video clip of their suspect stealing Jones's wallet. He passed it over the desk to Detective Johnson. "This is the "Arlina" we're looking for."

Johnson wolf-whistled. "Well, this is the driver's license photo of Arlina Hansen, who owns the silver Equinox in the camera footage your office provided us." Johnson delivered a blow-up of the SUV with a picture of the license plate as clear as if it were parked in front of them. The driver, unfortunately, was blurred.

"Does she have a daughter?" Miguel asked.

"Miss Arlina? No. Miss Arlina is a widow lady, no children," Johnson answered.

Tim ran his left hand over his jaw and pinched his bottom lip. He hid it, but his stomach felt like it flopped over. Did the Fayetteville Field

Office pull pictures of the wrong vehicle? He caught Berkstad standing in the corner of the office, his hands folded across his chest and a big smirk on his face as if Tim just earned an F on his report card.

Broady looked shell-shocked and sat silently in his chair.

Tim picked up his phone from Johnson's desk and reviewed the video footage Roxie had sent him from the officer's club parking lot. The clip showed the young "Arlina" getting into a silver SUV after kissing Jones. The bar's camera captured her license plate as she drove out of the parking lot. Tim compared the video with the print. The license plate matched.

"Should I pull my surveillance team?" Johnson asked.

"No." Tim shook his head. "Let's go interview Arlina. Is our search warrant ready?"

Johnson's mouth dropped open, and he rolled his chair back slightly. Tim wondered if the detective thought this a bad idea.

"Humor me," Tim said with a smile.

"Yessiree," Johnson reported. "I'll go get it."

~

Tim wanted to pass Berkstad off on Broady and Johnson so he could talk to Miguel privately, but Berkstad stuck to him like a shadow. Tim's intuition warning bells went off like a smoke detector in a house fire. Was his suspicion reasonable? Trusting Berkstad became harder to do. Berkstad had asked him not to tell anyone about the bribe offer. Tim couldn't honor that request. He understood Berkstad assumed he would, but as soon as he found time, he would forward the voice recording and details in an email to Elias.

They loaded into police cruisers, and after a short drive, pulled up stealthily behind the surveillance team down the street from Arlina Hansen's house. It was a small house on a quiet street lined with mature maple trees. The house reminded Tim of a cottage painted in watercolor, like the ones he'd find in one of his daughters' fairy tale books. A peaked roof covered a neat white house accented by dark green trim. Lovely, well-kept, and sufficiently watered flower beds lined each side of a stone pathway to a covered porch. Pots of pink and purple petunias hung from hooks along the porch railings. Wind chimes tinkled a soft melody in the warm, flower-fragrant morning breeze.

"We can't all go to the front door," Miguel said. "McAndrews and Johnson, come with me. Broady and Berkstad can head to the back with your uniformed officers in case our suspect squirts out."

Johnson nodded and reached for his pistol.

"Put that away. We won't need it to serve this warrant," Tim said. He couldn't imagine the mid-sixties church-going gardener pulling a gun on them, and he opened the gate to the white picket fence and walked through.

Johnson opened the screen door and rapped on the wooden one. Nothing like *the police knock* to get any occupants' attention. Tim rolled his eyes at the detective.

The door opened. In front of the men appeared a delicate woman in her mid-sixties. She was impeccably dressed and scooped her graying hair into a neat French Twist. Though lined with age, her face showed the grace of a contented life. She hadn't expected company and was slightly puzzled but smiled all the same. Tim stepped forward.

"Arlina Hansen?" He waited for her to nod. "Miss Hansen, I'm Tim McAndrews from the FBI. This is my partner, Miguel Gonzales, and Detective Johnson from the Fayetteville Police Department. We are here investigating a homicide. Do you mind if we ask you some questions?"

"Me? My goodness. Here in this neighborhood?" she said, alarmed. "I can't imagine I can be much help, but won't you come in?" She opened the door wide.

Tim pulled out his credentials and showed them to her.

"Miss Hansen, you shouldn't let strangers through your door without identification," Tim softly chastised her and smiled.

"Oh, my. I do know that," she blushed, hesitated, and read all three men's leather-bound IDs. She guided them into her living room. "Please sit down. I just made a fresh pot of coffee. May I bring you some?"

"I would love some, ma'am," Johnson said. "A dash of milk if you have it."

Anxious to get to the interview, Tim frowned at Johnson. But he also knew accepting her hospitality could help put her at ease. She hadn't taken Jones's wallet; he needed to discover the connection.

Arlina's house said a lot about her. She decorated it with florals, like her garden outside. An antique glass case displayed figurines that looked like they'd been collected over the years.

After serving Johnson, she sat on the loveseat across a claw-footed coffee table.

"I haven't seen anything in the news about a homicide…."

"Yes, ma'am. It happened in DC. Does the silver Equinox in your driveway belong to you?" Tim continued. He knew it did but needed her to claim ownership.

"Well, yes, it does." Unfortunately, she became skeptical—he could see it in her eyes. She scooted forward to the edge of her seat and set her coffee mug on a coaster on the coffee table. "But what does my car…?"

"We picked up video of your car leaving the Fort Bragg Officer's Club Thursday night. We believe our person of interest was there. We are interviewing everyone who visited the club Thursday night," Tim finished, catching her full stare.

She laughed nervously. "Oh, you don't want to talk to me. You want to talk to my niece. She borrowed my car to meet friends on Thursday night."

"Is she here?" Miguel asked.

"No. She only visited for a few days and went home late Friday morning. I took her to the airport." Arlina retrieved her coffee mug and sipped as if relieved.

"What's your niece's name? And do you know where she is now?" Tim asked.

"Her name is Terry…Tareeka Marlow. We call her Terry."

Tim sat up straighter. The name shocked—like a glass of ice water hitting him in the face. He struggled not to react. He didn't want to panic Arlina into warning her niece that the police and FBI were hunting for her.

Arlina continued, "She's home in DC now. She has to work tomorrow. We're so proud of her. Did you know she has a part-time internship with a very famous judge?"

"Excuse me for a second," Miguel said, stood, and exited through the front door. Tim knew he'd call Elias and the team. The team would locate and set up surveillance in case Miss Marlow learned of their visit to her aunt and decided to flee.

Tim smiled at her and nodded. Johnson glanced at him, lifting both eyebrows. Tareeka worked for Judge Waterford, which could easily mean she knew about Jones's adoption and that he would inherit a two-million-dollar insurance policy upon the Judge's demise. Did they conspire to kill her? It piled one more *bad-guy* card on Jones's stack. Tim battled with himself. He trusted Roxie's intuition and his own, but right now—things were not looking too good for Mr. Jaydon Lee Jones.

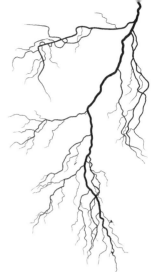

CHAPTER THIRTY-SEVEN

"WOULD YOU ALLOW me to take a DNA sample from you?" Tim asked. Arlina sat back and stared hard at him. "Will that help?"

"Yes, ma'am. It could help us eliminate Tareeka from involvement," he said, knowing it could go either way.

"Will it hurt?"

"No. You rub this Q-tip inside your cheek," he answered, pulling the kit from his pocket.

"Sure. I'll help any way I can." Arlina performed the task, and Tim inserted the swab into the kit's tube and sealed it.

"Would you allow us to search your car?" Tim kept the warrant in his pocket. He didn't want to distress Arlina and asked for permission instead. He smiled, keeping everything on a friendly level. He didn't need Arlina calling Tareeka the minute they left.

"Ma'am, does Terry—Tareeka—have a boyfriend?"

"I believe she does, but she doesn't talk about him much. My sister is afraid he might be married or involved in some criminal behavior. But I think Tareeka is too smart for that. Roseanna, my sister, watches too much TV. Everyone is suspicious in her book." She laughed.

"Does the name Wilford Kincaid mean anything to you?" Tim asked.

"Of course, it does. Willie is my cousin Effie's son. He's living in DC now, too, and he and Tareeka meet up occasionally."

"Do you think Tareeka is involved somehow?" The pitch to Arlina's voice raised an octave, and her eyes widened.

"We are weeding out the witnesses from the suspects," he reassured her with an open smile. It wasn't exactly a lie, but close enough to make him feel slightly ashamed. But without more evidence, he couldn't lay all his cards on the table.

"Oh, of course, I've seen that on TV. I watch crime shows, too," Arlina offered, looking down at the floor and back up with a smile. "You may search the car." Arlina was so naïve. Tim realized she wanted to do the right thing but wouldn't suspect her niece no matter what.

"Thursday night, do you know when your niece arrived home?" Tim asked.

"I don't. I take a sleeping pill some nights," she said. "But the car was here when I woke in the morning."

"What time was that?" Johnson asked. He picked up his cup and finished off his coffee.

"Oh, you're establishing a timeline, like on TV. Well, I usually get up around nine. Terry's flight was at 11:30."

"Thank you very much, ma'am. This is great coffee, by the way," Johnson added. Tim stood.

Arlina rose, walked Tim and Johnson to the door, and stepped on the porch with them.

"Thank you for your help, Arlina," Tim said. He nodded to Miguel, and an FBI evidence team moved in. Tim hoped to get latents matching the fingerprints in the Jeep and on Jones's wallet.

Berkstad appeared from the side of the house. "What's next?" he asked.

"We need to interview Jones's parents," Miguel said, peering over the top of the CSI officer processing prints from the steering wheel.

"Do you want me to wait here with CSI? I can meet you at police headquarters later," Berkstad said. Tim contemplated the offer. No way did he trust Berkstad. Tim decided to hand it off to the CSI supervisor overseeing evidence collection.

"I think we're good," Tim turned to a young CSI agent. "Make sure you mark these as from the car. Note the make, model, and license plate number on the envelope in addition to the case number." He lowered his volume so only the agent could hear.

"I can transmit an electronic file of these prints," the agent informed him.

"Do it." He gave the man Kandar's email address and patted him on the shoulder. He watched as the agent took pictures of the tape transparency with a high-resolution digital camera and emailed the results.

Another agent collected swabs of touch DNA to compare with the DNA gathered from the Jeep.

When they were finished, Tim walked to the porch.

"Thank you for your help," he handed Arlina his card. "If you think of anything, you can call anytime."

Tim stood on the driveway's edge and handed over the Buccal Swab to the Forensic Team as they packed up to leave. Berkstad strolled over.

"I think I'll return to the station with Detective Johnson," Berkstad said. "Lieutenant Broady can drive you to the Jones's house."

"You're sure?" Tim asked, furrowing his brow. Inside, he jumped for joy. But Berkstad's grin made the hair on the back of his neck stand on end. Miguel looked up from signing off on the CSI report and caught Tim's gaze.

"Let's get this over with," Miguel said, smiling.

The three men climbed into the camouflage-painted Humvee. From the backseat, Tim watched Broady enter the Jones's address into the GPS, close his door, and turn on the engine.

"That guy gives me the creeps," Broady added.

"Who, Berkstad? He gives everyone the creeps," Miguel laughed. "By the way, Tim, I called Elias, and our team's searching for Tareeka Marlow in DC. Elias said he'd get help from the Marshalls if he must."

"No. I mean, he *really* gives me the creeps. There's something sneaky and deceptive about him," Broady insisted as they pulled away from the curb.

"He's a spy, that's why," Miguel rhymed, laughing.

Tim couldn't help but chuckle. "He's a counter-intel guy."

"What's he doing with you then? Aren't you criminal profilers?" Broady continued, clearly rattled. "He stands around smirking like he's superior to everyone else."

"I wish we knew why he's around. We don't. He just shows up, and he's higher up the food chain. We have no choice but to let him tag along." Miguel turned sideways in his seat. When he turned back, he studied the side view mirror.

Tim noticed. Miguel's attention seemed glued to the mirror, not to the road ahead. "Turn right, don't signal," Miguel said suddenly. Tim twisted against his seatbelt and looked out the rear window. A black car, two lengths behind them, slammed on the brakes and nearly hit a car going in the opposite direction as they made the turn to follow. *Not good.*

"We have a tail," Broady announced. "Black sedan, North Carolina Plates."

"That's why Berkstad was so eager to return to the police station with Johnson," Miguel grinned. "Game on."

Broady's jaw tightened. "This isn't exactly the nimblest vehicle—but it's armor-plated, with bulletproof windows and run-flat tires."

In the rearview mirror, Tim saw a tight, determined smile curve his lips.

"Let's make sure they're following us before we get too carried away," Tim said, not eager to get involved in a chase or shootout. Too late; he heard Miguel pull the slide, chambering a round in his Glock. Tim would be in this fight whether he wanted to be or not. He called and informed Elias.

"I think we should try some simple turns and make sure," Tim said calmly after disengaging with his supervisor.

Broady nodded his agreement, moved to the left lane, and turned. The black sedan followed, staying around two car lengths behind. He then turned right onto a cross street. Again, the black car trailed them and continued through several consecutive and illogical turns designed especially for ferreting out a shadow.

After his next turn, Broady punched the gas, and the Humvee roared down the narrow two-way street. Up ahead, the signal light turned yellow—then red.

"Signal to turn left and go right," Miguel instructed.

When the light turned green, Broady executed the maneuver, crossing the right lane to do it. Tim held his breath as the car they'd cut off hit the brakes, smoking its tires. He heard someone scream, "Idiot!" and saw his one-finger salute in the air above the driver's side window.

The black sedan blasted through the intersection, but the sound of squealing brakes clued Tim they intended to pursue, no matter the cost to civilians and innocents. What was their purpose? Assassination? An abduction?

In the background, Broady's GPS demanded that he return to the route.

"Shut that thing up," Miguel said, glaring at Broady's profile. Finally, he reached over and ended the guidance.

Broady gunned the engine, speeding down the road, weaving around slower traffic. Unrelentingly, the black sedan copied each move. Tim cringed as one car barely escaped being scraped down the side by the sedan driver's misjudgment. At least it slowed their stalker down.

Tim watched out the rearview window until he could no longer see the car behind them. Broady suddenly whipped the Humvee into a grocery store parking lot.

Driving slowly, he crept down the aisles between parked cars, circled back and stopped short of the driveway that joined the street. The store building partially hid them from view.

"You've done this before," Tim commented.

"In Afghanistan," Broady said. "Sometimes, evasion was the only option."

The black sedan sped by, and they watched it accelerate down the road that led out of town.

"That's him. Let's go get 'em." Miguel's voice held a cold anger Tim didn't like, but had heard before.

"They don't know where we are headed. We should go to the Jones's house. Finish our interviews," Broady offered the alternative. "We shook them."

Tim wasn't so sure. When the car passed by, he thought he recognized the pursuers. They appeared to be the same team that chased him at the Sugar Maple Lodge. A desire for revenge sparked to life. They had leeway in the field to eliminate threats, and Tim was convinced these were Berkstad's agents.

"No. We need to end this—find out who they are and what they're after," Tim growled. "They won't expect us to come up behind them," he said.

Broady pulled into the right lane heading out of town. The road ahead darkened under branches of maple trees on either side. The trees seemed to reach for each other, as if the leaves longed to touch, and created an archway in shades of translucent gold and green, like stained glass.

In the distance, Tim could see the black sedan. The brake lights flashed on. They were making a U-turn.

Broady departed the roadway and retreated into the mouth of a driveway. Slowly, he followed the circle, facing the Humvee to the road and stopped. The camouflage paint did its job. The rig nearly disappeared in the dark and light patterns on the ground created by sunlight through the trees.

The couple in the black sedan proceeded toward them at a much slower pace than when they left town. Once they were closer, Tim could see them moving in the front seat as if trying to locate the Humvee. *Did they have a tracking device?* His heart beat faster. They had to, or they would've kept going. He reasoned.

Once the black car passed the driveway, Broady pulled out behind them. Tim watched their pursuers gesturing to each other when the Humvee loomed up in their rearview mirror.

"Forty Miles per hour. I'm going to PIT them," Broady announced and moved to the right side of the car. Tim remembered practicing the PIT maneuver (Precision Immobilization Technique) during his Tactical Driving Classes at Quantico. The same anxiety mixed with excitement rolled in his core. Executed perfectly, the PIT Maneuver stopped a fleeing suspect or terrorist immediately, and officers could move in for an arrest. An imperfect PIT could result in all kinds of unintended consequences, including death.

This pair's intentions were unknown, but their recklessness had already put lives in danger. They had to put an end to it.

The sedan's driver increased his speed, trying to avoid the inevitable. Broady was good at this. He held steady, kept up, and positioned his right front bumper just behind the sedan's left rear tire. He turned the steering wheel and accelerated. The mass and momentum of the Humvee spun the car in front of them around to the left and into the soft wet grass on the road's shoulder, facing in the opposite direction. The driver attempted a correction, but the car's two right tires sank into the soft earth, and the vehicle toppled onto its side. Both airbags deployed, filling the front interior with white.

Quickly, Broady braked and slammed the rig into reverse. Miguel and Tim released their seatbelts and left the Humvee before it stopped. Broady tossed a folding baton to Miguel. They raced to the overturned sedan.

Miguel smashed the driver's side window, and showers of safety glass spilled onto the turf. He cleared the rest away, unlocked the door and opened it. He cut away the airbag, sliced through the driver's seatbelt with his knife, and wrestled him to the ground. He rolled the dazed man to his stomach, quickly disarmed, and put him into flex cuffs.

The woman held her arms up, showing her hands were empty. Tim helped the woman out through the driver's door. He took the pistol from her shoulder holster and checked for another concealed at her ankle. He cleared both weapons and stuffed them in his pockets. A small cut on her bottom lip still oozed blood. Nothing serious. He cuffed her anyway and made her sit in the damp grass next to her buddy.

Tim recognized them. They'd followed him before and found themselves locked in the stairwell at the Sugar Maple Lodge. They hadn't learned their lesson and were disadvantaged once again.

"Are you looking for us?" Miguel asked as he searched the man for ID. When he found it, he handed it to Tim.

"Special Agent Roland Grimes, FBI Counterintelligence Division," Tim read out loud. "And you are?" He addressed the woman.

She shook her head no. Tim tightened his lips together and clenched his jaw. He explored the pockets of her suit coat and found her ID. "Special Agent Maggie White," he said. "Were you following us?" He wanted her to confess.

"Not us, you," she hissed at him, rubbing the blood from her lip on the shoulder of her white blouse.

"Why me?" Tim asked, frowning. She refused to answer and looked at anything other than Tim's face. "Did you hear me? Why me?"

"You're under surveillance. You kill us—another team will take over," Grimes yelled.

Tim looked in his direction, perplexed, and stepped in front of him. "Kill you?" Tim chuckled. He had no such intention and shook his head. "Surveillance for what?" Tim asked. "I'm FBI. We're supposed to be on the same side."

"That's our assignment—to watch you," Grimes defended, but he wouldn't look at Tim either. He lied. *Were they tracking his phone?*

"Bullshit!" Miguel menaced. "You know, and it's in your best interest to tell us."

"Who's your supervisor?" Tim asked.

"You're FBI?" White asked, confused. Tim could imagine the wheels turning a million miles a minute behind her eyes. "Wait a minute. We were told. . . ."

"Don't say anything!" Grimes warned.

Tim pulled out his ID and showed her. "Who's your supervisor?" he asked again. She shook her head, too afraid to cross her partner.

"You tell your boss I'm on to him. You tell Berkstad this must stop. Someone's going to get hurt, and it isn't going to be me. Got it?" Tim said his threat just above a whisper. He watched as the two stared at each other in surprise.

Tim motioned for Miguel, and they moved the two rogue agents to a shady spot under a tree. They walked toward the Humvee. Grinning as if he enjoyed the adventure, Broady stood by the driver's door.

"Wait, you aren't going to leave us here like this. . . ." White whined.

"Am I going to leave you in the middle of nowhere cuffed without transportation? Yes, ma'am, I am," Tim replied.

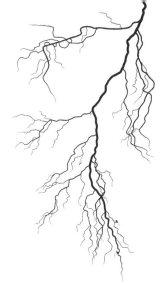

CHAPTER THIRTY-EIGHT

D ANI MOTIONED FOR Rachel to take her coffee and follow her to the outside covered patio. Towels in hand, Mike and the girls waited by the gate to the enclosure surrounding the pool. Dani pressed in the sequence that unlocked the gate, and the kids bounded through. After dressing both daughters in arm floaties, Dani sat at the table near the shallow end.

Mike had the deep end to himself and practiced diving from the board at the far side of the Olympic-sized pool. He needed friends, and Dani wondered if any kids his age lived nearby. Rumor had it the horse farm down the road was a boarding barn specializing in rich Hunter/ Jumper horse clients. They had the money to fit in, but did Mike inherit Miguel's horsemanship skill? She wondered. He was shy around her, but Dani noticed his eyes light up when the girls mentioned the horses.

School would start in two weeks; he could make friends there if he wasn't bored to tears by then. He was a smart, personable, and handsome kid.

Humidity lingered heavily in the air from the last few days of rain, and cumulus clouds formed and floated in the sky. The weather news for this afternoon predicted rain. It would be a hot, late August day. Summer held on tight, though Dani was restless for the cool mornings of autumn.

Rachel set her coffee mug down and relaxed in a chair at the table. Reading her sister's mood, Dani hesitated to bring up Miguel, but she had to.

SARAH VAIL

"Tim sure is a nice guy," Rachel started the conversation. It seemed awkward. Dani was afraid she'd seen them arguing this morning. Nothing like a morning spat to ruin the whole day.

"Rachel, Tim is Miguel's partner. He knows Mike is his son," Dani blurted out.

"Did you tell him? Why did you tell him?" Rachel set her mug on the table and leaned across it with eyes wide.

Dani shook her head, "I didn't. He's a detective, remember? He has eyes, and Mike looks like his dad," Dani sighed. "Tim thinks you should tell Miguel. Oh, Sis. Why didn't you tell him years ago? Why didn't you marry Miguel?"

"You know why. I couldn't. Dad and Miguel fought over him going into the Navy. Dad was sure he'd be killed or maimed, and I'd be a widow. He was just a seventeen-year-old kid. But, after the *incident* at Benghazi, no one could stop him. After he'd gone, Dad found out I was pregnant, and he was furious. You were only twelve, but at least you should remember all the tears, yelling, and door-slamming going on around you, do you?" Rachel asked.

"Yes, but you weren't that much older. You were only fifteen."

"Dad said I couldn't see Miguel again. I had a choice. Either I had an abortion or married Rob, or Dad would have Miguel charged with statutory rape," Rachel said. "I couldn't let Dad do that. I'd lied and told Miguel I was old enough. The thought of Miguel in prison—when we both participated. Dani, it was never rape. I loved him, and I couldn't give up my baby. I just couldn't. I married Rob, and that was that." Tears filled her eyes. "I tried to make a go of it with Rob. I really did."

"Dad treated you horribly. He was so unfair," Dani shook her head.

"Don't say that, Dani. He was a good father. He wanted the best for me. He found me a husband and covered up my mistake. He protected me the best he could."

"Rob Highland was nothing but a gold digger. He was twenty and knew exactly what he'd gain by marrying the boss's daughter," Dani grumbled. She stared hard at her sister. "Do you want to see Miguel?"

"He won't want to see me. He never wrote to me. Did you know that?"

"But he said he wrote you every week and called, but you wouldn't take his calls. Finally, he gave up—he didn't want to be a stalker." A

244

memory flashed in her mind of her father throwing some old letters in the fireplace at the ranch. *Were they Miguel's letters?* Had Dad stopped all communication? She didn't want to believe it. But she remembered how he'd reacted when Dani caught her ex-husband cheating. Dad had procured her lawyer and made sure Carl got far less than he wanted.

"I can't tell him about Mike. He'll hate me and never forgive me because I was so weak and scared," she said, pausing and staring into Dani's eyes. "Is this what you and Tim fought about this morning?"

"You weren't supposed to see that," Dani murmured.

"I should go. I don't want to cause any trouble. Especially for you and Tim."

Dani reached across the table and covered her sister's hand with hers. "I need you to stay. Miguel wants to see you. When I was at Sweitzer at Christmas, he asked about you. He still loves you. He never married, you know."

"We aren't those teenage kids anymore. Besides, everyone wonders about their first love," Rachel mused, her laughter mixed with sadness.

"Aren't you curious? Even a little bit?" Dani asked. "He's far more handsome than he was back then." She smiled.

"Is he?" She gazed out to the pool and seemed transported back to her past. The thoughts Dani read on her face were beautiful and painful.

"Tim could invite him when you're ready. You don't have to tell him about Mike—only if you want to. Who knows, it could be magical."

"Oh, God, Dani. You're such a Pollyanna. You always were," Rachel picked up her mug of coffee and sipped. Dani made sure her expression pleaded Miguel's case. Rachel tisked, "Okay. Invite him. But if we're both heartbroken and ruined by it—it'll be all your fault."

"You won't be. I promise. You won't be." Dani smiled. It was a promise she had no power to keep, but the thought of them together made hope well up inside. She'd always considered Miguel her brother; now, that might come true.

~

The interview with Jones's parents was like hunting for pirate treasure. Unfortunately, so far, they'd found an empty pit, Tim thought. Jones's parents hadn't told Jaydon he was adopted. He had no idea he was just about to become a wealthy man.

Tim stood at the end of the bed in Jones's childhood room. His mother explained she'd left it exactly as it was when he headed for college five years ago.

The walls of his room were postered with sports heroes and, oddly, the bookshelves were full of volumes about famous military generals from "Old Blood and Guts" Patton to "Stormin' Norman" Schwarzkopf, which shed some light on Jones's current Army career. Tim watched as Broady picked up one of the books and leafed through the pages. Beside the bookshelves, a sixty-inch television was mounted on the wall. Game controllers were stacked on a shelf. Tim assumed they were wirelessly connected to the computer on a small desk.

"Jaydon and his friends always played computer war games, and he'd especially liked the ones that featured special ops," she explained.

To Tim, Jaydon sounded like he'd been an all-American kid: good grades, a solid family, much like his own, and he had dreams. He didn't fit into the sociopath model.

"Do you know if Jaydon has financial problems? Problems with drugs or alcohol?" Miguel asked. "Gambling?"

"My Jaydon? Not my Jaydon. He is very opposed to drugs and the gang-thug culture. I think he might drink with his friends on the base, but never to excess," Mrs. Jones said. "I keep his books—in case something happens overseas," she almost choked on the second part of her sentence. "Jaydon is very frugal. He's saving up for a new house. I'll show you," she added.

Tim glanced at Miguel and then Broady raising both eyebrows. Maybe this wasn't such an empty treasure pit after all.

The men followed her to a small room set up as an office. A clean, dust-free walnut desk with a computer monitor, keyboard, adding machine, and hard-line telephone sat in the center of the room. She opened the center drawer and pulled out a leather ledger. Glancing through the pages, Tim noticed Jaydon's Army pay was tendered by direct deposit. Mom dutifully paid his bills and contributed to a savings account that had accumulated just short of twelve thousand dollars. Pretty good for a twenty-four or five-year-old.

"Out of the blue, Judge Waterford came to me one day while Jaydon was in grade school and wanted to contribute financially. She didn't want to disrupt his life but wanted him to have the best. We agreed. Any contributions were to be kept secret. Judge Waterford paid for all of Jaydon's college expenses above and beyond his baseball scholarship. Jaydon never knew," Mrs. Jones said. Tim could see she was proud of the boy she raised and tried to show her son in the most favorable light, especially to the FBI and police. It was understandable.

"He had an advantage over his friends," she commented. "Mrs. Waterford bought him a car, so he had no car payments. Jaydon thinks we bought it for him as a graduation present. Mrs. Waterford even promised to match his savings for a downpayment on a house when he was ready. I know it was selfish of me, but I wanted him to have all those things. So, whenever she offered them, I took it."

Tim licked his lips and nodded. Free money? Why not? He thought.

"Did Jaydon ever meet Judge Waterford?" Tim asked, looking up from a credit card statement showing Jaydon's monthly balances were always paid in full and on time.

"No. Mrs. Waterford said she didn't want him confused by her mistake. We took him home from the hospital right after he was born. She was only fourteen when she had him and his biological father—long gone." She waved her hand with a backward flip to emphasize her point. "Mrs. Waterford insisted he had a good life and family now. She didn't want him dreaming of a life that couldn't be or pining away over some no-account absentee father," Mrs. Jones wrinkled her nose and shook her head. "I have no empathy for deadbeat dads. I'm so sorry Mrs. Waterford is gone. She was a good woman."

"Yes. She would've been a great judge. Do you mind if I make copies of these?" Tim asked, lifting a bank statement. He'd have Kandar search for everything he could find, including any secret accounts Mom didn't know about. Tim didn't expect to find anything.

"Does the name Wilford or Willie Kincaid mean anything to you? Was he one of Jaydon's friends?" Tim asked.

Mrs. Jones looked puzzled. "Ummm, Willie Kincaid. No. I don't remember any friends by that name." There was no deception in her eyes.

"Does this Willie Kincaid have anything to do with Judge Waterford's murder?" She gasped. "You don't think Jaydon had anything to do with . . . ?"

"No, Ma'am, I don't. We want to make sure we clear him," he answered.

"Well, of course. I can make copies for you."

"We can make them and bring your originals back," Tim started.

Mrs. Jones cut him off. "You know I'm an accountant, don't you? I have a printer here. I do people's taxes." She smiled.

"That would be fantastic if you could make copies. It would save us some time. Does Jaydon have a fiancé or girlfriend?" Tim asked, watching her load a stack of papers into the copy feeder. He nearly held his breath, hoping she didn't mention Tareeka Marlow.

After stuffing the papers into a manilla envelope, Mrs. Jones grinned at him. "Jaydon has lots of girlfriends. Always has."

"Could you list their names and phone numbers if you have them?" He handed her a small notepad. "Did he bring anyone home to meet you?" Tim continued. "Anyone special?"

"No. Not yet. Jaydon wanted to get through his first tour before getting serious about a girl. His father and I are very proud of him, but we are worried sick about what he's signed up for. We tried to talk him out of Special Forces, but he's twenty-five—a grown man. He said he was making his own decisions." She exhaled a heavy sigh and jutted the envelope and notepad in Tim's direction. He took them with a nod.

"Thank you very much for your time. We'll get out of your hair," Miguel said.

"If you need anything, just call me," Tim handed her his card as they left.

Once in the Humvee, Tim buckled into the back seat behind Broady.

"Well, what do you think?" Miguel asked. Both he and Broady turned to look at Tim.

"Right now, I think I am wrong about Jones. He's not desperate for money. I'm sure he'll be happy to get it, but he's not in financial trouble," Tim set the envelope on the seat next to him and linked his fingers above his head. From what he learned today, Jaydon had returned to the bottom of his suspect list.

Miguel laughed. "Well, don't tell Roxie she was right. She'll never let us live it down."

"You were wrong. He's a good guy and a skilled and loyal soldier," Broady said defiantly, lifting his chin. "I can't understand why they took his wallet. How does that fit in?" Broady asked as he started the engine.

"So, if the theory is that they wanted the insurance money, how does that work?" Tim knew Miguel wanted to brainstorm.

They pulled away from the curb.

"What would you need to convince an insurance company you were the beneficiary of a life policy and were entitled to collect the money?" Broady asked.

"The death certificate, a copy of the policy, photo ID, a social security card, a birth certificate—I don't know, I've never had to do it," Tim answered. He'd call Kandar and get him on it.

"Wilford Kincaid and Jaydon looked a lot alike. Maybe they thought they could steal his identity to claim the insurance," Miguel said.

Tim sat quietly and deep in thought. "I think we're wasting our time following Jaydon. We're chasing the wrong rabbit."

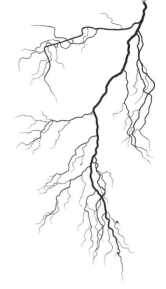

CHAPTER THIRTY-NINE

"WHO IS THE right rabbit?" Broady asked. Tim saw him glance into the rearview mirror and then return his concentration to the road. "We'll have to find more than we have right now to implicate Jones. He has an alibi—an airtight one," Broady said. Tim understood he defended his compatriot; it was reasonable but a little too fierce.

"We know Wilford Kincaid was one of our killers. His mistake—he tried to get to Jamie Randall, the boy who witnessed the body dump. We're pretty sure Tareeka Marlow is involved," Tim mused.

"But that doesn't stop Jones from being the Master Mind," Miguel added, earning a scowl from Broady.

"Why would he share his inheritance with a bunch of strangers? I don't see Jaydon in that role. He has too much going for him, and he would have been better off with Judge Waterford alive. She was very generous," Tim said.

"Guilty is what she was." Broady accelerated onto the freeway.

"Guilt might've been part of her motive, but the Judge had no other children. Maybe her motive was plain old motherly love," Tim offered the alternative. "Besides, her motive isn't important here. The bad guys' motives are. We aren't going to be victim blaming."

"If Tareeka knew about the insurance, she knew what Jaydon looked like. There was a picture album in the Judge's desk drawer. So, what if one day, while straightening up, Tareeka stumbles on the insurance policy, the box with Jaydon's actual birth certificate, and the photo album? She notices that Jaydon and good ol' Cousin Wilford look a lot alike, and the seeds of a get-rich-quick-plan germinates in her mind," Miguel said. "She didn't give a crap about Jaydon or Wilford. She just planned to get the money."

"Wow. That's cold-hearted." Tim whistled. "But possible. Statistically, though, women kill more often for love. Remember, Anton Williams, the Judge's clerk, said Carlton Waterford was having an affair, and the Judge planned to divorce him. What if the sultry Tareeka Marlow was his mistress, they planned to kill the Judge, cash in the insurance policy using Jaydon's ID, and run off to start a rich new life with no baggage. And as a bonus, they cut Jaydon out of his inheritance, assuming he'd never know the difference since he was adopted."

"Now, that's cold-hearted," Miguel said. "But typical. This certainly wouldn't be the first time it's been tried. I'm betting Judge Waterford never told her husband about the kid."

Dani's sister and her son Mike flashed into Tim's mind. He tamped it down. *I can't think of that now.* Tim shook it off.

"Why do you think Carlton Waterford is involved?" Broady asked.

"In his first interview, when the Judge was just a missing person, he spoke of her in the past tense," Tim said.

"That's not enough," Broady stared in the rearview mirror for a second.

"No. But he's lawyered up. And now we know there was a pending divorce and a mistress he forgot to mention," Tim chuckled.

"As if any guy would mention that to the cops when his wife is missing," Miguel laughed.

"What do you want me to do with Jones? He's waiting in the interrogation room in Fayetteville," Broady asked.

"Ask him if he knows Kincaid. We know he *knows* Marlow, even in the Biblical sense," Miguel said, while clearing his throat. "Ask him if he was involved with the Judge's murder. Give him a lie detector test. If he's lying, we'll at least know it," Miguel said.

"And if he passes?" Broady asked.

"Let's see if he volunteers for the lie detector test. If he does and passes, let him go. Just tell him not to leave town. If we have more questions and need to contact him, we will," Tim said. "We need to keep him cooperative."

For the rest of the ride to the police station in Fayetteville, Tim was silent. He watched the landscape pass by; green forests of maple trees slowly gave way to light industrial buildings and finally to the city. He heard Broady and Miguel discuss the case in the background but not their words. His attention had turned to Berkstad. What was he going to do about Berkstad? Tim was only an entry-level special agent with very limited experience. Though he had the requisite education for his job, Tim wasn't sure he was any good at it. If it came down to him or Berkstad, the latter man's time with the agency and experience would surely win out.

Tim knew he enjoyed a unique position. Dani's wealth meant if he lost his job, his family wouldn't suffer. But Tim loved the work. Solving the puzzles of crime tuned and sharpened his mind. Each time he and his team took down a criminal, he felt he served society. He was one of the white hats, the good guys. He helped citizens continue their daily lives with one less worry.

He wondered. Did Berkstad know the seventh floor authorized the search into his Congressman Patterson case files? Tim decided. Tonight at home, he would pore through the hacked information. He would discover if his suspicions of Berkstad's corruption were well-founded or built on sand.

What about Berkstad's claim he'd been offered a bribe to sabotage the Judge's investigation? Was it true or false? Tim had to admit his curiosity was piqued, but he also had to admit his intuition warned him Berkstad didn't like him. He had the distinct feeling Berkstad would set him up in a heartbeat.

Broady pulled into a parking space, and Tim's phone vibrated in his pocket.

"McAndrews," he answered, undoing his seatbelt, and opening the door.

"Tim, the bank records you wanted are in," Kandar said, with a tone of glee in his voice. "Carlton Waterford is flat broke. His fitness enterprise loses money every month. The Judge kept him afloat."

Tim chuckled. "So, if she divorces him, he's out of business?"

"Looks that way," Kandar said. "She's been supporting him for years."

"Interesting. I wonder if he's expecting to be the beneficiary on an insurance policy. Now, there's a motive for murder," Tim said, watching Miguel and Broady turn back to face him. "She was divorcing him."

"I'll have his call logs, text messages, and email this afternoon at the earliest or tomorrow for sure," Kandar reported.

"Good. Tell Elias and see if he wants to assign a surveillance team to see where Waterford leads."

"I already have," Kandar said.

"Thanks, buddy. See you in a few hours," Tim said, disengaging the call.

"What was that about?" Miguel asked.

"I'm liking Carlton Waterford more and more for the Judge's murder," Tim smiled. "Wait until you hear what Kandar just dropped," Tim said.

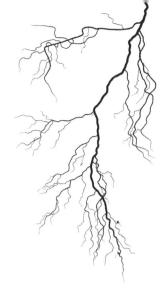

CHAPTER FORTY

"WHY DO THESE dirtbags think they are so much smarter than we are?" Miguel asked after hearing Kandar's report. Tim, Miguel and Broady disembarked from the Humvee. Tim grabbed the computer case he'd brought with him, and the men strolled across the parking lot toward the red-brick Fayetteville Police headquarters.

"They don't know all the information we can access," Tim shrugged. "We should keep it that way."

"I like to think our brilliant minds put all the information together to solve the crime, like Sherlock Holmes," Miguel chuckled.

"Of course," Tim laughed. "There's that."

"Hey, I agree," Broady said. "What do you want to do with Jones? Do you still want the lie detector?"

"I don't. His alibi is rock solid. He didn't kill anyone. Let him go," Tim said. "We know where to find him if we need him."

Tim held the glass entry door open as his comrades walked through. The officer at the reception desk recognized them and ushered them through to the detectives' division. They made their way to Johnson's office.

The door was closed. Tim knocked and twisted the knob. Johnson sat behind his desk, and Berkstad lounged lazily in one of the chairs in front of the desk, looking at them with a smug smile that made rage flash over

Tim like a lit match dropped onto gasoline. He'd learned to control the outward appearance of anger. The courtroom had taught him that—it was a practiced veneer.

Berkstad had sent those agents to follow him and who knows what else. He should have Broady check for a tracking device on the Humvee. He let out a slow breath, calming the fire inside.

"I need to talk to Berkstad in private. Can you leave us for a minute?" Tim asked.

Johnson stood, made an 'uh oh' face and said, "Sure, we can go grab some coffee."

Miguel picked up on Tim's wrath and seemed to know what was coming. Tim reassured him with a half-smile, but Berkstad's harassment had gone far enough. When the room cleared, Tim closed the door. He turned and braced one hip on the edge of Johnson's desk.

"What's up, Tim?" Berkstad asked as he slumped back into his chair.

"So, David, did you lose something?" Tim asked, a snarky grin creasing his face.

"Lose something?" Berkstad appeared puzzled.

Tim unzipped the computer case, pulled Special Agents Grimes and Whites I.D.s, badges, and pistols from his pockets, and set them casually on the desk. He waited until Berkstad made the connection. "You can find your *friends* on Highway 57 heading East, about seven miles from town. They're waiting and probably pretty pissed off."

Berkstad bristled, abruptly stood, and asked, "What have you done?" He started for the door. Tim blocked his escape, and Berkstad backed away.

"Oh, and you better order a tow truck. Unfortunately, they wrecked their car," Tim added. He paused and stared. "Berkstad, it's way past time for this shit to end. Stop following me, and don't ever put electronic bugging devices in my hotel room again. Got it?" He stepped aside, stifling the impulse to shove Berkstad back into the chair. Tim balled his fists at his sides.

"I don't know what you mean."

"You've been on my butt since I walked through the doors at Quantico. What's your problem with me?" Tim asked, poking him in the chest with an index finger. He expected to be accused of incompetence, accused of hacking Berkstad's files, accused of being an arrogant jackass, and formulated a rebuttal.

"Stay away from Roxie!" Berkstad growled. His posture changed. He was like a bull elk in rut, ready to charge.

Tim's mouth dropped open in shock, and he almost laughed, but Berkstad was serious. "What? Wait? Roxie? Are you kidding? Where's this coming from?" He was so surprised he had no words that made sense. They came out jumbled.

"She told me all about working with you in Seattle." Berkstad's eyes became black slits.

"Yeah, we worked together three years ago in Seattle. We were on the same task force. We caught the killer, closed the task force, and she took her dream job with the BAU and left for Quantico. So what?" This wasn't the defense he'd prepared for.

"You had an affair, and now you're here." Jealousy flushed red into Berkstad's face. "Don't even try to get her back."

"Whoa. Get her back? I never had her in the first place. We never even dated," Tim tipped his head, confused. "I'm married." The minute he said it, he wished he hadn't. Berkstad was married with three kids, and it didn't stop him from chasing Roxie. Tim could see he didn't believe it. "You're using FBI resources, having me followed, because you're jealous? You're obsessed. Man, you need to check yourself before you wreck yourself." Tim said, shaking his head. When Berkstad looked at him, his eyes were cold and dark and his jaw tight as if he were a dog ready to bite.

Tim's anger dissolved into pity. But love, real or imagined, battled money as the top motive for murder. A chill zipped along the top of his shoulders. Had Berkstad planned to kill him? Had he been waiting for the opportune time to strike? Is that why he kept showing up unexpectedly? It was possible. Tim forced himself to regulate his breathing. He vowed to be even more cautious from now on if this confrontation didn't end his career.

"Go rescue your agents. We will straighten this out in person with Roxie once and for all this afternoon at Quantico." Tim felt sorry for

David, but he wasn't the kind to be cowed. "For now, back the fuck off! We are supposed to be on the same team." He stepped aside and let Berkstad stuff his agents' equipment into his pockets and hustle from the room. Tim knew there would be consequences, but he didn't care.

Miguel, Johnson, and Broady filtered back into the room. Tim smiled at them, but concern made it insincere. Had Roxie told Berkstad they'd had an affair? When they worked on the task force together, he was a newly minted law school graduate who'd just passed his bar exam only days before they met. His first post-graduation job with the King County DA was as a liaison with the task force. He wasn't about to mess it up by jumping into a one-nighter with a pretty FBI agent he'd probably have to encounter again. It was self-preservation.

Still, he'd read her signals loud and clear. He let reason and the need for a job keep him in check and made himself scarce before anything could even get started. He never really thought much about Roxie after she'd gone to Quantico—until he accepted the job with the FBI Elias offered him. By then, life had changed. Dani swept him off his feet, and he'd married her, becoming a faithful family man like his older brothers before him. And Roxie? She was a team member, nothing more.

"We think it's safe to let Jones go. We just received some new info, and it's moved another suspect to the top of the list," Tim said, shifting his mind to work.

"Yep. The boys filled me in," Johnson lifted his eyebrows as if asking Tim to spill what happened between him and Berkstad.

Tim guessed they'd spied on them through the office window—he hadn't bothered to close the blinds. He glanced at his watch. "Will you deliver Jones back home?"

"Sure, we picked him up, we should take him back," Johnson volunteered.

"I have one question for him and then we can let him go," Tim said.

"Let's do it," Broady added. Tim saw he was anxious to get his man freed. Johnson stood and led them to the interview room. It was past noon, and Jones had been waiting since ten-thirty. Jaydon looked up when the detectives entered but didn't complain.

"Corporal Jones, I'm Tim McAndrews with the FBI. You know by now we're investigating the murder of Judge Evelyn Waterford," Tim said. "This is Special Agent Miguel Gonzales, and you know Lieutenant Broady, CID, and Detective Johnson."

Jones acknowledged them with a nod.

"I only have one question before we send you on your way," Tim stated. Jones quietly breathed a sigh of relief.

"Yes, sir. I'll answer your question if I can." He looked at Tim and Miguel one at a time as if trying to ascertain the question before it was asked. Tim didn't blame him.

"The girl you picked up at the officer's club Thursday night, do you plan on seeing her again?" Tim asked. Jones's jaw twitched, and his pupils darkened.

"She stole my wallet, rummaged through my house, and rained this shitstorm down on me. I have no plans to see that bitch again, sir."

"If she contacts you, will you let me, or Lieutenant Broady know?" Tim asked.

Jones didn't immediately answer, but not because he intended to deceive them. His whole face wrinkled with curiosity. "Did she murder this Judge Waterberg?"

"Waterford," Miguel corrected him.

"Sorry, sir. I can't seem to get her name straight," Jones said with a grimace.

Tim thought, *You'll get it straight when you're told about the money.* He glanced over at Miguel. Elias said it would be best if Judge Waterford's estate attorney explained Jones's new situation. Tim didn't want to be the guy that had to tell him he was adopted. Some kids were grateful. Others felt betrayed. It was his parents' job to tell him their family story.

Tim passed his card across the table to Jones. "Remember, if she contacts you, call us. We want to talk to her," Tim said.

"Me first," Jones snarled under his breath.

"Just call us. We'll take care of her. You won't have to lift a finger," Miguel said with a grin.

"Will I get my wallet back?" Jones asked.

"Yeah, sure," Tim said. "You can go. Detective Johnson will give you a ride home." They shook hands. Tim watched him leave the interview room, following behind the detective.

Let's get going. We have a plane to catch," Tim said.

Broady, Miguel, and Tim left the station.

Tim noticed the glances coming from Broady and Miguel, so he picked up his pace and walked ahead, swinging the computer case at his side. He grinned to himself. He intended to leave them hanging and say nothing until they were in the parking lot near the Humvee.

"So, what was the bruhaha between you and Berkstad?" Broady asked, almost ready to burst with curiosity.

"Bruhaha? I just updated him on our progress," Tim tried to keep a big smile from his lips.

"Ding, ding, ding, my B.S. meter is ringing," Miguel guffawed. "We saw you through the interior window. So, what was going on in there?"

"Not much. I just told Berkstad where he could pick up his agents," Tim said and smiled.

"And hopefully, you told him where he could stick them," Miguel added.

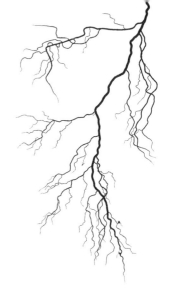

CHAPTER FORTY-ONE

TIM TOOK THE elevator to the basement at Quantico. He was anxious to see all the forensic evidence. He felt they were close to wrapping up this case.

"I can't wait to see Waterford's bank and phone records," Miguel said, rubbing his hands together and laughing like a villain. "I think we've got him."

"I hope the labs are back, too," Tim said. "And I hope I'm not fired for messing with Berkstad."

Miguel looked at him, pressing his lips together in a tight line. "Berkstad is messing with you. I can attest to that. And what if his stunt had come down to gunplay? What then? Did he explain why he had us followed? I mean, what was his reason? The hacked files?"

"Roxie."

"Roxie? What the hell?" Miguel seemed baffled. The elevator doors opened, and she appeared in the corridor.

"There you are. Reports are in from the lab. Elias is waiting for us—he said to go to the conference room as soon as you get here," she said, beaming, but the light didn't last. She twisted a strand of hair around an index finger. "What's wrong? You look like it's a hundred degrees, and someone stole your last cold beer. Where's David? Didn't he come back with you?"

"He took another flight," Miguel said. He wouldn't meet her gaze. Miguel had taken Tim's side. Tim didn't want there to be sides to take.

"Didn't the interviews go well?" she asked.

"They did," Tim answered but failed to elaborate. Tim studied her. Did she tell Berkstad that they'd had an affair in Seattle? If so, Roxie lied. He couldn't figure her out. What could she gain from that? He walked past her and up the stairs to the conference room.

"Well, aren't you going to tell me?" Roxie asked, reaching out and touching Tim's arm. He turned and shrugged her hand away.

"Isn't this why we're having a meeting?" Tim snipped and rapped softly on the door and opened it.

Folding chairs were placed on one side of a table in front of a large board that displayed a list of suspects and highlights of the evidence they had gathered. Each place at the table had a file folder, a yellow legal pad for notes, and a pencil in front of it. Along the west wall, another table contained the fixings for coffee and tea. A row of bottled water was stacked at the far end. Tim took a deep breath. They were going to be here for a while. He'd promised he'd be home for dinner. He glanced at his watch. It was only 3:30 so he decided to wait before calling Dani and breaking that promise.

Tim stepped forward to the whiteboard and swapped Carlton Waterford's name and picture at the bottom of the list with Jaydon Jones's at the top. Underneath the blank female silhouette with a question mark in the center, he wrote Tareeka Marlow and crossed out 'Arlina.' It might've been premature, but she was the logical choice for the seductress, pick-pocket, and unknown female abductor who left the lipstick-stained cigarette butt in the Jeep. He'd taken a Buccal swab from the real Arlina, and they could match her to her niece by mitochondrial DNA—since Arlina and Tareeka's mother were sisters and would inherit the same mitochondria from their mother.

Tim waited before he took a seat at the table as more team members filtered into the conference room. He avoided sitting next to Roxie, opened his folder, and began reading the reports. Completely absorbed in the information, he was surprised when Roxie motioned for Kandar to move and plopped in the chair next to Tim, placing a water bottle in front of him. Tim squinted at her, but they were partners, and he couldn't spend time trying to appease Berkstad's obsessive jealousy. He had a job to do.

Elias interrupted the conversations between team members. "Everyone, let's get started."

Tim looked up and noticed Elias had a stern and troubled look on his face. He didn't speak again until everyone was quiet.

"As you all know, the President has tasked us with finding Judge Waterford's killer. We originally developed a profile based on evidence at the scene of her abduction and the body dump site. There were at least two perpetrators; one driving the Jeep and one or two controlling the Judge in the back seat. We know that nine-year-old Jamie Randall had the misfortune of witnessing Wilford Kincaid and a second man disposing of the Judge's body at Little Crooked Creek.

"As of today, we have more information to add." Elias turned to the evidence board.

"First, the blood spatter in the back seat of the Jeep belongs to Judge Waterford, confirming she was killed there. We found two fingernail fragments under the back seat. These fit with the broken nails on the Judge's right hand. The nail polish is an exact color and chemical match to the polish she wore on her other fingernails. DNA, from skin cells found under her nails and from the fragments, match Wilford Kincaid with a 99.9 percent certainty.

"The DNA from the cigarette butts in the ashtray belonged to three people...." Tim looked up as Elias continued. His theory of three perpetrators was true. It surprised him, but Tim was learning to trust his instincts.

"...Two males, one being Kincaid, and one female. I see someone corrected our suspect list." Elias said, chuckling.

"Evidence Recovery found a nine-millimeter ejected bullet casing underneath the driver's seat in the Jeep. It matches the bullet recovered at autopsy and was fired from the pistol found in Wilford Kincaid's possession at the cabin. Wilford Kincaid was the registered gun owner, and we surmise he was the shooter in a struggle with the Judge."

"Cell phone geotracking puts three people connected to Judge Waterford at the restaurant at the time of the shooting. Wilford Kincaid, a woman named Tareeka Marlow, and Carlton Waterford. Waterford claims he was there to meet his wife for a Friday night dinner. But on the advice of counsel, he has refused to give us DNA for testing. We'll need to get a warrant."

The seemingly concerned husband just solidified his place at the top of the list. Why wouldn't he volunteer his DNA? Sure, the cops always had to rule out the spouse, but was there a better way? Tim wondered.

"Witness Anton Williams told us in his taped interview he believes Carlton Waterford was cheating on his wife. He suspects, without proof, the girlfriend is Tareeka Marlow. He testified that at last year's office Christmas Party, Carlton and Tareeka were real cozy."

"That's nothing. Everybody's drinking too much, flirting. That proves nothing," Roxie said.

"Yeah, but Carlton said he and the Judge had a great relationship, no problems. Tim and Miguel found paperwork confirming her intention to divorce him in her desk drawer in her chambers. She'd hired a divorce lawyer. We received Carlton Waterford's bank and credit card statements this afternoon. All three of his credit cards are maxed out to their limits. He has thirty-seven dollars and fifty-three cents left in his personal bank account, and his business account is overdrawn. Judge Waterford bankrolled him and had been doing it for years.

"He has motive—a new love interest, and the money tree was about to dry up," Elias paused and took a sip from a water bottle he'd earlier placed on the edge of the conference table. "He's arrogant enough to think he could get away with it.

"There is one thing that confounds me. Why did Marlow steal Jaydon Jones's wallet? Any ideas?" Elias asked. The team members all looked at each other.

"Maybe he intended to drop the wallet in the vicinity of the body—that way, Jones would be implicated in the murder. Jamie Randall interrupted his plan," Roxie proposed.

Tim contemplated her words. It was plausible.

"Jones is the Judge's biological son. We found his original birth certificate, the adoption dossier, and pictures in the Judge's desk. Jones stood to inherit what Carlton Waterford wanted and needed to get out of debt—a two-million-dollar insurance policy. The payout doubled if the Judge died by accident or violence," Tim said. "Kincaid was Tareeka Marlow's cousin. She probably promised to pay him if he helped them kill the Judge."

"I bet Marlow found the adoption papers and insurance policy just like we did. She assumed the policy and other accounts belonging to Judge Waterford named Carlton as the beneficiary," Miguel said, a big grin on his face. "Surprise!"

"Maybe she was caught before she could read the whole policy, assumed he was the beneficiary. She and Carlton could live happily ever after on the Judge's insurance," Roxie mused.

"You're sure Jones isn't involved?" Elias asked.

"He doesn't know he's adopted. He doesn't know about the insurance money. If he did, why would he share it with strangers? He has no debt and money in the bank. He's clean." Tim sat back in his chair and scrubbed a hand over his hair.

"Wait a minute," Tim said, thumbing through the pages in his file. "Marlow knew. She had to know. She found out who the beneficiary was on the policy. That's why she went to get Jones's wallet. They thought Cousin Wilford looked enough like Jones to fool the insurance company. She found the birth certificate and everything they'd need to get the payout without Jones ever being the wiser. It wouldn't surprise me if the night she pinched his wallet, she was supposed to kill him. Maybe she had second thoughts or failed."

Kandar raised his hand like a shy school kid.

"What is it, Kandar?" Elias asked.

"Detective Johnson from Fayetteville called to tell Tim and Miguel that Jones volunteered to take a polygraph after you left. He passed," Kandar said, sinking into his chair. "I recorded his call, and he's emailing the results. I just don't have them yet."

Tim offered him a high-five because he was grateful and to bolster Kandar's confidence.

"Oh, crap. We better call Johnson and tell him to get the Jones's in protective custody. They no longer have the ID. What if they kidnap the man? Or his parents? They may not give up on getting that money," Tim said.

"Kandar, call Johnson. Do it now," Elias said recognizing the urgency.

"Alright, what would you need from us, Tim, if you were still a prosecutor?" Elias asked.

Tim sat silently as he carefully read the evidence board and his notes. "I'd want stronger proof of the connection or affair between Marlow and Carlton Waterford. Can we get a warrant to tap their phones?"

Elias nodded, "Yes."

"I'd want DNA from both. I submitted a sample from Marlow's Aunt Arlina for mitochondrial this afternoon. But we should get a sample directly from her," Tim reported.

"Waterford's attorney says he won't voluntarily give DNA. We need a warrant," Elias said, rubbing his brow.

"Or a discarded item, cigarette butt, bar glass, fork, something like that. Of course, confessions would be nice," Tim lifted both eyebrows and smiled. Everyone agreed with nods.

"We can pick up Marlow for the theft of Jones's wallet. We have her on video," Roxie supplemented.

"Melissa, didn't you say we'd have printouts of emails and text messages by tomorrow?" Tim asked.

"That's what her provider promised," Melissa said.

"I want everything in hand before we pick up Waterford and Marlow. I want to refute every excuse they give with evidence. Box them into a confession. We should maintain surveillance until we have what we need," Tim said. "If they're in it together, they are in a tight spot. Now, they can't get the insurance money easily, and once they figure we're on to them, it's only a matter of time. They will run."

"Do you think Carlton Waterford is the mastermind?" Elias asked. Tim could see his boss was full of doubt. "He's a fitness coach and wouldn't have expertise in the Law. But he needed the Judge, and she was divorcing him."

"But Marlow—working with the Judge and in the courts might assume she does," Miguel said. "I pulled her college transcripts. She took business and computer program proficiency classes, no law."

Tim smiled. Miguel thought to do things no one else did. He admired his mind.

"Good job. This is really shaping up." Elias dipped his head and bit the bottom lip of his smile. "We'll keep both Waterford and Marlow under surveillance for a few more days until we have what we need. DC Metro is taking the overnight shift. I'll get our warrants started. Melissa, you can help me." Elias stood, ending the meeting. "The rest of you, go home, get a good night's sleep, and we'll start fresh at 7:00 AM tomorrow."

Elias's eyes brightened. Tim imagined he was looking forward to handing the killers over to the President, wrapped up with a pretty bow and in record time. Tim would to have to stick a pin in that bubble. After the room had cleared, except for Elias, Miguel and himself, Tim approached Elias.

"One more thing, though," Tim started.

Elias grimaced and tipped his head in Tim's direction. "What one more thing?"

"David Berkstad told me he received a call by an unknown person, offering a bribe if he'd slow-walk this case." Tim took a breath through his clenched teeth.

"What? When did he tell you this?" Elias asked. Miguel stared at Tim with rapt attention.

"This morning. I waited to run it by you, alone. In case you thought it was...."

"Bullshit?" Miguel interrupted, narrowing his eyes. "Wait a minute, that's why he had us followed. He wanted us to believe it was the guy offering the bribe."

"What do you mean someone followed you?" Elias was alarmed.

"We finished our interview with Arlina and were on our way to speak with Jaydon Jones's adoptive parents when we noticed the tail," Tim said.

"I take you lost them?" Elias asked.

"Yes. But not exactly in the way you might imagine." Tim cringed.

"How?" It was a question but alarm flashed from Elias's eyes.

"Lieutenant Broady, Army CID was driving. He *immobilized* them." Miguel said, with a tight smile on his lips as if he was trying not to.

"Exactly how did he do that?"

Tim swallowed. "A PIT maneuver. They lost control of their vehicle and ended up on their side in a ditch. We pulled two agents out of the car, found out who they were, cuffed them, and left them by the side of the road."

"And who were they?" Elias's voice raised an octave, not angry, but very curious.

"Counterintelligence Agents SA Roland Grimes and SA Maggie White," Miguel said. "They were pretty shocked when they learned we were FBI, too."

"I can't put this off any longer. I'm going to have to go to the Director." Elias's lips tightened.

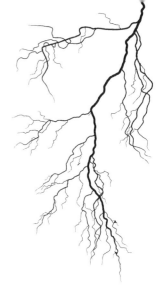

CHAPTER FORTY-TWO

TIM WALKED DOWN the mezzanine stairs from Elias's office to the main floor. His desk was next to the window with a view of the small park-like arbor outside. An afternoon breeze fluttered through the red, white, and blue petunias in the big terracotta pots. The two plain concrete benches in the shade of a huge maple tree looked inviting. He picked up his laptop and strolled to the glass door. He decided to give Berkstad until 5:00—a half hour from now to show up, discuss, and hopefully resolve his obsessive jealousy.

The bench wasn't nearly as comfortable as it had looked. Instead of quiet, the rapid-fire rounds from the nearby gun range interrupted the singing birds and rustling leaves. Occasionally, Tim caught the scent of burnt gunpowder wafting in the air. He opened his computer and queued his email.

"There you are," Miguel said and approached. "Want to get a beer?"

"Sure," Tim answered. He'd put it out of his mind all day, but he'd have to talk to him about Rachel and the boy some time. A little liquid courage wouldn't hurt, but he needed to keep his wits and say just enough not to betray Dani's trust. It was Miguel and Rachel's problem, and he had his own.

"What's this crap about you and Roxie?" Miguel asked.

"Berkstad's obsession. Roxie and I worked on a case in Seattle when I was a prosecutor. He assumes I'm trying to muscle in on his girl." Tim rolled his eyes.

"Has he seen your wife? I mean, Roxie's cute and all, but Dani...."

"He met Dani."

"Did you and Roxie even go out?"

Tim laughed. "No. I'm not that stupid. That's how you wreck your career—screw around with a co-worker. Goddard would've fired me in a heartbeat if he thought I hit on a task force member. I needed my job."

"Yeah. A woman scorned can be scary stuff," Miguel said, almost as if he had experience. Tim was intrigued but decided not to ask. "I don't date women I work with."

"I think that's a good strategy. Can you imagine battling at home and work?" Tim said, shaking his head.

"Especially this job." Miguel guffawed. "She gets mad at you, and in a gunfight with bad guys—it's, oops, friendly fire."

"Or she says she has your six and lets the bad guys shoot you," Tim chuckled.

"What are you guys laughing about?" Roxie came through the glass doors.

"Women," Miguel grinned.

"Want to go for a drink?" Roxie asked.

"Naw, I better not. I need to do my laundry, and Tim has to get home to his family," Miguel said, pretending seriousness.

Roxie studied him briefly, then seemed to take him at his word. "I'm worried about David. You shouldn't have left him."

"What's he doing hanging around us? Doesn't he have a department to run?" Miguel complained.

Tim agreed. But he knew exactly why—jealousy. He needed to confront it. "Did you tell Berkstad we hooked up in Seattle?"

Roxie stopped in her tracks and stared. Miguel lifted both eyebrows. "No," she said, but she wouldn't meet Tim's gaze.

He groaned. "Why would you do that?"

She pushed her lips out in a pout and looked at her fingernails. "When I first heard you were joining our team, he heard me talking to Melissa.

She asked about you. I said you were nice looking. Not exactly in those words, but we were joking around. He assumed the rest," she explained.

"And you let him?" Tim squinted at her and sighed.

"No. I told him we didn't date, wouldn't, and to get over it. But he's so…so…."

"Dangerously obsessed?" Tim asked, tipping his head to the side.

"Okay. I couldn't have put it better. I don't know what to do." Roxie looked at Tim, begging him to forgive her. "I'm sorry, Tim. I didn't mean for this to happen."

"I know," Tim answered softly. "We have very little control over other people. Just be careful."

"Roxie, you need to fix this. We are licensed to carry firearms. This jealousy crap could go very wrong," Miguel warned.

"You think I don't know that? Don't tell Elias, please," she implored.

"Berkstad will probably hitch a ride out of Pope on the 5:45 flight," Tim said. "Call him." Roxie nodded and reached into her jacket pocket for her phone.

"Tim, let's get going," Miguel said.

Tim closed his laptop and stood. He'd waited long enough for Berkstad to show up. He would've liked to clear the air once and for all. But he had other priorities. He needed to tell Miguel about Rachel, and he wanted to go home to Dani and the girls.

"Where are you going?" Roxie put her phone face down against her thigh. "I'll meet you there."

"Let's go to Red's place. It's a dive and never has many customers. And it's halfway between Miguel's place and mine," Tim said.

"Oh, ick. That place is filthy and it's far from my way home." Roxie complained.

"No one said you had to join us," Miguel replied.

"I'll wait here for David. I'll call if I'm going to stop by," she said.

"Good plan. We can hash over the case, and no one will hear," Miguel added.

~

Red's Place was a dive bar. The smell of stale spilled beer, grease, and dust hit Tim as he opened the door. Tim had learned about the saloon from Elias. He used this place to meet with informants from time to time. On weekend nights, the now-empty stage was populated with aspiring musicians singing and playing to dancers on the packed wood-parquet dance floor. But its dark corners were a perfect place to share secrets.

At the bar, an old, gray-bearded man, still wearing a crumpled felt hat, slumped over a shot glass. Besides Tim and Miguel, he was the only other patron. He gave them an uninterested glance as they passed by.

"Over here," Miguel said, sliding into a chair at a table in the corner next to the stage. Tim took the chair across from him. The bartender slowly sauntered over as if it annoyed him that they'd decided to patronize the place. They ordered whiskey and some greasy bar snacks.

"So, you think Waterford murdered his wife?" Miguel asked, not as a real question but as an odd conversational icebreaker.

"I do. I figure he met the killers in the parking lot, and when they drove away with the Judge, he staged her car and called 9-1-1 to report her missing," Tim said. "I think she came there to ask for a divorce, expecting it to be a safe public place."

"I wish there was video of the parking lot," Miguel said.

They rehashed several other aspects of the case, but no matter how much they talked about it, the case wouldn't move forward until they had phone records and DNA.

Their second shot of whiskey arrived, and Tim remembered after he took a sip, he hadn't eaten all day. The alcohol eased away the tension but also his inhibitions. Miguel ordered another round.

"Whoa. Slow down on the whiskey. We won't be able to drive," Tim laughed.

"Call Mitch to come get us."

Tim grinned. "I don't think Dani would appreciate me taking advantage of her pilot. Listen, I need to talk to you."

"Yeah, okay. What's up?" Miguel asked, retrieving the next shots one at a time from the bartender's tray and setting them down on the table.

Tim needed to proceed cautiously. He didn't want to betray Dani but didn't want to set his partner up for the hurt locker.

"Remember at Christmas you told me about your history with the St. Clair family?"

Miguel tipped his head slightly to the side. "Yeah."

"So, are you in a serious relationship with anyone right now?"

"Serious? No. I date a couple of women. They start to get too cozy, and I run for the hills. Roxie says I'm a misogynist." Miguel laughed.

Tim understood completely. It was his life before Dani.

"I'm just stuck." Miguel smiled. "I can't find what I'm looking for—I don't know what I'm looking for in the first place."

"Do you think you want a family?"

"And be like you?" Miguel laughed. "Yeah. I was raised to be all about family. I think about what it would be like sometimes. You aren't trying to fix me up, are you?"

"Maybe," Tim said with a grin. At Christmas, Miguel had bared his soul about Rachel. If he agreed to meet her, there could be magic again. But she could also crush his heart like a vice. He weighed it in his mind before speaking.

"Rachel and her son are here, visiting Dani. She wants to see you," Tim said. Miguel stared at him over the rim of his shot glass before slamming the contents. He set his glass on the table with deliberation as if hesitant to believe this news. Tim couldn't read him. Was he happy? Sad? Confused? Rachel had refused to see him for years.

"Now? After all this time, she wants to see me?"

"Think about it and come to dinner tomorrow night." Tim set his second and third shots of whiskey aside. He needed to be clear-headed. "She's getting a divorce."

Miguel laughed. "So, what am I? The consolation prize? Marriage doesn't work out—run back to good old Miguel? Fuck that."

"That's not exactly what happened," Tim said, reaching for a shot glass. He ran his fingers down the side of the glass but didn't drink it.

"What is?" Miguel asked, leaning forward across the table. "All I know is that I was off fighting a war, and she moved on. She didn't even answer my letters. I found out she married Rob Highland when I came home for a short leave over Easter. Her father wouldn't let me see her."

"As a dad, I wouldn't either. I'd be furious. She was only sixteen and pregnant," Tim said. As the words spilled out, Miguel's mouth dropped open in shock.

"I always hated Rob Highland —-sneaky bastard."

"Ahhh, I wouldn't blame him just yet." By the look on Miguel's face, Tim realized he'd just nuked his partner—not to mention his promise to Dani to let Rachel and Miguel work out their problem without any interference. "You argued with Simon St. Clair about enlisting. You joined anyway against everyone's advice—even your father's. Four months after you'd gone, St. Clair realized he had a problem to fix. He didn't want his daughter to be a young widow, raising a kid without a father. That's when he put a stop to you seeing each other. Dani says her dad paid Highland to marry Rachel."

"Paid him? No way. Rob was always after her. But it was my duty to join. To give back to the country that rescued my family. Do you think the kid is mine?" Miguel's breathing rate sped up.

"Only you know the answer to that. Is it possible?"

Miguel shrugged and stared into his bar glass. To Tim, it looked like a *yes-it's-possible.*

"I don't know what Rob looks like. I've never met him, but the boy looks a whole lot like you," Tim said, offering sympathy with a slight tip to his head.

"How long have you known?" Miguel's eyebrows lowered with suspicion.

"Since this morning. I waited to tell you. Broady and Berkstad were with us and didn't need to know."

"I have a kid?" Miguel's face broke open with a wistful smile. "Me? A kid?"

"Hold on. Maybe." Tim held up his palm, trying to slow down the assumptions. "A son. Fifteen. His name is Mike."

"Rachel named him after me? Really?" Both of Miguel's eyes widened with incredulity.

"Possibly. Dani said Rachel was very much in love with you. Teenage kids, first love. Powerful stuff."

"She named him for me? That's got to mean something. Can we get his DNA?" Miguel asked.

Tim stopped short for a moment and laughed. "Now, that's a typical reaction for an investigator. Of course," he smiled.

"I don't want to step in where I shouldn't," Miguel explained.

Tim could see Miguel's chest swelling with hope. Miguel knew he wanted Rachel. Admitting it after being rejected took a kind of bravery Tim clearly understood. Rachel would pick up his heart with care or stomp it into the dirt. Taking a chance when she might do the latter would be a hard choice.

"Just meet her and see where it goes from there. It's been a lot of years."

"What does she look like?" Miguel stared straight in his eyes.

"Very pretty. A lot like Dani, only with blonde hair."

"If it's my son, I want to see him. I deserve to see him. I should pay support," Miguel became contemplative, looking out to the empty dance floor as if imagining another world. If this were Tim's life, thoughts of how it would be to have a son played in his mind like a movie. He loved his daughters; they were jewels in his life. Having a son would add more treasure.

"Don't worry about that right now. I don't think she needs the money. Decide if you want to see her and let it go how it goes."

"Do you think I could walk away from my own kid?" Miguel asked.

Tim shook his head. "No." He didn't think that and expected Miguel's reaction to be what it was. Tim wouldn't be able to walk away easily, either.

"I've decided. Let's go to your place now," Miguel said. "I don't want to give her a chance to change her mind."

"Okay. Good point. I'll call Dani," Tim said.

~

Tim took the longer scenic route to the farm. Dani had asked for time so Rachel could doll herself up for Miguel's visit. Tim decided on the drive to ensure Miguel was sober when they arrived. Miguel watched the countryside pass by, sighing quietly from time to time. Tim could imagine all the thoughts racing around in his partner's head. Would she tell him why she wouldn't see him? Does she still have feelings for him? Would she still find him desirable? When he turned into the long driveway, he looked at Miguel.

"Are you ready?" Tim waited until he received his partner's nod. He pressed numbers into the security box, and the ornate wrought iron gates swung wide. Tim drove the car through, braking until the gates shut behind him.

With the potential that Berkstad and his rogue agents lurked around unseen, he needed to be careful. Berkstad pulled a *no-show* for their talk with Roxie. Berkstad wouldn't get over his jealousy until he faced it head-on. Tim wanted the mess cleaned up and out of the way.

Unsure of how Miguel's meeting with Rachel would go, anxiety rumbled around in Tim's stomach. He wanted happily ever after for his friends but knew life didn't always turn out that way.

As they rounded the last curve in the driveway, the pale, cream-colored stone house came into view. The late summer sun hung low in the sky, and a soft pink haze barely tinted the horizon, announcing the coming sunset. Below him, horses bunched at the pasture gates, waiting to be brought inside the barn for the night.

Looking forward to seeing Dani and the girls, Tim felt his whole body relax. He was home, and the farm was a beautiful place—his safe space.

Tim pulled forward into the breezeway between the carriage house and the main structure.

"Here goes nothing," Miguel said, reaching around to grab the go-bag he'd retrieved from his car. They'd left it in Red's Place's parking lot and would retrieve it sometime tomorrow. "You're sure you want to put me up overnight? You're sure you have room?"

"We have an extra eight bedrooms—I think there's room," Tim laughed.

"Do I look okay?" Miguel asked.

"Yeah," he answered. Miguel looked nice in his G-man suit and tie. Tim had always thought Miguel was nice-looking. His black hair was neatly trimmed, and his eyes were like dark chocolate. He was the epitome of tall, dark, and handsome. But Tim had to admit, he didn't really know what was handsome to women. "Rachel will be happy to see you. Don't worry. Just stay loose and go with it." *Was that good advice?* Tim had no idea. "I'll put your things in a room for you. Third door on your right at the top of the stairs."

They walked up the steps to the entry, and Tim opened the door.

Before he could shut it, Lettie and Chloe raced down the hallway and greeted him with leg hugs. He picked them up, one at a time, pointing to his cheek for a kiss.

"Mom said maybe before dinner, we can ride our horses. Can we? Can we?" Chloe bounced up to her toes in anticipation.

"We'll see. You'll need to change your clothes," Tim announced. "Lettie and Chloe, this is my friend, Miguel." Both girls were dressed in gowns copied from their favorite characters in princess movies. Lettie wore pink and Chloe blue. Dani spoiled the girls, but Tim didn't mind.

"Hello, Sir Miguel. My name is Princess Chloe, and this is my sister Princess Lettie. How do you do?" She curtsied.

Tim had to cover his mouth to keep from laughing out loud at her precociousness. Miguel played along and executed a sweeping bow.

"Your majesties," he said.

"Sir Miguel, will you be staying for dinner?" Chloe asked.

"With your permission, your grace," Miguel answered.

"I'll go tell Mom, I mean, the Queen," she answered. Taking her sister's hand, they dashed toward the living room.

"Well, I didn't know I was in royal company," Miguel teased. "I take it you're supposed to be the king in this scenario?"

"Only sometimes and only in this house. Everywhere else, I'm just a royal jackass," Tim laughed. "Thanks for playing along."

"My pleasure. My sister has three daughters. I don't get to see family as much as I'd like to."

"Maybe that will change," Tim said. "Shall we join the ladies?"

Miguel wiped his hand over his lips. "Lead on, your majesty."

Tim shook his head and laughed.

Dani stood when they entered the room. "Miguel, come in. I'm so glad you could join us." She walked over and kissed his cheek and then moved close to Tim, linking her arm through his. Instead, he put his arm over her shoulder and pulled her close to his side.

Rachel reclined on the sofa, resting on her hip with her shapely legs stretched comfortably to the side. She wore white shorts and a blue tank top showing off her newly acquired tan. Tim suspected they'd spent the day by the pool. Like Dani, Rachel was a beautiful woman. That they shared a similar genetic code was obvious.

When she saw Miguel, she sat up, and her mouth opened slightly with a small smile. An awkward blush raced into her cheeks. They had problems they needed to get through, but not once, not even for a second, did she look away from Miguel's face. Completely smitten, like Gatsby seeing Daisy after all those years, Miguel seemed to drink her in. The lost man wandering in the desert had suddenly stumbled on a pristine oasis.

Tim realized Miguel's feelings for Rachel hadn't changed since their teenage affair. If anything, they were more intense, fueled by his fantasies. Rachel wasn't a real woman to him—making heartbreak a very dangerous possibility. Tim was happy and frightened for Miguel all at the same time.

Dani hugged Tim tighter. When he looked at her, tears had welled in her eyes. Clearly, Dani wanted them together.

"Hi, Miguel," Rachel said, softly.

"Rachel. Nice to see you. May I sit?" Miguel asked, swallowing hard. He was ultra polite.

"Please do." She encouraged him by gesturing to the seat cushion beside her.

Before moving forward, Miguel sucked in a breath and slowly blew it out, giving Tim a *wish-me-luck* grin. Tim thought he had the right to confront her, but Miguel chose the better way. He truly loved her. Tim thought.

"I need to get changed. If you don't mind, we'll leave you two to talk for a while," Tim said, taking Dani's hand and leading her away. "We should keep the kids out of here." He pulled the double doors closed behind him.

"I agree," she said, leaning against his shoulder. "I'll tell Brenda the girls can have a riding lesson before dinner. Then I'll come up and help you change into something more comfortable," she teased. The expression on her face held a promise he could never resist.

Tim looked at her and smiled, "I have absolutely no problem with that."

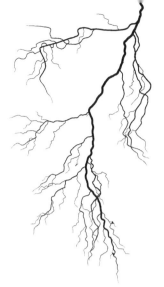

CHAPTER FORTY-THREE

T HE MORNING DRIVE had turned into a congested mess as Tim and Miguel made their way to the Metro DC Police Department. Tim wished he'd taken Elias up on the helicopter he'd offered. But, he liked the liberty of having a car.

Miguel had tuned the radio to a soft rock station and sang along with almost every song.

"I take it all is well with Rachel?" Tim asked, keeping his eyes on the road ahead.

"We're going to talk again soon," Miguel said cheerfully. "I didn't broach the subject of Mike with her. I'm hoping she'll bring him up."

"What did you think of him when you met him at dinner?" Tim flipped his right turn signal and turned into the Metro Police parking lot.

"He's a good kid. Smart and polite," Miguel grinned. "You're going to think I'm awful but. . .." He held up an evidence bag with a fork in it.

Tim laughed as he pulled into a space. "For DNA? At least you'll know."

As they walked toward the building, Tim's phone vibrated in his pocket.

"Kandar, Old Buddy. What have you got for me?" he asked, pressing the speaker button so Miguel could hear.

"The female DNA belongs to Tareeka Marlow. The second male sample is not in CODIS. He's never been arrested for anything," Kandar said.

"Are the call logs in?" Tim asked.

"In your email. Marlow was calling a burner, so I ordered those logs, too. I don't think you'll be surprised. Marlow and Waterford were using burners to talk to each other."

"I guess we have some reading to do," Tim said.

"Some of their messages are juicy. Even incriminating. Elias says we might be able to corroborate the texts with video from some of the places they met for dates."

"Sounds good." Tim smiled. He hoped the overnight crew had kept surveillance tight. The arrests were going to happen sooner than he expected. Then a lot of the real work would begin.

"He's calling Detective Cameron to update him."

"We're here. Call if you find more. I want this ironclad when we interview them," Tim said.

"You've got it." Kandar disengaged.

~

The police receptionist recognized Tim and Miguel and buzzed them through. They walked passed the busy detective's desks to Cameron's office.

"What? Right now?" He shouted into the phone while inviting Tim and Miguel in with a flick of his hand. "We're on it." He stood and grabbed his suit coat and wrestled it on.

"Tareeka Marlow just entered the courthouse and is headed for Judge Waterford's chambers."

"We have her DNA. Let's go get her," Miguel said.

"I can send an arrest team," Cameron offered.

"Not yet. I want her to think we want to talk to her to generate leads. She'll be more cooperative," Tim speculated as they left the station.

"She's after the insurance policy and the birth certificate," Miguel said.

"But we have all that stuff." Cameron picked up his pace.

"Once she discovers the documents are not there, she'll flee. Have the arrest team meet us there and be ready just in case." Tim worried

282

this could all go wrong. They had to get to the Judge's chambers before the sultry Miss Marlow found out the jig was up.

~

Courthouse security hurried them through the metal detectors when they showed their badges. The three men jogged to the Judge's chambers.

The outer door was open about an inch. Marlow was either here or had been here. Tim quietly shouldered it open. The anteroom was dark, but light filtered under the inner chamber's door. He could hear a soft female voice cursing and a rattling noise. Both increased in intensity as frustration and desperation set in. Someone, Miss Marlow perhaps, tried to force open the locked drawer in the Judge's desk.

Tim looked around the anteroom. Marlow's purse sat wide open in full view on her desk. He crept over and looked inside. Without touching it, he noticed the butt of a Glock 44, a small .22 caliber semi-automatic pistol, in the pocket designed for concealed carry.

She probably didn't have another. Tim decided to leave his weapon in its holster.

"One of us should approach her," Cameron said.

"I'll go," Tim volunteered. It was time to make their presence known.

Tim cautiously turned the knob to the Judge's chambers and pressed it open. The beauty that had pinched Jaydon Jones's wallet struggled to open the Judge's locked drawer and didn't notice him. Miguel and Cameron took up positions just outside.

"May I help you with that?" Tim asked. Tareeka stumbled back a step but rapidly regained her composure. She looked him up and down.

"Would you? I'm one of Judge Waterford's clerks. She's been—she died in an accident, and the chief justice wants to divvy up her cases. He asked me to get them for him. The ones in this drawer are the most urgent, and I can't get it open."

Oh, she was good. Quick thinking. And she'd sized Tim up in a heartbeat or thought she had. He evaluated the situation. Marlow's phone sat on top of the desk within reach. The screen showed a call was in progress and on speaker. Tim speculated Carlton Waterford coached her on what to look for. As she continued to tug at the drawer, Tim discreetly pushed the end call button on her phone. Waterford would call back, but she wouldn't be able to answer.

"Are you Tareeka Marlow?" Tim asked.

She hadn't expected him to know her name and studied his face. "I am," she answered. "Who wants to know?"

"Special Agent Tim McAndrews, FBI. We've been looking for you," he smiled and rounded the desk's corner.

"You have?" A startled look filled her eyes. Tim imagined her mind racing, trying to find an escape, trying to make a plan. She gulped. He could see her examining the door, calculating whether she could make it out before he caught her.

He reached under the desk where the secret compartment was located, pressed it upward, and the small brass key dropped into his hand.

He gave it to her.

"Yes. We've interviewed Anton Williams and were hoping you might be able to help us. Maybe you could help us generate a lead. I'd like you to come with me to DC Metro headquarters and answer some questions. Maybe you can help steer us in the right direction," he lied.

"I'd love to help, but I've got to deliver these files right away," she inserted the key in the lock and turned it. Tim knew once she discovered the drawer was empty, she'd panic. Any chance of her getting the insurance money would evaporate and vanish like a morning mist in sunlight.

"I'd really appreciate the help. The chief justice will understand," Tim delivered a smile as phony as a counterfeit twenty. "We can make it quick."

"And then what will we do?" Her voice took on a smokey, sultry quality. Tim had seen this movie before. They had the video stored on the computer at Quantico. While looking for other clues, he'd watched her seduce Jones and steal his wallet at least a dozen times. Tim decided he needed to check his pockets once she was in custody.

"Miss Marlow, I'm going to have to insist," he said with a broad grin.

She shrugged coyly. "Well, if you insist."

She stared at him momentarily, bent forward, and slid open the drawer. She straightened; her face contorted with disbelief.

"Oh, that's right. CSI emptied this drawer as evidence yesterday." He smiled. "Shall we go?"

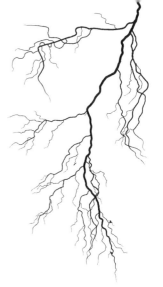

CHAPTER FORTY-FOUR

MISS MARLOW STARTED to round the judge's desk, opposite to how Tim guided her by his gesture. She was going to bolt, and, for some reason, he wanted her to try. He'd already let her find out the insurance policy and Jaydon Lee Jones's pre-adoption birth certificate were in the hands of the police. If she connected the dots, she'd realize that when she lied about the drawer's contents, she'd lied to the FBI. Lying to the FBI is a federal crime and a felony.

Suddenly, but not unexpectedly, she jigged around the desk and sprinted toward the door.

Tim announced it over his microphone attached to his communication gear. "She's running." Smugly standing back, he watched as Miguel and Cameron blocked the doorway.

"Miss Marlow," Miguel said. "You're being detained. Hands behind your back."

"Am I under arrest?" She whirled to face Tim and asked, her voice trembling with panic. Faced with three bigger and stronger men, she decided to comply.

"Why did you run?" Tim asked, shaking his head. They had more than enough probable cause but weren't ready to lay the arrest card on the table. He knew why she ran, but he wanted a confession and wanted her to name the third man.

"Am I under arrest?" She repeated, her gaze darted around the room. She still looked for a way to escape.

"Ma'am, we're just detaining you to ask you some questions," Tim smiled. "You made this harder than it needed to be."

"You can't arrest me. I didn't do anything."

Tim bit the bottom lip of his smile. Frantically, Marlow searched for an out. Running just made it all worse by confirming the investigators' suspicions.

"I certainly can. The minute you decided to run, you changed the game. Right now, I can charge you with resisting."

"Do you have a concealed carry permit for the Glock in your purse?" Miguel asked.

"How did you know…did you search my purse?"

"Didn't have to. I can see the gun's handle from here. Permit or no?" Miguel asked. "How did you get the pistol through the entry screening?"

Tareeka stared at the floor and didn't answer. Tim suspected she'd given one of the male guards the seductive treatment in return for a special favor. It wasn't that hard a leap to that conclusion. Marlow was a beautiful woman.

"I'll take that as a no on the permit," Miguel said. "An illegal firearm and resisting, that's serious stuff."

She looked up, and her countenance changed. In an instant, she closed her eyes in a long, slow blink and parted her full, red-painted lips in a sensuous smile. "Don't handcuff me. Please."

"You took that option off the table," Tim said. Without a doubt, she'd used her beauty and the unspoken promise of sex many times with great success. Tim chuckled to himself. All her game did for him was make him want to shower and wash away the evil.

Detective Cameron moved in and, taking one hand at a time, put his handcuffs on her wrists. The uniformed arrest team arrived. After the female officer patted Tareeka down, Cameron instructed them to take her to interrogation room two.

~

288

Tim called Elias from Metro Police Headquarters and told him they had Tareeka Marlow in custody. Elias wanted the honor of interviewing her. Judge Waterford was his friend. While waiting for Elias to arrive by helicopter, Tim followed his boss's prescription for a successful interrogation. One of Elias's favorite tactics was letting the suspect's imagination run wild by leaving them alone for an hour or so with the camera rolling.

As Tim watched the video feed, Marlow alternated between sitting at the table with her head resting on her arm and pacing the perimeter of the small room. Tim knew Elias was giving her time to make up lies that the evidence would easily refute. Sometimes a lie was as good as the truth. In court, that lie would further discredit any testimony by the suspect.

Tim's phone vibrated in his pocket. He expected a call from Kandar. The surveillance team following Carlton Waterford obtained a paper coffee cup from the diner near his fitness gym, where he'd stopped for breakfast. The cup was found in the trash can just outside and would be considered discarded property. Tim answered without looking at the caller I.D.

"McAndrews."

"Hi." It was a child's voice—familiar, but he didn't instantly recognize it. "It's Jamie. Do you remember me?"

"Jamie. Of course, I remember you," Tim said. He motioned, catching Miguel's attention. He held the phone against his hip and said to Miguel. "Get the agents watching over the Randall's at the safe house on the phone. Now." Tim knew his voice was full of panic. He scrubbed a hand over his hair, gathering his composure. He didn't want Jamie to be frightened.

"Where are you? You're not supposed to call out from the safe house. Is everything okay?"

"I'm just bored. I climbed out of the bathroom window," Jamie laughed.

"Where are you?" Tim asked again, forcing calm into his voice. His heart pounded, and Berkstad's bribe offer raced to the top of his consciousness. If it were true—what if they knew about Jamie? The boy was in danger.

"I'm at the pay phone at Quick Cart. I wanted some chips and candy. And I...I wanted to talk to you," he said.

"Jamie, I'm sending your safety team to get you. Don't move. Don't go anywhere," Tim said. "Can you see a street sign?"

"I can."

"What's the name of the street?" Tim asked. A quick glance informed him that Miguel was on the phone with the security team.

"Margnolia—no Magnolia," Jamie said. There was a pause. "Are you mad at me?"

"No. Jamie. No. I'm not mad at you. But you must return to the safe house with Agent Brady and Agent Cignoli. Put one of them on the phone when they get there. Don't go anywhere, and don't talk to anyone else."

"But they're no fun, and I was worried that you forgot me," Jamie said.

"I haven't forgotten you. I don't forget my friends," Tim said. He scrambled to the nearest detective's desk, rummaged through the top drawer, took out a yellow legal pad and a Sharpie, wrote QUICK CART MAGNOLIA ST in big letters, and held it up to Miguel. Tim hoped the store was close to the safe house. He had no idea where they were and needed to keep it that way.

"My Dad says I'll never get to see you again. He says you're too busy to talk to dumb old kids like me." Jamie's voice was full of hurt. Tim disliked Jamie's dad more than when he first met him.

"He's wrong, Jamie. As soon as my case is over, we'll get together. I promise," Tim reassured him. In the background, he could hear tires crunching on gravel, and car doors slam.

"Here, it's Agent Cignoli," Jamie said. Tim imagined him holding the phone's receiver out to the agent.

"Tim? The kid said he had to go to the bathroom. Little brat climbed out the window. He'd been complaining about needing to call his friend. That's you, I guess."

"Well, yeah. He takes matters into his own hands. That's why Jamie's in this mess in the first place," Tim laughed. "Did he hear you call him a brat?"

"No, Brady took him in the Quick Cart for some candy. Gees, I hate babysitting details," Cignoli whined.

"I wanted to make sure you found him and he's safe," Tim said.

"You tell him not to run away again."

"Put him on the phone." There was silence for at least thirty seconds.

"Hey, kid. Your friend wants to talk to you."

No wonder Jamie didn't like these guys. They didn't treat him with any respect. He might be a kid, but Jamie was human. And as for babysitting details—it was part of the job.

"Hello?" Jamie's voice held a dejected tone.

"Jamie, I don't want you to sneak away from the safe house. Do you understand me?" Tim asked.

"Are you mad at me?"

"No. I need you safe. If you want candy or whatever, just ask. And no sneaking out, no matter how bored you are. Promise me."

"I promise," Jamie was reluctant. *Oh, boy. Cignoli and Brady had their hands full.*

"All right. I've got to go back to work. I'll call you when I can," Tim said.

"Don't forget me," Jamie said.

"I won't forget you," Tim answered, disengaged, and sank into the chair in front of the detective's desk. *Never a dull moment in this job.*

When he looked up, Elias and Roxie had entered the detectives' division and were headed his way. Tim flipped the empty pages of the legal pad with his thumb. He was worried for Jamie.

He liked his theory that the husband murdered the Judge. But the thought that someone would pay Berkstad to slow-walk this case still bugged him like a mosquito bite he wasn't allowed to scratch.

"So, you found Miss Marlow," Elias said, grinning with satisfaction.

"And the surveillance team grabbed a coffee cup after Carlton Waterford threw it in the trash outside Mabel's Diner. Kandar put a rush on the DNA with the lab," Tim answered. He tried to focus, but his mind kept cycling back to Jamie and his safety.

Agents Brady and Cignoli were good men. He couldn't blame them for disliking witness protection duty. It was nearly as much fun as an overnight surveillance detail or watching grass grow.

"How long has she been in there?" Elias asked, tipping his head in the direction of Interrogation Room Two.

"About an hour," Tim tried to concentrate but remained distracted.

"Are you okay?" Roxie asked, sitting on the corner of the desk. "You don't look okay."

"Thanks a lot," he laughed, trying to throw off her concern. She narrowed her eyes at him.

"Okay, here's what we're going to do," Elias said. He seemed to ignore Roxie's evaluation of Tim. "I'm going in and going to make nice. I'll ask simple questions. Ask if she feels she's been treated fairly and such."

"You're the good cop," Roxie smiled.

"Tim, you and Roxie are going to be the bad cops," Elias said, handing him a folder. "This has all the pertinent evidence we'll use to extract...I should say coax a confession."

"Should we have Metro pick up Carlton Waterford?" Tim asked.

Elias tented his hands and pressed his lips into a tight line. "Did Kandar give you an ETA on the DNA?"

Tim shook his head. "Probably later today."

"We could play them off each other," Roxie said, shrugging her shoulders.

"Miguel, go with Melissa and pick up Carlton Waterford. Tell him we have a few more questions for him," Elias said. "When I ask you for a cup of coffee, you and Roxie come in. And bring coffee. Are you ready?"

"I'm ready," Tim answered.

Tim and Roxie sat side by side, watching the video feed of Elias's interrogation. Within minutes, Elias had Tareeka Marlow completely relaxed. They laughed together, discussing Miss Marlow's impressions of her former boss. Tim had so much to learn. He would've probably caused her to clam up and run for legal counsel by confronting her right at the start.

Roxie broke his concentration by placing her hand on his forearm. He glanced at her.

"David didn't come home last night, and he isn't picking up when I call him," she said, barely above a whisper. Worry colored her voice, but she didn't look at him. "It's been close to twenty-four hours. He's never left me this long without communicating."

Berkstad had probably gone home to his wife and kids. Tim decided against saying that out loud. "And?"

"You have to help me, Tim. I have a bad feeling about it," she answered. The urgency in her tone concerned him. He'd learned not to dismiss a woman's intuition. He tried his hardest not to care; Berkstad was a jerk. But he cared about Roxie, just as he cared for his other team members.

"Did you ask Kandar to geolocate his phone?" Tim asked. It was an extreme measure, but Tim thought it might be good for her to find out her prince charming was really a creep. He suspected his phone would ping off the cell tower closest to the home he shared with his wife and kids. As harsh as it was, Roxie needed to be hit with a bucket of ice water to help her get her head screwed back on straight. She deserved better than Berkstad. "Go do it. I'll cover with Elias."

Roxie stood, bent forward, and kissed his cheek. He flinched away from her and scowled.

"Mr. McAndrews?" Tim turned at the sound of his name. "You have a call from the Trask County Sheriff's Office. Line three," a detective from the main floor said as she stood in the viewing room doorway.

What now? Tim wondered. He punched the button for line three. "McAndrews," he answered.

"Tim, it's Shannon. Shannon Cleary."

"I know. I recognize your voice. What's up?"

"Listen. Remember those posters you had us put along Route 45 in the gas stations and truck stops?" Deputy Cleary asked.

"Yeah."

"A trucker just came forward. He picked up a hitchhiker on Saturday night. He picked *her* up after he passed through Crystal Falls City before the flood and close to the campground. He didn't think anything of it until he saw one of our posters at the Mile Two Hundred Truck Stop," Cleary said.

"Really?" Tim quickly thumbed through the evidence folder and found a copy of the poster with the sketch artist's rendition of Jamie's smaller man. Underneath the picture, it read, 'Have you seen this man? Call an anonymous tip to Crime Stoppers.' Immediately, he looked at the live feed from the interrogation room. Wow! How had he missed that? He couldn't stop the smile swelling from his insides. The picture looked a whole heck of a lot like Tareeka Marlow without all her glamour makeup.

"Well, well," he said. "Jamie's small man is a woman." He imagined Marlow in camouflage clothes and a blue baseball cap.

"Yep," Cleary said. "He confirmed that she's the woman he picked up when I showed him her driver's license picture."

"Detective Cleary, you are a rockstar," he said. "Thank you." He disengaged and leaned back in his chair. They had her. The stack of evidence was overwhelming. The cigarette butt with her lipstick and DNA in the stolen Jeep's ashtray, her text messages proving the affair with Carlton Waterford, the videotapes of her stealing Jones's wallet, her attempt to gather enough information to cash in the insurance policy, and now the witness placing her near the scene of the body dump gave Tim more than enough probable cause to search her apartment. Since she was in custody, he decided to get a warrant. He just hoped the Assistant District Attorney and a judge would feel the same way.

Tim stood and knocked on the interrogation room door. Elias answered.

"May I speak with you for a minute?" Tim asked.

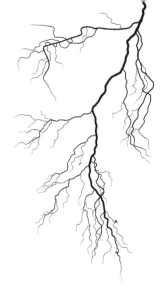

CHAPTER FORTY-FIVE

FTER ELIAS HEARD the new evidence, he made a few phone calls, first to the district attorney handling the case and then to Judge Martin Redfield for search warrants for both Marlow's and Waterford's residences.

A little disappointed he wouldn't get to play 'bad cop' for the second half of Marlow's interrogation, Tim was very eager to see what they would find at her apartment.

Roxie would help Elias finish the interrogation and hopefully obtain a confession. Carlton Waterford would be a harder nut to crack. So far, there existed no direct evidence of his involvement. In his gut, Tim knew he had his wife murdered. But gut feelings weren't evidence. Sure, the man was flat broke, facing destitution from a divorce and a philanderer. That didn't make him a killer. Tomorrow, when the DNA results from the discarded coffee cup were in, if the DNA matched the third cigarette butt in the Jeep's ashtray, Carlton Waterford would have some explaining to do.

They'd already confirmed the Jeep's owner did not know any of the participants who'd stolen his vehicle. Waterford's cigarette butt didn't walk there and jump into the ashtray. Tim suspected at some point, after the theft and before the Judge's body was dumped, Carlton Waterford sat in that Jeep, smoking a cigarette.

Detective Cameron pulled his cruiser to the curb in front of Marlow's apartment building. The Pinecrest Terraces appeared to be a very upscale apartment complex. Much too pricey for a woman making an entry-level law clerk's salary.

"Why do I get the impression someone is paying Marlow's rent?" Tim asked as he looked over at Cameron and lifted an eyebrow.

"Maybe this is why Carlton Waterford is broke," Cameron laughed.

"Ya think?" Tim chuckled, unbuckling his seatbelt. "It wasn't on his bank statement, though. He probably paid in cash."

A black and white parked behind them. The two patrolmen inside would serve as backup. The apartment's manager met Tim and the detective inside the lobby door.

"You must be Detective Cameron?" The manager approached them with an outstretched hand.

"Yep. This is Special Agent McAndrews, FBI and Patrol Officers Bengetti and Somers." Cameron reached inside his suitcoat and produced the search warrant.

Tareeka Marlow's beautifully decorated apartment confirmed that her rent was being supplemented at the very least. It fit what Tim had learned about Carlton Waterford's narcissistic self-assessment. As described by Anton Williams, Judge Waterford's senior clerk, Carlton fancied himself a *gangsta*, dressing the part in fancy suits and expensive shoes—all at the Judge's expense. He was nothing more than a "broke-ass pretender."

Tim wondered what Marlow, the gold-digger, would do when she found out. He bet she'd turn on Waterford faster than an ice skater in a sit spin.

"I'll start in the second bedroom. You take the master," Cameron said. And they parted ways.

Marlow's room looked like the bed chamber of a queen. Gossamer netting hung from the canopy's structure and was tied at each of the bed's corner posts with white satin ribbons. The bed was covered with a white satin quilt with elegant squares of hand-crocheted lace. *Expensive.* Tim thought. He put on a pair of Nitrile gloves.

He started searching the bedside table on the right side of the bed. The alarm clock and a cell phone stand were placed on top, and he surmised it logical that she'd keep anything important in the drawers underneath. He found an address book inside the top drawer. What he found intrigued him. Several of the president's top cabinet members and phone numbers were listed inside, opening a whole new can of worms. Was Marlow one of D.C.'s notorious call girls? Or maybe a blackmailer? He slipped the book into an evidence bag.

In the bottom drawer, he found four different colored burner phones. He laughed to himself. Carlton Waterford might be surprised to learn that he wasn't the only lover in Miss Marlow's stable.

A search of the second bedside table and dresser yielded nothing of interest. He opened the door to the walk-in closet. Marlow's clothes hung on both sides of an aisleway neatly arranged by color. One side held dresses and gowns, the other an array of more casual garments. A white wicker clothes hamper stood out at the very back against the wall as the only messy element in her closet. A camouflage jacket spilled out from under the top. And there on a shelf, just above the hamper, sat a blue baseball cap, matching Jamie's description of the clothes worn by the second man.

Tim felt his iPhone vibrate in his pocket.

"McAndrews," he answered.

"Tim, it's Kandar. DNA is back early. They gave us priority. It matches the cigarette butt from the Jeep. It's Carlton Waterford's with a one in a trillion certainty. I thought you'd want to know," he said.

"Yes. Great. Thanks, buddy," Tim said and disengaged.

~

Tim and Detective Cameron from the DC Metro Police arrived at the large red brick home where Judge Waterford used to live. Built in the antebellum style, the structure was embellished by a traditional porch with white columns. Set back from the road, the house was surrounded by beautifully manicured lawns, trimmed hedges, and weed-free flower beds.

Simultaneously with this raid, another team served a search warrant on Carlton Waterford's Fitness Gym. Tim suspected Waterford underestimated the police, not to mention President Tomlinson's regard for the Judge.

They walked up the cobblestone path to the home's front door and knocked. A young woman dressed in a taupe uniform with a lace-trimmed white apron answered. The apron had *Quality Clean Maids* embroidered on the front, and she held a stereotypical faux feather duster.

"Good morning, Ma'am. Detective Cameron and Special Agent McAndrews from the FBI. We're here to search the premises," he announced.

Her eyes widened, but after the surprise subsided, she stepped aside. She refused to take the warrant, so Cameron casually dropped it on a living room coffee table. He motioned the CSI team to follow.

Inside, the house was neat, clean, and organized. The furnishings were comfortable, revealing the Judge's easy-going style. Still, nothing seemed out of place. Tim stood for a moment, trying to imagine her daily routine.

CSI detectives would box up Waterford's computer, banking records and correspondence. Tim sat down behind the desk in the home office. He opened the left-hand drawer, searched through the file folders, and found *another* insurance policy that originated only a month ago. *Two million wasn't enough?* He thought.

He thumbed through the document, and realized the bottom-line signature didn't match others Tim had seen on documents in the Judge's chambers. He shuffled through the drawer, found an envelope with some canceled checks, and took out one with the Judge's signature. The insurance policy's signature line contained a scrawl that was not Judge Waterford's. To Tim, this indicated that the policy was a fraud and added fuel to the theory that her murder was premeditated. Her husband planned to kill her for at least a month before he did—maybe longer. He would forward these papers to an FBI document examiner for comparison.

They found Waterford's burner phone in a bedside nightstand. He'd only called and received calls from one number. That would be easy to trace. Tim bet they'd find that number belonged to Tareeka Marlow.

Kandar would head up the search on the computer.

"Well, that's it then. We got 'em," Cameron said, the left side of his mouth curled in more of a snarl than a smile. "They would've gotten away with it if Jamie Randall hadn't seen them dump the body. You're the profiler, how do you think this all went down?" Cameron asked.

Tim stared at the detective for a moment and then said, "Waterford was in financial trouble and having an extramarital affair. He wanted to get rid of his wife, but he completely depended on her. She'd kept his business afloat for years. He couldn't survive if he just asked for a divorce. I bet he knew Marlow would boot him if she found out he wasn't the breadwinner he pretended to be," Tim sighed. There was some satisfaction that they'd caught the Judge's killers, but Tim couldn't shake the dark sense of sadness. "I think Calton found out the Judge planned to divorce him. Maybe Judge Waterford confided in Marlow, and she warned him. That spurred him to try to find out if there was an insurance policy. When looking for that, Marlow stumbles on Jaydon Jones, and from the pictures in the Judges drawer, realizes good old cousin Wilford, looks near enough to Jaydon they might be able to fool the insurance company.

"When we trace the geotracking on her burner phone, I bet we'll find she checked out Jones several times," Tim continued.

"They put their plan in motion. She heads for Fort Bragg and steals Jones's wallet," Cameron added.

"The next day, Marlow, Carlton, and Kincaid swipe the Jeep from Samuel Greer's driveway, kidnap, and murder the Judge. Carlton helps them but stays behind at the restaurant parking lot to stage her car and play the grieving husband. He deserves an award for acting like he wanted to locate his missing wife," Tim shook his head disgusted. "And like you said, if it hadn't been for Jamie collecting crawdads, they might've had time to clean it all up and get away with it."

"Naw. We would've found out. It just would've taken longer," Cameron said. Tim joined him in a big smile.

"Well, shall we get back to the station?" Tim asked.

"Yep. I'm anxious to hear them explain this stuff," Cameron laughed.

~

Tim walked through the door to the detective's division at the Metro Police Headquarters with Detective Cameron on his heels. The constant buzz of a busy police station filled his ears.

Tim had taken pictures of everything they'd gathered. He'd emailed Elias and Roxie a copy of the pictures as soon as possible and handed the evidence to the crime lab for processing.

Roxie emerged from the interrogation room, glanced up, recognized Tim, and smiled.

"Thanks for the pictures. I think she's getting ready to break," Roxie said. "She's going to flip on Waterford."

"Without a deal?" Tim asked. He hadn't seen the ADA assigned to the case.

"Elias doesn't think the DA will give her a deal until forced. Surprisingly, she hasn't asked for an attorney," Roxie said. "You'd think she would."

Tim passed her the folder with pictures of Marlow's camo gear he'd taken when CSI pulled it from the clothes hamper in her closet.

"CSI found red spots on the left shoulder of Marlow's camo jacket consistent with high-velocity blood spatter. The presumptive phenol-phthalein test was positive for blood. The lab will do DNA analysis to confirm the blood is Judge Waterford's," Tim said.

"So, you think...." Roxie started.

"We know the Judge fought for her life. The broken fingernails told us that. Now we know Tareeka Marlow sat in the right front seat when the Judge was shot and had turned to watch," Tim reported.

"Do you want to confront her?" Roxie asked.

"No. Go ahead. Get a confession, Roxie. I believe Carlton Waterford is the mastermind. I'd like to have Marlow's confession to that before we tackle his interview."

"You've got it," Roxie said, tapping Tim on the shoulder with the folder. She opened the door to the interview room, briefly held Tim's gaze, and then entered the room, closing the door behind her.

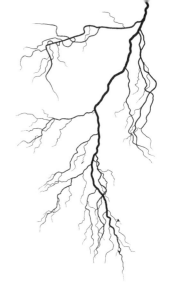

CHAPTER FORTY-SIX

T IM STIRRED AWAKE to the sound of his phone vibrating in its charging station. He reached for it, trying not to disturb Dani, who snuggled against his side, her head resting against his shoulder.

It was 1:00 AM, and the call was from Roxie.

"McAndrews," he answered softly but not quietly enough. Dani turned away from him and burrowed down into the covers.

"Tim, it's Roxie," she started.

"I know." He grabbed the silk robe from the bedpost, slipped from bed, and walked to one of the chairs in front of the fireplace at the far end of the room.

"Marlow finally confessed," she said. "She's named Carlton Waterford as the mastermind."

"You're calling me because—you don't believe her?" Tim asked in a subdued tone. He slid his arms through the sleeves of his robe, tied it, and sank into a chair but stayed on the very edge. He looked back, making sure he hadn't disturbed Dani.

"Tim, she never asked for a lawyer, didn't even protect herself by asking for some consideration in exchange for giving him up," Roxie answered. "That's not reasonable for a woman working in the criminal justice system."

"Maybe she feels guilty," Tim stated. "We have so much evidence against her. Maybe she thought the DA wouldn't negotiate. Did Miguel and Melissa pick up Carlton Waterford?"

"They couldn't find him. He eluded his surveillance team."

"Damn. That's not good."

"Elias called the Marshalls. They'll find him." Roxie's voice was confident. She remained on the line but silent. She had more to say.

"Anything else you want to tell me?" he asked, anticipating her answer, cringing.

"David still hasn't called. The last place his phone pinged was in Fayetteville. Tim, something's happened to him."

He sighed. "Call his wife. If he's not there, call Fayetteville Police, and report him missing. Did you talk to Elias?"

"I did call Fayetteville. No. I didn't tell Elias," she said softly. "Why do you hate David so much?"

"Because he's worse than a pest. He said he had Congressman Patterson under surveillance, and not one of his agents reported that Patterson roofied and raped fifteen-year-old girls. Patterson was sleeping with a Russian spy—they caught that. How'd they missed the little girls?"

"No one is perfect, even *you* make mistakes."

"That's what you're using as an excuse? No one's perfect? Roxie, it's one thing not to recognize a person in disguise and another to ignore child abuse," Tim raised his voice. When he turned to view Dani, he realized Dani was sitting up. He never meant to wake her. He groaned.

"Do you really believe he ignored child abuse?" Roxie asked. "Do you actually believe that?"

Tim didn't readily answer. Yes. He believed it. Was he ready to turn that into a formal accusation? No. He had no concrete proof. Yet.

"Roxie, go home. Get some sleep. I'll see you in the morning. If Berkstad still hasn't contacted you, I'll help you find him," Tim moderated his voice. He waited until she disengaged and then hung up. Berkstad caused him problems in the middle of the night, no less.

"I'm sorry, Baby. I didn't mean to wake you," Tim said to Dani, returning to bed.

"It's okay." She reached for him, and he slipped under the covers. Her skin felt deliciously warm. "Who called? Not Elias, I hope." She cuddled against him.

"Roxie. To tell me our suspect confessed. Why didn't you want it to be Elias?" Tim asked.

"Because he makes you go to work every time he calls." She kissed his cheek. He turned his head, making her next kiss meet his lips.

He wrapped his arms around her. "We have about five more hours before I go back to work. And if Elias calls, I won't answer."

"Ummm, I like that," she said.

~

At the Metro Police Department, Tim turned to see Miguel walking into the Detectives' Division with Carlton Waterford. He hadn't handcuffed the suspect.

Waterford wore an expensive light grey suit, black shirt, and a pale gray silk tie. His leather shoes matched his tie, as did his fedora. The only dab of color was a single magenta feather reaching upward from the hat band. *Who comes to a police interview dressed like that?* Tim wondered. Clearly, the man was spending the money he anticipated from the insurance policies before he had it.

Tim had been too busy to watch the news. Elias had shut down all information to the usual sources at the president's behest. Maybe Carlton didn't know Wilford Kincaid was dead and that their plan to cash in an insurance windfall died with him.

The transcripts of text messages between Carlton and Tareeka confirmed their affair. And though they talked cautiously about their plans to kill the Judge, it was all there. It perfectly matched the timeline of the murder and neighborhood security videos.

Miguel escorted Carlton Waterford to the interview room. Detective Cameron offered him coffee and, when he accepted, left him in the locked room to wait. Elias was on his way. Tim would volunteer to be 'bad cop' for this interview.

Tim greeted Elias just as he hustled into the video surveillance cubby by the interrogation rooms. He looked through the various camera feeds.

"Is that Carlton Waterford?" Elias directed his question by looking from Detective Cameron's face to Tim's and back again.

Tim grimaced as he nodded.

"He looks like a pimp wanna-be," Elias chuckled. "How long has he been here?"

"About fifteen minutes," Tim answered.

"No attorney?" Elias asked. But the words weren't even a second old when Waterford's attorney strolled in. Elias discreetly frowned at Tim and then made nice to the attorney.

"Morning, Bill," Elias said.

"Morning. Are you charging my client with a crime?" Bill Dooley asked. His face was pinched as if he knew the answer but hoped what he believed wasn't true.

"First-degree murder. Conspiracy to commit first-degree murder for starters," Elias said with a condescending smile.

"He won't be answering any questions," Dooley said.

Elias shrugged. "That's his right." Elias reached into his suit coat's inside pocket and retrieved a piece of paper folded into three sections. "This is a warrant allowing us to collect Carlton Waterford's DNA." He handed over the document.

Tim thought Waterford's attorney's countenance fell noticeably. He almost disappeared into his suit jacket. He couldn't refuse to turn it over this time, and he knew they wouldn't be asking if they didn't know the answer already.

"We'll give you a few minutes to confer with your client," Elias announced.

Dooley pressed his lips together and hardened his jaw. This was not the news he wanted to tell his client. Tim was a little disappointed he wouldn't get to play his part. The attorney went into the room.

"Tim, I need you to do something," Elias said. His brow lowered, and his mouth turned stern at the edges.

"Whatever you need, sir," Tim said.

"First, cut out the 'sir' crap." Elias tipped his head, and a small smile broke through, but it was fleeting. "I need you to take Miguel and Roxie and get back to Quantico. A helicopter will take you to Fayetteville. Trace Berkstad's supposed route and see if you can find him."

Tim tried to mask his displeasure. He wasn't sure it worked.

"He's been missing for twenty-four hours. I called his wife, and he didn't go home last night. He hasn't returned to DC Headquarters, and even the director is worried." Elias placed a hand on Tim's shoulder. "Do this for me?" He asked, but it wasn't really a question.

"Sure," Tim answered.

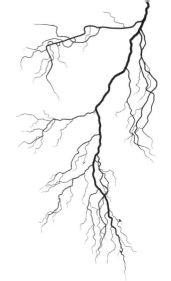

CHAPTER FORTY-SEVEN

ROXIE WAS ANXIOUS the whole drive to Quantico. When Tim looked to the back seat, he noticed her fidgeting with her suit coat's hem and nervously staring out the window. She loved Berkstad. Just because he and Miguel didn't like the guy wasn't reason enough to discourage her feelings. *You love who you love,* Tim thought. If Roxie was that worried about him, Tim would do what he could to help her.

They arrived at the parking lot and headed for their offices in the basement. Tim decided to call Kandar before they committed to a helicopter ride to Fayetteville. He lagged behind and let Miguel and Roxie go before him toward the building.

"Kandar, it's Tim. Can you ping Berkstad's phone again? I just want to be sure...."

"Well, give me a gold star! I've got him. He's twenty-five miles North of here, close to the Bradford on the Potomac," Kandar answered.

"Is that a hotel?" Tim asked.

"Boy, is it. A famous one. That's where Nicholai Solenov, the billion-aire philanthropist, supposedly lives. I understand he has the whole top floor," Kandar answered.

Tim stopped short and traced his thumb along his upper lip. "Can you think of a reason Berkstad might be there?"

"Of course, there is a reason," Kandar said, excitement in his voice. "He's Counter-intel and conspiracy theories contend Solenov is still loyal to Russia—a spy. He supports all kinds of purported activist communist front groups with his billions. He's sowed so much discord and chaos that he's banned from entering several European countries."

"Do you think Berkstad's in danger?"

"I don't know. Elias might."

"Elias is closing out the arrest of Carlton Waterford with DC Metro. He asked me to find Berkstad. I'm almost at the office. Can you gather everything you can find on Solenov for me? Thanks, Buddy," Tim said. He disengaged.

Tim looked across the expanse of the parking lot at the building in front of him. The sky above was rain-washed and crystal blue. The billowing puffs of an early morning thunderstorm receded in the distance.

What ifs began to circle in his mind, like vultures over carrion. In the last few days, Berkstad had mentioned the prospect of Tim joining Counter Intel several times. And he'd mentioned a bribery plot. Tim had wanted no part of either. But what if Berkstad really needed his help and was in danger? Had he let his dislike of the man interfere with his job? He pushed the guilt that tried to swamp him away. He couldn't think about that now. He had to concentrate on how to fix it.

Tim picked up his pace to rejoin his partners, ready to cross through the entry doors. They stopped and turned as if looking for him.

"What happened to you?" Roxie glared at him and pushed her bottom lip out in pretend annoyance.

"Kandar pinged Berkstad's phone for me. He's twenty-five miles north near the Bradford on the Potomac." Intrigued when Miguel and Roxie exchanged glances that screamed like a siren, Tim continued, "What do you know that I should know?"

"Nicolai Solenov," they replied in unison.

"Yeah, the billionaire Russia ex-pat who funds a bunch of activists. I've heard of him, but really—who is Solenov?" Tim asked. Again, the alarmed look passed between Roxie and Miguel.

"Not here," Roxie said, putting out her arms and encouraging him and Miguel back into the parking lot.

Tim faced her when they were far enough away from the building. "Tell me," he insisted.

"I met him once, he tried to get me to join CI. He's just a randy, rich old man. What I'm about to tell you is all based on hearsay. It might not be true," Roxie said, taking in a deep breath as if preparing for a speech. Tim lowered his chin and stared hard into her eyes.

"Rumors are that Solenov immigrated to America—some say escaped to America—from Stalin's Russia in 1946. He was seventeen and brilliant. The conspiracy theory says he made his fortune by manipulating currencies in countries rebuilding from the devastation of World War II. He runs some big Hedge Fund. Many believe he's secretly still loyal to the communist ideals and is really a plant. He used American Capitalism to get rich but hates American Capitalism. He does everything he can to destroy it," Roxie said.

"Remember the Warner Brothers, Loonie Tune Cartoons of Ralph the Wolf and Sam Sheepdog? Where they'd time-clock in, beat the hell out of each other for eight hours and clocked out at the end of the day?" Roxie asked.

"With a 'Good night, Ralph. See you tomorrow, Sam. I loved those cartoons as a kid," Miguel said.

"Friendly adversaries. . . ." Tim's thoughts drifted.

"When the Cold War ended, the then FBI Director Roberts and Solenov agreed to stop spying on each other. David took over Counter Intel ten years ago. He said Solenov changed—he developed a crazy 'god' complex. After all, he is ninety-four.

"Solenov claims he was anointed from birth and chosen to *save* the world. Money does that to some people. Success in one thing deludes them into believing they are brilliant in all things, and they should rule the world," Roxie said, her brow wrinkled with worry.

"David thinks Solenov is insane—being a whacko is one thing, but being nuts and rich doesn't mix well. Solenov started funding organizations that stirred up chaos. He supported and encouraged riots. Now, he's funding the campaigns of anti-law enforcement politicians. David felt he might go further—to murder and genocide. He had Counter-Intel keep a close eye on Solenov."

"Solenov became the epitome of a comic book villain. He even looks the part," Miguel added. "Rumors still swirl that he's bought off some of the supervisors on the seventh floor."

"So, if Solenov found out he's the target of Berkstad's spy program—is Berkstad in danger?" Tim asked.

"Damn," Miguel said. "Berkstad's a shit, but he's one of ours."

"Tim, we have to go save him," Roxie pleaded.

Tim linked his fingers together and rested his hands on his head. What if Berkstad was one of the bought-off supervisors? He decided not to reveal his thoughts to Roxie. What if Solenov was behind the bribery scheme Berkstad told him about?

"We're going to need Elias's input, and we're going to need help," Tim said.

"I can get us in," Roxie said. Her whole body seemed weighted with a burden too heavy to bear.

"How?" Tim asked.

"I met him once. He likes me."

~

Tim finished dressing by slipping the tiny tie-clip camera in place. The device was a digital video and audio recorder and would send the information in real-time to Kandar's computers. He would watch from the hotel room and monitor the feed. Tim wasn't sure the device would get past Solenov's bodyguards, but he needed to try.

Roxie paced back and forth behind him, watching his reflection in the sliding glass door to the balcony outside the hotel room.

"Can we hurry up? You look pretty enough," she complained.

Tim rolled his eyes. "Kandar, do you have sound and video?" The surveillance team occupied a room directly underneath Solenov's penthouse.

"It's good now," Kandar replied. "Remember the code word is 'hot.' If you get into trouble, just say 'hot,' and we're in there in seconds."

"Roxie, we are not authorized to go until everything is set up." Tim watched the horizon on the other side of the steel blue river for the helicopter. A four-man Hostage Rescue Team (HRT) would land on the helipad on the hotel's roof. If he said the code word, they would repel down to the balcony off Solenov's penthouse, break through the glass, and come to the rescue. If Berkstad was a hostage, they would get him out. That was the plan anyway. The best case was to find Berkstad and get him out without incident.

Elias explained that Solenov wouldn't kill Berkstad himself, but he might have someone else do it for him. The director and no one in Berkstad's department could think of a reason Solenov would want him dead. He'd made no ransom demand. Tim felt Roxie knew, but wouldn't say. Every time he asked her a question, she became like a nervous school girl, lying to the principal.

Ramping up Tim's anxiety, Berkstad's phone had stopped pinging his location an hour ago. He didn't tell Roxie. It would only add to her stress. Once again, Tim checked his pistol.

Through the hotel window, he saw a small black speck across the river growing larger. The UH-60 Black Hawk carried the FBI's Hostage Rescue Team (HRT). The pilot would circle and approach the helipad from an angle that the occupants of the penthouse couldn't see. Though the helipad was private to the hotel's permanent guests, Solenov was only one of several others authorized to use it. Any noise would be dismissed, but a shiny, black chopper with an FBI Logo wouldn't be.

"They're on the pad," Kandar reported.

"Let's go, Roxie," Tim said, and she bolted toward the door.

They rode the elevator to the penthouse floor, exchanging glances—Tim trying to get Roxie to talk, Roxie avoiding the obvious. Adrenaline flowed. The doors opened to a lobby elegantly decorated with mahogany wainscoting and crown moldings. A beautiful young woman sat behind an ornate desk with a computer. *The gatekeeper*, Tim assumed.

Roxie approached her, but the young blonde looked past her to Tim. His suit coat was buttoned, so his badge and shoulder holster were covered, but still, the girl studied him with suspicion. Tim knew he had FED written all over him.

"Roxie Stauffer and Tim McAndrews to see Mr. Solenov," Roxie snapped.

The girl cued up her computer calendar, glared at Roxie, and then slowly, deliberately punched in a numeric code that opened the front door to the suite. Tim wondered if that action alerted Solenov's bodyguards. Only one way to find out.

A large man in a dark suit met them just inside the door. He wasn't exactly a butler, but for the moment, he played that role.

"Weapons, please," he said cordially, but menace radiated from his eyes. Roxie readily complied, so Tim cautiously handed over the pistol from his shoulder holster. The pistol at his ankle, he intended to keep. The guard didn't pat them down. He knew they carried back-ups, but he didn't ask for them. Tim reasoned as he studied the man that if he and Roxie were going to die in a gunfight, it would be in Solenov's best interest to be able to claim self-defense. Tim watched as the man slipped the weapons into the top drawer of the mahogany entry table. Tim wanted to know where to find his service pistol if or when that time came.

"Mr. Solenov is in the library," the man said, gesturing with an open palm to his left.

"Thanks, Rodney," Roxie said. It surprised Tim that she knew his name. He narrowed his eyes at her but didn't ask. He sucked a breath through clenched teeth. Trust was necessary in partnerships. Now, he wished Miguel, instead of Roxie, was with him confronting Solenov. He gave Rodney a quick smile and nodded as he passed by.

Roxie pressed open one of the double doors to the library. The room, filled with ambient light from a bank of windows on the west wall, contained hundreds of leather-bound volumes stacked on polished hardwood shelves. They reached up to the thirty-foot ceiling. A small one-person elevator cage with an electric motor allowed a reader to roll to a shelf and grab any book he might want.

Behind a hand-carved antique mahogany desk sat Nicolai Solenov. He looked incredibly old, almost as if someone had animated a long-dead corpse. Tim thought.

"Roxanne, my beautiful FBI agent, what brings you here to see me?" Solenov asked, analyzing and evaluating Tim as he stood before him. "And who is your friend?" His cold glare seemed as if he was envious of his youth. "This isn't the illustrious Special Agent McAndrews David's been bragging to me about, is it?"

Tim felt an icy chill down to his bones. Nickolai Solenov was a sociopath. He oosed charm, but it didn't mask the hate sparking behind his eyes.

"It is, Tim McAndrews, Nickolai Solenov, Nickolai—Tim McAndrews," Roxie announced.

Tim stepped forward and carefully shook the older man's hand. Like a raven's claw, Solenov's skin was cold, rough, and dry, and Tim forced himself not to recoil.

"To what do I owe this pleasure?"

"David is missing. No one's heard from him for two days," Roxie said.

"I'm so sorry, Dear. What can I do to help?" Solenov's eyes darkened like polished onyx in sunlight. He wasn't sorry, and he had no intention of helping. Tim thought.

"Well, Nickolai, we tracked his cell phone, and it led us here. We found his car in the parking lot," Tim challenged and watched a devious smile curve the old man's lips.

Solenov chuckled. He studied Tim's face. "I must admit, I'm very impressed with your young man, Roxanne. My sources tell me you've arrested Tareeka Marlow and Carlton Waterford and charged them with first-degree murder in Judge Waterford's case. That's record time for an arrest, isn't it?"

Roxie whirled to look at Tim, but he didn't react. The flattery was hollow. He knew Solenov shouldn't know that. Elias hadn't released anything to the press. He was under orders to let President Tomlinson do the honors first thing tomorrow morning.

"She is one of mine. Did you know that? Yes, Tareeka is one of my best operators. She does whatever I ask."

Tim forced his breathing to calm, but still could feel his heart pounding in his chest. He remembered the address book from the drawer in her house and the ten members of Congress and three senators listed inside. Tim imagined Tareeka had something on each and every one of them, and they were blackmailed into doing Solenov's bidding. No wonder she didn't try to make a plea deal—she thought she'd be safer in prison. Tim decided to push.

"Did you tell Tareeka to kill Judge Waterford?" Tim asked, his voice a controlled calm.

A slow smile spread across Solenov's face, deepening the wrinkles in the skin at the corners of his eyes.

"Berkstad said you were sharp. But David wasn't able to convince you to join us. What a shame," he said, his voice trailing off as if it was an afterthought.

Was Berkstad dead? The question briefly entered Tim's mind. He shook it off. He couldn't let Roxie know he thought it.

"Did you ask Marlow to kill Judge Waterford?" Tim asked again, with more force this time.

"I asked President Tomlinson to reconsider his choice, but he wouldn't change his mind. Judge Waterford would never bend to our agenda. I had my own candidate for the Appellate Court, and getting rid of her was easy. Carlton needed money and an affair to boost his ego. And you've seen Tareeka. She could turn anyone's head. I suspect—even yours," The old man dropped his head back and laughed. "Yes, I told Tareeka to kill Judge Waterford. I told her exactly how to do it, too."

Tim contained his astonishment. Solenov had just confessed to being a conspirator in the murder. And he had it on tape.

In his peripheral vision, Tim saw Roxie fidgeting, but he couldn't look away from Solenov now. Tim tipped his head slightly in an affirmative gesture.

"Oh. My. God." Roxie said just above a whisper.

"You thought of every detail. I'm impressed. Are you the one who offered Berkstad a bribe to scuttle this investigation?"

Tim was met with a stare that tried to rattle his composure. It worked, but he refused to show it. "You ordered the bugging of my room. You're the one who followed us in Fayetteville...." Tim smiled. "What did you hope to gain from that?"

The older man chuckled. "You're a married man, and blackmail is a priceless tool. I thought if you couldn't resist being alone overnight with the beautiful Roxanne—or, at the very least, Deputy Cleary, I'd own you. I needed to determine if you were prone to the typical young man's weaknesses. I do whatever I have to do to get my way."

Tim wanted to look at Roxie. Was she in on it? He kept his attention on the old man.

"Roxanne didn't know I used her in this way. Forgive me, dear," Solenov said.

Tim knew Solenov wouldn't have told him if he intended to let Roxie and him leave here alive.

"Where's David Berkstad?" Tim asked again.

Tim alerted as Solenov slowly opened the middle desk drawer and set Berkstad's iPhone, badge, Glock, and magazine on the desk's shiny surface. Now, he knew. David was dead. He glanced at Roxie. She hadn't made the connection. Solenov pressed a button mounted on the corner of his desk.

"Is it *hot* in here? I suddenly feel *hot*," Tim said. He grabbed Roxie's arm and pulled her back toward the door, remembering it opened inward. He stepped in front of her. It bought him a few seconds.

Tim's perception of time slowed. The biggest man he'd ever seen, outside of linemen on the football field, burst through the door, leading with a semi-automatic pistol. He turned to face them, pointing the gun barrel at Tim's chest.

In a smooth movement, Tim stepped forward, grabbed the pistol's barrel, ducked out of the line of fire, and twisted downward—hard. The big man yelped in pain, but managed to pull the trigger. Tim felt the heat from the round as it raced from the firing chamber. The sound was deafening, but the bullet lodged in the library's far wall. Tim had control of the weapon. The next moment, he glimpsed the huge fist coming for his face. Muscle memory from training took charge, and he ducked below the blow. The giant lost his balance and lurched forward toward Roxie.

"No!" Tim scrambled to get between them.

Pop-pop, in rapid succession, broke through the ringing in his ears. The smell of burned gunpowder and hot lead wafted in the air. The huge man stopped his forward momentum, clutched at his chest, and crumpled to the floor as if his bones had turned to water. Roxie stood frozen, armed with her concealed backup.

Outside of the library, Tim heard breaking glass. The hostage rescue team came through the sliding glass doors.

"Here! We're in here!" Roxie screamed.

Tim raced forward and swept his arm across Solenov's desk, sending Berkstad's gear crashing to the floor, but out of the old man's reach.

Solenov sat paralyzed. His eyes turned black and soulless.

"Where is Berkstad?" Tim demanded. "Where is he?"

The old man let out a demonic cackle. "I'm afraid Berkstad has left this world. And my beautiful Roxanne just killed the only man who knows where the body is buried." A sick smile curved his thin lips as if he enjoyed being cruel to her.

Tim's heart broke for his partner and friend. Roxie loved David. She had loved him enough to get involved with him even though he was married with three kids. She'd jeopardized her career for him.

"Nicholai Solenov, you are under arrest for conspiracy to commit murder and the first-degree murder of Judge Evelyn Waterford. You are under arrest for the murder of David Berkstad. Stand up." Tim pulled handcuffs from under his suit coat and placed them around the man's frail wrists.

"You can't arrest me. You can't prove I did anything," he hissed.

"I have you on tape. You're not the only one who knows how to use electronic surveillance," Tim shook his head, and smiled, watching the man's bravado turn to fear.

Two members of the hostage rescue team burst through the library doors and took Solenov into custody. Tim looked at them and knew his face reflected his desperation.

"Is he here?" he asked. "Berkstad? Is he here?"

The lead man shook his head no. "All clear."

Berkstad was dead. Tim turned his attention to Roxie. She stood in the corner as if frozen in place. The pistol, still smoking, pointed to the floor. He went to her, tracing his hand slowly down her arm, removing the gun from her hand. Roxie trembled and slumped against his shoulder, and tears began to flow. He cradled her against his chest until he saw Miguel at the doorway. He would send her home in Miguel's care.

"You're okay, Rox. It's all going to be okay," he whispered as he petted her dark hair. He knew it wasn't true.

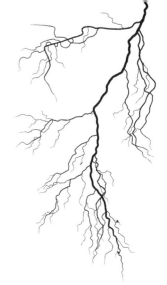

CHAPTER FORTY-EIGHT

TIM HADN'T SLEPT well all night. Yesterday's scene played over and over in his dreams. He'd called in a CSI team, and they'd combed over every inch of Solenov's house searching for evidence. Elias had them search each of Solenov's three cars. They found blood in the trunk of one vehicle. It tested positive for human blood. Further examination would likely confirm it to be Berkstad's.

Elias had CSI pull the car's GPS system from the dash and deliver it to Kandar. They would search for Berkstad's body, until they found it. Elias had graciously relieved Tim from that duty, and he was grateful.

Elias gave Roxie a month of paid leave, though neither he nor Tim thought it was long enough. No one really ever recovers from the death of a loved one. Elias promised Roxie that Berkstad's wife and children would never know that she was his paramour.

There was one consolation—Nicholai Solenov would never rule the world, and Carlton Waterford and Tareeka Marlow were going to prison for life with him.

Dani snuggled up against Tim's side. Her smooth, soft, skin was warm and comforting. She stirred awake and braced herself up on one elbow.

"How long have you been awake?" she asked, moving so her head rested on his chest, and he could look into her eyes.

"Not long," he answered.

She bit her bottom lip. She knew that wasn't true, but he knew she wouldn't ask for information he couldn't tell her.

"What's the plan for today?" She kissed his shoulder and stirred up longings he wasn't sure he was ready for, but still wanted. She wouldn't let him stew in negative thoughts for long. Her touch, as ever, was intoxicating.

He stroked the back of his fingers along her cheek. "I'm going to release a little boy, Jamie Randall, and his family from protective custody this morning. Get them settled at home. And this afternoon, I'm taking my girls on a long, peaceful, horseback ride and then to dinner anywhere you want."

"Are you working this weekend?" she asked, tracing an index finger outlining his lips. He closed his eyes, enjoying the sensations racing through him.

"No. This weekend is ours." He was emphatic.

"And what are your plans before breakfast?" she asked, nibbling at his neck provocatively.

"You know exactly what they are," he grinned and pulled her as close to him as he possibly could.

If you enjoyed this novel, please leave a review on
Goodreads and/or Amazon.com.

Other mystery/suspense novels by this author include:
James Street
Snow Country Lane
Old Schoolhouse Road
Lightning Ridge Road

And Coming Soon, "The Legend Of Flying Horses", a historical
fiction novel, elements of which are based on true events.

ABOUT THE AUTHOR

Sarah Vail spent forty years in private industry before retiring to Coeur d'Alene, Idaho to write mystery-suspense fiction. To keep her writing interesting and authentic, she has continued her education in Creative writing, Copy Editing, Criminal Justice, Forensic Science, Criminology, Criminal Interrogation, Weapons Handling, and World History. Ms. Vail is active in a critique group where she hones her craft. Her current mystery suspense novels, *JAMES STREET, SNOW COUNTRY LANE, OLD SCHOOLHOUSE ROAD and LIGHTNING RIDGE ROAD* are offered in hardcover, softcover, and ebook formats, and are distributed by Ingram and available on Amazon and sold by booksellers everywhere.

www.sarahvailauthor.com

Printed in the USA
CPSIA information can be obtained
at www.ICGtesting.com
LVHW051206230324
775289LV00001B/3